Julie Ellis is the bests *Wind* and *The Velvet* vationist and research various environmental is working on her next

JULIE ELLIS

The Hampton Women

Grafton

An Imprint of HarperCollins*Publishers*

Grafton
An Imprint of HarperCollins*Publishers*
77–85 Fulham Palace Road,
Hammersmith, London W6 8JB

Published by Grafton 1992
9 8 7 6 5 4 3 2 1

A catalogue record for this book
is available from the British Library

ISBN 0 586 21048 2

Set in Times

Printed in Great Britain by
HarperCollinsManufacturing Glasgow

For Roberta Lawrence
a great English teacher
and a beautiful human being,
with love

Acknowledgements

I would like to thank, again, Mr Franklin M. Garrett, historian of the Atlanta Historical Society, for having written his invaluable book, *Atlanta and Environs*, and for his courteous assistance and that of the staff of the Atlanta Historical Society during my research in Atlanta. Among those on the staff I wish particularly to thank librarian Eugene Craig, always tireless and gracious. Also, my thanks to Faye Gamel, Cherie Taylor, and Mary Froehlich of the library staff.

My gratitude to Leonard Dinnerstein for having written his magnificently researched book, *The Leo Frank Case*, and to Harold H. Martin, for having written his concise and informative history, *Georgia*. My thanks, also, to the staff of the Library of Congress, to the sergeant at arms of the House of Representatives, to the Genealogy Room of the New York Public Library, the librarians of the New York Historical Society, to Mrs Edith G. Sanders of the Atlanta Public Library, Mr James J. Foster of the Steamship Society Library at the University of Baltimore, Mr James Wilson of the Staten Island offices of the Steamship Historical Society, Mrs Pressey and Mrs DeWitt Peltz of the Metropolitan Opera Archives, and Mr Green of the Epiphany Branch of the New York Public Library.

My thanks to my son Richard for researching on my behalf at the various libraries at Columbia University, and to my daughter Susie for an assist in copy editing.

Caroline

1

The South was jubilant on this Inauguration Day of 1913. In every hamlet, town, and city this was an occasion for celebration. At precisely 1:23 P.M. this afternoon Virginia-born Woodrow Wilson took his oath as the twenty-eighth President of the United States. After almost half a century in the shadows of the Confederate defeat, Southerners lifted their heads in pride. Five Southerners would grace Wilson's Cabinet. William Jennings Bryan, the idol of the South, would be his Secretary of State. Texan 'Colonel' Edward Mandell House would undoubtedly be his most trusted adviser in the White House.

Southerners had been flocking to Washington since Friday. Atlanta had sent a huge contingent, including 175 cadets from the Georgia Military Academy, to attend the Inauguration. On Sunday the famous Atlanta Journal Special, carrying only Atlanta passengers, sped towards the Capitol.

In Hamptonville, once an independent mill village, now a part of Atlanta, Caroline Hampton sat hunched over her desk in the Hampton Mill annexe and contemplated the potential of the South. She had done well by the mill since her grandfather's death, fifteen years ago, yet she was dissatisfied. The Hampton Mill should be the largest – the most powerful – in the South. The time to mould the mill as she envisioned it was *now*.

With characteristic sudden decisiveness Caroline reached for the telephone. In moments she had an architect on the phone and had made an appointment for him to come to the mill the following morning. She leaned back in her chair, pleased.

At thirty-three Caroline appeared ten years younger. Her hair, worn in a soft pompadour and drawn back into a Psyche knot that emphasized the delicacy of her features, remained the colour of a spring sunset. Her eyes were the luminous blue of her girlhood. Carrying three children – Liz, who was now twelve, ten-year-old Josh, and five-year-old Francis – had added a slight, provocative fullness to her small, slender figure.

Rarely, and then only in the privacy of Hampton House, did she allow her face to reflect her inner anguish, ever close to the surface, since her realization shortly after his birth that her younger son, Francis, was an 'unnatural' child. To Atlanta she was the beautiful, dynamic Caroline Hampton, granddaughter of the founder of the Hampton Mill, and wife of her distant cousin, the handsome, highly respected state legislator Eric Hampton.

Wilson was President. But for her, Eric would be taking office today as congressman from this district. Because of her refusal to move to Washington, Eric had ignored the importuning of Jim Russell, his law partner and political manager, the urging of Senator Bolton and a powerful clique in the party, to run for Congress last November. Eric *should* move beyond the confines of the State Legislature, but how could she uproot Francis from the only place he felt secure?

She started at the light knock at her open door. Andrew, her distant cousin and longtime superintendent of the mill, stood there, an anticipatory smile on his lean, ascetic face. At forty-three he was still slender, his hair slightly streaked with grey.

'Dinner at seven?' he asked. Away from the mill, Andrew was painfully shy, almost a recluse, except for his devotion to the theatre and the opera; but he enjoyed festive occasions at the elegant Hampton House, which stood barely a hundred yards beyond the mill.

'Seven,' Caroline confirmed. 'Liz is so excited. It's her first grown-up party.'

Andrew inspected the wall clock.

'Wilson has been sworn in by now. The first Southern-born President elected since Abraham Lincoln.' Andrew smiled in wry amusement. 'We didn't do too well with him.'

Andrew left Caroline's office. She leaned back in her chair, tired, her throat tightening in tension. She had been at the mill since seven, as usual. She dreaded tonight's dinner. The conversation was certain to revolve about the Inauguration. That was all that would be discussed in Atlanta tonight.

This was the first dinner party in Hampton House in eleven months. The occasion had demanded it. As a politician's wife, she knew this. All over Atlanta, parties were being given tonight. Only a few weeks ago Jim had told her, with his characteristic bluntness, that entertaining was important to Eric's career. Had he forgotten that fifteen years ago it was *she* who had instituted the campaign teas when Eric was running for the City Council?

'Caroline, it's two-thirty,' Ellen reminded her from the doorway. At three sharp, for the past three years, she had left the mill early to spend time with Francis.

'Thank you, Ellen.'

Caroline's eyes followed Ellen's tall, full figure until she disappeared down the hall. Ellen had been left a widow at twenty-eight, with a six-year-old child. She had gone to school to learn typing and stenography. Her job at the Hampton Mill was her first. In the seven years that Ellen had been Caroline's secretary, she had become a

11

trusted friend. Though their lives were dissimilar, Ellen – more than anyone else she knew – understood her inner turmoil.

Caroline's eyes moved to the clock. Dr Adams would be arriving at the house at three. Last night, when they fought about her bringing in another doctor, Eric had accused her of sacrificing Liz and Josh in her efforts to help Francis.

'Caro, you've done everything you can for Francis. For God's sake, remember you have two other children. You owe them a decent life, too!'

She frowned, visualizing Francis' terrible tantrums, which would break out after moments of such sweetness. Neither Liz nor Josh brought school friends home any more. They were ashamed of Francis. Not just the tantrums, she forced herself to acknowledge. All his bizarre behaviour.

In a burst of restlessness Caroline rose to her feet. She would leave now so that she would have a few moments to check with Mattie about dinner preparations. For three days Mattie and Elvira had been cooking and baking. Seth, retired three years now, came – as always on festive occasions – to supervise the party preparations.

All at once Caroline was nervous about meeting Dr Adams. Eric and she had approached so many doctors with hope, only to be told there was no hope.

She left the mill and drove the short distance to the house. Walking up the steps to the veranda, she could hear Francis in a screaming fit in his bedroom. She went out to the kitchen to talk with Mattie and Elvira, then into the dining room, where Seth was laying the dinner table. As they discussed which wines to serve, Caroline became aware of a sudden quiet upstairs. The tantrum was over.

When she walked into Francis' bedroom she found him

listening to his music box. She knew not to disturb him. That would thrust him into another tantrum. He ignored her arrival. Sometimes he seemed to look right through her.

'We're having the dinner party tonight,' she reminded Patience. Her eyes betrayed her anxiety.

'You don't need to fret about Francis tonight,' Patience soothed. 'Last time I was down to Plains to visit my aunt, she give me this medicine. It won't hurt Francis none,' Patience said firmly. 'It'll give him a good night's sleep, and there won't be no yellin' to mess up yo' party.'

Caroline hesitated. 'Just this once,' she stipulated, then snapped to attention. A car was stopping before the house. 'That must be Dr Adams.' Caroline's heart pounded. Marian Bolton had spoken about Dr Victor Adams with such confidence; she had been instrumental in persuading him to set up his practice in Atlanta. But famous specialists had come to Atlanta to see Francis before and offered no hope.

'I'm Dr Adams.' A warm, deep voice touched by a Boston upbringing filtered up to greet her. 'Mrs Hampton is expecting me.'

'Yessuh,' Roland said with quiet respect. 'She'll be right downstairs. She say I'm to show you to the parlour.'

'Roland, wait please,' she called down impulsively. 'Dr Adams, would you like to come directly up to Francis' room?' Instinct rebuked her. She should have offered Dr Adams a cup of coffee, a glass of wine; but she was impatient to learn his initial reaction to Francis.

'That would be fine, Mrs Hampton.'

Dr Adams strode across the wide foyer and up the stairs. A tall, slender young man with dark, unruly hair and ascetic features. A warm, sensitive man, Caroline decided. Instinctively she trusted him.

'Francis is quiet right now. He may have a tantrum if

13

we disturb him. He *will* have a tantrum.' She forced herself to be honest.

'We won't disturb him,' Dr Adams reassured. 'Let me just observe him.'

Caroline opened the door to Francis' bedroom. He was listening to a music box. Patience looked up from the dresser where she was putting away clothes. Almost as deeply as she herself, Caroline realized, Patience hoped that this latest doctor could help Francis.

'He's a handsome child,' Dr Adams said softly. 'These children usually are.' Caroline lifted her face to his in astonishment. 'Mrs Hampton, there are many children like Francis in this world.'

'My two older ones are fine,' Caroline stammered.

'You have older children?' He stared in disbelief.

'Liz is twelve and Josh is ten. We thought at first that Francis was . . . normal.' She refused to use the currently fashionable 'unnatural child'. 'Though he screamed so much even as an infant.' Francis was unaware of their presence. He sat motionless except to rewind the music box at the required intervals.

'Let's go downstairs and talk,' Dr Adams said after a few minutes.

'You don't need to examine Francis?'

'I know Francis.' Dr Adams' smile was compassionate and reassuring.

They went downstairs and into a large, square parlour that had changed little since the General's death almost fifteen years ago. The same massive pier mirror hung between a pair of velvet-draped windows. The same fine French antiques, the handsome six-octave piano, adorned the room. Over the Carrara marble mantel hung the painting of the General's wife, Caroline's grandmother. Dr Adams scrutinized the portrait.

14

'I would think the lady was you, except for the gown,' he said. 'She belongs to an era before your time.'

'She's Louisa Hampton, my grandmother,' Caroline explained.

'You haven't spent all your life in Atlanta,' Victor surmised while they seated themselves in chairs before the fireplace. Roland had started a fire in the grate against the chill of the afternoon.

'I lived in London until I was eighteen,' Caroline confirmed. Her speech retained the flavour of England. 'There had been a family feud.' No need to explain that her father, aghast at a war that would pit family and friend against one another, had fled to London at the outbreak of the War Between the States, and for this had been disowned by his father, General Josiah Hampton. 'When my mother died, I came to Atlanta to make peace with my grandfather. My father had died years earlier. I never met my grandmother. The General was my sole surviving relative.'

'You loved him very much.' Victor's voice was tender.

'Very much.'

'But what we must talk about right now is Francis,' Victor summed up crisply. 'I want to know everything about him from the moment he was born. Any tiny detail you recall,' he instructed.

Caroline talked rapidly, her words tumbling over one another in her rush to share the agony of the past five years with this sympathetic young doctor. At intervals he nodded or interrupted with a succinct question.

'There are times when he seems fine, and then . . .' She gestured in despair. 'He goes out of control. He does strange things. He hurts himself. But he's not stupid.' Her eyes dared Victor Adams to contradict her.

'Children like Francis are usually fine-looking and bright,' he told her. 'And some of them can learn. I discovered this when I saw the work that Dr Montessori was doing in Rome with these children. I was excited by it. I knew this was how I wanted to spend my life.'

'Dr Adams, do you believe you can help Francis?' She trembled at the prospect.

'I can make no promises,' he cautioned. 'But I want to try. It'll be arduous, discouraging – and possibly fruitless. It may be a year before we'll see even a slight improvement.'

'Please try,' Caroline whispered. 'We'll do anything you say. Please, work with Francis.'

In the large, high-ceilinged corner bedroom that she shared with Eric, Caroline pulled a delicate yellow Charmeuse dinner dress over her head, with care so as not to disarrange her hair. Tonight, when she particularly wished Eric to arrive home early, he was late. He knew Dr Adams was coming. He was deliberately late.

Caroline swung about with a start as the bedroom door opened and Eric walked inside. For one dispassionate moment she regarded him without speaking. At thirty-nine Eric was still one of the most handsome men in Atlanta. He had a rakish charm that fascinated women.

'You're late,' she began.

'It won't take me long to dress.'

He strode to the eighteenth-century American high-boy, pulled a shirt from a drawer, and took out a suit from his closet. Caroline struggled against the recriminations that threatened to spill forth. Didn't he care to hear what Dr Adams had to say?

'Jim told me the suffragists parading in Washington yesterday were almost stampeded. They complained the police did nothing to help them,' Eric reported while he tossed aside the clothes he had worn to his law office. He was still lean and flat and muscular.

16

Caroline frowned. At this moment she didn't care to talk about the suffragists.

'Eric, I saw – ' she began, but he interrupted with a chuckle.

'I'm in sympathy with the suffragists, but why the devil do they wear such abominable clothes? It might help their cause if they appeared more attractive.' He inspected his face in the mirror. 'I don't need to shave again, do I?'

'You do not need to shave.' Caroline's voice crackled. 'You need to listen to me. Turn around and look at me,' she ordered, and he complied, eyes reproachful. 'I saw Dr Adams today. We spoke for a long time. Eric, he believes he can help Francis.'

'Caro, how many times have we heard that?' Eric lost his good humour. 'Does he have a pipeline to God?'

'He knows about children like Francis. Eric, he's willing to try.'

'He's willing to experiment on Francis with some newfangled ideas!' Eric shot back.

'Don't you want to meet Dr Adams?' Caroline challenged.

'No. I don't want to hear a fairy tale,' Eric rejected. 'I spoke with Dr Dimon today. He feels we should send Francis away from the family. He's learned about a sanatorium down in Americus.'

'Francis is not going to a sanatorium!' Caroline was furious.

'Caro, you've been through so many disappointments.' The tenderness she cherished in Eric warmed his voice. 'We've brought the finest specialists to Atlanta.'

'I want Dr Adams to work with Francis one year, Eric. Give Dr Adams one year to help Francis.' Her eyes held his, daring him to deny her this.

'Caro, it's wrong to expose Liz and Josh to another

17

year of Francis' behaviour,' he rejected. But his face told her that deep within him was a flicker of the hope she felt. 'All right,' he capitulated. 'He'll have his year with Dr Adams. But we'll move Francis into a small house with Patience and a trained nurse. You'll be able to see him every day,' he cajoled.

'Francis stays with us.' She felt sick at the thought of moving him away. That poor, troubled baby. 'You know he would be terrified in some strange surroundings!'

Eric's attention was diverted by the sound of a car pulling up before the house.

'We'll talk tonight.' His face was set. 'You'd better go on downstairs. I'll only be a few moments.'

Frustrated that Eric was avoiding further confrontation, Caroline left their bedroom and moved towards the stairs. She was angry at Eric, yet filled with guilt. Except for her insistence on remaining in Atlanta with Francis, Eric would be in Washington tonight. He would be taking his seat in the new Congress. Almost from their first meeting she had encouraged Eric to forge ahead in politics. To strive to fulfil the General's dream of a Hampton in the White House. There were those high in the party that were convinced this could be.

Only she held Eric back.

2

Eric struggled with his tie before the bedroom mirror. Hell, he was in no mood for this dinner party tonight. He stared at his reflection, seeing the years racing past. He was almost forty, going nowhere as long as Caro was so adamant about staying here in Atlanta with Francis.

But was it Francis, or was it the mill? With disturbing frequency this question plagued him. She was allowing the mill to become an obsession with her. Eric reached for his jacket, pulled it on, and left the bedroom. Arriving at the foot of the stairs, he heard Caro in conversation with Marian Bolton in the parlour. They were talking about Dr Adams. He wished to hell Marian would stop giving Caro false hopes.

'Papa!' Liz called from the top of the stairs. 'Am I late?' She hurtled towards him, her red-gold hair falling to her waist in a satin sheen, eyes incredibly blue.

'No, honey,' he reassured her. 'You're early.' His eyes rested on his oldest child with pleasure. She was already as tall as Caro, with a faint swelling of young breasts beneath her frock that elicited a blend of tenderness and disquietude in him. Whatever Liz did, she did with such intensity.

'Do you like my dress?' She whirled about to display the dainty blue satin and *point d'esprit* net frock.

'It's beautiful,' Eric declared.

'Don't you think I look at least fourteen?'

'At least,' he agreed solemnly, reaching for her hand. 'Come with me while I have a drink before the others arrive.'

'Don't you wish you were in Washington right now?' Liz's eyes searched his. She heard too much, he thought. They must be careful about the way they talked before the children.

'I'm happy to be right here in Atlanta,' he lied.

He loved Atlanta with a passion, but he knew the place for him at this point in his career was the Capitol. Maybe Francis would be unhappy for a few days if they left for Washington. After that he would forget. And there'd be months each year, when Congress was not in session, that they'd be back in Atlanta. Washington would be a fine experience for Liz and Josh.

Eric seated himself before the fire in the library while Liz went through the ritual of pouring him a glass of wine. He heard a car pull up before the house. Anticipating the arrival of guests, Seth was already moving across the foyer and to the door.

'Good evenin', Mist' Russell,' Seth greeted the newest arrival.

'Good evening, Seth. How're you feeling these days?'

'Mighty good,' Seth boasted, face and figure belying his eighty-three years.

'Liz, go tell Mr Russell I'm here in the library,' Eric ordered. 'Then present yourself to Mrs Bolton.'

'You want to talk to Mr Russell without me around,' Liz interpreted.

'Go,' he ordered with mock sternness.

Jim appeared at the library door. His face radiated pleasure.

'This is an important night for the South.' His voice was detached, a forewarning to Eric he was about to launch an attack. He sat down in the chair opposite Eric. 'Two hundred thousand visitors are up there in Washington celebrating the Inauguration. And you and I are sitting here in Atlanta.'

'It's like you said.' Eric bluffed high spirits. 'An important night for the South.'

'When the hell are you going to wake up?' Jim demanded with sudden irascibility. 'You've got to take a stand and move up from the Legislature. Another term and you'll be frozen there for life.'

'There's still the governorship,' Eric hedged. 'An honourable position.' With the governor's mansion right here in Atlanta.

'Fuck the governorship. You're in no position to try for it. You know that, Eric. Tom Watson still dictates the Democratic nominees for governor. We're against everything that son of a bitch stands for now, and you've made that clear.' Jim leaned forward, thrusting a hand through his ruddy crop of hair, still untouched by grey at fifty-four. 'You'd carry Atlanta and Columbus and maybe Savannah. You're too progressive for the rural masses, plus you're a pacifist. Watson would castrate you. You've got a seat in Congress and a senatorial seat waiting for you, Eric. Evans is seventy-three and ailing. He wants out of Congress. I've talked to Bolton. By the end of this new term he'll be panting to retire. He's sixty-one and in Washington for twenty-seven years. He's had all he wants. He only ran for this term to hold the Senate seat for you.'

'The senator will retire if Marian agrees to it,' Eric observed.

'She'll agree,' Jim insisted. His blue-grey eyes were bright. 'Think about it. If we make the right moves, you'll be a presidental candidate in 1928.'

'That's an enticing prospect,' Eric admitted. He heard cars drawing up before the house. Jim and he would have to join the others in the parlour in a moment. 'Caro brought in some smart-ass doctor from Boston who's set up practice in Atlanta. He's going to work with Francis.

I told Caro, one year with this doctor and we've got to accept reality. I don't love the boy less for being realistic.' His voice betrayed his exasperation. 'One year, Jim, and Caro's got to agree to go to Washington with me.'

'It's time,' Jim said. He was pleased.

The formal dining room at Hampton House was the one room in which Caroline had made major changes. Its original regal elegance had become relaxed with the addition of Chinese wallpaper. The draperies and the seats of the Philadelphia chairs had been replaced to repeat the delicate yellow of the wallpaper. A French Empire ormolu chandelier hung over the Philadelphia banquet table, supplanting the ornate crystal chandelier.

Eric sat at the head of the banquet table, resplendent with the Hamptons' finest table linens, Louisa Hampton's Spode china and Waterford glass, and the silver that had been saved from the Yankee invaders at Hampton Court by her quick thinking.

At Eric's end of the table Caroline had seated political friends. In addition to small, portly, grey-haired Marian Bolton, there were Judge Colquitt, three fellow legislators, a councilman, and their wives. At the lower end, surrounding Caroline, were Liz, Sophie – once the General's trusted assistant at the mill and now Caroline's and in residence at Hampton House for over forty years – Andrew, Jim Russell, and David and Noah Kahn. The Kahn brothers had been Caroline's friends since her arrival in Atlanta. Noah had attended tonight's dinner without his adored wife, Rae, now in her third pregnancy.

'The senator told me when Mr Wilson took his oath, the Annapolis boys were on his right, West Point on his left, and the Culver Black Horse Troop from the military academy right there in front. And when the Georgia troops and cadets passed by the President's reviewing stand, Mrs Wilson rose to her feet and waved.' Marian glowed in triumph.

'In the Senate the South has more than half the Democratic majority,' Jim reflected. 'In the House, more than two-fifths.' Intercepting the meaningful exchange between Eric and Jim, Caroline tensed. At a time when the South was coming into its own at last, Eric sat here in Atlanta instead of in Washington.

'Remember, also, that we hold most of the committee chairmanships.' Eric's voice brought her back to the dinner table. 'All but two in the Senate, and the same in the House.'

'Half a century ago we were prostrate and bleeding from our wounds.' Judge Colquitt's face was zealous. 'Now we have returned to the house of our fathers.'

'At last Reconstruction is over,' Eric said. It was like a benediction.

Caroline barely tasted the superb artichoke soup. She withdrew from the general conversation to talk with Noah and David about the trouble in Mexico.

The dinner was going well, Caroline assured herself, despite her personal unease. The fillet of bass was followed by crisped duckling with tangerine, served with a raw mushroom salad. For vegetables there were baked potatoes and new asparagus.

Why did Liz persist in glancing towards the ceiling that way? Was she expecting the chandelier to fall on the table? Then all at once Caroline felt sick in comprehension. Liz was afraid that Francis would awaken and disrupt the party.

Now she was assaulted by a recall of Liz's eleventh birthday party. She had insisted that Francis sit at the table on this special occasion, despite Liz's vociferous objections. At the precise moment when Liz leaned forward to blow out the candles on her birthday cake, Francis had smashed the cake with his football.

Caroline's face softened while she listened to the private conversation between Liz and David Kahn. Knowing David's shyness, she had placed him next to Liz, who could draw a mummy into conversation.

'I'm not far along in my research,' David confided to Liz, as though she were a contemporary. 'But every moment I'm not in the classroom or preparing for the next day's teaching, I work at it.'

After earning his doctorate in physics at the University of Chicago, David had turned down a professorship at Harvard to return to teach in Atlanta. He had done this out of gratitude to the General, Caroline was convinced. She could still remember the look on David's face, almost fifteen years ago, when he learned that Josiah Hampton's will provided for his college education.

'Did you read the article in Sunday's *Journal* about Mrs Pankhurst?' Sophie was deliberately stemming the general conversation away from the Inauguration. Dear Sophie. 'I loved what she said when that correspondent, Shepherd, asked her to explain to American women why English suffragettes are blowing up houses and burning down buildings. "We're fighting the War Between the States over again – only it's white slavery this time, not black!"'

'I read that article about Mrs Pankhurst,' the youngest of the legislators' wives said with a vivacity that elicited a glare of reproach from her husband. 'She said, "Tell the women of America that we are doing the same thing American men did back in '76 when they threw the English tea into the Boston harbour and rebelled against English rule."'

'Hear, hear!' Jim approved. 'I'm for giving the ladies the vote, and the sooner the better.' He turned to

Caroline with a glint in his eyes that should have fore-warned her. 'And may you ladies have the franchise when Eric runs for the House of Representatives next year!'

Caroline felt encased in ice. Eric had made no commitment to run for Congress! *Had he?* Without discussing it with her?

'Congressman Eric Hampton!' Judge Colquitt's voice was jubilant. The dining room was charged with excitement. 'Let's drink to that.' He reached for his wineglass.

'Wait, Judge,' Jim commanded. 'This calls for champagne.'

Pale but composed, Caroline watched while Eric summoned Seth from the doorway.

'Bring six bottles of champagne up from the cellar, please,' Eric told him. 'The Dom Perignon, Seth. And have Elvira bring the Waterford goblets.'

The atmosphere was electric. Only Sophie appeared uneasy. Sophie was aware of the tensions between Eric and her, Caroline realized, and was anxious. What was Eric doing to them? What was he doing to their marriage?

Seth arrived with the Dom Perignon. Glasses were filled. Judge Colquitt rose to his feet, glass in hand.

'To Eric Hampton, the next congressman from Atlanta!'

Caroline's hand was unsteady when she lifted her glass. Her smile was a reaction commanded by her brain. Eric and Jim had plotted this before the dinner was arranged, she fumed in silence. This was why Eric was so eager to have an Inauguration Eve dinner. Eric Hampton had tonight announced his candidacy for a seat in Congress, which would be made available at his request.

Changed into a maroon flannel dressing gown and slippers, Eric tossed another log on to the fire in the grate.

The evening had turned cold, with a sharp wind echoing through the still-spare winter trees and rattling the shutters. Eric crossed to draw the draperies at the windows, pausing at the last to inspect the grey-red· clouds that clustered in the sky. They might have snow tonight despite the narcissus that bloomed in such fragrance throughout Atlanta.

He was tired and tense, and facing a battle with Caro. Didn't Caro know what it did to him to see Francis like that? Francis was his child, too. He would give ten years of his life to see Francis normal.

Eric turned to the door at the sound of voices on the stairs. Caro was talking to Patience. Then he heard the doorknob turn. He reached for his pipe, dropped into the lounge chair again. Caro would be in a rotten frame of mind.

Caroline walked into the room and closed the door behind her. Her eyes were ignited in rage.

'How could you allow Jim to announce your candidacy in that melodramatic fashion? Without a word of warning to me!'

'Caro, I never expected it. I was as startled as you.'

'Jim wouldn't have dared without your approval,' Caroline retaliated.

Eric sighed. 'It was an insane misunderstanding.' He frowned, groping for words.

'You didn't deny it!' All the rage she had been compelled to disguise through the evening was spilling forth.

'I told Jim about your bringing in this new doctor,' Eric began, trying to placate her. 'I said we were allotting one more year to bringing about some improvement in Francis. Jim assumed that at the end of the year we'll go ahead with my political blueprint. He didn't – '

'You let Jim make a formal announcement before Judge Colquitt and the others,' Caroline interrupted.

'Without saying a word to me before we went down to dinner!'

'Caro, you're not listening to me,' Eric protested. 'I'm not running for office. I won't be officially campaigning for at least twelve months. Francis will have his year with that doctor from Boston.' Caro was always so logical, except where Francis was concerned. She had to understand that life must go on for the rest of the family. 'It'll be over two years before we make the move to Washington. Provided I'm elected.'

'You know you'll be elected,' Caroline said impatiently. 'The party will see to that.'

'Caro, listen to me. Since Francis was a few months old, he has monopolized our lives.' Eric strained to keep his voice even. 'You knew that Congressman Evans has been warming that seat in the House for me for the past two terms. He wants to retire. He's not going to wait beyond this term. *I want to go to Congress from this district.*'

'You're planning ahead as though Francis didn't exist,' Caroline accused.

'We agreed to one more year,' Eric reminded with the calm politeness that sometimes exasperated Caro. 'We'll find a small house nearby, where we can visit with Francis every day –'

'I won't allow that! I won't let him be shunted out of his own home. I won't desert Francis.' Her voice broke. 'It's my fault he's the way he is. God is punishing me for loving you before I had the right.'

'Caro, don't drag up Tina after all these years. You know we had no marriage. You know what she was.' On the honeymoon he had discovered Tina's infidelity. Half of Atlanta had known about her scandalous behaviour from the time she was fifteen.

'I look at my poor, darling baby, and I know it's my

27

fault he's like that.' Caroline closed her eyes in anguish. 'My fault.'

'Caro, stop it.' He rose to his feet and grasped her by the shoulders. 'It's not your fault, nor mine. It's God's will, and we have to live with it.'

'Eric, why?'

She held her face up to his. How beautiful she was. Again Eric was conscious of how deeply he loved his wife. Christ, he'd been with a lot of women before he married Caro, but he had not touched another since. No need, when Caro came to him with a passion that matched his own.

'Caro, stop torturing yourself,' he ordered.

He brought her to him, his mouth reaching to comfort her in the most potent fashion he knew. For a moment she was limp in his arms. Then her hands crept about his neck. He felt himself grow hard against her.

'Wait, honey.' His eyes met hers with promise while he pulled loose the pins that held her hair in a fashionable French knot, and allowed the mass of red-gold hair to fall about her shoulders. 'Wait,' he reiterated, and went to lock the door. He had nightmares about one of the children walking in on them in the midst of their making love.

He locked the door and turned around. Caro was struggling with the hooks at the back of her dress. Her face was flushed, her mouth slightly parted. She had willed herself to forget about Francis. This little while belonged to them.

'Let me,' Eric commanded, and walked to her.

Carefully he released each hook of the yellow Charmeuse dinner dress, pulled the silken material away from her velvet white shoulders. His mouth dropped to burrow in the crevice between throat and shoulder, knowing this

28

was an erotic area for her. His hands moved around to caress her high, full breasts.

'Eric, it's chilly in here,' she said after a moment.

'Come closer to the fire. I'll throw on another log.'

Eric threw another log on the fire and coaxed the grey-edged logs into orange brilliance. Caro stood beside him, her dress sliding from her shoulders, eyes closed. For now, nobody in the world existed except the two of them.

A cosy warmth spilled into the room from the fireplace. Eric crossed the room to turn off the lamps. Motionless before the fire, her hair cascading down her back, her dress displaying the rapid rise and fall of her breasts, Caro waited for him. He felt as overheated tonight as he had been at sixteen.

He drew Caro to him. His mouth sought hers. While her arms reached to encircle his shoulders, he pulled her free of the silken folds that kept her from him. Dress and undergarments fell into a heap at her feet. He pulled his mouth away. His eyes swept over the voluptuous nudity. With a body like this, her capacity for passion, Caro could have been one of the great French courtesans.

'It's indecent for you to be so beautiful at your age,' he teased, his hands moving about her body.

'Eric, love me. Please.'

His mouth imprisoned one taut nipple. No rush. He was good enough to take his time, he thought with pride. His hands were at her pelvis, arousing her with the skill that came with years of their learning each other's needs.

'Eric, I want you in me,' she whispered, all of her abandoned to emotion. It pleased him that she could talk to him this way.

His mouth left her breast to roam the route they had learned to enjoy. Her hands cradled his head. Her body was hot from the heat cast by the logs, reflecting his own inner heat.

'Eric,' she whimpered. 'Oh, Eric!'

He stripped off his robe and the single garment beneath, and lifted her in his arms. Caroline buried her face against his shoulder while he carried her to the bed, threw back the comforter, and lowered her to the sheet.

'It's like ice,' she protested.

'Not for long,' Eric promised, his hands caressing her slight form.

Only now did Caroline open her eyes.

'Eric, I want you in me,' she reiterated. She moved beneath him, her hands tugging at his shoulders.

'Oh, Caro, baby.' He moved with her in towering intensity.

Suddenly Caroline stiffened beneath him.

'Francis,' she cried out in alarm. 'He's having a bad spell!'

'Patience can handle him.' Eric's voice was ragged.

Caroline marshalled all her strength to wrest herself free. She darted towards the closet for a robe. With a groan Eric rolled over on the bed, watching while she pulled on the robe and ran out the door.

In the next bedroom Francis screamed like a woman in hard labour.

Eric stood in the centre of the room, inspecting the neat piles of clothes he had laid out on the bed. The door of the closet that normally held his wardrobe was ajar, advertising its emptiness. The drawers of the highboy were pulled out, their contents removed.

Damn, he'd had all he could swallow of being brushed aside every time Francis decided to throw a tantrum. Caro allowed no room in her life for her husband. He was playing second fiddle to his son. He would feel less frustrated if she had taken a lover.

His face taut, Eric lifted an armful of clothes from the

30

bed and left the room. Walking past Francis' door en route to the guest room at the far end of the hall, he could hear Caroline and Patience talking in muted tones while they struggled to quiet Francis. He must have awakened the entire household.

Eric made three trips between rooms until all his personal attire had been removed from the bedroom he had shared with Caroline for thirteen years. From this night forward he would sleep alone. He would run for Congress in November of next year. If need be, he would leave Atlanta to live alone in Washington during the long months when Congress was in session.

Would Caro even be aware of his absence?

3

Caroline stood beside Francis' bed, gazing down at his small, inert form. His face seemed angelic in sleep. Serene, poignantly appealing. She reached out to brush the dark, curling hair from his forehead.

'He's gonna sleep now, Miss Caroline,' Patience said.

'You go to sleep, too,' Caroline urged.

She left Francis' room to return to her own, conscious now of utter exhaustion. She opened the door softly, anxious not to awaken Eric. But the lamp on the night table spilled light across the empty bed. The sheets had been changed, the bed neatly turned down.

Almost strangled with shock, Caroline stared at the drawers of Eric's highboy, pulled wide and emptied. His open closet door revealed the deserted pole. She flinched, visualizing the passionate moment she had aborted. Yet she had to go to Francis. She had to go to her child in agony.

Her eyes focused again on the empty bed. This couldn't be happening to Eric and her. Her initial instinct was to run to the guest room and seek out Eric. Yet even as she moved towards the door, her pride ruled over instinct.

No. She was not in the wrong to run to Francis. Tonight her first obligation was to her child. She tossed aside her robe, pulled a nightgown from a drawer, and slid it over her head before the dying embers in the grate. It was past two. In four hours Elvira would be coming into the room with her morning tea.

The sky was rosy with early dawn before she fell asleep. She awoke from habit at six. Immediately the memory of last night assaulted her. She reached with one hand to Eric's side of the bed. Why was he behaving so illogically? He was demanding that she choose between Francis and him. She loved both of them. Needed both of them.

Caroline pulled herself into a sitting position, thrusting the pillow behind her back as Elvira came into the room.

'We had us a sprinklin' of snow last night.' Elvira offered her usual weather report. 'But it looks like it's gonna be warmer today.'

'I hope so, Elvira.' Caroline forced a smile.

She drank her English tea, laced with fresh sweet cream, seeking solace in its warmth. Heat was coming up in the radiators in noisy, welcome gasps. Later in the morning a breakfast tray would be brought to her from the house.

Caroline planned each day with care. The hours at the mill, the hours with Francis, the hours with the other two children and Eric. Before Francis the nights had belonged to Eric and her; now the shadow of Francis lay in the bed with them.

With sudden urgency Caroline left the bed and prepared for the day. Hoping to encounter Eric and learn that he regretted last night's hasty departure, she dressed with record speed and went downstairs. Sophie sat alone in the small octagonal breakfast room, cheerful with Chinese wallpaper. She smiled in welcome when Caroline came into the room.

'Eric left early. He said he wanted to go over a brief before he met with a client who was coming in early.' Sophie's voice deepened in compassion. 'You had a bad time with Francis last night.'

'One of his worst spells. But Dr Adams feels he may be able to help Francis.' Caroline sat at the table while Sophie finished her coffee. In a few minutes they would leave together for the mill. Eric had left the house early

33

to avoid seeing her, she tortured herself. How long would he keep up this absurdity?

'Caroline, don't raise your hopes too high,' Sophie pleaded. Sophie, like Eric, feared that she would be hurt again.

'I have faith in Dr Adams,' Caroline insisted. 'He's arranged to spend an hour with Francis five days a week. Nobody's ever worked with him on such a concentrated basis.'

'When is the architect coming?' Sophie changed the subject.

'At ten. I'd like Andrew and you to be there,' Caroline told her.

'You're sure you want to go ahead with it? We're having trouble finding hands to work the equipment we have.'

'We have more orders coming in than we can handle without expanding. We can't stand still, Sophie. We have to move ahead.' Wasn't that what Eric said about himself? *Caro, I can't spend the rest of my life in the State Legislature.* 'We pay the highest wages in the South. We'll find workers. We're almost a legend.'

'We're losing workers to other mills who aren't so choosy about the age of their workers,' Sophie shot back.

'I won't hire children under fourteen.' Caroline's face was set. There were mills that hired children even below the legal age of twelve. She remembered what Asa Candler told a convention of labour reformers five years ago: *'The most beautiful sight that we see is the child at labour; as early as he may get at labour, the more beautiful, the more useful does his life get to be.'* She heartily disagreed with the Coca-Cola manufacturer. 'Those children belong in school.'

'A lot of their parents don't agree with you,' Sophie pointed out drily. 'They leave us and go to a company

34

that will hire them and their children. Every year it's harder to hang on to enough labour.'

'We'll manage,' Caroline hedged. 'You'll see.'

Caroline took pride in the way the Southern cotton mills were outstripping those in New England. The Northerners were reluctant to scrap machinery that was still in good working order, ignoring the greater efficiency of the new equipment. By the end of the decade, she predicted, the Southern mills would monopolize the textile industry.

The morning in the mill sped past. At ten sharp the architect arrived. Caroline sent word to Sophie and Andrew to join them in her office.

'I'm disturbed about building yet another annexe,' Sophie said bluntly, ignoring the reproachful stare of the architect. 'Our mill village houses are occupied to capacity. Where will we put new workers? If we can round them up.' Her eyes moved from Caroline to Andrew, knowing he must support her in this.

'It's dangerous,' he admitted. He was, as always, unhappy at disagreeing with Caroline. 'If we're drawn into war, there could be trouble.'

'Wilson is a man of peace. He won't let us become involved in war,' Caroline rejected. Like many Americans, Eric and she were worried about the situation in Mexico. Eric had come back from the Spanish-American War a stern pacifist. 'I want to go ahead with the annexe. If need be, we'll build more houses.'

'You'll *have* to build,' Sophie warned. 'Where else will workers find housing they can afford? Not in Atlanta with rents rising every year.'

'You have the land.' The architect was delighted at the prospect of enlarging his assignment. 'The houses can be ready when the annexe is complete. We can go into immediate production.'

35

Only part of Caroline's mind focused on the meeting. At three Dr Adams would be coming to the house. She had to believe that he could help Francis. Until Francis was a normal child, she was in bondage. It was wrong of Eric to stipulate that Dr Adams was to have only one year to achieve a cure. He would have as long as he needed, Caroline swore.

At ten to three Caroline left the mill and drove to the house. Francis was in his room with Patience. She was holding his hands as she sang to him, which told Caroline that he had been in one of his head-banging periods. She knew not to try to talk to him. With a faint smile for Patience, she sat in the slipper chair by the window.

At the sound of Dr Adams' arrival Caroline rose to her feet and went to the door of Francis' room to wait for the doctor.

'Francis has been banging his head against the wall again,' Caroline explained while they walked together into the bedroom.

Victor gazed intently at Francis, who gave no indication that he was aware of anyone's presence in the room.

'We must find a small football helmet for him to wear,' Victor decided after a moment of concentration. 'Well-padded inside so that he can't hurt his head. Do you suppose you can find something like that?' His dark eyes were matter-of-fact.

'If I can't, I'll have one made,' Caroline promised. How absurd that she had not thought of something so practical herself.

'I want you to leave me alone with Francis for an hour,' he explained gently. 'Don't be disturbed at whatever you hear in this room. Whatever I'm doing will be to help Francis.'

'I know.' She was drawn to his honesty, his sensitivity. 'Patience, we'll leave Francis with Dr Adams,' she said.

'Yes'um,' Patience accepted.

'I'll be waiting in the library,' Caroline told Victor Adams, and left Francis' bedroom.

Caroline sat in the library, trying to concentrate on the morning's *Constitution*. At intervals Francis emitted a piercing scream, then was quiet again. Was he frightened of Dr Adams? she asked herself guiltily. But Dr Adams brought hope. *Dear God, let him be able to help Francis.*

Liz and Josh returned from school. Hearing their voices, she called them into the library and explained that from now on Dr Adams would be here every day at three to spend an hour with Francis.

'Then you can listen to me practice my music,' Liz said with satisfaction. 'Leave the library door open so you can hear me,' she ordered, heading for the piano in the parlour.

'Mama . . .' Josh was all at once sombre.

'What, honey?'

'Will I ever be like Francis?' His dark eyes were fearful as they searched hers.

'No, Josh.' Her throat tightening, Caroline reached to draw him close. How vulnerable a little boy could be. 'You'll never be like Francis. And someday he'll be more like you. You'll see.'

'Liz says when we grow up and get married, our children will be like Francis.'

'No, Josh!' She spoke with an intensity that startled him. It unnerved her to discover that Josh and Liz harboured such fears. 'Liz and you will grow up and marry and have fine, healthy children. Liz is mistaken.'

'I'm going up to my room.' Josh appeared relieved. 'Who wants to listen to that awful piano practice?'

Slightly more than an hour later she heard Dr Adams call to Patience. Simultaneously Liz abandoned her practising to go up to her room. Caroline stood in the doorway of the library, awaiting Dr Adams' appearance. She heard him talking briefly with Liz on the stairs.

'Was Francis difficult?' she asked when he approached.

'We have much work ahead of us,' he stated gently. His dark eyes rested on her. 'I met Liz. I can't believe you have a twelve-year-old daughter.'

'I'll have Elvira bring us coffee while you tell me about Francis.' Fighting against a surge of self-consciousness, she reached for the pull to summon Elvira.

They talked over coffee, absorbed in the task that lay ahead. Caroline relaxed in Victor Adams' warmth, his earnestness about his work.

'This house used to be full of the laughter of children.' Caroline's face was pained in recall. 'But in this last year both Liz and Josh have given up bringing any of their friends home. They're ashamed of Francis.' She hesitated. 'My husband feels we ought to arrange for Francis to live away from the house, but I can't – '

'No, you mustn't,' Victor interrupted. 'He should not be put through any serious change. Each move in his routine must be orchestrated with care.'

She would do whatever Victor Adams ordered, Caroline swore to herself while she listened to his schedule for Francis. This was Francis' chance for a normal life. Nobody – not even Eric – could be allowed to stand in the way.

Caroline napped briefly before dinner, a rare occurrence for her. Waking, she dressed and hurried downstairs. Josh and Liz were already in the dining room, fighting to claim Sophie's attention. Sophie glanced towards the door as Caroline approached.

'Eric called a few moments ago to say he'll be detained downtown. We're not to wait dinner for him.'

'Then I'll tell Mattie to serve.' Caroline concealed her

sharp disappointment. Eric was sulking. When he drew within himself, refusing outward battle, he was exasperating.

After the nightly battle to ship Liz and Josh off to their rooms to study, Caroline retired to her own. She lay alone in bed, reviewing sales figures Sophie had prepared for her. All the while, she was conscious of every minute sound on the floor below. When she heard Eric arrive home, she laid aside the sales figures. He was talking with Roland. Now he was coming upstairs.

Her heart pounding, she listened for his footsteps down the hall. She waited for him to open the door and come to her. He was walking past her room, his footsteps muted in deference to the hour. Moments later she heard a door down the hall open and close. Eric had gone into the guest room.

It wasn't just her preoccupation with Francis that infuriated him, Caroline forced herself to rationalize. He was irritated because she persisted in refusing to go to The Hague peace conference with him in August. He knew it was impossible for her to leave Atlanta for a month, even if Francis was well. In August the farmers were picking cotton. The mill needed her. She would remain.

Had Eric resented her independence all through the years? Her mind hurtled backward. Eric had been shocked when she took over selling, as the General had done. But who else was there to handle this? Not Sophie. Not Andrew. And Eric was frank in his distaste for the mill. Without her at the helm he would have been forced into forsaking politics and law to take over the mill.

If she had not forsaken London for Atlanta – if she had not managed in that chaotic year and a half before the General's death to win her grandfather's affection – Eric would have inherited the Hampton fortune. Did that

39

upset him, despite all his protestations? In truth the Hampton fortune was *theirs*, in trust for their children and their children's children. Did it irk Eric that she was not beholden to him for her very existence?

Only in this last year had she come to realize that Eric resented her being able to function in a man's world. Sometimes at social gatherings, when she became engrossed in textile talk with other mill operators, she could sense his disapproval. Did that make her less of a woman? In bed she was Eric's wife, the woman who loved him.

Tonight she lay alone, fully awake and passionate. For a truant moment she considered darting down the hall to the guest room. She wanted Eric to make love to her tonight. She *needed* that. But no, she would not crawl to him.

To outward appearances Caroline's life seemed little changed in the weeks that followed the Inauguration. Eric gave no outward indication that a rift existed between them, though with growing frequency he would phone the house in the afternoon to report that he would be detained downtown for dinner. Caroline remembered with disconcerting vividness how often Eric had been absent from the dinner table in the tumultuous final two years of his marriage to Tina, who had died in a fire in Paris.

Could he be considering a divorce? No, she forced herself to acknowledge. A divorce would kill him politically. Nor would he subject the children to that disgrace.

Night after night she sat at the dinner table and tried to ignore Eric's absence. When he was home, he was polite, seemingly solicitous of her welfare, yet there was a frightening wall between them that had never before existed. Each night she lay alone in bed, hoping he would come to her.

Tonight Caroline dressed with infinite care for the opera, which they were attending with Marian Bolton. She listened all the while for sounds of Eric's arrival. Fearful he would not be here in time. She tensed at the sound of the doorbell. Roland was going to the door.

'Good evenin', Mist' Eric.'

Caroline took a deep breath. She wouldn't have to make excuses for Eric's absence. He was bounding up the stairs. Of course, he would go with her to the opera with Marian. Marian brought news from Washington.

With coat and purse in tow, Caroline went downstairs to wait for Eric. He was already in the reception hall. He inspected her green Charmeuse satin frock, cut with charming simplicity, daring only in the slight slit of the skirt, as decreed by fashion.

'You look beautiful, Caro.' For an electric instant his eyes held hers.

'Thank you.' Caroline's heart pounded. Why didn't he grasp her by the hand and run back upstairs with her to their bedroom? Seven weeks had gone by since Eric had made love to her.

'I told Roland to bring the Pierce Arrow out front. It'll only take ten minutes to drive to the Boltons'.' He pulled the door wide for her, and they walked across the wide veranda to the waiting Pierce Arrow.

In tacit agreement they hurried through dinner with a speed that elicited reproachful clucks from the Bolton maid. Marian ordered the Packard brought to the front of the house while they collected their coats.

Marian's chauffeur deposited them before the auditorium-armoury, where opera lovers were arriving in impressive numbers. Eric positioned himself between Caroline and Marian and guided them into the quietly elegant main hall, which had a seating capacity of more than five thousand. The horseshoe-shaped arena was surrounded by boxes, a dress circle, and two balconies. For Opera Week the balcony rails were adorned by bright-coloured fringed bunting hung in swags.

'I love Offenbach,' Marian said while they took their seats. 'His music is so tuneful.'

'He's a woman's composer,' Caroline mused. 'Sentimental and romantic.'

Caroline leaned back in her seat, willing herself to forget her personal torment in the magic of the Offenbach music. Gilly and Bori were in top voice. This was the Metropolitan Opera in its most brilliant performance. Yet Caroline was ever conscious of Eric's restlessness.

At the intermission at the conclusion of the first act, Caroline, Marian, and Eric abandoned their seats to stroll among the enthusiastic operagoers.

'Gilly and Bori are superb!' a man to Caroline's right exclaimed. 'Not only is Bori's voice miraculously flexible, but she's young and beautiful as well.'

'You mustn't overlook Rothier and Carl Jorn,' his companion rebuked. 'The whole company is fantastic.'

'Caroline, you must tell me,' Marian coaxed. 'How do you feel about Victor Adams?'

'Marian, I'm so grateful that you brought him to us.' Caroline ignored Eric's expression of annoyance. 'Victor's patience with Francis is phenomenal.'

Marian hesitated. 'Does Victor feel he's making any progress?'

'He said it'll be a long road,' Caroline told her. Eric's face tensed. He swung his head away, pretended to be absorbed in the colourful assemblage. She could not – *would not* – censor her conversation to please Eric.

'Caroline, honey! And Eric!' A light, girlish voice – though its owner was past thirty – halted their return to their seats. 'And Mrs Bolton. How nice to see you all tonight.'

Leonora Carlyle – small, dark-haired, with doll-like features and wide blue eyes – hovered before them. Caroline compelled herself to be cordial, though she detested Leonora. Eric seemed amused by her.

'Mama's here with me,' Leonora effervesced, and turned to beckon the florid-faced mountainous Mrs Kendrick, who was a distant cousin to Tina. Local gossip insisted that not only did Mrs Kendrick live with her daughter during Leonora's ten-year marriage to Judge Carlyle, but that she accompanied the couple on their European honeymoon. Since the judge's death four years ago, Leonora was said to be on a frenzied search to replace him. 'Mama,' Leonora called fretfully, because Mrs Kendrick seemed reluctant to disengage herself from her male companion, 'please come say hello to family.'

Caroline's cordiality was strained. Tina's cousin was hardly family. Eric, too, was irritated by this reminder of his first wife.

Mrs Kendrick bore down on them with the grace of a rhinoceros.

'Isn't the performance breathtaking?' Her eyes skimmed over Eric and Caroline to rest on Marian. The senator's wife ranked above a mere legislator.

Caroline was aware that Leonora's gaze had settled on Eric. Leonora looked at every man as though he were the most magnificent animal she had ever encountered.

'The opera's charming,' Marian agreed. Thirty years as a politician's wife had trained Marian to be polite to everyone, though Caroline knew she had little liking for either Leonora or her mother. 'I believe it's time to return to our seats.'

Caroline and Marian remained in their seats during the next intermission. Eric excused himself; of late he had become addicted to pipe-smoking. Caroline was glad for this little time alone with Marian, to talk about Victor's efforts with Francis.

When the curtain fell on the epilogue, the audience rose to their feet. The cast took endless curtain calls. At last, convinced there would be no more curtain calls, the audience slowly moved out of the auditorium, satisfied they had witnessed grand opera's greatest success in Atlanta thus far.

At the Bolton house Mary was waiting to serve them coffee and petits fours in the huge double parlour, where a fire had been laid in readiness for their return. While Eric and Marian launched into an absorbed discussion of the unhealthy situation in Mexico, Caroline grew anxious. Was Francis all right? He had suffered such a bad spell when Victor was with him this afternoon. Her face grew hot as she recalled what had happened. Francis had deliberately urinated on Victor.

'Eric, it's late,' Caroline interjected apologetically, earlier than she would have on other occasions. 'I'm concerned about Francis,' she confided to Marian.

'Patience is with him.' Eric's voice was testy. Her colour high, Caroline rose to her feet.

'I'll drive myself home. Marian, you'll send Eric home in your car?'

'George will drive you home,' Marian substituted, disconcerted by Caroline's departure alone. 'I'll feel more comfortable.' It was a gentle reprimand to Eric, though Caroline knew Marian enjoyed talking politics far into the night, despite her declarations of distaste for the Washington life.

'You don't mind, Caro?' Eric was casual.

'I don't mind at all,' Caroline assured him sweetly. She

44

minded. She was furious that Eric could be so lacking in concern for Francis.

'I'll see you to the door, Caroline.' Marian's smile was conciliatory.

4

Eric leaned forward in his chair, his third cup of coffee growing cold while he talked at length with Marian about the senator's political future.

'Jim's right,' Marian assured him. 'Harry will retire from the Senate after this term if he knows you're running for his seat. I want him to retire,' she said vigorously.

'Miss Marian,' the Boltons' longtime houseman intruded, knowing he would not be reprimanded for this liberty. 'It's way past midnight. You has the ladies comin' in for a Memorial Day breakfast in the mornin', and you always say you needs to get your beauty sleep when you is entertainin'.'

'Isaac, you're right.' Eric rose to his feet. 'I've been here an unconscionably long time.'

'I've enjoyed every minute,' Marian told him. 'I hope Caroline won't be angry that I've kept you so long.'

'Would you mind if I make a phone call before I leave?' Eric grinned. 'Jim will be relieved to hear that you're in favour of the senator's retiring. Everybody knows he won't do that without your approval.' He moved forward to kiss her good night. 'Thank you for a beautiful evening.'

'Eric . . .' All at once she was serious. 'Give Victor Adams a chance with Francis.'

'Dr Adams will have his year,' Eric promised. But at the end of that year he would be actively campaigning for Congress. When the time came, he would go to Washington. With or without Caro.

Eric went into the library to phone Jim. He spoke

briefly with Jim, hesitated a moment, then reached for the phone again. When the operator came on the line, he gave her the number scrawled on the paper Leonora Carlyle had slipped into his hand while they talked during the second intermission at the opera. She pretended to want his advice about seeing a piece of property left her by the judge. But her eyes told him exactly what she wanted of him.

'Hello.' Leonora's sweet Southern voice greeted him as casually as though it were high noon. She had said, '*Call as late as you like – I never go to sleep until dawn.*'

'I can be there in fifteen minutes,' he said without identifying himself. 'Are you sure we won't disturb your mother?' The implication was that they would be discussing Leonora's property.

'Mama always has a glass of sherry at bedtime. The Battle of Atlanta could be fought again, and she wouldn't know, once she's between the sheets.' The way she said 'between the sheets' set his teeth on edge.

'I'm on my way.'

Isaac saw him out. He slid behind the wheel of the Pierce Arrow and drove through the night-empty streets to the Carlyle house on Peachtree Road. Judge Carlyle had built the house for his first wife, who died on their third wedding anniversary. The official report claimed she had been killed when she intercepted an intruder. It was widely believed that she had killed herself.

The judge, then a member of the City Council, remained a widower until he was fifty, when he married seventeen-year-old Leonora Kendrick. The mother had promoted the marriage, Eric surmised, because the Kendricks were strong on family position and weak on money. Eric pulled up before the Queen Anne-style house, its ground-storey walls of rough masonry, the two upper floors shingled. The windows of the upper floors

47

were dark, but one lower wing of the multiple facades of the house was illuminated.

Eric left the car and walked up to the entrance. Leonora pulled the door open as he reached the stairs. She stood there in the spill of light, wearing an ivory brocade robe fastened to the throat but designed to display every curve of her body.

'I have coffee waiting for you.' Leonora might have been entertaining a suitor in midafternoon.

'Strong, I hope.' His eyes were seeing past the ivory brocade robe. One cup of coffee and she would be flat on her back. These last celibate weeks had been trying. He would be happy to dispense with the coffee and give the lady what she wanted.

She led him down the wide corridor, dotted with Tabriz prayer rugs, to a room whose function defied definition. The walls were covered with a delicate floral wallpaper. A pair of green velvet upholstered armchairs flanked the marble fireplace, where a log smoldered in the grate. An English oak top table on three turned legs had been drawn between the chairs and set with two Haviland cups and saucers and an elaborate silver service. At one side of the room a four-poster canopied bed sat between two tall, narrow windows.

'The judge used this room in the two years before his death,' Leonora told Eric, gesturing him to a chair before the fireplace. 'When he was unable to climb the stairs.'

'Tell me more about this property you're considering selling,' he prodded while she poured coffee for him.

'It's the house where the judge kept his handsome young boys.' Leonora startled him with her candour. 'It's rented now. Mama thinks I ought to hold on to it. She says that the way Atlanta is spreading out into the country, that land will be worth a fortune in ten years.'

'Your mother's probably right.'

48

'The judge never laid a hand on me,' Leonora told him. Her smile was disdainful. 'At regular intervals he talked about my giving him a child, but he could never bring himself to perform his husbandly duties.'

'You encountered no problem in acquiring substitutes,' he said.

'No,' she admitted. 'But for a long time I've thought about you. I was sure there would be a night for us.'

'A night,' he pinpointed. He had no intention of becoming involved with Leonora Carlyle.

'Right.' She surprised him with her ready acquiescence. 'In my position I have to be discreet. Mama and I are looking for a successor to the judge.' Her eyes had an arousing way of lingering on his crotch. 'Too bad you're attached. You're handsome, important, rich and young enough.' Her eyes were laughing now. 'I'm sure you're young enough.'

'Honey, I'll be young enough for the next thirty years,' Eric boasted. 'Would you like a demonstration?'

'I thought you'd never ask,' Leonora set down her cup, walked the few feet between them, and sat across his thighs.

Eric cleared his throat. His body reacted instantly. She was built like Caro, he thought unwarily. Passionate like Caro. Leonora lifted her face to his; and while he reached for her already parted mouth, he felt her hand seeking him.

His mouth was hard on hers, his tongue darting into the hot, moist crevice. His hands sought the buttons of the brocade robe and released them, one after another, to the waist. She wore nothing beneath.

'Take off your robe,' he ordered, lifting her to her feet.

He began to strip. Mama would not disturb them, whether she slept or not. This was Leonora Carlyle's way of life. Gossip was correct.

'Eric, you act as though you were in a whorehouse.' Leonora's eyes scolded him, but she was removing her robe.

'A very exclusive, private whorehouse,' he amended with an audacious grin.

'I ought to throw you out.' Leonora pretended to sulk.

'You won't. You're an overheated bitch who can't get enough. But I promise you one thing, sugar. You won't forget tonight for a long time.'

Leonora stood before him, wearing only a diamond-studded wedding band. His eyes dwelt on her high full breasts, crested with enormous nipples, moved to the narrow waist and curving hips. The thighs not long enough for true beauty, but he was sure there would be passion between them.

'You talk a lot, Eric,' Leonora taunted. 'Show me.'

He swept her off her feet and carried her to the bed. Had the judge died in this bed? he mused. But no matter. The judge had no taste for women. Pity, when he had this at his disposal.

Eric dropped her on to the bed and sat on the edge. His hands rippled over the warm velvet of her body. Tonight would be theirs alone. Leonora was husband-hunting. She couldn't afford to boast that she had slept with Eric Hampton, even if women did talk like that.

'Eric, stop wasting time.' Leonora reached with a small, slim hand to fondle him.

'Damn you, Leonora!'

He lifted himself above her and thrust within her, abandoning restraint.

'Don't fret, Eric,' she murmured. 'We have all night ahead of us. We can do everything.'

The passion stored in him for several weeks demanded release. He was rough with her, intent only on his own satisfaction. He talked to her in the gutter language he

50

had not used in bed for fifteen years. Feeling himself swelling within her.

'No!' she rejected when he made a move to withdraw. Unexpectedly she giggled. 'Don't worry, Eric. I can't conceive. The judge never knew that, but what did it matter? Stay.' Her hands were active, coaxing him into fresh heat. 'Eric, make me scream. *Make me scream!*'

When Eric lay limp and exhausted above her, she prodded him on to his back and began the ritual she had learned through a varied apprenticeship. It would be a night they would both remember.

Eric noticed the first grey streaks of dawn filtering through the drapes while he dressed. Leonora had fallen asleep, naked and satiated. There was a raw, early-morning chill in the room. He pulled the satin coverlet across Leonora's body, and stared at her in odd detachment. This was the first time in over thirteen years of marriage that he had been unfaithful to Caro. He felt no guilt.

Caroline awoke at eight, mindful that today Eric and she were to take Liz and Josh to the Confederate Memorial Day parade. What time had he come home last night? She had been so tired she had fallen asleep moments after settling herself in bed.

She frowned, hearing Liz and Josh fighting in the hall. Sophie insisted she was too easy with them. If she was, it was because she felt guilty about her constant involvement with Francis and the mill, which took up so much of her time.

'You tell Mama that, and I'll beat your brains out!' Liz screeched. 'I didn't tell Lou Ellen we were moving to Washington next year!'

'You did, too!' Josh accused.

Caroline pulled on her robe and hurried to the door.

'Lower your voice, Elizabeth,' she commanded. 'You, too, Josiah.' She used their formal names only when she was angry. 'You'll wake up everybody in the house.'

'Mama, you're not even dressed, and we're supposed to go to the parade,' Liz wailed.

'The parade won't start until two this afternoon,' Caroline told her. 'We'll leave early, though, so we can find a good spot to watch from,' she soothed. 'Now, go downstairs and have your breakfast.'

As she had promised, Caroline marshalled Liz and Josh into the automobile shortly before one o'clock. Roland would drive them into the city and wait with the car until after the parade. She was irritated that Eric had not emerged from his room. He had agreed to accompany the children and her to the parade. It had been a ritual with them since Liz was three.

On impulse she asked Roland to drive first to Andrew's cottage, midway between Hampton House and the mill, on the chance that he might like to go to the parade with them. Andrew was delighted at the invitation.

'What a beautiful day for the parade,' he said with quiet pleasure while they drove away from Hamptonville. 'The perfect time of year to honour the Confederate dead.' The earth was lush with greenery. Flowers bloomed in glorious splendour on every side.

'Andrew, we must do something to stop this wholesale stealing of our workers.' Ten men had already left. Caroline was oblivious of the splendour of the April day. 'Do you have any idea who's responsible?'

'Todd Murdoch,' Andrew told her. 'I got it out of one of the men when the family and he were vacating their house this morning. Murdoch lures them away with offers to hire their children under twelve as well as themselves. They want those extra pay envelopes each week.'

'That's illegal,' Caroline rejoined, and sighed. 'Not

52

that the law is ever enforced.' She had never met Todd Murdoch, but she had heard much about him. He was reported to be ruthless, hard-driving, and hardworking.

'Andrew, we can't let this go on,' Caroline pressed. 'We're not alone in losing workers. I spoke to Arthur Bradley and Ed Swift. They're being raided, too.'

'Who's Murdoch?' Liz abandoned her private discussion with Josh about last night's parade to eavesdrop on her mother and Andrew.

'A man who owns a mill in Atlanta.' Caroline shot a warning glance at Andrew. They would terminate the discussion for now.

Roland left them a few blocks from the parade area. They walked to an advantageous point on Peachtree. Already the sidewalks were jammed with humanity. Traffic had been detoured. Caroline felt a poignant closeness to her grandfather, dead almost fifteen years. She visualized the General riding down this same street, his back ramrod stiff, his head high, rain streaming down his face.

Visitors who had come from all over the South to hear the opera were part of today's crowd to honour the Confederate dead. No parade in Atlanta ever radiated such warmth – and such sadness – as the one on Memorial Day, Caroline thought, honouring the Confederate dead while remembering the infamy of the Fall of Atlanta.

All at once the sound of martial music alerted the crowd. The parade was moving. Andrew dropped an arm protectively about Caroline and Liz as the onlookers surged forward in their enthusiasm.

A platoon of police appeared first to clear the way for the grand marshal, General Nash. Cheers filled the air while the general and his staff moved along Peachtree en route to Oakland Cemetery.

'Here comes Governor Brown,' Andrew told Josh and Liz.

The governor was followed by the infantry divisions, college cadets, the Boy Scouts. The superintendent of the public schools commanded the second division of the parade, made up of the Red Men's drum corps, the Red Men, high-school and grammar-school boys. A seemingly endless column of marchers, sprinkled generously with lively bands.

Liz shrieked approval when the ladies' contingent appeared. Daughters of the Confederacy, Children of the Confederacy, Colonial Dames, the DAR, and Daughters of 1812. Even a group of ladies from the Home for Old Women.

The stars of the parade, who brought tears to the eyes of many a spectator, were the proud old Confederate veterans themselves, most of them on foot. Only a few capitulated to the years and rode. Each year their number grew smaller.

'Caroline, look to the left on the other side of the street,' Andrew whispered. 'The tall man wearing a brown homburg.'

Caroline's eyes found the man Andrew indicated. He stood inches above the others about him. He appeared to be in his mid-thirties, handsome in an earthy fashion, flamboyant in dress.

'Who is he?' she asked Andrew.

'Todd Murdoch.'

Gazing at Murdoch, Caroline could feel the power he exuded. He was here in Atlanta to disrupt the whole textile industry, for his own advantage.

'What do you know about him, Andrew?'

'He grew up in Chicago, where his father was a meat packer. I understand he married into a Massachusetts textile family. When his wife died, he sold his mill up there and moved here.'

'Call a meeting of the mill operators,' Caroline decided on impulse. The others were as upset as she. 'Arrange it as soon as possible. We can't let Murdoch come into Atlanta and behave like a privateer.'

'Mama, you're not watching the parade,' Josh scolded.

'Darling, I'm watching,' Caroline placated. 'It's the best Memorial Day parade ever.'

The family had just sat down to breakfast on Sunday morning when Roland came into the room to tell Eric that Jim Russell was on the telephone.

'Go ahead without me,' Eric said, pushing back his chair.

He went into the library, confident that Jim had not called him to pass the time of day. 'Good morning, Jim.' He sat behind the desk.

'Have you seen the extra the *Constitution* brought out this morning?' Jim asked.

'No.' He was instantly alert. 'What's happened.'

'It's probably irrelevant, but I thought of Liz right away. Some maniac killed a thirteen-year-old girl in Atlanta. It was a brutal, sadistic murder.'

'Good Lord!' Eric flinched. 'How much do the police know?'

'She was found in the basement of the National Pencil factory about three this morning. Her name was Mary Phagan. She worked in the factory. Even the police felt sick when they saw the body. Both eyes were bruised, cheeks slashed, head caked with dried blood. A piece of rope and a strip from her underskirt were tied around her neck. Her clothes were torn, fingers out of joint. The body was so covered with grime the police didn't know if

55

she was white or coloured until they looked under her stockings.'

'Any suspects?' Eric asked.

'The police took the night watchman, who discovered the body, to the police station. They questioned the plant superintendent. He's also part-owner of the factory. Name's Frank.'

'Leo Frank,' Eric pinpointed. 'I've heard Noah mention him. The police don't think Frank killed her?'

'They're not making any statements yet. But I thought you ought to know.'

'Thanks, Jim. We'll keep a close watch on Liz.'

Eric returned to the breakfast table, reminding himself that he had promised to play 'catch' with Josh and Liz. He'd take the two of them to a baseball game next week. He felt a surge of sympathy for the parents of the murdered little girl. Their lives would never be the same again.

It was almost an hour before Eric was able to draw Caroline into the library to tell her about the murder. Why did she look so stricken when he said he had to talk to her? What was she expecting? For a moment guilt brushed him. No. She couldn't know about Leonora. Nobody knew.

'That poor little girl.' Caroline shivered. 'Nobody in Atlanta is going to sleep well until her murderer is caught.'

'This is a garish reinforcement of a favourite Southern conviction. "It's a disgrace for women and girls to work in the mills, side by side with men,"' Eric mocked.

'That's archaic,' Caroline dismissed. 'It isn't degrading for women to work in factories. It's an economic necessity.'

'Try telling that to the rural families that pour into Atlanta hoping to better their lives with factory jobs.

Mary Phagan's death proves the factories are evil. The city is evil.' Eric pulled his pipe from his jacket pocket, packed it with tobacco while he squinted in thought. 'Caro, they come here from the farms, and what do they find? They're forced to live in slums. Working conditions in Atlanta are among the worst in the country. They work a sixty-hour week, with half an hour for lunch. Mary Phagan earned ten cents an hour. You and I know that children work in this city for twenty-two cents a week!'

'Not in the Hampton Mill!' Caroline flashed.

'No.' Eric's voice was gentle. He knew how Caroline fought to improve conditions in their mill village, despite much hostility from their stockholders, fortunately a minority voting block. 'But we have no factory inspectors. We know how many owners ignore the laws against hiring young children.'

'I saw Todd Murdoch at the parade yesterday,' Caroline said in recall. 'He's stealing workers from almost all the mills, and hiring their children as young as ten. He doesn't care that it's illegal, and neither do they. They want the extra pay envelopes.'

'We passed legislation, but everybody ignores it. Caro, the unions are going to have to come in and raise wages and shorten hours before the situation improves. If a man makes a living wage, he's not going to try to push his ten-year-old child into the mill.'

'I hope they catch the fiend who killed Mary Phagan.' Caroline's voice was uneven. 'I pray they catch him before he kills another little girl.'

5

Sunlight poured into Caroline's office while she sat hunched over the morning *Constitution*. Normally she read the newspaper after dinner. It was morbid, but she felt compelled to read every word that spilled across the front page, even the sickening revelation that Mary Phagan was a child, a year older than Liz.

'Isn't it awful?' Ellen walked into the room, notebook in hand, and closed the door behind her. 'Everybody on the streetcar this morning was talking about the murder. They all think it was the Negro night watchman.' Ellen grimaced. 'They're saying she was molested before she was murdered.'

'Eric told me that yesterday afternoon when the watchman was brought out of the factory, two or three thousand people had gathered outside. Some of them yelled, "He ought to be lynched!"' Caroline shook her head. 'How do we make people understand that lynching is murder?'

'I was so worried about Janet last night.' Ellen sat in the chair beside Caroline's desk. 'She was visiting a girlfriend when I heard the newsboys running through the streets with the extra. I was terrified of her coming home alone later, even though she was only a block away.'

'I know. I look at Liz, and I'm scared. How can we be sure they're safe?'

Both women started at the knock on the door.

'Come in,' Caroline called.

Andrew opened the door. 'I've set up a meeting with the operators for Friday night. Here at the mill at eight.'

When Caroline returned to the house at three, Patience told her that Dr Adams was already with Francis. The last week he had been spending as much as two hours a day with him. Caroline sensed that he felt he was on the brink of a breakthrough, though there was no visible change in Francis' condition.

Caroline sat in the library to wait for Victor while Patience brought her mint tea. In a few minutes Liz and Josh charged into the room, full of questions about yesterday's murder.

'Don't they know who killed Mary Phagan yet?' Liz demanded avidly.

'They'll catch him, won't they?' Josh asked.

'They'll catch him,' Caroline said. Eric had been scathing last night in his assessment of the Atlanta police force's capabilities. In the past two years about eighteen Negro women had been murdered in Atlanta. Not one murderer had been brought to justice. But Mary Phagan was white. The populace was outraged that 'the sweetest and purest thing on earth – a young girl' had been attacked. No Southerner could rest until she was avenged. Hoping to change the subject, Caroline commanded, 'Liz . . . Josh, tell me what happened at school today.'

After an interval, Caroline shipped Liz off to practice, while Josh escaped to his room. Caroline's mind dwelt on Eric. It irked her that she must be the one to mend fences. It was Eric who had moved out of their bedroom. But tonight, she decided, she would push aside her pride, go to the guest room, and knock on Eric's door. She should have taken the initiative weeks ago.

When Victor came down from Francis' room today,

they talked over tea about the horror of Mary Phagan's death. Atlanta was outraged by the murder. While they talked, Caroline heard Eric arrive. Victor and she had been so engrossed she had been unaware of the time.

'Eric just came home,' Caroline rose to her feet. 'I'd like you two to meet.' It was time.

'Of course.' Victor smiled, yet Caroline sensed his unease. Did he suspect that Eric disapproved?

'Eric,' she called down the hall while he headed towards the stairs. 'Please come in and meet Dr Adams.'

He paused a moment before striding towards the library. She could tell he was annoyed. Yet Eric ought to meet the doctor who was treating Francis. Even Liz and Josh seemed to look upon Victor as a member of the family now.

'Eric, I'd like you to meet Dr Adams,' Caroline was determinedly cheerful. 'This is Francis' father.'

'I've been looking forward to meeting you, sir.' Victor seemed at ease as Eric and he shook hands, but the atmosphere was suddenly tense.

'Caroline has told me how optimistic you are about Francis,' Eric said. Damn him! She had made no such statement.

'Eric, I told you Victor warned me it will be a long haul.' Colour flooded her face. 'We can't expect miracles.'

'How long has it been?' Eric inquired with deceptive politeness. 'Since the Inauguration, I believe? About eight weeks?'

'About that,' Victor agreed.

'And you've made some step forward?' Eric challenged, the scorn in his eyes contradicting his polite smile.

'None,' Victor said. 'It's a matter of trying ways of

reaching through to Francis. So far I've not found the proper way.'

'Papa!' All at once Liz was hurling herself into the library. 'Is that the afternoon newspaper?'

'Will you excuse me, please?' Victor was apologetic. 'I should be stopping by to see a patient in the hospital. I'm glad to have met you, Mr Hampton.'

'My pleasure.' Eric nodded in farewell.

'Liz, you are not to read the *Georgian*,' Caroline ordered, but Josh and she were devouring the photograph of Mary Phagan that graced the front page.

'She was pretty,' Liz decided, all at once sad.

'Very pretty,' Eric agreed, scrutinizing the photograph. 'It's hard to believe she was not quite fourteen. But your mother's right.' He pulled the newspaper away from Liz. 'You're not to read all the gory details of Mary Phagan's death.' He turned to Caroline. 'The police questioned David's friend, Leo Frank, all this morning again. He wasn't arrested, but I hear he's hired the Pinkerton agency to conduct a private investigation, since the factory's involved. He's also hired a lawyer.' Eric shook his head. 'That wasn't wise.'

'You mean people will think he's guilty because he rushed out to hire a lawyer without even being arrested?' Caroline was troubled.

'It's likely. Every little detail is being picked up and magnified a thousand times. Every new edition of the *Georgian* has more inflammatory material.'

In the midst of dinner Eric announced that he had to go downtown for a committee meeting of his peace group.

'Again?' Sophie clucked. 'You might find it more convenient to move yourself into the Georgian Terrace Hotel.' Caroline's fork clattered to the floor. 'You only come home to change clothes.'

'Sophie, you're being sarcastic,' Eric reproved. 'You

know we're preparing for the peace conference in The Hague. It's less than four months away, and we have a lot to accomplish.'

'We'll hardly know you're away.' Sophie shrugged.

'Papa, take me with you to The Hague,' Liz pleaded. 'I've never been on a big ship. School will be out. I could go.' Her eyes shone with anticipation.

'I can't do that, honey,' Eric said gently. 'I'll be busy with conference business every minute.'

Caroline lowered her eyes to her plate. For weeks Eric had tried to persuade her to go with him to The Hague. In addition to the conference sessions, there would be receptions and dinners. Fascinating people from all over the world would be attending. She would love to go to The Hague, but Eric ought to understand she had other responsibilities.

Eric left while Elvira served dessert. Caroline struggled to conceal her disappointment. Why did he have to go downtown again tonight? Those meetings were more and more frequent, with the conference less than four months away, and they dragged on forever. She had been on the verge of trying to reconcile with Eric, but she knew now she would probably be fast asleep before he came home.

Caroline went upstairs when Sophie retired to her room. She looked in for an instant on Francis, as was her custom. How desperately she wished Victor could bring about some improvement that she could show to Eric! In the spill of moonlight she saw that Patience was still awake.

'He fine tonight, Miss Caroline,' Patience whispered. 'Did Dr Adams tell you? He teachin' Francis to count. With blocks. Francis count to four now.'

'Dr Adams didn't tell me.' Her voice was tender. Victor must be waiting until there was something more impressive to report. But she *was* impressed. 'I'm so pleased.'

'Yes'm. He gonna teach Francis all kinda things.' Patience's confidence in Victor matched her own.

On impulse Caroline walked to Francis' bed, brushed her mouth against his warm soft cheek. Dear God, let Victor help him. Let Francis have a normal life.

'Good night, Patience.'

'Good night, Miss Caroline.'

Caroline went into her own room and prepared for bed. She pulled open a window to allow the spring night air into the bedroom and sat in a chair by the window to read Theodore Dreiser's newest novel.

When Eric had not returned by eleven o'clock, Caroline went to bed. Tomorrow, she vowed, she would insist that Eric be home for dinner. She would tell Mattie to prepare the roast duck that was his favourite food, with early green peas and wild rice. She would make sure he stayed home all evening. And later she would go to the guest room and show Eric he had a wife who loved him.

Tuesday seemed to drag on interminably. All through the day Caroline's mind devised excuses to keep Eric home this evening. In addition to his favourite duck, she had told Mattie to make a pecan pie for dessert. She would come down to dinner in the new green dimity dress, one of those she had bought at Rich's in a hurried excursion in preparation for the approaching hot weather. Eric and she had not played chess for years. Tonight she would coax him into a chess game.

At three she left the mill for the house. Victor was upstairs with Francis. She went out to the kitchen to consult with Mattie about dinner.

'Mist' Eric gonna like dinner tonight,' Mattie prophesied with a mischievous glint in her eyes. Mattie knew tonight's dinner was a peace offering.

Victor spoke briefly with her over tea, with Liz practising scales in the background, and rushed off to make a hospital call. She left the door to the library open. Liz liked that. Within a few moments Liz switched from scales to the Tchaikovsky piece. A smile lighted Caroline's face. Liz played with such feeling.

Liz finished her piano practice and came into the library.

'I'll study down here,' she decided, 'instead of going up to my room.'

'Fine.' Caroline understood. Liz was waiting for Eric to come home with the *Journal*. All of Atlanta waited for a headline that would identify Mary Phagan's killer.

Caroline was about to go upstairs to change for dinner when Eric arrived. Liz pounced on the *Journal*, which he carried under one arm. Her eyes swept the headline.

'The police have arrested the superintendent. That's the Mr Frank that David knows!' Liz said indignantly.

'He's being detained until after the inquest,' Eric amended.

'He's in jail!' Liz retaliated, and sat on the edge of the sofa, absorbed in the story.

'Eric, what's this?' Caroline was reading over Liz's shoulder. '"WITNESSES POSITIVE MURDERED GIRL WAS SAME WHO CREATED SCENE AT THE TERMINAL STATION ON FRIDAY."'

'Two gatemen told the *Journal* that a young girl who created a scene at the station on Friday morning was Mary Phagan,' Eric explained. 'She was crying and carrying on. She dragged a young man off the Washington sleeper. They recognized her from the photograph in the *Journal* yesterday morning. To be sure they were not making a mistake, they went down to Bloomfield's chapel

64

to view the body. They're convinced the girl was Mary Phagan.'

Caroline started at the sound of the doorbell, being rung with an air of urgency. Roland was hurrying to respond.

'Are you expecting someone?' Eric asked curiously.

'No.'

'It's David.' Liz recognized his voice and ran into the hall. 'David, we're in the library.'

David rushed to the library. His face was pale, his eyes stricken.

'Eric, have you heard?' he asked. 'Leo Frank's been arrested!'

'It's here in the *Journal*,' Eric acknowledged.

'Lucille Frank was at the station when Leo was being questioned. Then Lanford, the Chief of Detectives, came out and said he was being held. They wouldn't even allow Lucille to see him!'

'Papa, can they do that?' Liz demanded.

'If Leo isn't cleared, Atlanta won't be safe for any Jew.' David declared, his voice uneven. 'It'll be like the pogroms in Russia and Poland. A man came into Noah's store this morning, ranting, "All the Jews ought to be driven out of Atlanta!"'

'Liz, go upstairs and wash up for dinner,' Caroline told her, unnerved by Liz's preoccupation with what David was saying.

'Mama, it's early,' Liz protested, her eyes darting to her father for support.

'Liz, go upstairs.' Caroline spoke with an authority that Liz resented but respected.

'You treat me like I was five years old!' Liz stalked out of the library in a rage.

'David, there will never be a pogrom in this country,' Caroline maintained. 'I know you have painful memories, but it can't happen here.'

'Caro, we can't close our eyes to growing signs of racism in this country,' Eric said. 'Look how Southern segregation laws have been increasing. Now we have legalized housing segregation, segregation on streetcars. We even have separate elevators here in Atlanta. And we can't ignore racist feelings in this country towards the Jews. Several years ago fifteen hundred shoe-factory workers threatened to strike in Massachusetts unless nine Jewish employees were dismissed.'

'In Russia Mendel Beiliss is imprisoned on charges he killed a twelve-year-old Christian boy in order to use the child's blood in a religious ceremony,' David interrupted bitterly. 'And it's starting here in Atlanta with Leo Frank.'

'It's not just that he's a Jew,' Eric analysed. 'He's also a Northerner and an industrialist. To the illiterate Atlantan, all Jews are city people, and the city is evil. Leo Frank is an employer, and hence the enemy. David, I'm concerned,' Eric admitted.

'Be concerned not only for Leo Frank. Be concerned for Atlanta's Jewish community, too.' David was grim.

'I'm sure they are in no danger,' Caroline injected.

'For God's sake, Caro, open your eyes!' Eric ordered. 'We have a racial situation right here in Atlanta, and it's going to get worse if Leo Frank goes to trial. You're so involved in the mill and with Francis that you can't see anything else!'

Caroline flinched as though Eric had slapped her. How had she deluded herself into believing she could break down the wall between Eric and herself? How dare Eric talk to her this way in front of David!

Forcing a smile, Caroline turned to David. 'David, would you excuse me for a few minutes? I must talk to Mattie about dinner.'

6

Caroline dressed for dinner in compulsive haste, striving to erase from her mind the memory of Eric's voice lashing at her in such hostility. She had been so eager to reconcile with Eric. She had planned tonight with such care. She had not recognized the distance between them. Eric looked at her with the eyes of a stranger. With a last glance at herself in the mirror, Caroline went downstairs to await dinner.

Eric sat alone in the parlour. At Caroline's appearance he glanced up from the law journal he was reading. His eyes were sombre. He didn't even notice her new dress. Five years ago he would have noticed.

'Mama!' Liz shrieked from somewhere in the hall. 'Mama!'

Caroline suppressed a wave of impatience and crossed to the door. Liz was running towards her, clutching a battered teddy bear in her arms.

'Liz, you must learn not to scream that way,' Caroline chastised.

'Francis does,' Liz retaliated. 'All the time.' She held up the teddy bear. 'Look what Francis did to him. He pulled out his eyes and pulled off his ears!'

'Liz, you're twelve years old. Don't you think it's time to forget about playing with teddy bears?' She always felt defensive when confronted with one of Francis' misdeeds.

'I don't play with teddy. He sits on my bed!' Liz was on the point of tears.

'Where was Patience?' Eric demanded.

'She must have dozed for a few minutes,' Caroline guessed. 'Francis kept her up most of last night.'

'Never mind, Liz,' Eric consoled, drawing her to him. 'It's almost May. The end of the month we'll be going up to Hampton Court.'

'Not this summer,' Caroline said quickly, and was immediately defensive again. 'Victor feels it would be bad for Francis to take him away from here. He has to be in Atlanta for his treatment.' Her heart was pounding.

'Is Dr Adams running this house?' Eric asked with quiet sarcasm. 'Is he to tell the family where to spend the summer?'

'Eric, we have to do this for Francis. This one summer,' Caroline specified. More, if need be, but she would face that later.

'Do you remember how devilishly hot it gets in Atlanta in the summer?' Eric challenged. 'The fans just blow around hot air.'

'Thousands of people stay in the city all summer,' Caroline pointed out.

'Because they have to,' Eric pounced. 'My children don't have to remain in the heat. We have a country house.'

'It would be bad for Francis to move him from familiar surroundings at this stage of his treatment. Victor's positive about that. He would slide backwards.'

'I haven't seen any progress,' Eric said flatly. Liz was solemn, her gaze shuttling between parents. 'All right, Caro, you stay in Atlanta with Francis. I'll take Liz and Josh and go up to Hampton Court until I have to leave for The Hague. At least, let them be comfortable until then.'

'What about my teddy bear, Mama?' Liz inquired, her smile angelic. 'Will you buy me a new dress to make up?'

'I'll buy you a new dress,' Caroline agreed, her head pounding.

She would drive up to Hampton Court every Sunday. Patience would be able to manage Francis for the day. It might be relaxing to be alone in the house for a few weeks, without having to be a referee between Josh and Liz, without facing Eric's anger.

Eric sat at dinner, aware that Caroline had chosen the menu to please him. She had dressed to please him. Now she acted as though he wasn't even at the table. She kept talking with Sophie about the new parcel-post system the government had just inaugurated.

He was sure Caro was furious with him for speaking out that way in front of David. He'd been upset. He spoke without thinking. But damn, it was the truth.

'What's happening at school?' Eric turned first to Liz, then to Josh.

They burst into speech simultaneously, fighting for his attention. All that was required of him was to listen. His mind focused on Caro. She was shutting him out of her life. Didn't she miss being with him? In all the years, she had never once pushed him away. No phony excuses, no air of conferring a favour on her husband. She was always ready to make love. This was one of the things that made their marriage so special.

Was it *his* fault that Caro had allowed Francis to disrupt the high moment of their passion? Was he less of a man than he was five years ago? Hell, no. Leonora Carlyle was proof of that.

Was there some other man? Caro was beautiful. She looked like a girl, despite the three children. Young enough for a man of Victor Adams' age. That son of a bitch was handsome enough to turn almost any woman's head. Was Victor Adams the reason Caro showed no indication of missing her husband in bed? Instantly he was ashamed. Not Caro.

Sitting in the parlour after dinner, he pretended to be absorbed in the law journal he had been reading earlier. Caroline was talking with Sophie about a meeting on Friday with other mill operators. His thoughts wandered to Leonora Carlyle. He wasn't in love with her, but she satisfied a need. He desired his wife, but he refused to resume a relationship that took second place to his child.

In sudden decision Eric rose to his feet.

'I'm going to drive over to Jim's house. He might have some news on the inquest.'

'David's so upset about it,' Caroline said to Sophie. 'He knows Leo and Lucille Frank.'

'If there's anything special, I'll call you,' Eric fabricated. Striding towards the library.

He carefully closed the library door and went to phone Leonora.

'Would you like to discuss that piece of property again?' he asked.

'I'd adore it. But don't come over for another hour. I have to get rid of some people. Dull people,' Leonora purred. 'You'll be much more interesting.'

'I promise.' He chuckled. No strings with Leonora. They both knew that. 'I'll be there in an hour.'

He left the house and drove to Jim's place, which was conveniently en route to his primary destination. Caro knew that, as an ex-newspaperman, Jim had a way of picking up news before it hit the headlines. Eric's leaving the house would create no problem tonight.

He found Jim in his kitchen. 'I'm going downtown,' Eric said. Jim would assume he meant to the peace-movement office. 'I just stopped off to have a cup of coffee with you.'

'You know all this involvement in the peace movement

70

could act to your disadvantage,' Jim reminded, going to the range for the coffeepot. 'If a war situation should arise.'

'Jim, I want to go to Congress so I'll be in a position to fight against our involvement in war. Whether it's with Mexico or the Balkans or whatever. The peace movement is what motivates me, Jim.'

For a while they dissected the Balkan situation, with both men dubious about the imminent cessation of fighting. Then Eric checked his watch and rose to his feet.

'See you at the office in the morning.'

When he approached the Carlyle house, Eric saw that the entire house was dark except for the wing where the judge had spent his last years. Leonora was waiting for him. Tonight she wore a white lace negligee with ruffles outlining the low neckline and sleeves. It was obvious she wore nothing underneath.

'It's so warm tonight,' she complained, leading him down the hall to the late judge's room. 'I chilled some champagne.'

A ceiling fan whirred softly overhead. The scent of early roses filtered through the open windows. Eric stood in the middle of the room while Leonora poured Dom Perignon into tulip glasses. His shoulder blades ached with tension. He wasn't built for a celibate life. But he'd have to watch himself with Leonora. He couldn't afford to allow her to become a habit.

'I'm leaving for New York tomorrow,' she told him. 'So this is a going-away party.' Leonora handed him a glass. 'To tonight. I don't know if there'll ever be another.' Her smile was provocative. 'So let's make this night wonderful.'

'Do you plan to live in New York?' He lifted an eyebrow in astonishment.

'I'm going to New York to shop, and then with Mama

71

to Saratoga Springs so she can take the baths. I hear many rich men go there.' She sighed. 'All old and fat, no doubt.'

'I don't doubt that you'll find yourself a rich husband,' Eric drawled. 'You're prime stock.'

'Take off your clothes, Eric. I want to remember how a young man looks.' She set down her glass and began to unbutton the lace negligee.

'Why must the judge's replacement be rich?' Eric asked. 'The judge left you well provided for.'

'I have extravagant tastes. The judge's estate is in trust. I detest limitations.' She stood before him, naked except for her white satin shoes.

Eric tossed aside his own clothes while Leonora watched. They were like a pair of gladiators in the arena, he mused. Damn if he would return to Caroline's bed until he knew they could enjoy an uninterrupted night together. Nor did he have a taste for whorehouses. Leonora was a fine convenience.

'Pity you're married.' Leonora moved to him, slid her arms about his shoulders, and thrust her body against his. 'You wouldn't consider a divorce. You have political ambitions.' It was a statement.

'You're clairvoyant.' His hands settled about her curvaceous rump, but his thoughts wandered. He ought to be lying in bed with his wife instead of nuzzling this hot little bitch. But why was he feeling guilty? It was Caro who had driven him to Leonora.

'Are we going to stand here this way all night?' Leonora reproached. Her eyes were curious when they met his. *What was the matter with him?* He ought to be erect by now.

'Let's try out the bed,' he suggested self-consciously, and pulled her hands from about his neck.

Her teeth settled at his shoulder, nipping lightly. Her

eyes laughed as she held her face up to his for a moment, then dropped to her knees, her hands fondling his thighs. He grunted when her mouth closed in on him. In seconds he'd be ready for Leonora Carlyle.

Caroline strove to eliminate discussion of Mary Phagan's murder before the children. All of Atlanta seemed obsessed by the case. By the end of the week the governor had ordered ten companies of the state militia to stand by to protect Leo Frank and Newt Lee, the night watchman. The newspapers were inflaming the city.

Friday evening Caroline confiscated the *Journal* before Liz and Josh could read the latest lurid reports on the case. It disturbed Caroline that no word was said about the incident at the railway station. Seven suspects had been arrested. The man whom Mary Phagan was said to have pulled off the Washington sleeper was not one of them.

Caroline left the house with Sophie for the meeting at the mill. The lights were on in the conference room, the rest of the mill blacked out. Andrew had arrived early to set up the room for the meeting. A dozen operators were arriving to discuss their common problem. Every mill in the area suffered from Todd Murdoch's piracy. He had aggravated an already serious labour problem.

Caroline sat at the head of the conference table, flanked by Andrew and Sophie, and listened to the grievances of the operators, none of whom seemed to be aware that Todd Murdoch was responsible for their difficulties.

'Last week I lost my ten best weavers. They took their pay envelopes and moved out of the village. No notice to me. No word as to where they were going. These weren't drifters,' Ed Swift emphasized. Men who would use any excuse to move on, sure there was a job waiting for them

73

somewhere else. 'These workers had been with me for anywhere from six to twelve years!'

'Ed, we know who's stealing our workers,' Caroline told him, and felt the excitement this announcement generated. 'Andrew pinned down a man who left us last Friday. Todd Murdoch's responsible.'

'That young bastard?' an operator twice Murdoch's age exploded. 'Pardon me, Caroline . . . and you, Miss Sophie,' he apologized, 'but I haven't trusted that man since he first set foot in Atlanta.'

'What do we know about Murdoch?' Sophie interjected.

'His father was a Chicago meat packer who went broke through wheat speculation when Todd was eighteen. Todd and his brother were brought home from Exeter and went to work to feed the family,' an operator contributed. 'Then the two brothers and their father went to Alaska, struck gold, and returned to Chicago. Todd gambled away his share, moved to Massachusetts, married the daughter of a textile mill owner. My wife's sister married a man up in Lowell and told us all about him.' He hesitated. 'There's a little more she told us, if you ladies will pardon me talking so frankly . . .'

'Go ahead, please,' Caroline urged. 'We need to know everything we can about the man if we're going to fight him.'

'Six years ago, my sister-in-law tells me, Todd discovered his wife playing around with another man. Todd killed him. I don't have to tell you, nobody was going to throw him into jail for that. His wife died six months later, giving birth to the dead man's child. You know the rest. He bought the mill here a year ago and wants to take over the textile industry in this state.'

'Let's appoint a committee to go to Todd Murdoch and

order him to stop this pirating,' Caroline said. 'If he wants a fight, we'll give it to him.'

'Caroline, he's killed a man,' Ed Swift reminded. 'He has no respect for ethics. I don't think talking is going to do much good. We need fresh legislation against stealing labour.'

'That will take too long to put through,' Caroline objected. 'We've got to warn him we won't take this lying down.'

'You may have noticed Bill Turner isn't here tonight,' one of the operators said uneasily. '*He* figured Todd Murdoch was hiring away his workers. I didn't believe it then. Bill went to Murdoch last week. Old Bill's a hothead. He went there waving a pistol he brought back from San Juan Hill. Murdoch broke his arm for him.'

'I'll go as a committee of one to talk to Mr Murdoch,' Caroline decided, her eyes ablaze. 'I doubt that he'll break my arm.'

For a few minutes there was an outbreak of shamefaced protests. Then, at her insistence, it was agreed that Caroline would approach Todd Murdoch as their representative. After all, she was the wife of a legislator who would introduce fresh legislation against pirating workers, as well as a mill operator herself.

At ten the following morning Caroline was received by Todd Murdoch in his thoroughly masculine office. Caroline had seen him at a distance at the Memorial Day parade. She was not prepared for the magnetism he exuded.

'Mr Murdoch, we know you're stealing our workers,' she began, and he interrupted with an indulgent laugh.

'Sugar, this is business. No Marquis of Queensbury Rules.'

'We in the South observe business ethics. We won't allow this thievery to continue, Mr Murdoch. We're gearing ourselves to fight for stronger legislation. My husband is prepared to sponsor the bill. Once it's passed, we'll see that it's enforced.' His eyes surveyed her with a blatant admiration that unnerved her. 'In the meantime, if you keep this up, you'll bring on the kind of opposition that could lead to bloodshed.'

'Not my blood.' He chuckled. 'And why is a beautiful woman like you bothering herself with running a mill?'

'I do a good job of operating my mill,' Caroline bristled.

'I'd be happy to take it off your hands.' His smile was indulgent. 'At a fair price.'

'The Hampton Mill is not for sale!'

'It's one of the finest mills in the South. I could make it the largest and the best,' he boasted. 'There's not just my money involved.' His eyes glistened with confidence. 'I have access to funds to buy out every mill in Georgia.'

Caroline tensed in fresh awareness. Todd Murdoch was after power; he wanted to control the textile industry.

'You've bought one mill,' she said. 'Be happy you have that.'

'Now, why would a beautiful woman want to be bothered with running a mill?' His eyes strayed to the accelerated rise and fall of her breasts. Colour sprang into her cheeks.

'Does it make me less a woman because I do?' she challenged.

'Not for me,' he assured her. 'Though to some men it's like taking the fuzz off a Georgia peach. But I'm telling you right to your face, Caroline Hampton. If you weren't the legislator's wife, I'd be courting you till you promised to marry me.'

His laughter followed her as she stalked from his office. Todd Murdoch was an arrogant, uncouth boor, Caroline told herself. But she was disturbingly aware of him as a man.

7

May sped past with disconcerting swiftness. Caroline was swept up with fresh hope for Francis, though some of Victor's decrees were discomforting. He had decided, now that Francis always wore the football helmet – even in the summer heat – that Patience and she were to walk away from him when he had a tantrum. They must ignore him. When Francis began to bite the back of his hands because he could do no injury to his head, Victor ordered gloves for him. His tantrums seemed to be of shorter duration, less frequent. Caroline was hopeful.

David Kahn was frequently at the house, knowing that Caroline and Eric were sympathetic towards Leo Frank. Atlanta was overrun with groups of investigators independently pursuing evidence about Mary Phagan's murder. Eric complained that everybody – including the police, detectives, and Solicitor General Hugh Dorsey – was more concerned about finding evidence that would hang Leo Frank than in learning the truth about the murder.

'I hear Mr Scott told one of his associates that "unless the Jew is convicted the Pinkerton detective agency will have to get out of Atlanta,"' David reported bitterly the evening before the grand jury was to hear the case. Pinkerton detective Scott had been spending a lot of time on the case, but he admitted that he had come up with no conclusive evidence or clues.

'I can't bear some of the stories that are running around town,' Caroline frowned in distaste. 'Folks are saying Lucille is ready to divorce Leo. That he has another wife in Brooklyn. That he murdered his first wife. That he's a pervert who goes out on the streetcar lines pulling off young girls.'

'Some people say he's a Catholic, and all the Catholics are for him,' David said. 'Others complain he's a Mason, and all the Masons are defending him. And of course there are those who know he's a Jew and insist the Jews are all out for him.'

'I wish somebody other than Hugh Dorsey was the prosecutor,' Eric admitted. 'Dorsey has lost two important cases. For a man who's as politically ambitious as Hugh Dorsey, that's a desperate situation. He'll do anything to win a conviction.'

Four weeks after the murder the grand jury met to consider an indictment of Leo Frank. On the following day, after less than ten minutes of deliberation, the jury gave Hugh Dorsey the indictment he needed. Liz refused to come to the dinner table when her father reported the verdict.

The next morning Eric prepared to leave for Hampton Court with Liz and Josh. Caroline stood on the veranda with them while Roland piled their luggage into the car. She had come home from the mill to be here. Josh, she suspected, was uneasy at leaving her behind.

'I'll be up to Hampton Court on Sunday,' she promised with a final hug and kiss before he climbed into the car. 'Be good.'

Caroline stood alone on the veranda until the car disappeared from view, then climbed back into the Hupmobile to return to the mill. Her feelings were mixed. It would be relaxing to be alone in the house with Sophie and Francis for a few weeks. No battles to referee between Liz and Josh. No silent accusations from Eric. Yet already she dreaded the separation, which had hardly begun.

Tonight Sophie and she would dine with Andrew in the summerhouse behind his cottage. She suspected Andrew had extended the invitation to delay her coming home to a half-deserted house.

Driving back to the mill, Caroline reminded herself how she had coped with what had seemed an impossible way of life in those months when Eric was trapped in marriage to Tina. She had sworn to herself, '*The mill will be my life.*' Now it would be the mill and the children. She must be realistic. She had lost Eric.

Early Sunday morning, after a week that seemed interminably long, Caroline prodded Sophie into the Hupmobile and settled herself behind the wheel of the car.

'I don't know why you don't have Roland drive us,' Sophie grumbled. 'It's a long, hot trip. You could relax.'

'I want Roland at the house in case of any emergency,' Caroline explained. 'He's the only one of the servants who knows how to drive.'

Sophie's face softened.

'You're worrying already about Francis. He'll be fine with Patience.'

In the afternoon Victor would be at the house, Caroline reminded herself. With Eric and the children away, Victor had decided to see Francis every afternoon. His dedication was wonderful. He pretended to be cool and analytical about his work with Francis, but she felt the depth of his tenderness, his affection for her small son. In such a short span of time Victor had become an integral part of their lives. Except to Eric.

Hampton Court was beautiful this time of year. Driving up the long roadway lined by pecans and dogwoods, Caroline remembered her father's descriptions of Hampton Court in those years before she came to Atlanta.

How he had loved the huge white house that rose before them now – tall and stately behind a circular driveway flanked by evergreens, its eight massive round white columns reaching up from the veranda to support the roof. How she wished that Papa could have lived to see it again! How she wished that Mama and he might have known their grandchildren.

'There's Josh!' Sophie waved to the small figure leaning over the railing of the filigreed balcony above the entrance.

The screen door was flung wide; Liz hurled herself with terrifying speed across the veranda and down the steps.

'Mama, you're late!' Liz scolded, kissing Caroline and Sophie in turn. 'You said you'd be up early.'

'Honey, we're here for breakfast.' Caroline laughed. 'Were you expecting us at the crack of dawn?'

The day fled past, with Liz reproachful when Caroline announced that Sophie and she must leave for Atlanta after an early dinner.

'I hate driving at night on these roads,' Caroline said, feeling a wrench at leaving Hampton Court after a day enveloped in family. She wished that there might have been a little time alone with Eric. 'But Aunt Sophie and I will be up again next Sunday.'

Caroline devised a summer pattern of living, until Liz and Josh would return to Hampton House and Eric would leave for The Hague. Once a week Sophie and she had dinner with Andrew at his cottage. On Saturday evenings Andrew came to dine with them. On other nights Sophie and she spent hours wrapped up in mill business, studying reports and sales figures, dissecting the items Caroline clipped from the financial pages of magazines and the large-city newspapers to which she subscribed.

Caroline sensed intuitively that the country was sliding

from a healthy economy into what could become a depression. The message was scrawled between the lines of the financial reports. The Hampton fortune had increased under her leadership, but Caroline was forever fearful of some national disaster that would annihilate the empire she was building. The empire necessary to assure her that Francis would be forever cared for in the finest style. She was obsessed by the need to provide for her youngest child.

Her thirty-fourth birthday arrived. Andrew invited Sophie and her for dinner that night, surprising her with a birthday cake.

Caroline was disappointed that Eric had forgotten her birthday. It was the first time in all the years that he had not remembered. Only the June of '98, when he had been in Cuba with Roosevelt and the Rough Riders.

Work on the mill annexe and the new houses was proceeding on schedule, though Sophie fretted about the costs. Caroline refused to be pessimistic about the short-age of mill operators. When the annexe was completed, they would find workers. The word circulated from mill to mill; the Hampton Mill was known to be one of the most progressive in the nation. And for the time being it appeared that Todd Murdoch had abandoned his labour piracy.

Eric drove into Atlanta twice each week for several hours to confer with Jim about their clients and to consult with the peace group. Before he drove back to Hampton Court, he phoned Caroline to report on the children. Josh was happy to spend each day reading or walking along the river. Liz rode every morning, swam in the afternoon with Josh and two young daughters of the household servants. In the evenings she played the piano and complained about the dullness of life at Hampton Court. Each time Eric phoned, Caroline hoped he would decide to remain in Atlanta for the night. He was always in a rush to return to the plantation.

Caroline looked forward to her meetings each afternoon with Victor, hopeful of fresh encouragement. Francis' tantrums were diminishing in frequency and were of shorter duration. Perhaps the others in the household might not realize this, but Patience and she noted the change and were joyful.

One afternoon early in July, when she realized Victor had lingered far beyond his normal time with Francis, she impulsively invited him to remain for dinner. Victor still lived at the Georgian Terrace and took most of his meals in the hotel restaurant.

'Please stay, Victor,' she encouraged.

'I'd like that very much,' Victor accepted.

They went out to sit on the screened portion of the veranda until dinner would be served when Sophie arrived from the mill.

'I'm part physician and part educator,' Victor declared whimsically while they discussed Francis' progress. 'Next week I'm going to work with Francis so that he'll begin to walk up and down the stairs properly. He's counting to ten now, and he understands,' Victor emphasized. Eric had insisted Francis only parroted. 'Patience and I work together with him with spools of thread. Soon he'll learn their colours.'

'Victor, I'm so grateful.' Caroline radiated her pleasure.

'We have a long way to go, Caroline,' he cautioned. 'And there may be setbacks.'

'You're helping Francis. You've given me hope, Victor. That's the most precious gift in the world.'

'A gift from Dr Montessori,' Victor said conscientiously. 'And remember, her methods are effective, too, with children who have no special problems. When she held her first international teacher-training class in Italy last January, students came to her from all over the world.' Victor elaborated enthusiastically on the Italian doctor's work.

'Why is the United States so unresponsive to Dr Montessori?' Caroline asked.

'She's a woman ahead of her time. As you are.' His eyes were rich with tenderness. Caroline was conscious – again – that to Victor she was not only his patient's mother, but a woman he admired. 'Still, I understand there are almost a hundred Montessori schools in the country now.'

Caroline interrupted, her eyes shining. 'Victor, I'd like to start a Montessori school in the village, for the younger children. For the three- to six-year-olds. Not only would it be helpful for the children, but day care would free some of the mothers to work in the mill. They'll appreciate another pay envelope.'

'You'll encounter some heavy objections,' Victor warned, but Caroline sensed his excitement at the prospect of a Montessori school in Hamptonville.

'Will you help me?'

'We'll have to wait until the fall,' Victor temporized. 'And there'll be parents who'll complain that the children are too young. They'll resent the school for interfering with their parental rights. But we'll try, Caro.' She was startled by Victor's use of the diminutive that was seldom used except by Eric.

'I'll talk to Grace and Henry Roberts. I know they'll work with us.' The long-time minister of Hamptonville and his wife were devoted to the welfare of the mill workers.

The possibility of a school for the three- to six-year-olds was a challenge. With Grace and Henry's support, Victor and she could persuade the mill-village parents that the school was important. An extra pay envelope for a mother freed by the school would be strong motivation, Caroline reassured herself.

At intervals David dropped by for an evening's talk about developments in the Leo Frank case. Atlanta's three leading newspapers bombarded readers with sensational stories. Extras were frequent. Throughout the South the Leo Frank case was headline news. Tensions in the city were alarmingly high.

'Caroline, all the newspapers are convinced Leo's guilty,' David said with quiet desperation. 'Thank God, there are some people in this city who don't feel that way. Did you see the letter in the *Georgian*? That man came right out and said that the case against Leo was weak, and the evidence points unmistakably towards Conley!'

'David, the truth will come out in the trial,' Caroline insisted.

Caroline was silent about Eric's growing pessimism as the prosecutor built his case. The insistence of Conley, the Negro sweeper at the pencil factory, that he had helped Leo Frank carry Mary Phagan's body to the cellar, was putting a noose about Frank's neck. His family cook, after twenty-four hours of grilling, had signed a damaging affidavit, duly reported in the headlines. When she was released, she repudiated the affidavit. News of this was relegated to a back page of the newspapers. Frank's situation appeared grave. But an innocent man could not be convicted in this country, Caroline told herself. Eric was being overly cynical.

On July 11 Leo Frank's lawyers contrived to have word reach the *Georgian* that they had obtained an affidavit from an insurance agent who had tried to sell Conley insurance on the day Mary Phagan was murdered. The affidavit stated that Conley, annoyed and probably half-drunk, had threatened the insurance man with a gun: '*I've killed a girl today. I don't want to kill nobody else.*' The agent said he had gone to the police and to some of the factory officials on the Tuesday after the murder to report this, but nobody was interested. The newspapers – and the police – were interested now.

When Caroline next went up to Hampton Court with Sophie, Eric told her he would return to the Atlanta house with Liz and Josh on the following Sunday.

'I've promised David and Noah that I would be there for the trial, though God knows what difference that'll make,' Eric said.

'Eric, the jury can't convict Leo Frank!' Caroline said. Liz looked stricken.

'If it does, his lawyers will appeal.' Eric betrayed none of his inner doubts.

All this Sunday Caroline was restless. She chided herself for being inattentive to the children. Normally she devoted every moment to them, determined to make them understand how much she loved them, that she missed them. But this Sunday a vague uneasiness nagged at her all day. She was worried about Francis.

Relief surged through Caroline when, at last, Sophie and she were in the car en route to Atlanta. The day had been overcast. She had clutched at the possibility of rain to push dinner ahead an hour, guilty at the children's reproaches yet feeling a compulsion to return to Hampton House.

'Stop worrying about Francis,' Sophie ordered, and Caroline started. 'When you look like that, I know you're worrying about him. We've been coming up all these weeks, and Patience has managed, hasn't she?'

'Sophie, Victor *is* helping Francis.' All along, Sophie

had been noncommittal. Now Caroline let her eyes leave the road for an instant to seek Sophie's assent.

'Could be,' Sophie allowed, permitting herself a wisp of a smile. 'Francis sure counts up a storm.'

'And Victor's teaching him to walk up and down the stairs one at a time. Won't Liz and Josh be surprised when they see that?'

It disturbed her that, to Liz and Josh, Francis was someone to hide. She longed to see affection for Francis a part of their lives. Later, Victor said, he would enlist their help in working with Francis.

Turning into the driveway of the Atlanta house, Caroline spied Victor's Pierce Arrow parked at one side.

'Something's happened to Francis!' Suddenly her heart was pounding. 'Victor's here!'

Caroline slammed on the brakes with a recklessness that was foreign to her, pushed open the door, and darted towards the house. Victor had heard the car come up the driveway. He was emerging from the foyer to greet her.

'It's all right, Caro,' he soothed, sensing her awareness that something had happened to Francis. 'Francis fell down the stairs. But at his age, bones heal very quickly. It's a fracture of the left ankle. He'll be back on his feet in two weeks.'

'*He fell and I wasn't here.*' Caroline was white with shock. 'Let me go to him – '

'He's asleep.' Victor prodded her towards one of the stalwart rockers that lined the veranda. 'Sit down, Caro. I want you to understand that you mustn't make a fuss about this accident.'

'Victor, he broke his ankle.' Caroline tried to mask her involuntary reproach.

'That was part of the learning process. When the ankle is healed, he'll walk again. Caro, you don't want to wrap him in cotton. You want him to be normal.'

'Yes,' Caroline whispered. Looking scared, Patience came out with lemonade for them. 'Patience, he's going to be fine,' she soothed. 'It was just an accident.'

'He's sleepin' now,' Patience reported. 'I'll go up and sit with him.' Patience turned to Victor. 'We're gonna keep on with the learnin' games when Francis gets better?'

'We'll work tomorrow, just as always,' Victor said matter-of-factly, and Patience left them with a smile. 'I've just received another box of toys from Nienhuis in Holland. They'll be a diversion for Francis while his ankle is mending. Nothing's *changed*, Caro.'

'I know, Victor.' She forced a smile. For all his show of confidence, Victor was afraid she might remove Francis from his care.

Much later, after she had sat by Francis' bed for a while and was confident that he slept without pain, Caroline left his bedroom. Patience took her place beside the bed, wielding a large palmetto fan. Caroline went to her room to phone Eric. He must be told about Francis' accident, and reassured that there was no serious damage.

'Francis will be fine,' Caroline consoled Eric after she had explained about the accident. 'At his age a fracture heals fast.'

'Francis shouldn't have been on the stairs alone!' Eric said angrily. 'Where the hell was Patience? She knows he's not to be left alone.'

'He wasn't alone,' Caroline explained. 'He was with Victor. He just got excited about being able to manage the stairs properly and tried to take them too fast. He tumbled down before Victor could catch him.'

'He might have broken his neck!'

'He didn't.' Caroline struggled to be realistic. She, too, had been upset about the accident. 'Eric, it's part of the learning process.'

'And if he breaks his neck, will you say that same thing?' Eric demanded.

'Don't be ridiculous!' Caroline shot back in anger.

'Caro, I want you to stop this nonsense with Victor Adams,' Eric ordered. 'I don't want that man in the house again.'

'He's helping Francis. Even Sophie admits that.'

'I don't want that man in my house,' Eric said ominously. 'Tell him.'

'No,' Caroline rejected. 'It's my house, too.' Colour suffused her face.

'Oh, excuse me.' Eric's voice was rich with sarcasm. 'I forgot for a moment. Of course, it's *your* house.' Caroline heard the faint click of the phone at the other end.

'*Our* house,' she cried out futilely into the dead phone. How could Eric, who was so bright and compassionate, be so intractable and stupid about Victor?

Of course Victor must continue to come to the house and work with Francis. Victor offered them hope. None of the fine, expensive specialists that Eric had brought from New York and Chicago and Philadelphia had been able to do that. No matter what the consequences, Francis must remain Victor's patient.

8

On the sultry Sunday afternoon following Francis' fall down the stairs, Eric returned to Hampton House with Liz and Josh. Hearing the Pierce Arrow pull up before the house, Caroline hurried to the foyer to welcome them. Liz and Josh were shrieking insults at each other as they walked up the stairs and across the veranda to the front door. They were hot and tired from the dusty drive. Georgia had not seen rain in weeks. This weather was horrendous.

'Will you two shut up?' Eric yelled, following behind them. 'You haven't stopped fighting since we left Hampton Court!'

'Elvira,' Caroline called from the screen door she had pulled wide. She turned her head to see Elvira, smiling fondly, moving her heavy frame with the speed reserved for emergencies or special occasions. She, too, had heard the car approach.

'Miss Caroline, don't them children look jes' good enough to eat?'

Caroline pulled them to her for a warm kiss.

'Elvira, would you please take them out to the breakfast room and give them some lemonade? They'll cool off sitting under the ceiling fan.'

'Mama, Liz has been a pig all day,' Josh hissed. 'She thinks she's so grown-up.'

'You're such an infant,' Liz shot back. 'You don't know anything.'

'Out to the breakfast room!' Eric thundered, and bent

to kiss Caroline. A perfunctory kiss demanded by the occasion, Caroline thought.

'Eric, come out to the side veranda. There's a bit of a breeze from the river right now,' she cajoled.

'Later. Right now I want to see Francis.' He was polite but withdrawn.

Caroline stood at the foot of the stairs, gazing upward in silent anguish even after Eric had disappeared into Francis' room. He blamed her for Francis' fractured ankle, which Victor said was healing beautifully. He still resented her reminding him that this was her house, too. She winced recalling how he had hung up on her. He'd thought she was throwing her inheritance in his face. *She wasn't*. She only insisted on sharing. That was what marriage should be.

'*I don't want that man in my house*,' he had said, as though she were a chattel. Oh, she despised the arrogance of men! Eric pretended to be so aware of the rights of women, but like all other men, he was convinced the ultimate decision was the prerogative of the husband. She would not bow down before her husband's wishes when she knew he was wrong. Francis was her child, too. She would fight for what was right for him.

After dinner David and Noah arrived at the house at a summons from Eric. They were followed forty minutes later by Jim. They gathered together on the side of the veranda to talk in sombre tones about the opening of Leo Frank's trial tomorrow morning.

Caroline was irritated that Eric insisted Liz be allowed to sit with them. She was concerned about Liz's involvement in Mary Phagan's murder.

'I wish to hell the trial had been postponed until cooler weather,' Jim said. 'Psychologically it's bad in the heat.'

'The trial will become a circus,' Noah warned. 'Every

Jew in Atlanta is fearful of repercussions. There's such bitterness building between Jews and Gentiles.'

'Noah, Jews have always been an important part of this community,' Caroline protested. 'They're highly respected.'

'When the police arrested Leo Frank,' David said hotly, 'they evoked all the silent prejudice against Jews and Northerners and strung it out into the open.' Liz gazed at David as though he were a prophet, Caroline thought. Why must a tender little girl be exposed to this ugliness? Yet how could the children in the city be isolated from what dominated the thoughts of every resident?

'Between the newspapers and the police, Leo's going to have a rough time, even with Rosser and Arnold as his attorneys,' Eric pursued. 'Let's pray that reason prevails.'

In the morning Caroline sat at her desk struggling to concentrate on the architect's progress report on the mill annexe and the new houses. But her mind was focused on the comment she had overheard one of the workers make to another as she walked to her office an hour ago. *'Sure that jury's gonna find Frank guilty. The police all think he's guilty. And Mary Phagan was one of us folks.'*

Ellen came in and took her place beside the desk, notebook propped against one knee in preparation for the morning's dictation.

'They'll be fighting for seats in the courtroom this morning,' Ellen guessed. 'How long do you think the trial will last?'

'Eric figures two weeks at the most.' In two weks Eric expected to be on a train bound for New York, where he would take a Holland America ship to Rotterdam.

'I hope so.' Ellen sighed. 'I feel so sorry for his wife.'

This Monday seemed to drag on forever, Caroline told

herself while she clock-watched for the hour to leave the mill. She was impatient to hear from Eric exactly what had happened in the courtroom. To her relief, Eric arrived home early, only minutes after Victor had left the house.

'How did the trial go?' Caroline asked, striving to conceal her anxiety.

'Like Noah predicted last night,' Eric said disgustedly, removing his jacket and loosening his tie. 'By seven o'clock this morning, people were pushing their way into the courtroom. Every seat was taken. Women were there, dragging children along with them.'

'Don't tell your daughter that,' Caroline exhorted while they headed automatically for the library, their oasis on a hot day by virtue of the ceiling fan installed there. Upstairs Francis was screeching. 'Ice cream, ice cream, ice cream!' He was frustrated at being restrained by the cast on his foot. 'Liz is furious because I wouldn't let her ask David to take her with him to the trial.'

'There was a mob hanging outside the courthouse all day. Their mood was so ugly, twenty police officers were called up to guard the courtroom. Somebody suggested that the spectators be searched for dangerous weapons.' Caroline flinched. 'From twelve-thirty to two o'clock when the court recessed, the courtroom looked more like a picnic at Grant Park than the place where a man was on trial for his life. Caro, you wouldn't believe it.' Eric grimaced in distaste. 'Most of the spectators came equipped with sandwiches, cold chicken, cake. Everything for a picnic but cold drinks.'

'What about the case itself?' Caroline asked while they seated themselves in chairs drawn up beneath the fan.

'This is the first day.' But Eric appeared unhappy. 'Dorsey is out to show that the blood spots on the floor and the strands of Mary Phagan's hair in the lathe nearby prove the murder occurred opposite Frank's office, and therefore he's guilty.'

'Nobody knows for sure that the blood spots were human blood. Nor that the strands of hair are Mary Phagan's,' Caroline protested. Jim and Eric had emphasized this last night. 'And that's flimsy evidence to convict him on!'

'There are a lot of angles that are not receiving proper treatment.'

'Papa!' Liz's voice was shrill as she darted into the library. 'Tell me about the trial!'

Caroline hurried Liz and Josh into the car. They were to accompany Eric to Terminal Station. Roland was approaching with Eric's luggage.

'Where's Papa?' Josh asked.

'He went to the library to make a phone call. He'll only be a minute.' Caroline tried to sound matter-of-fact. In truth her head was pounding with the knowledge that Eric would be away for a month.

'Mama, why does Josh always have to sit by the window?' Liz complained. 'You spoil him something awful.'

'You can sit by the window, too,' Caroline soothed. Josh tended to complain of carsickness if he was not sitting beside an open window. 'I'll sit in the middle.' When would the children outgrow their incessant bickering? 'Here comes Papa now.' Eric would sit up front with Roland.

At the station passengers were already boarding Eric's train. The imminent separation elicited an unexpected arousal in Caroline. Eric kissed Josh and Liz, then leaned forward to brush his mouth lightly against hers. Involuntarily her arms closed in about him.

'Eric, we'll miss you.' Her mind hurtled back through

94

the years. Eric, en route from Washington, DC, to San Antonio to join Roosevelt and the Rough Riders, had phoned from this very station to say the train was briefly in Atlanta. *'Caroline, I love you.'* There had been time for him to say little more, but she clung to those four words during his absence. How had they allowed this absurd chasm to develop between them?

'Take care of the children and yourself.' Eric's eyes left her face to search among the crowd for the other delegate from the Atlanta peace group who would be travelling with him. 'I'll write you.'

Eric disappeared into the Pullman car. The children watched eagerly until his face appeared at a window. Caroline's gaze moved about the cluster of people saying their final farewells. All at once she stiffened. Standing tall among those at the entrance to the next car was Todd Murdoch. He was staring intently at her, a hand at the elbow of a lady about to board the train. He smiled and nodded in greeting. A sardonic, amused, challenging smile.

Her face hot, Caroline swung her eyes to the window of the Pullman car where Eric was in pantomimed conversation with the children. Her heart was pounding. How ridiculous to allow Todd Murdoch to unnerve her this way. He was crude and coarse, yet she was conscious of the magnetism that he generated even at this distance.

Caroline focused on the Pullman window. Slowly the train began to move along the track. Liz and Josh waved exuberantly. Caroline joined them. Not until the train was out of sight would the children agree to leave the station and return to the car.

Who was the woman with Todd Murdoch? Caroline wondered. She was quite pretty. Was he preparing to take himself a second wife? He was rich and handsome; there would be many Atlanta ladies happy to marry him, despite the rumours that he had murdered a man in Massachusetts, or maybe because of them. Atlanta ladies would consider it romantic that he had defended his honour.

In New York Eric and his fellow delegate, the distinguished Judge Dimon, left the Doric temple that was Pennsylvania Station and took a taxi uptown to the low red-brick Plaza Hotel that sat at the entrance to Central Park. For dinner they travelled to Delmonico's at Forty-fourth Street and Fifth Avenue. For both the judge and Eric it was a sentimental journey.

The judge sat across the table from Eric in the elegant Louis XVI yellow-and-green main dining room and reminisced about the earlier Delmonico's.

'For close to twenty years I managed to dine once a year in Delmonico's,' the judge confided with an expansive smile. 'I was in the old Delmonico's on Twenty-sixth Street when Oscar Wilde, in town for the opening of *Patience*, complained about his bill.'

'When I was at Princeton and money had just arrived from home,' Eric reminisced, 'my roommate and I would head for New York and Delmonico's. We thought we were terribly sophisticated.' He chuckled. 'Then we'd go to the theatre, have supper at Rector's, and end up with breakfast at Jack's. After that we had only enough money to get us back to the campus.'

'What about between supper at Rector's and breakfast at Jack's?' The judge's eyes twinkled.

'We acquired feminine companionship,' Eric assured him.

The following day Eric and Judge Dimon went to the pier to board the *Rotterdam*, lead ship of the Holland America Line. They stood before the two-masted, two-

96

funnelled vessel and admired its elegant lines, its impressive 650-foot length.

'Twenty-four thousand tons,' the judge said with respect, 'and it can do eighteen knots. It has three elevators.'

'It'll be a restful week on the seas,' Eric mused while they went through the routine of boarding ship. 'And cool.' Atlanta had been a furnace when they left, and New York was little better.

'I rather wish we would stay a day in Plymouth and Boulogne-sur-Mer.' The judge was good-humouredly regretful. 'But we'll be there only long enough for passengers to disembark and freight to be unloaded.'

Eric made a mental note to write home before they arrived at Plymouth. The letter could be mailed from there. There would be little time in The Hague for letters, with three events – one on top of the other – during their visit to the city. The Universal Peace Congress, the Interparliamentary Union meeting, and the opening of the Peace Palace.

At dinner that evening, in the elegant dining room – where the menu included *Suprême* of sole d'Orléans, duckling with port-wine sauce, and sweetbreads à la Toulouse – Eric was aware that the decidedly attractive dark-haired young woman at the far end of their table was intent on being introduced to him. She contrived to be introduced first to his companion, the portly Judge Dimon. 'I suspected right off that you were en route to The Hague,' Serena Mayo said enthusiastically. 'We pacifists have a special sense about one another.' Her eyes moved with plotted impersonality to Eric. 'Are you going to the peace congress, too, Mr Hampton?'

'Yes. The judge and I are delegates from Atlanta,' Eric explained.

'I'm from Chicago,' Serena told him. 'I had to fight for

the place,' she admitted. 'They resented sending a woman. I used some minor blackmail.'

Eric laughed, though the judge was startled by her candour.

'The Hague will be more interesting for your presence,' he assured her. She was tall, slim, with just enough fore and aft to arouse him. Her emerald eyes met his with a disconcerting directness. It was clear that Serena Mayo anticipated extracurricular activities on board ship and in The Hague.

The judge, as Eric had expected, retired early. Serena suggested a walk on deck. He assumed it was not to continue their discussion about the Peace Palace and Andrew Carnegie.

They strolled in silence for a few moments, enjoying the splendour of the night. The sky was splashed with stars. Moonlight lent a golden glow to the deck. Music filtered from the first-class saloon. Serena slid an arm through his.

'When I'm on board ship, I always feel as though I were on another planet, with no past, no future,' Serena said effervescently. 'Does that sound immoral?'

'That depends upon what you call immoral.' Eric chuckled, his eyes telling her he held a liberal view of the subject. This girl was no Leonora Carlyle, but her message bore an amazing similarity. The voyage and the ten days in The Hague appeared promising.

'Being a suffragist, I can hardly be a prude,' Serena began.

'That hasn't hampered many of your fellow travellers,' Eric pointed out.

'I'm a suffragist and a pacifist. Does that seem incompatible to you?' she asked.

'No,' Eric said. 'I suppose you might call my wife that. She's a suffragist who doesn't believe in violence. She's been quite disturbed by some of the action of the English suffragists.'

'All right, you've told me you're married. We've got that out of the way.' The amazing emerald eyes were laughing at him. 'Why isn't your wife with you?'

'She's involved with other situations,' he said drily.

'Then that makes you fair game,' Serena concluded.

'Are you always so candid?' Eric asked good-humouredly.

'It simplifies life.' She shrugged. 'I'm not married. I wouldn't tie myself down in such a mundane situation. Men are fine as long as you don't take them seriously. As long as they can't put you down and give you orders. I told you I was a suffragist,' she reminded. 'Any objections?'

'You're the most damned attractive suffragist I ever met,' he said. 'And I am in sympathy with the cause.'

'As long as it doesn't interfere with your private life,' Serena derided.

'What the hell do you mean by that?' Eric frowned in annoyance.

'It's the standard male attitude. Like with my mother, when she remarried after my father died. Her second husband was so loud about supporting women in their demand for the vote. But he thinks women should vote the way their husbands tell them! That's what I hate about men – they've got to have the final word.'

'But you find other things to like about them,' Eric teased.

'They have other talents,' Serena conceded, her smile whimsical. 'So let's not waste three or four days playing games.' She lifted her eyes to his with a glint of anticipation. 'Would you like to sleep with me?'

'At this moment, there's nothing I'd rather do.' Eric

silently congratulated himself on having acquired a single stateroom.

'I'm sharing my cabin.' Her eyes were inquiring. 'I couldn't afford a single cabin in first class.'

'My cabin.' He couldn't wait to take this girl to bed. 'No problem, Serena.'

They walked hand in hand to his cabin. He switched on the light and locked the door. She switched off the light and reached for him in the darkness.

'Nobody has made love to me for almost a year,' she told him. 'Does that surprise you?'

'Yes,' he admitted.

'I have to be attracted to a man. But once I've decided, there's no need to wait.' In the darkness her mouth met his.

For a few moments he was satisfied to probe her hot, eager mouth while his hands familiarized themselves with her body. If she had not been with a man for almost a year, it was not for want of suitors.

'Take off your clothes,' he said, releasing her.

'No!' Her voice was furious. 'Not just like that.'

'You asked me if I wanted to sleep with you,' Eric shot back.

'I'm a woman,' Serena told him, fumbling for the light switch. 'Not just a receptacle for your passion. When I make love, I expect to share a beautiful experience.'

'Serena, I'm sorry.' His first instinct had been right. This was a special woman. 'Please stay.' He turned off the light and reached for her again. 'That damn candour of yours misled me. You're young and beautiful, and I want to spend the rest of the night making love to you.'

'*With* me,' she corrected, allowing him to pull her close again.

His mouth burrowed at one ear, moved along her slender throat. He drew her body tautly against his while

100

his hands manipulated the hooks of her dress. The soft fabric fell to her waist. He drew her camisole over her head and tossed it aside in the darkness. His hands found her breasts and were followed by his mouth.

'Eric, let's go to the bed,' she whispered after a few minutes, and his hand found hers in the darkness.

She laughed softly when he collided with a chair, but a moment later he was lifting her on to the bed. A hand reached out to fondle him, and a low sound of excitement escaped him. He couldn't wait to burrow within that passionate body.

Eric and Serena lay in each other's arms far into the night, alternately talking and making love. After the arid months in the guest room at Hampton House, Eric marvelled at such richness. Serena satisfied him physically, stimulated him mentally. She offered him the gift of herself with no demands, no stipulations. He felt unfettered, twenty-five again.

The days on shipboard moved past with a wonderful sameness. During the day Serena joined the judge and him at meals and for strolls about the deck or heated conversations in one of the saloons. Serena was articulate and well-informed; he relished arguing with her about the powder keg that was present-day Europe.

'Germany is the world's greatest military power. Why in hell does she need a large navy unless she has aggressive designs on England?' Serena challenged. 'The English will starve to death if they can't import food!'

Deliberately he would take an attitude in which he did not believe, just to bait her, enjoying her indignation, her logical denunciation. It had been this way with Caroline in those days before Francis usurped her every thought.

Eric suspected that the judge – an earlier riser –

recognized the reason Serena and he never appeared at breakfast. They arrived at the luncheon table separately, moments apart. Judge Dimon was philosophical. Eric would be away from home for a month. A man as young as Eric, with his appeal to women, could be expected to avail himself of diversion. Serena made it clear, even to the judge, that she was aware of Eric's marital commitments.

The evening before the ship was to dock at Plymouth, Eric wrote a letter to Caroline. The *Rotterdam* included many Americans among the passengers, with the same destination as Judge Dimon and himself. Eric described the general optimism of the delegates, though he himself harboured reluctant scepticism.

'I pray that we can make lasting achievements,' he wrote Caroline. 'Jim and I have talked long and uneasily about the way the nations in Europe have become armed camps over the past fifty years. We're part of a civilization that believes that armaments are the only guarantee of peace. Yet we've seen that to prepare for war is not the road to peace.'

From Plymouth the *Rotterdam* steamed ahead to Boulogne-sur-Mer, and thence to Rotterdam. At the bustling port of Rotterdam, Eric and Judge Dimon shepherded Serena to the train for the brief ride to The Hague.

'The Hague is an intriguing city,' Judge Dimon said expansively. 'Did you know, it was originally a hunting lodge belonging to the counts of Holland?'

Eric and Serena were content to sit back in the immaculate train and listen to the judge grow eloquent about their host city. Eric knew the judge would not be staying at the hotel where he had reservations. Judge Dimon had been in The Hague at the conference in 1907; for sentimental reasons, he would stay at the same hotel.

They arrived in The Hague, three miles inland yet

surrounded by the North Sea. Eric was amused by Serena's delight in the broad streets crossed by picturesque canals and lined by shops and dwellings, by the charming architecture – half-Dutch, half-French.

Eric and Serena parted from the judge and headed for Eric's hotel, which was close to the Nordende Palace. Serena clucked in disapproval when they were escorted through gloomy corridors to their room, though from their windows they had a view of the garden behind the palace.

'Stop bitching,' Eric reproached when they were at last alone. 'The bed's comfortable.'

'Let's try it out,' Serena ordered ebulliently, and tossed herself across its width, knowing Eric would not dawdle for a second invitation.

9

Caroline sat defensively erect in her chair while Andrew, naming each account in turn, spread across her desk the cutback orders received by the Hampton Mill in the past few days. This was a roll call of their major accounts. The seriousness of the situation was reflected in Andrew's voice.

'Every company is cutting back ten to twenty per cent on their original orders,' Sophie pointed out. 'I can't understand it. Can the trouble in the Balkans have that much effect on the economy in this country? I thought when the Treaty of Bucharest was signed twelve days ago, the European situation would become more relaxed.'

Andrew sighed.

'There's still a terrible uneasiness throughout Europe about the Balkans.'

'And we can't ignore the Mexican trouble either,' Caroline reminded. 'For all Wilson's avowal to keep the peace, a lot of Americans are worried that we'll be dragged into the war down there.' If war came, they would face a shortage of materials for building machinery. They ought to order equipment for the annexe now, at current prices. 'But we're not the only mill receiving cutbacks.' Caroline propelled herself into an optimistic facade. 'I spoke to Ed Swift several days ago. He's running into the same situation. The other operators may not admit it, but they're getting cutbacks, too.'

'Caroline, we ought to hold up on the annexe and the houses for a while.' Sophie was visibly apprehensive.

'I think that would be a bad move,' Caroline rejected. 'Look at the way construction prices are soaring. If we delay building for eighteen months, I'd wager costs will rise another ten per cent.'

'Cut down on the size of the annexe,' Sophie urged. 'At this stage you can do it.'

'The new annexe as it's planned will double our capacity.' A dream she had nurtured for fifteen years. 'Sophie, that would make us the largest operation in the South.'

'And double our problems,' Sophie shot back. 'I've been worrying for weeks. Where do you expect us to find hands to work in that new annexe?'

'We'll find them,' Caroline insisted. 'The farmers are starving to death up in the hills.'

'Mary Phagan's murder will frighten a lot of them away,' Andrew warned. 'The farmers have long been terrified of the high crime rate in Atlanta. They figure the mill operators are exploiting their women and children as cheap labour. Now a little girl was murdered in a factory. They'd rather starve on the farms.'

'They'll come when they know there are jobs and decent houses waiting for them.' Caroline was convinced of this. 'We won't just sit back and wait for them to come. We'll go out to the farms and offer them jobs.'

'I hate to dampen such enthusiasm,' Sophie said drily, 'but with cutbacks we're not going to need a larger capacity. We can handle the current orders without even running overtime.'

'This is a temporary situation. We have to look ahead.' Caroline paused. 'I plan to place an order immediately for the equipment for the annexe.' Sophie looked out-raged. 'They won't deliver for at least a year,' Caroline cajoled. 'But we'll contract at current prices.'

Andrew appeared uneasy.

'Add that to the cost of putting up the annexe and the houses, and you're obligating yourself to a tremendous expenditure.'

'We may be moving into a depression,' Sophie reminded. 'A few bad years, and you could jeopardize the mill.'

'We must expand now, or it'll never happen.' Caroline was adamant. 'Our economy is changing. Prices are going to spiral. Sophie, it's *now*.'

'You're forever giving in to the workers and raising wages,' Sophie grumbled. 'And our taxes have become insane.'

'The General built outside of Atlanta all those years ago to avoid paying city taxes,' Caroline conceded. 'But with the city expanding in every direction, it was inevitable that we'd become part of Atlanta.' The wages they paid were the highest in the state. Other operators complained. 'But we're making a comfortable profit, Sophie.' She strove to be realistic.

'It's useless to argue with you. You're as stubborn as your grandfather was, once you make up your mind,' Sophie told her. 'I remember the years when Josiah and I would sweat out every payday,' Sophie recalled. 'Though the workers never knew that. I don't want to see you lose what your grandfather built.'

'I won't lose,' Caroline promised. She could not allow this to happen; the mill was a sacred trust for her children.

When Sophie and Andrew returned to their offices, Caroline found herself assaulted by misgivings. On almost every occasion Andrew sided with her against Sophie's conservatism. Was she taking on more than she could handle? *Was her judgement going astray*? For the first time in fifteen years Caroline felt her self-confidence wavering.

At three Caroline was walking into the house. She had

106

seen Victor's car outside; he was upstairs with Francis. Reason told her it was absurd to desert the mill at three every afternoon to sit here while Francis was upstairs with Victor, yet she felt compelled to be here. She looked forward to talking with Victor afterwards over glasses of iced tea.

In the afternoon stillness Victor's voice filtered down the stairs to her while she headed for the library. 'Patience, no,' Victor said firmly. 'Francis must learn to dress himself. Now, let's try it again, Francis,' he urged. 'Put this hand into the sleeve . . .'

Caroline settled herself beneath the ceiling fan in the library. Elvira came into the room with a tall glass of iced tea.

'It's powerful hot, Miss Caroline. I figured you'd be wantin' somethin' to drink right away.'

'Thank you, Elvira.'

Caroline reached for the morning's *Constitution* and began to read. She was upset by the articles on the Leo Frank trial. David told her that each day when Prosecutor Dorsey left the courthouse, the crowds hanging around outside applauded his appearance. How could the jury convict a man who was obviously innocent?

In a surge of irritation Caroline tossed aside the newspaper and picked up the March issue of *McClure*'s magazine from the top of a stack of back issues.

Caroline flipped through the pages of the magazine, stopped short at an article by Burton Hendrick. Her eyes sped over the words while her mind rejected the contents. Burton Hendrick wrote about the supposed activities of a Jewish conspiracy that sought to seize the country. He listed industries which he claimed, 'the Jews absolutely control.' This was the kind of muckraking writing that appealed to the illiterate elements of the country. It was dangerous.

Restless, she reached for the *Constitution* again. She would read the newspaper until Victor came downstairs.

'You look very sombre.' Victor's voice startled her.

'I was reading about the trial.' Caroline raised her eyes to his. 'It's incredible that it's gone on for four weeks.'

'I hear they expect the case to go to the jury tomorrow.' Victor sat down beside her, his expression grave. 'The mood in the city is alarming.'

'You were trying to teach Francis to dress himself today.' She withdrew from disturbing contemplations. Here was the core of her life. 'Do you think he'll learn?'

'I believe he'll learn,' Victor said carefully. 'We must concede that Francis has moved backwards in certain areas since his accident, but this is temporary. We must keep pressing ahead.' His eyes searched hers. 'You understand this, don't you?'

'Of course, Victor.'

'You're sure you want me to continue working with Francis? I've asked myself this a hundred times since he broke his ankle.'

'Victor, you've given me the only hope I've ever had. Of course I want you to continue working with Francis.' Her smile was luminescent. 'And we must start setting up the Montessori school in Hamptonville very soon.' This would convince Victor that he had her full support.

Caroline and Victor spoke with mounting excitement about the new school, though both were aware that they would face hostility from some of the mothers when the service was offered.

'I talked with Grace and Henry Roberts,' Caroline reported. Victor knew that Henry had long served as minister in Hamptonville, and in the days before the schoolhouse was built and staffed, doubled as teacher. Grace was devoted to the children, and much loved by them. 'They're so enthusiastic. They'll do everything possible to help.'

'I've ordered toys from Nienhuis in Holland,' Victor told her. 'My contribution to the school.' How warm and compassionate he was, Caroline mused.

'Grace thought it would be practical to serve a hot lunch to the children. She's offered to do the cooking.' The food would cost little. 'I worry that so many of the children come down with pellagra.' No cure was known for the sickness that affected so many in the South.

'Not just pellagra,' Victor pointed out. 'I've studied the health reports. More than half of the white school-children in this area and close to three-quarters of the Negro schoolchildren suffer from malnutrition and anae-mia. Poor diets, Caro.'

'It shouldn't happen.' Caroline recoiled from the image of undernourished children.

'The schools could help the situation,' Victor said hesitantly. 'I'm talking about the entire city school system.'

'How?' Caroline felt a surge of excitement.

'By serving free hot lunches. Milk,' he pursued. 'I've discussed this with the school authorities. They're sym-pathetic, but there's the problem of funds. I understand the requests for welfare in Atlanta have been climbing sharply for the past three years. The relief warden expects them to be even higher in the coming winter.'

'Victor, we'll start serving free hot lunches and milk in the Hamptonville school,' Caroline resolved, her mind in action. 'There's storage room in the school that can be converted into a kitchen.' With orders being curtailed, she ought to be trimming their budget, her mind exhorted. Was she moving too fast? Where she had never doubted her instincts, now she wavered. But this was for the children. Let Hamptonville lead the way.

Caroline heard a car pull up before the house. That would be Liz returning from an afternoon of swimming. Liz raced down the hall and charged into the library.

'Liz, don't run like that in this heat,' Caroline remonstrated. 'Go out and tell Mattie to give you some cold strawberries and cream.'

'I don't want anything.' Liz collapsed into a chair.

'You're looking mighty pretty, Liz,' Victor told her. 'The image of your mother.'

'I think I look like Papa,' Liz disputed, and sighed. 'I wish he'd taken me with him to The Hague.'

'Liz, would you like to help us work with Francis?' Victor asked, apparently on impulse.

'Me?' Liz was startled.

'You're his sister.' Victor waited for her assent. Caroline knew that Victor meant to include the whole family, eventually, in Francis' treatment.

'No,' Liz rejected, and rose from her chair. 'Maybe I will have some strawberries.'

Caroline saw Victor to the door and returned to the mild comfort of the library fan. A few minutes later Liz joined her, cradling a bowl of strawberries and cream.

'What time do we leave for the party?' Liz wanted to know. She was pleased that she – but not Josh – had been invited to Rae Kahn's surprise birthday party for David tonight.

'About a quarter of eight.'

'Will there be a lot of people we don't know?' Liz probed, all at once uneasy.

'Just several professors from the college where David teaches,' Caroline soothed.

'Is Victor coming?'

'He doesn't know David,' Caroline reminded. She must introduce them. They would enjoy each other's company.

'I heard Katie's mother say that Victor hardly ever accepts invitations anywhere. She said everybody invites him because his father is a judge and his mother an Italian countess. Is she really a countess?' Liz seemed intrigued by the prospect.

'She was until she married Victor's father and became an American citizen.' Victor was too involved in his work to allow himself to be engulfed in local socializing, Caroline surmised.

'Victor likes you,' Liz said softly. 'He likes you a lot.'

'I'm very fond of Victor.' Caroline was disconcerted. Her first instinct was to reproach Liz for calling Victor by his given name, but Victor felt this was proper, since Francis had been taught to do this. 'He's like a member of the family now. And it wasn't very nice of you to tell him you didn't want to help with Francis.'

'Papa says Victor isn't doing anything to help Francis.' Liz was deceptively sweet.

'Papa doesn't understand.' Caroline's voice was sharp. 'But you'll see, Liz. Francis is going to improve. He's going to be just like other children.'

Eric should be more prudent in the way he talked before the children. They shouldn't be aware of the strained relations between their parents. Already, Caroline suspected, Liz – so mature for her age – was taking sides with her father.

The neat white turreted Queen Anne house on Piedmont Road, where Noah and Rae lived with their three children, while Noah's brother David occupied the attic apartment, was brightly lighted when Caroline parked in the driveway behind a line of cars.

111

Small, round, and pretty, David's sister-in-law Rae opened the door for them, gestured for quiet, and led them into the comfortable parlour where several of David's colleagues were talking in conspiratorially hushed tones.

The parlour offered an uncluttered pleasing arrangement of Victorian furniture. The piano was a rosewood Steinway that dated back to 1845. Noah had done well for himself financially. His store on Decatur Street had expanded several times in the past fifteen years, and now there was the second store in Marietta. Noah and Rae were delighted that the new baby, born five weeks ago, was a girl. Their younger son was exactly Francis' age, the older almost eight.

'David has no idea about the party because it's Friday night. He would never expect me to give a party on the sabbath. But God will forgive me,' Rae said, her dark eyes guilt-free.

Noah introduced Caroline and Liz to David's fellow teachers while Rae went up to bring David down to the parlour on some pretext. Caroline and Liz added their beribboned packages to those neatly stacked atop a circular paper-mâché table inlaid with mother-of-pearl, which stood between two windows. At the sound of David's and Rae's voices on the stairs, Noah positioned the guests at each side of the door.

'Surprise!' they chorused as David and Rae walked into the parlour. At the double doors that led into the dining room, the family maid stood grinning, birthday cake with candles in her hands. 'Happy birthday!'

Momentarily bewildered, David stared about at the smiling faces in the parlour.

'David, didn't you remember it's your birthday?' Liz ran to him and threw her arms about him.

'I didn't remember,' he acknowledged. 'Between

spending every day in the courtroom and working in the evenings, I forgot. Thank you all!' His face radiated pleasure. 'This is a true surprise party.'

Rae marshalled the guests into the dining room, determined that the trial would not be discussed. Tomorrow the prosecutor would wind up his summation. Tonight they would forget that Leo Frank's life hung in the balance.

Caroline watched while Liz contrived to sit beside David. Liz was developing so quickly! In the past four months her breasts had swelled to curvaceous proportions. Caroline suspected that at any moment Liz would come to her to confide that she had begun to menstruate. She had carefully explained to Liz the changes that took place in a young girl's body at her age. At first repelled, Liz now waited with anticipation for this signal that she was no longer a child.

'David, blow out the candles,' Liz ordered ebulliently. 'Every one of them. But first make a wish.'

Sitting across the table from Liz, Caroline observed the new softness in Liz's eyes when they rested on David. A chill darted through her as she interpreted that look. First love. *But Liz wasn't yet thirteen.* No, she was wrong. Caroline chastised herself. David was like an adored older brother; that's all it was.

While they were yet at the table, Jim arrived and apologized for his lateness.

Despite Rae's determination to keep the mood light, talk kept coming back to the Leo Frank case.

'I was in court earlier in the week when Leo took the stand in his own defence.' Noah's voice was impassioned. 'For four hours he spoke. How can they doubt the man's innocence? The *Constitution* said his voice "carried the ring of truth in every sentence."'

'I was there that day,' Jim said. 'When Leo stepped down from the witness box, I thought: He's acquitted himself. The jury is spellbound. They *know* he's not lying! And then reason returned to me. The jury will be ruled by the passion of the mob, and they won't be appeased until Leo hangs.'

For a moment a painful pall settled on those in the room. 'David, you'll be there in court on Monday?' Caroline's heart was pounding.

'On Monday Dorsey will finish his summation. The state has changed the normal order of procedure in order to let the prosecutor speak last. The case will go to the jury. I'll be there,' David assured her.

'May I go with you?' Caroline asked. 'I'd feel uncomfortable alone.'

'Mama, take me with you!' Liz's face was incandescent.

'Liz, no,' Caroline refused. 'A courtroom is no place for a child.'

'I'm almost thirteen,' Liz tossed back. 'And there are children there lots younger than me. Ask David.'

'Liz you're not going.' Caroline was firm.

'Papa told me how you went to stop a lynching when you were just a girl.' Liz recalled. 'He said you stood there before all those awful people and – '

'I was nineteen, Liz,' Caroline interrupted. 'And I couldn't have succeeded. Papa arrived and stopped it.'

'I was there,' David said, caught up in recall. 'Your father said afterwards that your mother looked like an American Jeanne d'Arc, standing there before that angry mob.'

'You wouldn't do it now,' Liz accused her mother. 'You've changed. You'd think up all kinds of reasons not to do it!' Liz jumped to her feet. 'Can we go home now?'

'In a few minutes, Liz.' Caroline's throat was tight. She could do nothing to please her husband or her daughter. *Had she changed? Was she so different?* She turned to the others. 'I can't believe the jury will convict Leo Frank.'

'Think about it, Caroline. We've been through four months of sensational newspaper reporting,' Jim said. 'It would be impossible to assemble a jury in Atlanta that wasn't aware of those stories. We know that prejudice and perjury abound in that courtroom. But this is not just the case of a man being tried for murder. It's the outcry of the frightened rural masses who've left the farms for the city, hoping to find better lives and instead discovering themselves living in crime-infested slums.'

'Leo is being crucified as Alfred Dreyfus was crucified in France,' Noah declared. 'Because he's a Jew and a Northerner.'

'I can't believe that!' Caroline protested. 'This is a civilized city.'

'Caroline, you're so in love with Atlanta and your dream of the New South that you don't want to recognize the bigotry that infests not only Atlanta but also this whole country,' Jim accused. 'There is a growing segment of this nation that is building up a hatred towards Jews, blacks, Catholics, immigrants – anybody who doesn't fit the white Anglo-Saxon Protestant mould. And if we don't rise up to fight it, it'll grow worse.'

White and shaken, Caroline rose to her feet.

'It's late. Liz and I have to go home.' She turned to David. 'I'll drive by and pick you up on Monday morning. We'll go to the courthouse together.'

10

Tense and tired from lack of sleep the previous night, Caroline sat beside David in the front seats they had managed to snare for themselves by arriving at the courtroom at an early hour. Caroline recoiled from the almost festive mood of the onlookers.

Suddenly the throng burst into a spontaneous noisy demonstration. Caroline swung about in her seat. It was impossible to see what was happening. Many of those in the rear of the courtroom had leapt to their feet. Some blocked the aisle.

'Dorsey's arriving,' David explained. 'The star performer.'

'Why doesn't Judge Roan stop them?' Caroline asked when the demonstration continued.

'The only way he can do that is by clearing the courtroom.' David's eyes settled on Judge Roan. 'He's calling the sheriff over now.'

The spectators watched while Judge Roan conferred first with the sheriff, then with the defence attorneys, Rosser and Arnold. When the spectators realized that Dorsey was ready to continue his summation, cut short by Roan on Friday aftenoon, they lapsed into a tense quiet.

The prosecutor began to speak. At intervals Caroline's eyes sought David's, but David was transfixed by Dorsey's oration. His eyes never left Dorsey's face. Caroline knew from the sounds outside the courtroom that a huge crowd had gathered around the building. They could hear Dorsey speaking. At intervals there was applause.

Dorsey spoke for three hours, with not one person relinquishing a seat despite the heat of the morning, the discomfort of sitting so long on uncomfortable benches. The chimes of the Catholic church nearby rang at noon, as Dorsey finished his summation.

'Guilty! Guilty! Guilty!' the prosecutor intoned, the church bells accentuating each of his concluding words. Caroline felt herself encased in ice.

Judge Roan charged the jurors. They left the courtroom. David took Caroline to a nearby restaurant for a lunch that neither of them wanted.

'David, will they find him guilty?' Caroline asked while they waited to be served. She knew the answer.

'The lawyers will appeal.' David struggled to hide his apprehension.

'Will the jury be long out?' Caroline asked.

David shrugged.

'Who can say?'

'Will we be allowed to return to the courtroom to wait and see if the jury returns today?' Caroline pursued.

'Yes,' David told her. 'There'll be a few people there. Reporters, mostly, and Leo's friends.'

'We'll go back.' Caroline was decisive. Maybe a miracle would happen.

As David predicted, the courtroom was sparsely populated. Caroline and he sat down for the long wait. Four hours after the jury left the courtroom, word came that a verdict had been reached. Neither Leo nor his attorneys appeared.

Caroline turned to David. 'Shouldn't Leo be here? And where are his attorneys?'

'This must have been prearranged,' David surmised. 'Judge Roan may have been afraid of a riot if they were here.'

The twelve men filed to their seats. Every eye was galvanized to them.

'Oh, my God,' Caroline whispered. From the haggard looks on the faces of the jurors she could read the verdict. The foreman of the jury rose to his feet.

'Guilty.' The word seemed wrung from him.

While the judge made an effort to poll the members of the jury individually, a reporter leaned his head out the window to shout the verdict to the crowd that had congregated about the courthouse all day beneath the blazing August sun. A joyous outcry rent the air and rose to a frenzied crescendo that was to be repeated throughout the city.

'Close the windows!' Judge Roan ordered.

Caroline and David sat frozen to the bench while Judge Roan questioned each member of the jury. Each time, the juror questioned replied, 'Guilty.'

'Let's get out of here,' David said tersely, a hand at Caroline's elbow.

Outside, Caroline and David pushed their way through the mob that had accumulated to almost four thousand. Men and women alike were screaming themselves hoarse with approval. *Leo Frank was found guilty.* Judge Roan would sentence an innocent man to hang, Caroline thought in anguish, and citizens rejoiced.

While Caroline and David fought to break free of the screeching horde of humanity, they heard a fresh crescendo of joy surge through the crowd, who ignored the mounted police who tried to disperse them.

'Like Cossacks!' David muttered, pale with recall of pogroms.

Hugh Dorsey had emerged from the courthouse. Three men lifted him to their shoulders and carried him over the heads of the cheering mob to his office across the street.

'Rosser and Arnold should have demanded a change of venue,' David reiterated. How many times had he said that? Caroline asked herself in compassion. 'The case was tried in the newspapers before Leo ever set foot in the courtroom. There was not one juror among those twelve men who would have dared to free Leo! They would have been ostracized in this state!'

Right at this moment Leo Frank must be hearing the verdict. His wife would learn that he had been found guilty. Why wasn't Eric here today? Caroline mentally berated. She needed Eric to share her sorrow.

Eric and Serena lay in sublime silence in each other's arms in his otherwise dreary hotel room. A light blanket protected them against the dank chill of the day. Eric stiffened at the intruding sound of hymns emerging from the Nordende Palace, close enough to be viewed from the hotel windows.

'Dammit, more hymns? Is the queen praying for the Americans to go home?' Eric jeered.

'Shut up, Eric,' Serena scolded. 'So they sing hymns half a dozen times a day. If we went to more social events instead of indulging our sordid desires, we wouldn't hear them.' Her eyes laughed at him.

'We only missed the concert at Scheveningen, and that would have been a ghastly cold ride. And a couple of receptions,' he conceded. 'We'll surely be at the opening of the Peace Palace tomorrow.' Two days later, he thought involuntarily, he would be on a ship sailing for home.

'I'm going to hate being alone.' Serena read his mind. She was staying another week, then going to London, where she planned to research an article on the English-women's approach to suffrage.

'Why don't you junk that interview with Emmeline

Pankhurst and try for passage to New York on my ship?' Eric persuaded.

'I have a commitment,' she reminded.

He pulled her closer to him, feeling passion well again in him. But there was more than passion between Serena and him. The peace movement bound them together. Ideologically they were one. He could spend the rest of his life alternately making love to Serena and arguing about the most viable routes to world peace.

'This has been a very special time in my life,' Eric said after a few moments.

'A special time for me, too.' Serena's hands moved between them. Her eyes were appraising. He suspected that if he voiced the words, she would invent a reason to come to Atlanta.

'Do we have to dress and go down to dinner?' He'd prefer to spend the evening right here, with the feel of Serena's bare skin against his own. He had not thought it possible to make love as often as Serena and he made love – but he had spent so many deprived nights in the guest room at Hampton House.

'To a late dinner,' she stipulated.

'Serena, you're like nobody I've ever known.' He lifted himself above her, separated her thighs with one of his own. 'You're the most exciting, passionate, fearless woman in this world.'

'Stop talking so much,' she ordered, her voice uneven. 'Do what you do so well.'

When they at last went down to dinner, Eric discovered his high spirits in retreat. He was enmeshed in the realization that in two days he would be on his way back to Atlanta. To a life that had become alarmingly empty. He was almost forty years old. *What had he accomplished?* Caroline didn't need him. All she needed was the mill. Even with the children she felt it her right to make decisions. Like this business with that bastard Victor Adams. If he didn't know Caro as well as he did, he would suspect the handsome young doctor was sleeping with his wife.

'You're tired from this madhouse week,' Serena intruded on his introspection.

'Not at all,' he contradicted, for a moment irritated. At forty he wasn't decrepit. Self-consciously he dismissed this. God, he was getting thin-skinned. Fifteen years difference between Serena and him meant nothing when they were in bed. Serena knew that. 'It's been a fascinating week.'

Eric and Serena awoke to a day that was shining gloriously. Bells were ringing throughout the city. They arose and dressed swiftly. Both were caught up in the meaning of the opening of the Peace Palace, truly one of the greatest events in the history of the world-peace movement. This was a reaffirmation of peace in a world that was threatened by war.

'I feel absurd wearing evening clothes in the morning,' Eric complained as Serena handed him his white gloves and high hat, that were *de rigueur* today.

'Typical American attitude,' Serena mocked, reaching for one of the orange-dyed rosebuds she had bought at a florist's on the Moelenstraat last night. The other would adorn the jacket of her suit. Today everyone in The Hague – even horses and dogs – would wear a touch of orange. 'We're lucky to have seats.'

'The Peace Palace auditorium is rather inadequate for the situation.' Eric's smile was wry. 'Especially with all the pushy Americans owning no credentials, demanding seats.'

Eric and Serena had breakfast at the hotel and joined the throngs in the street. The usual cool weather had been supplanted by a summer heat more familiar to Americans. Eric was amused by Serena's delight in the garb of the women from the country, who strolled along the street – knitting as they walked – in dresses extended by multilayered petticoats, hair framed by headpieces of lace and gold.

'Eric, look at the wreaths across the street!' Serena glowed with discovery. 'Those baskets hanging from them have real flowers.'

Watchful of the time, they sought out a taxi for the long ride to the Peace Palace. Arriving at their destination, they discovered that those fortunate to have been allotted seats were already filing past the magnificent bronze doors into the architectural gem that was the Peace Palace, made possible by the generosity of America's Andrew Carnegie. Walking into the hall they observed the majestic staircase, which Serena recalled had been designed to resemble the grand staircase of the Paris Opera House.

'Serena, look at this,' Eric ordered. Just inside the entrance had been placed a Latin motto in mosaic. "*Sol justitae illustra nes*,"' Eric read and translated, "Sun of justice shine upon us." All at once he was sombre. 'I should like to photograph that and send it to the court that's trying Leo Frank.'

'Do you suppose the trial is over?' Serena asked. Eric had told her in detail about the travesty of justice being enacted in Atlanta.

'I wish I knew.' His voice was edged with exasperation. 'There was nothing in the New York papers, and surely nothing here.'

Eric and Serena followed the crowds into the great court of the palace, where the opening ceremonies were to be held in the presence of HM the Queen, HM the Queen Mother, HRH Prince Hendrik, Mr and Mrs

Carnegie, the Administrative Council, and members of the Permanent Court of Arbitration. They took their seats and waited with keen anticipation.

Despite the excitement of the occasion, the eloquence of the speeches, Eric encountered difficulty in focusing on the ceremonies. In two days he would be leaving Serena behind. Since the evening he had met Serena in the dining salon on the *Rotterdam*, he had cut himself off from the past, except at unwary moments. He was reluctant to relinquish the new relationship.

When they left the Peace Palace to return to the city, it seemed to Eric that Serena clung to his arm with a poignant regret at their imminent separation. But there could be no more for them than this, he admonished himself.

'Did you hear the story the woman behind us was reporting so gleefully?' Serena demanded, her head on his shoulder when they had at last ensnared a taxi.

'I heard a lot of stories,' Eric teased her.

'Idiot!' She lifted her head and gazed at him in a mixture of reproach and provocation.

'Don't look at me like that unless you want to be raped right here in the taxi,' he warned.

'It's only rape when the lady protests,' Serena reminded. 'This lady requests.'

'Bad for the driver's morals,' he chided, confident that the man spoke only Dutch.

'The story,' she picked up. 'One of our compatriots arrived at the Peace Palace with four friends. They sat right down in the seats being reserved for the queens. They were unseated, or course. How could they be so gauche?'

'Dizzy from the excitement of the occasion,' he drawled. 'I think tonight we'll have dinner in our room.'

123

How the hell was he going to survive without Serena? It was madness to feel this way about a woman.

'Tonight we are going to be received at the palace,' Serena reminded. 'Judge Dimon is arranging it.'

Though the card arrived, summoning them to Nordende Palace, Eric and Serena remained at the hotel. Tonight Serena was uncharacteristically quiet but characteristically passionate. Dammit, Eric swore, if she would say one word again about his remaining longer in Europe, he would arrange it. To the devil with plans! Yet he knew if he dallied longer with Serena, he might never return to Atlanta.

The following morning Serena woke him in the manner that had come to delight him. He had never been one to indulge in morning lovemaking until Serena entered his life. Caroline was up at six to rush off to the mill.

'What are you thinking?' Serena demanded effervescently, sprawled in naked warmth above him.

'Let's have breakfast, lunch, and dinner here in the room,' he suggested, his smile rakish.

'No.' She astonished him by the swift rejection. 'You have exactly twenty-four hours left in this country. Today we are going to be tourists.'

Despite his protestations, Serena took Eric to the fine fifteenth-century Gothic St Lawrence, the most famous church in Rotterdam. Hand in hand they stood before the tombs of the Dutch admirals Cortenaer, Witte de With, and Van Brakel. From St Lawrence they went to the Schielandshuis, the meeting house built in the late seventeenth century by Jacob Lois. They visited Hendrick de Keyer's beautiful statue of Erasmus, the great Rotterdam humanist placed on the Grote Market in 1622. They strolled through the zoological and botanical gardens before Serena capitulated and allowed them to return to the hotel for dinner.

When they went up to their hotel room after dinner, Eric realized that this would be the last time Serena and he would come through this door together. Tonight would be the last night that he would lie in this bed with Serena in his arms. The awareness lent a special intensity to his lovemaking. How was he going to survive in the old life that had become a travesty? *Could he survive?*

Caroline sat between Liz and Josh on the rear seat of the Pierce Arrow, listening for sounds of an approaching train while Roland sought a parking space. They were early, of course; but she was too impatient to wait at home. The days of loneliness had strengthened her resolve to reconcile with Eric. In twenty minutes the train from New York should be pulling into the multiple-towered, monumental Terminal Station.

Roland parked. Caroline and the children left the car and walked across the plaza into the large waiting room. In the cavernous interior of the station the summer heat seemed to have diminished. Caroline seated herself on a bench while Liz and Josh restlessly explored.

'Mama, let's go out and wait by the tracks,' Liz ordered imperiously after a brief inspection tour with Josh. 'I want to be right there when Papa arrives.'

'Liz, the train won't be here for at least ten minutes,' Caroline protested, but she rose to her feet. Like Liz and Josh, she was eager to see Eric. Tonight she would make him understand how desperately she had missed him.

The waiting room was becoming crowded as the arrival time of the New York-to-Atlanta train approached. Others, too, were leaving the waiting room to go out behind the station to wait for the train in the track-covering shed, which was artfully concealed by a facade of Renaissance Revival arcades.

'The train's coming!' Liz darted forward, like others around them.

'Mama, are you sure Papa's on this train?' Josh asked, clinging to her arm.

'He telegraphed from New York yesterday,' Caroline reminded. 'He'll be on this train.'

They waited by the track while the train chugged to a stop. Passengers began to step down. Porters appeared with bright smiles, hands outstretched for baggage. The air vibrated with the sounds of lively greetings. Josh moved forward, impatient to catch sight of his father.

'Papa!' Liz shrieked. 'Papa!'

Caroline felt her heart pounding as she strode towards Eric, conscious that his eyes had been seeking her. She must make him understand how much she had missed him. She must tear down the wall that had grown between them. She loved Eric enough to take the initiative.

'Eric, we've missed you.' Her eyes were luminescent as they feasted on his face.

'You look beautiful,' Eric said softly, and bent to kiss her. A gentle kiss, when she wished to be kissed with passion.

Caroline sat silently in the car while Liz and Josh plied their father, sitting up front beside Roland, with questions about his trip. Eric was glad to be home, she told herself. He missed them, too.

'How has Francis been?' Eric interrupted Liz to ask.

It was a perfunctory question, Caroline thought, and was irritated. Eric still maintained a closed mind. Nothing she would say about Victor's progress with Francis would penetrate his consciousness.

'Francis is fine,' Caroline reported. Eric would ridicule the admission that Francis had learned to put on his jacket in the proper fashion. Yesterday – in the presence of Victor and Patience – he had demonstrated this new

126

skill, and beamed with pride when she applauded and hugged him for this accomplishment.

'No repercussions from the ankle?' Eric prodded.

'Why should there be?' Her smile was strained. He still blamed *her* for that fractured ankle. 'Mattie is preparing your favourite dinner.' She strove for lightness. 'Roast duck and wild rice.'

Not until Eric and she were sitting in the library with frosty glasses of lemonade in hand, and Liz and Josh had gone their separate ways, did Caroline bring up the Leo Frank trial.

'I didn't want to talk about the trial in front of the children because Liz had been so upset over the outcome –'

'Rotten decision, but what was expected,' Eric interrupted. 'I phoned Jim from New York and he told me.'

'I gather from David that Rosser and Arnold are deep into preparations for an appeal.' Caroline fought to keep her voice casual. *He had phoned Jim but had sent her a telegram.* In all the time he was gone, she had received just two letters – the brief one from New York and the scarcely longer one mailed from Plymouth. Liz and Josh had each received a souvenir postcard from The Hague.

'God knows the defence has ground to appeal for a new trial.' Eric was emphatic. 'Jim told me Rosser and Arnold have a number of affidavits from people who swear they heard two of the jurors utter prejudicial remarks against Frank before the trial began.'

'They're certain to get a new trial?' Caroline pushed.

'Leo Frank will have a new trial,' Eric conceded, yet his eyes were grave. He drained his glass of lemonade and rose to his feet. 'I'd like to go up and see Francis.'

Caroline refrained from telling Eric that Francis would be sitting down to dinner with them. For the past three weeks, Victor, Patience, and she had been working together with Francis to prepare him for tonight. They had gone through endless pretend meals with Francis in his room. Last night Francis had come downstairs for a dress-rehearsal dinner, to the astonishment of Sophie and the children. He had been so delighted by the experience, so proud of his new skills. Josh had been touchingly solicitous of his younger brother.

Caroline dressed for dinner with infinite care. She had ordered that red roses be cut for the table, because Eric's favourite flowers were roses. The Haviland china was to be used, and the Waterford glassware. She had taken the precaution, however, of instructing Elvira to set Francis' place with his favourite plate and silverware, lest demands on him be overwhelming.

Caroline sat at the table with deceptive casualness, but her eyes revealed elation when she saw Eric's astonishment at the sight of Francis. She had placed him between Josh and Eric, to point out his independence of her. Sophie was beaming in approval.

'We have a party, Papa. You come home.' Francis was breathless with accomplishment.

'I'm glad to be home, Francis.' Eric's eyes were tender. 'I missed you all.' He wasn't comfortable with Francis at the table, however. Caroline sensed he was gearing himself for an outburst.

Should she have told Patience to stand behind Francis to help him? He could handle a fork, but cutting with a knife still eluded him. No, she was right, she reinforced her decision. To have Patience standing by would show Francis that she was anxious about his behaviour. Besides, Josh had been coached to help him.

She made a point of not watching Francis, though she was aware that Josh was patiently cutting Francis' roast duck for him. At regular intervals Eric's gaze settled on his youngest child. *Dear God, let everything go well.*

Liz and Josh were spilling over with questions about Eric's trip, each impatient for the other to finish in order to launch a fresh question. Pleased at being in this situation, Francis was content to listen. As always, Eric treated the children's queries with respect. Gradually his wary expectation of a painful outburst from Francis was subsiding.

Dinner was going well. Caroline congratulated herself. Tonight was a spectacular success for Francis. Pride pushed away the tension that had gripped her. Eric talked about the ocean voyage home while Elvira and Roland cleared the table.

Elvira came back into the dining room with a silver tray laden with white, pink and chocolate petits fours.

Then, without warning, 'Don't want cake!' Francis screeched, his face growing crimson in rage. 'Ice cream! Ice cream!' He began to beat on the table with his spoon in a raucous accompaniment to his verbal demands.

'Stop that, Francis!' Liz shrieked. 'You ruin everything!'

'Patience will give you ice cream, Francis,' Caroline told him over the din. Patience was standing by in the kitchen for just such an emergency. She would hear Francis' carrying-on and come. 'Patience will get you ice cream,' she reiterated, pantomiming to the others that they were to ignore Francis' tirade. Masking her disappointment, inwardly cringing before Eric's irritation, she chose a petit four and passed the tray on to the others. *Why hadn't she thought to serve ice cream for dessert?*

Patience came into the dining room, lifted Francis from his chair, all the while murmuring promises of ice cream, and carried him from the room. In a few moments they could hear his shrieks subsiding. The coveted dish of ice cream had been presented to him.

After the dinner the family – except for Francis – sat in

the parlour and listened to Liz play Debussy's *Clair de Lune*, which she had recently learned. Then she left the piano to settle herself on the arm of her father's chair. Josh was deep into a book Eric had picked up for him in New York. Sophie who was morbidly afraid of travel by ship, questioned Eric in minute detail about the ocean voyage.

'Dinners were like those in the finest hotels in the world,' Eric rhapsodized. 'If I hadn't used restraint, I would have gained ten pounds on the voyage. One night,' Eric said reminiscently, 'there was the finest chateaubriand I ever tasted. I should have taken you with me, Sophie,' Eric teased. 'You would have loved every minute of it.'

'You should have taken Caroline with you,' Sophie said in a rare unwary moment.

'I tried to.' Eric's smile was quixotic. 'She turned me down.'

Clutching at her self-possession, Caroline rechannelled the conversation. 'I'm anxious to read *The Human Slaughter House*.' This was the book Eric had bought in New York for her. 'I understand the Kaiser banned it in Germany.'

'It's ironic that the Kaiser is expected to be a prominent candidate for the Nobel Peace Prize.' Eric grimaced. 'The man who built the German Army into the most powerful military force in the world.'

'Noah says that someday David will win a Nobel prize in physics,' Liz contributed, her face incandescent.

'I would not be at all surprised,' Eric said seriously. 'David's brilliant.' And Liz was captivated by him, Caroline thought, and was disturbed. *She was a little girl*.

'I don't know about the rest of you, but I'm going upstairs to my room and go to bed,' Sophie announced, dabbing at her forehead with a linen handkerchief. 'I

130

can't wait for this hot weather to be over.' Sophie was making an effort to leave her alone with Eric, Caroline interpreted.

Minutes later Caroline ordered Liz and Josh off to bed, encountering the usual protests that they did not have to arise for school the next day.

'Off,' she insisted, and walked with them to the door, where each kissed her good night, though not without reproach.

'Mama, I'm almost thirteen,' Liz reminded. 'You still treat me like I was a baby. Some girls are out working when they're thirteen. Some even get married!' Liz charged down the hall in defiance.

For a moment Caroline stood watching the children's retreating figures. By the time they began to climb the stairs, they were battling about some insignificant incident of the day. Liz's words ricocheted in her head. *Some girls are out working when they're thirteen. Some even get married!* Did Liz entertain such absurd notions? It was impossible to read her volatile young mind.

Alone with Eric, she felt a surge of anticipation. Eric had been away from home for almost a month. Surely now he would forget the stupid barrier he had erected between them.

'Mattie left a pitcher of lemonade in the icebox,' she said, her voice strained. Why didn't he get out of his chair and take her in his arms? 'Or perhaps you'd like coffee?'

'Nothing, thanks.' Eric seemed absentminded. Perhaps he was tired, she alibied in disappointment. Too tired to make love to his wife? her mind taunted. After all these months? 'I think I'll call Jim before I go upstairs. We spoke just a few minutes when I phoned from New York.' He smiled. 'I couldn't wait to get to Atlanta to hear about the trial. Though I suspected the outcome.'

'Jim will give you all the details.' Caroline rose to her feet.

'Goodnight, Eric.'

In her room Caroline threw open all the windows, grateful for a faint breeze from the river. For weeks she had been looking forward to this night, when she would go to Eric and make him understand that she loved him. Needed him. She had always prided herself on the openness of their marriage. She had never felt a reticence in expressing her passion. A touch of her hand at Eric's shoulder, a glow in her eyes, told him that she was eager for him to make love to her. Why was it so difficult for her to make that move now?

Through the open windows, in the night stillness, she could hear the faint sound of Eric's voice. His words were indistinguishable, but she knew he was talking to Jim. They would talk for a long time. In a sudden decision, she moved into her bathroom and ran a tepid tub. Out of the tub she slipped into a white batiste nightgown with Valencienne-lace inserts and a ruffled neckline. She loosened her hair to fall about her shoulders in a red-gold cloud, then placed an off-white China silk negligee across the bed, to be worn when she walked down the hall to Eric's room.

She pulled a slipper chair to the window and waited for the sound of Eric's footsteps in the hall. The heat of the day was at last in retreat, the air fragrant with the scent of wild roses. She leaned forward, enjoying the light breeze that washed her face.

She stiffened into alertness. Eric had stopped talking with Jim. Her mouth parted in a subconscious smile, she turned her head towards the door. Eric was walking up the stairs. She heard the muted sounds of his footsteps in the carpeted hall. Then the faint sound of his door opening and closing.

Caroline rose to her feet and reached for the negligee, pulling it on as she crossed to the door. She felt eighteen again. Tonight she would batter down the absurd wall between Eric and her. Her life would become whole again.

Her heart pounding, she stood before the door of the guest room and lifted one hand to knock. Instantly the door was opened.

'I was too restless to sleep. I heard you come upstairs.' She struggled to maintain her poise. 'Did Jim have anything new to tell you about Leo's appeal?' She was stammering. What was the matter with her?

'It'll probably be heard towards the end of the month.' Eric closed the door behind him. For a moment his eyes met hers. She was conscious of a curious appraisal. Then he was walking across the room to pick up the glass of lemonade he had brought up with him. 'It's so damnably hot here after The Hague.' He took a deep swig of the lemonade.

'I was in the courtroom the last day of the trial,' Caroline continued self-consciously. She saw Eric's start of astonishment. Didn't he know that she, too, was upset about the injustice shown to Leo Frank? 'I went with David. Liz was furious that I wouldn't let her come with us.'

'I thought about it all the time I was away. When we . . . when I walked into the Peace Palace, I saw a Latin motto set in the floor in mosaic. It translated "Sun of justice shine upon us." I wanted to photograph that and send it to the court that was trying Leo.'

'I sat there in the courtroom and I couldn't believe what I saw and heard.' Caroline shuddered. 'I was ashamed that so many people in our city could behave so abominably.'

'The case is far from settled, Caro. There are people in Atlanta who are prepared to fight for justice.'

Suddenly the atmosphere in the room was tense. Caroline and Eric discussed the case, but their eyes carried on a separate conversation.

'Eric. I wanted you there in the courtroom beside me.' She reached a hand out to touch his arm. 'I felt so alone.'

'You're not alone now.' He reached out to bring her to him.

'Eric I love you.'

His mouth came down to hers. Her body relaxed against his. Everything was going to be fine with them again.

His mouth withdrew, then delayed to kiss her eyelids before he spoke.

'Let me lock the door, Caro.' His age-old admonition, lest the children walk in on them in lovemaking.

Caroline slipped out of her negligee and lay back against the pillows on the mahogany four-poster bed. She was trembling when Eric came to lie beside her.

'I never saw you look more beautiful than tonight,' Eric told her, his hands at her breasts.

'Darling, I've missed you.' Caroline welcomed the weight of the leg he moved across hers. 'I've felt so empty.'

'You won't be now,' he promised, his mouth lowering itself to burrow in the hollow between her breasts.

She felt the weight of his body above hers and closed her arms about his shoulders. His legs manoeuvred to separate her own. Eagerly she flexed to receive him.

'Sssh,' Eric cautioned, aware of the passion welling in her, matching his own.

'Eric, love me. Quickly.' Her voice was an imploring whisper.

She stifled the sounds of her passion as he thrust

himself within her, knowing that in a few moments this pleasure would escalate into exquisite ecstasy. This was the way it was with Eric and her.

Suddenly the night quiet of the house was splintered by a shriek from Francis, audible even this far from his room. The shriek was followed by another. Subconsciously she froze. *Not now. Dear God, not now*.

Eric pulled away from her.

'Caro, you'd better go to Francis.' His voice was cold. 'Today was too much for him. When is that damn doctor going to learn Francis can't be pushed so far?'

11

A breeze from the river filtered into Francis' bedroom, lifting the light summer drapes away from the windows so that silvered moonlight spilled across Francis' small face, tranquil now in sleep. Caroline stood beside the bed, suffused with love for this youngest, troubled child.

'Patience, he was doing so well all through dinner,' Caroline said in frustration. 'Up until Elvira brought in dessert.'

'He's better, Miss Caroline. We dassn't expect him to be all well yet,' Patience cautioned. 'Dr Victor, he'll be right proud of Francis, you jes' wait and see.'

'Good night, Patience. You go to bed now, too.' She smiled in affection and left the room.

Caroline walked with quick, small steps down the long stretch of hall to Eric's room. At the door she hesitated. No, it was absurd to knock. She reached for the knob and opened the door. The room was in darkness. Eric lay sprawled diagonally across the bed. From his regular breathing she knew he was asleep.

She closed the door to Eric's room and returned to her own, struggling to repress the disappointment that coursed through her. Their aborted passion was fully alive again in her – but Eric slept. She sat in the slipper chair beside the window and stared, unseeing, into the night. Eric had *told* her to go to Francis. He hadn't tried to stop her.

He was tired from the long train trip from New York, she told herself. It was natural that he fell asleep. Yet she had been so sure he would be waiting for her return. She had expected tonight to be different from the night when Eric had moved into the guest room. Nothing had changed.

When Victor arrived at the house the following afternoon, Caroline was waiting in the foyer to report on Francis' behaviour the previous evening. Breathless from tension, she waited for his assessment.

'Caro, we expect Francis to fall backwards at moments,' Victor reminded calmly. 'All through dinner he was fine. That's progress. And we're going to see more and more times when Francis behaves well, until the good times far outweigh the bad times. I'm delighted by the way he's responding.' His smile was warm and positive.

'I've talked with Josh,' Caroline told him. 'He's willing to spend some time every afternoon playing ball with Francis.' Victor had explained that he would stand behind Francis, guiding his arms to catch and throw, with Josh being the other player. He wished Francis to have the experience of playing with another child. 'Josh is pleased that you asked for his help.'

'Good,' Victor approved, moving towards the stairs. 'We'll start tomorrow.'

Caroline went into the library. Despite Eric's cynicism, she would continue to do whatever Victor asked. Francis' welfare took precedence over everything else.

She settled herself under the ceiling fan to go over the reports Andrew had given her. Cutbacks in orders continued to come in, mirroring the decline in business throughout the country. Costs for construction on the annexe and the houses were running higher than anticipated. Over Sophie's objections and Andrew's exhortations she had gone ahead and placed orders for machinery.

137

She finished reading the reports and focused on the problem of replacing Ellen. This morning Ellen had told her that her longtime friend Charlie had asked her to marry him.

'I didn't dare tell him that I'd like to keep on working. He's so strong about the wife's place being in the home.' Her smile was rueful. 'But we won't get married until you've found another secretary. Charlie understands that.'

Caroline started at the sound of the phone ringing. Marian was calling.

'I have a favour to ask,' Marian said after preliminary chit-chat.

'Anything,' Caroline said.

'I received a letter from the seamstress who sews for my niece out in New Orleans. A sweet, hardworking woman with a very pretty daughter. I gather the daughter was just jilted by the young man she expected to marry, and the mother feels if she comes to Atlanta and gets a job here, she'll forget. She knows shorthand and typing. Do you suppose you could help her?'

'Ellen's leaving to get married,' Caroline told Marian. 'I might have a job for her in my office. I can't guarantee to hire her, but if she's coming to Atlanta anyway, I'll be glad to talk to her.'

'I'll write her mother tonight,' Marian promised. 'I have a feeling she'll be fine.'

Maureen Vauban stood before the mottled mirror that hung over the dresser in her cheap furnished room in an unfashionable section of Atlanta and inspected her reflection. The message the mirror sent back was reassuring; she was eighteen and beautiful of face and figure. Honey-haired, green-eyed, with the pert features of her Irish seamstress mother and the vivacious charm of the elegant

French father who had never acknowledged her. In a few moments she would leave to call on Mrs Hampton, who might hire her as a secretary.

Maureen picked up her crocheted purse, which contained a letter of reference from a New Orleans banker on whom her mother had once bestowed her favours. Though Maureen had never served as the banker's stenographer, the reference gave her some sense of confidence. She smoothed the demure bodice of her white dotted-swiss frock, chosen to impress Caroline Hampton with her refinement. It was urgent that she be hired for this job. She had only funds enough to pay her rent for three weeks and her food for a matching time, if she were frugal. There was no going back to New Orleans. Her mother had been blunt about that.

Maureen left her room and went out into the heat of mid-September Atlanta. Her landlady had explained how she could reach Hampton Mill, at the same time making it clear that she disapproved of a roomer who would consider such a demeaning place of employment. Maureen was in no position to be choosy.

She found the streetcar stop and waited for one to arrive. Today she was beginning a whole new life. Her objective, to catch a rich Atlanta husband. She would never be able to marry well in New Orleans. Too many people knew the stigma of her birth.

She had vague memories of her father, who had been one of Louisiana's wealthiest landowners. New Orleans gossip maintained that Maureen resembled her father more than did his legitimate offspring. He had been murdered by his wife when she discovered his 'second family.' With her funds cut off and a five-year-old daughter to support, Maureen's mother had speedily married Claud Vauban, a handsome New Orleans gambler. Two years after that marriage, from which Maureen acquired her last name, Claud walked out when his wife balked at supporting him in the fashion he had arranged. He had decided his beautiful Irish wife should entertain gentlemen of discerning taste willing to pay well for her favours.

A streetcar appeared and stopped for passengers. Maureen walked to the back of the car and sat down. A woman across the aisle was screaming at a pretty little girl of about three.

'You're gonna get it when we're home,' the woman warned, her voice strident.

Maureen clenched her teeth, visualizing her mother making similar threats, and carrying them out. From the time they were left destitute at her father's death until she was old enough to fight back, her mother had beaten her regularly. Yet when the rich New Orleans ladies came to have their dresses made, Mama could be so sweet and loving. Always carrying on about how hard she worked to support her little girl – who more often than not concealed bruises received at her mother's hand beneath the dainty white dresses in which she was dressed.

After she was twelve, Mama never hit her. She knew better. Nor would she accept her mother's admonition that she marry the first Irish dockhand who asked for her hand. Her sole vivid memory of her father was the day he had taken her to his mansion in the elite Creole section of the city, at a time when his legitimate family was visiting up in Saratoga Springs, New York.

Hand in hand with her handsome debonair father, she had walked in wonder through the huge, high-ceilinged rooms with their magnificent antiques and fine wall hangings. She had kicked off her shoes to feel the thickness of the rugs beneath her feet. She had known then, though she was only five, that someday *she* would own such a house. Three weeks after that visit her father was dead, and the weekly remittances ceased.

Nobody would stop her, Maureen vowed. She would discover a very rich man who could not bear to live without her. But she would not be stupid like her mother. Her price would be marriage. She would live the way her arrogant half-sisters and half-brothers in New Orleans lived.

Maureen alighted at the last stop of the streetcar, accepting directions from the conductor about the location of the Hampton Mill. She would have preferred to work for a man; but if Caroline Hampton would hire her, she would jump at the opportunity. Mrs Bolton had told her that Mrs Hampton's husband was a member of the State Legislature. He would be both rich and powerful.

She walked swiftly, conscious of the time. The day was pleasant, a harbinger of autumn, though they would be sweltering again tomorrow, Maureen thought in distaste. She frowned at the sight of the large unprepossessing brick building with endless opaque windows that came into view. The Hampton Mill. An annexe sprawled at one side of the structure. A much larger annexe was in a state of construction.

In a plateau adjacent to the mill buildings were rows of small white houses, each a depressing duplicate of the other. The mill village, Maureen surmised.

She approached the mill, flinching at the noise of the machinery. She opened the door and walked inside. Her nostrils tingled at the unpleasant scent. The humidity, which was essential to the operation of a cotton mill, was overwhelming.

Fighting her revulsion, she asked a worker for directions to Mrs Hampton's office. The woman pointed down a long corridor that would lead into the annexe. Maureen was conscious of the stares that followed her progress.

The door to the office was open. Oblivious of

Maureen's approach, the woman at the desk was engrossed in a ledger spread before her.

'Mrs Hampton?' She had not expected Caroline Hampton to be young and beautiful.

The woman at the desk looked up with a ready smile. 'Come in, you must be Maureen Vauban.'

'Yes.' Maureen returned the smile, managing an aura of shyness. 'Mrs Bolton said I was to be here at nine o'clock.'

'Sit down, please.' Mrs Hampton was intent on putting her at ease.

With appealing charm Maureen talked about her newly acquired skills, her supposed employment at the New Orleans bank, and her belief in the future of women in the business world. Instinct told her this would please her prospective employer. Then Mrs Hampton dictated a letter and called for her present secretary to show Maureen to a typewriter so that she could transcribe it.

When Maureen returned to Caroline's office, perfectly transcribed letter in hand, she hesitated at the open door. Caroline was in absorbed conversation with a pleasant-looking man.

'Come in, Maureen,' Caroline ordered. 'Maureen, this is my cousin, Mr Hampton, who is the mill superintendent. Maureen may be replacing Ellen.' Her cousin, Maureen noted; not her husband.

'I hope we'll be seeing you around here,' the superintendent said shyly, and turned back to Caroline. 'I'll let you know when the new dyes arrive.'

'Fine, Andrew. I hope they're an improvement on the last. Andrew Hampton left the office. Maureen handed the typed letter to Caroline and stood before the desk. Caroline quickly scanned the test letter, looked up in approval.

'I'm sure you'll do,' she said. 'Sit down, Maureen, and

I'll tell you just what will be required of you. If you like, you can start tomorrow. That way you'll have some time with Ellen to help you before she leaves.'

'Oh, Mrs Hampton, thank you so much!' Her eyes glowed in gratitude. But not too effusive, her mind cautioned. Caroline Hampton would hate that. 'I really need the job.'

Half an hour later Maureen left the mill. She would loathe working in that awful place, yet she knew she was fortunate to have found a job so quickly. Waiting for the streetcar, she decided she must phone Mrs Bolton immediately and report on what had happened. She would learn from Mrs Bolton if Andrew Hampton was married.

12

Summer gave way to autumn, Caroline's favourite season of the year, which always seemed to her filled with fresh promise after the long, hot Georgia summer. She was relieved that Liz and Josh were back on a school schedule, because during the summer months she was especially aware of her daily absence from the house. Guilt plagued her despite her rationalizations.

Appearing the exemplary husband, Eric accompanied her along with Liz and a reluctant Josh, to Ellen's wedding. She was delighted that Ellen's daughter, Janet, and Liz seemed to find pleasure in each other's company, particularly since Liz's friend Katie had just left for boarding school.

Now Eric and Jim were planning the campaign for Congressman Evans' seat in the 1914 election. Right after the first of the year the congressman would announce his retirement. At the same time Evans – and the party – would indicate their support of Eric.

Night after night Caroline lay sleepless, grappling with the realization that the breach between Eric and her was widening. He meant to go to Washington without her. Recurrently she asked herself if she could bring herself to leave Atlanta and the mill, even if Francis' condition permitted taking him with them.

Andrew and Sophie were efficient and knowledgeable, but they didn't have her vision for the Hampton Mill. With Wilson in the White House – with tariffs so favourable to the cotton manufacturers – now was the time for the Hampton Mill to expand. Running the mill, enlarging its capacity, and improving the mill village were a compulsion with her.

Within the next two years she was determined to set up a health service within the village, and to add a library wing to the school. Expansion would make this possible.

At the end of October Leo Frank's attorneys presented his request for an appeal before Judge Roan. Rosser and Arnold argued that the evidence did not warrant conviction, that the prejudicial atmosphere in Atlanta denied Leo Frank a fair trial. 'It is the most horrible persecution of a Jew since the death of Christ,' Arnold declared.

Judge Roan denied the appeal. That evening Caroline sat in the library while Eric, Jim and David dissected Judge Roan's decision. Only in moments such as this, Caroline thought, was there any real closeness between Eric and her.

'I hear Judge Roan has issued a statement that says he's thought about this case more than any other he's tried – and he's not convinced of Leo's guilt.' Jim's face was sombre, his eyes reflective.

'Then how could he deny Leo a new trial?' Caroline was outraged.

'Because obviously the jury was convinced,' Eric pointed out.

'That has to be reversed!' David said forcefully. 'They can't hang an innocent man!'

'It'll have to be reversed by a higher court.' Eric was fatalistic. 'Judge Roan was afraid to grant a new trial. He was afraid we'd have a riot in Atlanta.'

'It'll go to the state Supreme Court. Maybe then Leo will get a fair trial,' Jim told them. He rose to his feet. 'I have to be in court in the morning. David, I'll drive you home.'

Only now did Caroline discover that Liz had been hovering outside the library door.

'Liz, you're supposed to be up in your room studying,' Caroline rebuked.

'I did my homework.' Liz lifted her chin in defiance and turned to David. 'I think that Judge Roan is just awful.'

'He won't have the last word, Liz,' Jim said in an effort at optimism. 'Don't you worry your pretty head about that.'

'Liz, I've been thinking about taking Janet and you to see *Ben Hur* when it comes to Atlanta,' Caroline said while Eric walked with David and Jim to the front door. 'Would you like that?'

'I'd rather see Pearl White.' Liz was candid.

'You'll see her again, too,' Caroline promised. Why did she feel it so urgent to woo her own daughter?

Maureen left her rooming house in the still-dark early morning and hurried through the raw chill to the streetcar stop. She loathed the shoddy rooming house, her prying landlady, the mill. Despite the arrival of winter weather, the mill was excessively hot and humid. A tropical jungle, insanely noisy. The lint that pervaded the air was a constant source of annoyance to her. The faces of the workers that mirrored their bleak existences were an ever-present threat to her because she was only one step above them. Only her financial need keep her at the Hampton Mill.

The streetcar arrived and she pulled herself aboard, finding a seat in the rear. Each day in the office was a depressing repetition of the previous day, yet her sharp mind warned her that this was not the time to seek other employment. Business conditions were poor; she heard this on every side.

She stared out of the streetcar window. How stupid she had been to expect to find herself a busy social life in

146

Atlanta! The only men she met were the potbellied roomers at the house where she lived, and the mill workers. She was nobody in Atlanta. Mrs Bolton had talked to Caroline Hampton about a job for her, but she wasn't inviting her seamstress's daughter into her home for social gatherings.

At the end of the line Maureen left the streetcar and headed for the mill, its thousands of opaque windowpanes lighted against the dreariness of the morning. Her stomach churned at the prospect of another day inside the mill. She had been working there almost three months. *She had accomplished nothing*.

Shoulders hunched against the cold, the likes of which she had never encountered in New Orleans, Maureen considered her situation. She was letting too much time go by without accomplishment. But the first few weeks she had been nervous about her ability to hold on to the job; her earlier confidence had evaporated when Ellen left and she was on her own. At the end of the day she was too tired to think clearly.

She had proved herself on the job. Caroline Hampton was satisfied with her work. Now it was time to do what she had come to Atlanta to do. It was going to be harder than she expected. Still, she wasn't without prospects. Andrew Hampton was accessible, polite, and friendly.

So far they had exchanged nothing more extensive than greetings and talk about the weather. But Maureen's confidence in her appeal was strong. She could make Andrew Hampton notice her; all she had to do was decide that he merited this.

What about Eric Hampton? Maureen mused. What kind of a man allowed his wife to spend long hours every day managing a cotton mill? Was the legislator too busy with government and his law practice to care what his wife did?

She would work late tonight, Maureen resolved in sudden decision. Addie, the toothless old cow who cleaned up the offices after the mill shut down for the day, was supposed to be a terrible gossip.

A little past six in the evening, with the machinery mercifully quiet, Maureen dawdled over her filing. She could hear Addie moving into Caroline's office with her mop. In a little while she would come in here.

Maureen glanced up with a welcoming smile as the small, spare, stoop-shouldered woman of indeterminate old age approached the doorway.

'I'll come back later, miss.' Addie turned to go.

'No, please come in,' Maureen coaxed. 'I'm through working. I'm just stalling on going out into the cold.' She reached into her muff in a gesture that appeared spontaneous but was planned. 'Would you like to share a candy bar with me? I just love sweets.' She broke the bar in two and handed one piece to Addie.

'Oh, I got a awful sweet tooth.' Addie's face brightened as she reached for the candy. 'Been like that all my life.'

'Where do you live in the mill village?' Maureen displayed a lively interest in continuing the discussion.

'In a room behind the company store,' Addie explained, happy to socialize. 'When my old man died of the pellagra and my sons moved away, Miss Caroline fixed it up for me to do the office cleanin' and live there. She even give me some dishes and pots from the big house. I been workin' for Hamptons for goin' on sixty years.'

It was easy to prod Addie into talking about the Hampton family. Only now did Maureen realize that Andrew lived in the small pretty cottage near the mill.

An elderly coloured woman kept house and and cooked for him, Addie reported.

'Most of the mill belongs to Miss Caroline, but Miss Sophie and Mr Andrew, they own shares, too.'

'Did Miss Caroline's husband run the mill before he went into the Legislature?'

'Mr Eric?' Addie grinned indulgently. 'He wouldn't have nothin' to do with the mill, even when the General was alive. That's one fine-lookin' man. Still young enough to turn the head of a girl as young and pretty as you. And what a hellion he was before he settled down with Miss Caroline! She's his second wife,' Addie said with a knowing glint in her eyes.

Maureen listened in rapt attention to Addie's story of Eric Hampton's beautiful first wife, who had killed her lover and then run off to Paris with her brother.

'That Miss Tina, she was no good,' Addie was emphatic. 'She got what was coming to her when she was killed in a fire over there in Paris. It worked out good for Mr Eric. He didn't have to wait for the divorce to go through to marry Miss Caroline.'

Scanning the Atlanta *Journal* that evening in the dreary light of her bedroom, Maureen focused her attention on a familiar name beneath a group photograph. So Eric Hampton was involved with one of those crazy peace groups. She wouldn't have expected him to be, from the way Addie had described him. Maybe it had something to do with politics.

She scrutinized the photograph. Addie was right. Eric Hampton was a fine-looking man. She could enjoy being married to a man like that. She still smouldered at the memory of her mother's relationship with Jacques Beauchamp, whose blood had bequeathed her a yearning for high living but not the assets to support it.

Normally Maureen fell asleep moments after her head

touched the pillow. Tonight she lay wide awake staring at the paint-peeling ceiling. It would not bother her one bit to take Eric Hampton away from his wife. Caroline irritated her. She was polite and considerate, Maureen assessed, yet to Caroline Hampton she was no more than somebody to order around in the office.

During the next few days her impatience to meet Eric Hampton accelerated to a painful intensity. When Caroline gave her a complicated contract to type, Maureen knew the time to meet him had arrived. Caroline left the mill at three. The contract had to be ready for signing tomorrow morning. Maureen would, of necessity, have to go to Hampton House for help in unscrambling some of that complicated legal language. But not until quite late, when Eric Hampton was sure to be home.

Shortly past six Maureen pulled on her coat, reached for her muff and the envelope holding her notebook and the pages she had already typed up. She strode down the noisy, humid hallway and out into the sharp night cold. The sky was clear, the moon a sliver of silver. Tightening her collar about her throat, she walked in the direction of Hampton House. The east wing of the house was brightly lighted. The drapes were drawn tightly at the tall narrow windows across the front of the house. Maureen mounted the stairs and crossed to the door. She rang the bell. A young coloured man pulled it wide so that she could walk into the immense high-ceilinged reception hall.

'May I please see Miss Caroline?' Maureen asked. 'I'm her secretary.'

'I'll tell her you is here,' the young man said hesitantly. 'Would you wait here, miss?' He was apologetic about not showing her into the parlour, but she worked in the mill. Mill employees were not received at Hampton House.

While she waited, she could hear a man's voice in conversation with Miss Sophie. They were in a room down the long hallway. Moments later the young coloured man came into the reception hall and beckoned her to follow.

'Miss Caroline say for you to come into the library. Down this way, miss.'

She followed him, pinpointing the male voice. She managed a glance into a room at the side. She recognized Eric Hampton from the newspaper photograph. Addie had been right. A fine-looking man.

'Miss Caroline is in here.' The gentle-voiced servant gestured to a room on the right. Caroline sat at a desk strewn with papers.

'I'm sorry to disturb you this way.' Maureen was appealingly apologetic. 'But I know this contract has to be ready for signing in the morning, and I just couldn't figure out three sentences.'

'I should have gone over it with you, Maureen. I'm sorry you're being detained so late at the office.' Caroline gestured to a chair beside her.

In a few minutes the sentences in question, involving complicated legal phrases, had been clarified. Again Caroline apologized and personally conducted Maureen to the door. She wasn't going to meet Eric Hampton.

'Mama, isn't dinner ready yet?' an imperious young voice demanded from the staircase.

'Shortly, Liz,' Caroline told her. 'Go inside and talk to Papa and Sophie.'

That would be her daughter, Maureen decided. Spoiled and wilful, she guessed. And undoubtedly a snob. All Southern young ladies were snobs.

'I'm sorry to have disturbed you,' Maureen apologized again at the door.

'Thank you for having the good sense to come here,' Caroline told her. 'You were using your head.'

Maureen walked away from the house towards the mill. She hated families who lived in big, beautiful houses. Nobody ever laid a hand on Liz Hampton, she'd bet. Caroline would blanch at the idea.

At the mill Maureen returned to her office and sat at the typewriter to complete the contract. In an odd fashion she was glad to be at the mill tonight, surrounded by the clatter she normally detested. She dreaded going home to her furnished room. She couldn't go back to New Orleans if she wanted to; Mama had made that clear.

'Maureen, you're still here?' Andrew hovered in the doorway.

'I'm just finishing up that contract for Miss Caroline,' she explained. 'It has to be ready for the meeting tomorrow.'

Andrew seemed to be in silent debate.

'Come to my office when you're finished,' he decided. 'I'll drive you home. It's too cold to stand out and wait for a streetcar.'

'Thank you, Mr Hampton.' Her smile was dazzling. 'I do appreciate that.'

13

Caroline parked the Hupmobile in front of the house and remained behind the wheel for a few moments, inspecting the red-berried, glossy-leaved wreaths of holly that hung at the front windows and graced the front door. She felt little Christmas spirit this year, though for the sake of the children she must make a pretence of festivity.

Christmas gifts had been bought in one frenzied foray through Rich's and lay colourfully wrapped and beribboned in a corner of her closet.

She would love to invite Victor to Christmas dinner; but considering Eric's attitude, she knew she mustn't. Probably Victor would be with Senator and Marian Bolton for Christmas dinner. Marian would make sure he wasn't alone.

She left the car for Roland to drive into the garage and went into the house. Tonight Eric and she were going to hear Helen Keller speak at the auditorium-armoury. They had been nowhere together for weeks. So many evenings Eric went back downtown after dinner – to meet with Jim to work on his campaign plans or to the peace-movement office.

She walked into the library, and was surprised to discover Eric sitting before the fireplace, absorbed in a book. He glanced up at her approach.

'Marian phoned a few moments ago,' he told her. 'She'll pick us up with her car.'

'Fine,' Caroline pulled off her coat and went to stand before the healthy blaze in the grate.

'I had a long session with Jim and some of the party

'leaders this morning.' Eric's offhand air alerted Caroline to trouble.

'Has Evans changed his mind about not running for another term?'

'Evans won't run. But I'm running into an absurd situation. On account of the Mexican problem.' His tone was sarcastic.

'What about the Mexican problem?' Caroline demanded, dropping into the chair opposite Eric.

'The party's inner circle is insisting I disassociate myself from the peace movement. There are factions that could need American protection in Mexico.'

'Americans with heavy investments in Mexico,' Caroline expanded. 'Eric, what will you do?'

'Fight them.' He appeared undisturbed. 'Nonviolent fighting. Nobody is going to redesign my ideology.'

'How serious is this?'

'I'm going to have trouble pinning down the nomination if I won't recant. And I won't,' Eric reiterated.

'Wilson is dedicated to peace,' Caroline said in exasperation. 'He won't let us be dragged into fighting in Mexico.'

'Nobody can deny Wilson wants peace. He's made that clear.' Eric's eyes rested appraisingly on Caroline. 'Sometimes I can't believe Wilson has been in office almost a year. But he has.' The atmosphere was suddenly heavy.

'Barely ten months,' Caroline's throat tightened. Eric was reminding her of his stipulation that Victor was to have one year to work with Francis. 'Here comes Elvira with my tray.' Caroline strove to keep her voice even.

'Mattie fixed you a chicken sandwich,' Elvira said, putting the tray on a small table, which she set up before Caroline.

'Thank you, Elvira.'

'Jim said that every seat for the lecture tonight has

been sold,' Eric commented. 'That was to be expected. Helen Keller is from northern Alabama – her father was a Confederate officer who fought through the war. His mother – Helen's grandmother – was a second cousin of Robert E. Lee. That must fill the hearts of the United Daughters of the Confederacy with delight,' Eric drawled.

'Did you know that Mark Twain said Helen Keller is the most marvellous woman who has existed on earth since Joan of Arc?' Knowing about the tremendous obstacles Helen Keller had overcome fortified her confidence that Francis would one day be a normal child. 'I was so delighted when Marian invited us to go with Victor and her.'

Eric froze.

'You didn't say that Victor Adams would be with us.'

'I thought I had,' Caroline stammered. 'I was so excited when Marian called to invite us. I may have forgotten to mention that Victor was coming, too.'

His face grim, Eric reached for his book. He was dismissing her. When the phone rang, Eric rose to answer it. The call was from Jim.

'All right, Jim,' he agreed. 'I'll meet you there at seven-thirty sharp.' Caroline stared in dismay as he put down the phone.

'Eric, we're hearing Helen Keller tonight.'

'I can't make it, Jim's set up some crucial meeting. Take Liz with you. She'll love to go.'

Caroline struggled to conceal her fury. Eric was *glad* of an excuse not to go to the lecture. Because Victor was going to be present.

'I'll ask Liz as soon as she comes home.' Eric could have insisted Jim schedule the meeting at another time.

Liz was very excited about going to hear Helen Keller.

All through dinner she debated aloud what to wear to this Saturday-night event.

'What's the difference what you wear?' Josh jeered in disgust. 'It's just a dumb old lecture.'

'There'll be two thousand people there!' Liz told him. 'Helen Keller is famous.'

At the scheduled time the Bolton chauffeur arrived at the front door to say that the car and Mrs Bolton awaited them.

'Eric has a meeting that came up at the last moment,' Caroline apologized while she settled herself beside Marian, 'but Liz is replacing him if that's all right with you.'

'Honey, of course it is,' Marian assured her. Her face lighted as Liz climbed into the car. 'Liz, you look so pretty. And so grown-up!'

'Thank you, Mrs Bolton.' Liz beamed.

'How was Washington?' Caroline asked.

'Most of the time deadly.' Marian uttered a sound of distaste.

'Has there been a lot of talk about the White House wedding?'

'Not everybody's enthralled at contributing money towards the diamond necklace that's being bought for the youngest Miss Wilson's wedding present.' Marian's voice was acid. 'The senator and I didn't contribute, though everybody in government was urged to give. This right at the time when Mrs Wilson and her oldest daughter had agreed to be officers of the Society for the Prevention of Useless Giving!'

The car pulled up before Victor's hotel, where he was waiting, and then headed for the auditorium-armoury. Crowds were swarming into the hall where Helen Keller was to speak. Caroline's eyes roamed about among the spectators, resting with compassion on the children and adults who were blind, who were deaf and dumb. Here to find courage in Helen Keller's accomplishments.

Caroline leaned forward expectantly when Mrs Macy was being introduced.

'She's been at Helen Keller's side since Helen was barely seven years old,' Marian whispered. 'And she's thirty-three now.'

Mrs Macy talked first about Helen's childhood.

'At that time,' Mrs Macy explained, 'Helen was expressing her wants in the most primitive way. If she wanted bread and butter, she went through the motions of slicing bread and spreading butter over it. If she wanted ice cream – and she very often did – she would make as though she were turning a freezer.' Tears filled Caroline's eyes. Instinctively she turned to Victor. His eyes met hers in silent understanding.

When Helen Keller came forward to speak, a chair positioned before her, the two thousand people in the auditorium waited in reverent silence. She spoke with hands outstretched towards those two thousand people whom she could not see. Her voice was low, laboured, sometimes unintelligible, but every individual in the auditorium sought to understand.

'The world needs more light,' she said, and no one cared that her voice was monotonous and difficult to hear. 'More knowledge. More love. My teacher has told you how a little word dropped from her hand touched the darkness of my mind, and I knew joy and light and happiness.'

Caroline's eyes blurred as Helen Keller continued to speak. What a wonderful intellect, and it might have been lost to the world except for Helen's determination and Mrs Macy's help.

'We cannot live alone,' Helen Keller told the audience, whose applause she could not hear. 'We can't do anything alone. We must unite our hearts, our hands, and our brains to end the cruel conditions under which many of our fellow men live. It is more difficult for ignorance to think and insensibility to feel than it is for the blind man to be taught to see the splendour of the sunset.'

Helen Keller held out her hands, and her mother came to stand with her as two thousand people applauded. After the programme was finished, the blind, the deaf, and the dumb among the audience eagerly crowded on to the platform to grasp her hand, to be able to say that they had touched Helen Keller. To Caroline's astonishment, she saw tears in Liz's eyes.

When they were pushing their way through the crowd and towards the door, Liz spied David with Noah and Rae.

'David!' she called exuberantly.

They managed to meet for a few moments of conversation.

'Wasn't she wonderful?' Liz asked David.

'A great lady,' David said gently.

'Did you see Andrew?' Rae asked.

'No.' Caroline was startled. 'I didn't know he was planning to be here tonight.'

'He was with a girl,' Noah told them. 'A very pretty young lady.'

'I doubt that it was Andrew,' Caroline said. 'Probably someone who looks very much like him.'

Eric sat across the table from Jim in the large country kitchen that, after hours, served as a private office. Jim brought over the percolator and poured coffee for them.

'It didn't go well,' Eric assessed. 'They expected me to be the ass-licking party man. Dammit, you'd think by now they'd know how I operate.'

'They're talking national politics,' Jim reminded.

'You're supposed to be anxious to move up the line. Eric, they see you as a presidential candidate in eight or ten years. Bolton's brought about that thinking. But they want to be damn sure they're putting their money on a winner.'

'Or somebody they can control?' Eric scoffed.

'They're the most powerful men in this state, all of them dedicated to pushing a Georgian into the White House. Moving you from Atlanta to Washington is the first major step. At the next election, you could run for Senate. Provided they're sure of you. We'll have one hell of a battle if that tight little clique that just left here decides against you.'

'I won't withdraw from the peace movement. I won't play games,' Eric reiterated. 'Bryan still opens his mouth loud and often about the need for peace.'

'Bryan was appointed Secretary of State. He didn't have to be elected. But we do have some favours of our own to call in,' Jim conceded. 'Favours that might affect some of those gentlemen who just left here.'

'I want to go to Congress.' Eric's face was resolute. 'On my terms. I won't be a slave. I'll be my own man.' Sometimes he felt less than that in his own home. A house that was legally his wife's property. How would Caroline feel about going to the White House, if that should arise? It would be a home that *he* had bought for them.

An hour later Eric left Jim's house and settled himself behind the wheel of the car, ambivalent about his destination. He pulled out his watch. It was not yet nine-thirty. Some nights, even Saturdays, there were workers at the peace-group office till midnight. He might as well drop by there for an hour.

Driving downtown through the cold night, Eric allowed his mind to close in on his conversation with Caroline this

159

afternoon in the library. She knew damn well what he meant when he brought up that Wilson had been in the White House close to a year. That damn prig, Victor Adams, had been in *his* house for close to a year. It was time Caro prepared herself to give the doctor his walking papers.

Caroline had deliberately plotted that little party this evening. Probably with Marian's help. The two of them were determined to cram Victor Adams down his throat. Thank God, Jim gave him a legitimate excuse to pull out. If Jim hadn't called, he'd have figured out something else. Caroline was not going to manipulate him any more.

He turned off Peachtree and drove to the run-down building where the peace group maintained its head-quarters. Lights were lit in their second-floor offices. He parked and left the car. Climbing the stairs to the offices, he could hear the hum of voices.

Eric opened the door and walked inside. A cluster of women was seated at a long table, stuffing letters into envelopes. They were so busy talking they were unaware of his arrival. Two men were in avid conversation with a woman who sat on the corner of a desk, her back to him.

'Say, Eric!' one of the men greeted him in jovial spirits. 'We were just telling this young lady how impressed you were with the goings-on at The Hague.'

The young lady turned around, and Eric froze. What in hell was Serena doing in Atlanta? His head was all at once a kaleidoscope of their weeks together. The memory triggered alarm. Guilt was a knife at his throat.

'I found The Hague fascinating too.' Serena was smiling at him with no indication that they had ever met.

'This is Eric Hampton,' the man introduced him. 'Serena Mayo.'

'Hello, Eric Hampton,' Serena extended one hand.

'Hello, Serena Mayo. Welcome to Atlanta.' Eric had

160

regained his composure. Their hands met in a secret message that sent a tingle through Eric's six-foot frame.

After pretending to compare their experiences in The Hague, Serena announced that she must leave.

'Do you have a car?' a woman who had joined them asked. 'This is a bad neighbourhood to look for a streetcar on a Saturday night.'

'I'll be glad to drive you wherever you're going,' Eric offered.

'California,' Serena flipped, and everybody laughed.

His hand at her elbow, Eric and Serena walked down the dreary, warped stairs to the street. They maintained a stolid silence until they were in the car.

'Why in hell didn't you let me know you were coming here?' Eric demanded.

'I wanted to see the look on your face when you walked into the peace headquarters and found me there.' She laughed.

'Honey, you don't know how much I've thought about The Hague.' In the darkness of the car he pulled her to him and kissed her, his body pulsating to be with her again. He had shifted about in bed so many nights, wishing he could relive their days – and nights – together. How many mornings had he awakened, remembering her favourite way of starting the day? 'Where are you staying?'

'I have a house.' Her voice was a caress. 'You can chase me through eight rooms. Four upstairs and four down. I won't be hard to catch.'

'Where is this marvellous place?' He was impatient to make love to her. But he wouldn't think beyond tonight. This could not continue.

'Piedmont Road. The house belongs to a woman I met in London. When I decided to come to Atlanta, I wrote to Grace Lamont and made arrangements to rent the house.' Eric released her and started up the car. 'It was closed up and a foot deep in dust, but it's fine now. I use the lower floor. I can stay as long as I like.'

'What brought you to Atlanta?' he asked.

'I missed you in bed. When I was offered an assignment to write on suffragism in the South, I grabbed at it. Atlanta was the logical locale. I told you, I can't sleep with just any man. He has to be special.'

'I'm flattered. Where do we go on Piedmont Road?'

They arrived shortly at the broad-gabled, dormered, shingled house where Serena had been living for the past week. She had been in Atlanta a whole week, he marvelled; and he had not been aware of her presence. He parked in the driveway with a moment of misgiving. But there were many Pierce Arrows in Atlanta. Who would know that it was Eric Hampton's car parked in this dark driveway?

Arm in arm they went into the house. Serena led him directly to the downstairs bedroom, overly furnished, its walls darkly papered. A grim, forbidding room with too many lamps.

'Can you bear this room?' she mocked, standing beside the ornate, heavily canopied four-poster bed.

'Sugar, I don't see a thing here but you,' he told her, drawing her to him. He'd have to tell her they couldn't see each other after tonight. Hell, his mind reproached, she had accepted this assignment because of him. But The Hague had been different. Then he was three thousand miles from home.

'Eric, are you sorry I came to Atlanta?'

'Don't be crazy.' He brought his mouth down to hers. No better method of shutting up a woman.

'You're learning,' she complimented him. 'This time you didn't tell me to take off my clothes the minute we were alone.'

'Take off your clothes,' he ordered. 'Do I have to do everything?' He crossed to switch off the lamp. He could not relax entirely in this situation. Not when Hampton House was no more than a mile to the north.

In a moment he felt Serena's warm hand on his naked thigh. His own hands found her breasts in the dark. Nobody even knew they were in the house; every room was dark. Why the hell was he so concerned? He had gone to Leonora Carlyle's house – twice – without worrying like a nineteenth-century old maid.

'You're sure you're not angry that I came to Atlanta?' she asked after a few moments, her voice uneven.

He reached for her hand and brought it to him.

'What do you think?'

'Take me to bed, Eric.'

He swept her into his arms and felt his way to the bed, swearing as he stumbled against a footstool. He dropped her on to the bed and lay down beside her, his hands familiarizing himself with her again.

All at once he was aware that she was lifting herself above him. His hands reached up to find her breasts as she straddled him.

'You're my prisoner,' she taunted, one hand fondling him.

'Do you hear me complaining?' How had he survived without Serena all these weeks?

'Didn't you miss this?' she demanded, bringing him to her.

'What do you think?'

The sounds of their passion mingled as they moved together. They were back in The Hague, Eric told himself. Yet he was ever conscious that he would have to account for his hours away from home.

* * *

Eric and Serena sat on a mound of cushions Serena had tossed on the floor before the fireplace. The firelight from the blaze Eric had started in the grate was their only illumination. They sipped the rum-laced coffee Serena had made and brought into the bedroom, each content with the other's silent presence.

'Serena, this isn't The Hague,' Eric at last punctured the cosy silence. 'We'll have to be careful.' How long would she be here? Only until she finished the assignment, he coddled his guilt. Three weeks, a month? 'I'm after the nomination for congressman from this district. It's going to be a hell of a lot more difficult to sew up than I expected.'

'And a juicy scandal would throw you right out of the race. I understand that.' Her voice was grave. 'We'll be so careful. Nobody'll ever suspect.' She pulled herself to her feet and set her cup and saucer on the mantel. 'I wish you could stay all night,' she admitted, 'but reason tells me you ought to leave. How long can you be at a peace meeting?'

'Tonight I was at Jim's house for a political confrontation,' he told her with a rakish grin. 'After the others left, we talked. We talked a long time.' Humour lit his eyes.

'I'll be at the peace movement's office most nights,' Serena told him. 'You'll have no trouble finding me.'

14

On New Year's Eve Caroline scheduled a late family dinner, with Andrew invited as always. Caroline ordered a sumptuous menu: grapefruit, turtle soup, broiled Georgia shad Chattahoochee style, wild turkey with oyster sauce, green peas, yams, salad à la Taft, and for dessert petits fours and Filipino ice cream.

This year – for the first time – Liz and Josh were allowed to stay up to see in the new year. Liz had inveigled her father's support for this, and Caroline had capitulated. In the family tradition, Eric opened a bottle of champagne shortly before midnight. Liz was ecstatic, Josh wide-eyed in astonishment, when their father presented each of them with a goblet half-filled with the pale, bubbly liquid.

'To 1914,' he toasted, and the family drank as the church bells pealed in the new year.

On New Year's Day Caroline, Eric, and Sophie went to the Boltons' open house. Eric disappeared with the senator after the first few minutes. There would be much of that between now and Election Day, Caroline reminded herself.

In a small, drab, poorly furnished room a thirty-minute streetcar ride from Hampton House, Maureen Vauban spent New Year's Day sprawled across her sagging bed reading old issues of the *Ladies' Home Journal*, lent to her by Mrs Ryan, her landlady, and examining the expensive attire on display in the current issue of *Vogue*.

In a fit of rebellion Maureen hurled the copy of *Vogue*

across the room. It landed in a reproachful heap on the tattered hooked rug. She lay back across the bed, visualizing herself in the new dresses which were causing such consternation among the clergy for their daring. Skirts were transparent, though an underlining protected the wearer from view; but skirts were climbing above the ankles. The décolleté allowed was flattering to a bosom as lush as hers.

A fresh wave of depression rolled over her. She had not been prepared for the loneliness of a New Year's Eve in a strange city. Everywhere there were parties. Riding home on the streetcar last night, she had eavesdropped on conversations around her that rippled with planned festivities. She had been depressed all evening knowing she would be sitting down with Mrs Ryan and other luckless boarders to a New Year's Eve dinner of stew or macaroni and cheese or spaghetti. After dinner she had gone to her room and written a long, sentimental letter to Mama. Knowing it would not be answered.

On holidays nobody should be alone. The whole city was closed except for restaurants and theatres, where people went in pairs or in parties. *Nobody was alone.* Even this morning she had felt self-conscious, going out into the near-deserted streets to mail the letter to Mama.

Most folks were asleep after last night's partying. She heard the new year come in alone, in bed in a flannel nightgown. She was eighteen years old, and most men thought she was beautiful; but she spent New Year's Eve alone in this rotten furnished room. She would be glad when the holiday was over, even though it meant going back to work.

Where was she going to make friends in this fancy city? Not with the mill folks or the roomers here in the house, Maureen rejected.

Back home Mama and she had no friends. Mama was

too uppity to make friends with their neighbours, and the ladies who came for sewing weren't inviting Mama to their houses. Not the seamstress who had whelped Jacques Beauchamp's illegitimate daughter.

She had come to Atlanta knowing only Mrs Bolton. She had expected to make friends, to have a busy social life in the city that everybody talked about as being so modern and exciting. Maybe she ought to look for a job in another office, where she might meet an eligible single man – or a rich widower.

The senator's wife hadn't invited her to her open house today, she thought vindictively. Mrs Bolton could have asked her.

She didn't have to be alone, Maureen thought in her own defence. Half a dozen of those bulls at the mill were panting to spend their piddling savings on a New Year's Eve with her.

She must have been out of her mind to write to Mama last night. She hated that old bag. What did Mama ever do for her except beat her up? From the time she was seven she was working when she wasn't in school. Cleaning the house, running errands. She was delivering to the customers by the time she was ten, doing plain sewing at eleven. She didn't owe Mama anything.

She left the bed to cross to the paint-chipped dresser and pull out of the top drawer the small box of chocolate cherries she had bought as a Christmas treat for herself and doled out one at a time. She pushed her pillows against the headboard of the bed, made herself comfortable with the candy box at her right. She ate in reckless abandon, finishing the contents that had been destined to last another two weeks.

All right, be realistic. Eric Hampton was out of her reach, but she saw Andrew every day. He liked her. He enjoyed spending the evening with her when they went to hear Helen Keller. Addie said he owned part of the mill. He had lots of money, even though he lived in that small cottage.

She would make sure that Andrew asked her out again. A whole new year lay ahead. Nineteen-fourteen would be different from all the others. *She would make it different.*

January sped past, cold and bleak. Business conditions had dropped to depression level, though President Wilson dismissed this as 'psychological in origin'. To families scrounging to keep food on the table and the rent paid, Wilson's words were of no comfort.

In New York City, Philadelphia, Chicago, and Cleveland, municipal lodging houses were packed every night. Labour riots were breaking out, strikes growing in an intensity that was bringing forth a national conference on unemployment in New York the following month. Henry Ford's announcement of the five-dollar, eight-hour workday had summoned the unemployed from every section of the nation, though the Ford Company could accommodate only a few thousand.

Early in February Wilson abandoned his policy of 'watchful waiting' and lifted the embargo on guns to the Mexican rebels. *El Imparcial* taunted that Wilson was coming out into the open as the friend of the bandit Villa. They labelled him 'the Wicked Puritan with sorry horse teeth.' Just two weeks after the lifting of the arms embargo, Scots-born William Benton, a cattle rancher in Chihuahua, Mexico, was executed by Pancho Villa's firing squad. Benton had been living in Mexico for thirty years. He owned a 150,000-acre ranch that he had developed into a showplace. He was hardworking, proud, and hot-tempered. Repeated raids on his herds sent him to Villa to accuse him of cattle stealing. Villa ordered Benton to be killed that same night.

All over America and Europe people were outraged by the murder of Benton. Newspapers in the United States, Canada, Paris, and London reproached the United States and reminded Washington it was morally responsible for Mexican behaviour. Under the Monroe Doctrine the United States rejected European intervention on the American continent.

Like many others, Eric feared the United States would be forced to take action in Mexico. Only now, discussing the seriousness of the situation in the bedroom of Serena's rented house, did he learn that Serena had spent three years, in her late teens, living in Texas, on the Mexican border.

'Eric, you know we'll have to intervene, or turn our backs on the Monroe Doctrine,' Serena voiced his thoughts.

'I hope we manage not to do that,' Eric hedged. 'I know about all the Americans owning huge tracts of land on the border who're just waiting to add northern Mexico to the United States. I know how many Americans feel we must have Mexico because it's so rich.' His eyes were contemptuous.

'Neither Wilson nor Bryan understands Mexico.' Serena sighed. 'Wilson sends John Lind as his special emissary. A man who doesn't speak Spanish and doesn't bother to learn.'

'I heard that Van Hintze, the German minister down in Mexico, offered to support the Huerta regime if Huerta would promise to cut off oil to England in case war breaks out in Europe.' Eric reached for Serena's hand. 'Remember all that beautiful talk we heard in The Hague in August? Will it mean anything, Serena?'

'I'd like to go down to Mexico.' Serena was contemplative. 'I speak Spanish fluently. I have some understanding of the people.'

'Stop talking,' Eric ordered, reaching for her. 'I have to leave in forty minutes.' He didn't want to think about Serena's going to Mexico. He knew she had finished her current assignment. There was no real tie to hold her here. Except himself.

In February Leo Frank was denied a new trial by the Georgia Supreme Court by a divided vote of four to two. The defence, already working in preparation for a new trial, now had to prepare another appeal. They hired the famous detective William J. Burns to help clear Leo Frank.

The defence released information that several affidavits had been secured from prosecution witnesses that repudiated their earlier testimony. The newspapers were quick to publish these retractions.

The Atlanta *Journal* published an account reporting that the state biologist concluded that the hair found on the lathe – one of the prosecution's main pieces of evidence – was not Mary Phagan's hair. He said he had told this to Hugh Dorsey, who brushed aside this conclusion.

The jubilation on the part of Leo's friends and defence was short-lived. The retractions were repudiated. Eric and Jim, like others knowledgeable about Georgia law, suspected that the prosecution might have pointed out the Georgia statute providing the death penalty for anyone swearing falsely in a capital case. On March 7 Leo was again sentenced to die. The hanging was scheduled for April 17.

Three afternoons after the sentencing, Eric arrived home an hour earlier than usual. He walked into the library, where Caroline sat listening to Liz practise the piano.

Simultaneously Caroline heard Victor talking to someone in the hall. He must have finished working with Francis and come downstairs. She listened, puzzled. *He was bringing Francis into the library.* Involuntarily her eyes swung to Eric. She lived in fear of Eric's making some outrageous demand about removing Francis from Victor's care – because she would refuse to do this.

Her face grew tender when Victor appeared in the doorway with Francis, one small hand in his.

'How nice to see you two.' Caroline managed an air of levity.

'Francis has something to show you all,' Victor said matter-of-factly. 'Francis, go over to the desk here, and write your name on this piece of paper.' He reached into his jacket pocket for paper and pencil. 'Then show it to your mama and your papa and to Liz. Take your time, Francis,' Victor encouraged.

His face appealingly ingenuous, Francis darted to the desk and seated himself. Caroline watched him grip the pencil and laboriously move it over the paper. Eric could not deny that this was progress.

'Victor, please sit down,' Caroline invited. 'I'll have Elvira bring us tea.' She struggled to conceal her nervousness. She was ever conscious of Eric's ultimatum. Only one year – which was quickly drawing to a close. *Please, God, don't let him say something awful.*

'Thank you, no,' Victor demurred. 'I have to be at the hospital for a consultation in about twenty minutes.' Caroline doubted that this was true. He sensed the hostility that emanated from Eric.

'Write name,' Francis announced in triumph, and hurried to show the paper to Caroline.

'Francis, that's beautiful.' Caroline inspected the rough

171

block letters that spelled his name. 'Show Papa.' But she pulled him to her for a congratulatory kiss before sending him on to Eric.

Caroline watched while Francis presented the paper to his father. His face noncommittal, Eric inspected the printing. Was he expecting perfection? Caroline asked herself defensively while Eric continued to view the offering. Francis was six years old. How many six-year-olds without Francis' problems could print well?

'It's very nice, Francis,' Eric approved. 'Take it to Liz. I think she's finished her piece.'

'I'll see you tomorrow, Francis,' Victor said, his smile encouraging. 'We'll learn to write some more.'

'Don't you find spending so much time with Francis a drain on your medical practice?' Eric asked Victor. Though his voice seemed casual, Caroline tensed. She knew Eric well enough to catch the vitriolic undercurrent. 'We wouldn't want to feel we were shortchanging your other patients.'

Her face drained of colour, Caroline stumbled to her feet. Eric must not antagonize Victor.

'This house has been my laboratory, Mr Hampton,' Victor said, his tone conciliatory. 'Whatever Francis and I accomplish together, with the help of the family, will be passed along to other families. Francis is learning, but so am I. As for the time, I'm at my office for two hours on five evenings a week, so my patients are not being deprived.' He was polite but wary. 'If you'll excuse me now, I must go over to Grady Hospital.'

'I'll see you to the door,' Caroline offered. She didn't trust herself to face Eric.

'Did you really print your name, Francis?' Liz's voice followed them into the hall, where Patience waited to be summoned to take Francis back upstairs. 'Show me how you do it.'

172

'Patience, bring Francis' dishes down to the kitchen,' Caroline said on impulse. 'Francis will have dinner with us tonight. I'll tell Mattie.'

'Yes, Miss Caroline.' Patience's eyes lighted.

Caroline walked with Victor to the door.

'Francis will be fine at dinner,' he prophesied. 'It'll be a reward for his having learned to write his name. He's doing well, you know.'

'Thanks to you,' Caroline said, pleasure washing over her. 'Victor, I'm so happy about him.'

'We'll keep working, Caro.' He smiled, pressed her arm for an instant, then hurried across the veranda and down the stairs to his car.

Victor knew what Eric had been saying, Caroline realized. He cared too much about what he was doing to acknowledge a subtle insult. A crisis had been averted between Eric and Victor. Temporarily.

Caroline walked down the hall and out towards the kitchen. Passing the library, she saw Liz and Francis, their heads bent over a piece of paper, both absorbed in Francis' printing efforts. Eric was settled in an armchair reading the newspaper.

Patience came into the kitchen with Francis' dishes.

'Miss Sophie, she jes' come home. She say she want to talk to you up in her room.'

'Thank you, Patience.' Sophie must have had a call from their equipment supplier, she surmised.

She knocked at Sophie's door, then walked inside at Sophie's summons.

'Caroline, remember the night you heard Helen Keller speak, and David said he saw Andrew there with a young lady?' Sophie's voice was ominous.

'Yes, but –'

'I suspect it *was* Andrew,' Sophie told her. 'Just as I was preparing to leave my office, I heard him talking with

Maureen. She's having dinner with him at his cottage, if you please. And after that they're going to the theatre.'

'She must have been seeing him all this time.' Indignation brought colour to her cheekbones. 'Sophie, I'm going to fire her.'

'You can't do that,' Sophie warned. 'She'd run crying to Andrew. She's out to marry him.'

'Andrew?' Caroline stared in disbelief. 'He's been a bachelor for so many years.'

'Sugar, every man's a bachelor until some girl gets her hooks into him and turns him into a married man.'

'What does Andrew know about her?' Caroline was aghast at the situation. 'What do any of us know? Only that her mother sews for Mrs Bolton's niece in New Orleans.'

'Andrew doesn't care about that,' Sophie pointed out. 'Maureen's young and beautiful. She can be utterly charming.' Sophie's sarcasm was obvious.

'Andrew's more than twice her age,' Caroline protested, feeling as protective towards him as she would towards one of the children. She had hired that girl.

'He's a man, Caroline. I'm worried about Andrew's welfare,' she admitted. 'But there's nothing we can do but stand by and watch.'

'What a pretty cottage, Andrew,' Maureen said admiringly when they approached the small, pristine white house, where smoke spiralled in welcome from the chimney.

'It's my refuge from the world,' Andrew told her. 'My palace in miniature.' He put a hand at her elbow as they started up the steps to the small veranda. 'We'll be properly chaperoned,' he assured her, his smile shy.

'Phoebe won't leave us alone for a minute. She's so pleased when I have company, which is very rare.'

Andrew opened the door. They walked into a small foyer and were greeted by tantalizing aromas from the kitchen.

'Mist' Andrew?' Phoebe's excited voice preceded her bulky figure. Her face shone in delight. 'My, do we have us a beautiful young lady for dinner.'

'Phoebe, we'll have to eat right away.' All at once Andrew was self-conscious. 'We're going to the theatre.'

'Yessuh. I'll have dinner on the table in a couple minutes.'

She was here in Andrew's house. At last. This was the beginning of a campaign to make her Mrs Andrew Hampton. The Hamptons were one of the fine old families of Atlanta. From the looks of this house – the beautiful antiques and the Oriental rugs and what Maureen intuitively guessed were fine old paintings – Andrew must be well-off.

Wouldn't it astonish some folks back in New Orleans to know she was being squired by Andrew Hampton? Wouldn't it astonish Caroline Hampton?

15

Eric stifled a yawn while he gathered together papers strewn across his office desk. He was due in court in forty minutes. Slightly past two A.M. last night he escorted Senator Bolton and six guests high in the Democratic party from the Hampton House parlour to the front door.

The senator had called in favours. Jim and he had done likewise. This was not unethical. The support of those men was essential if he was to win the nomination, which a year ago had seemed so positive. Within forty-eight hours he would know if he would run for Congress in November.

He frowned at the intrusion of his telephone.

'Hello.'

'Have you missed me?' a silken feminine voice inquired. This wasn't Serena. She was too bright to call him at the office.

'Who is this?' He managed to mask his irritation.

'Leonora.' She sulked. 'I've been gone a long time.'

'I gathered,' he said warily.

'From Saratoga Springs Mama and I went to Europe. We roamed around for months. In Paris we met a mutual relative.'

'Oh?' He was impatient with this chitchat.

'Your former brother-in-law and my cousin,' Leonora amplified. 'Chad. We saw him at Maxim's. He – '

'Leonora, I have to leave for court in a few minutes,' Eric said, forcing himself to sound polite.

'Don't you want to hear about Chad?'

'Not particularly.'

'I have a recurrence of interest in selling that piece of property we talked about before.' Her voice was a sultry invitation.

'I'm sorry. Right now I'm all tied up.' He had not meant the words to sound so brusque.

'Your loss,' she said coldly. 'Call me if you change your mind.'

'Good-bye, Leonora.' Leonora was a dead interlude in his life; he had no intention of reviving it.

While he thrust papers that would be required at court into a briefcase, Jim charged into his office.

'You know what those son-of-a-bitching Mexicans have done now?' Jim dropped himself into the chair that flanked Eric's desk. 'Excuse me, I refer to the Huerta Mexicans. Those bastards supported by the British oil interests.' His contempt was eloquent.

'The British have withdrawn their recognition of Huerta.' Eric reminded. 'Under duress from Wilson. I'll admit. But what's happened?'

'Take a look at this.' Jim thrust the morning's *Constitution* before Eric. 'In the middle of one of the world's richest oil fields the *Dolphin* – one of our gunboats being used by Rear Admiral Mayo as his headquarters – had to run out of oil. A whale boat went in to get it. An inexperienced ensign and sailors were in a restricted area, even if they were unarmed. They were arrested and marched through the streets to the headquarters of Colonel Hinojosa. He released them immediately and had them escorted back to their boat. There was an apology to the American consul.'

'And now Mayo's making all these demands?' Eric was incredulous. 'A formal expression of regret, the arrest of the officer responsible for the incident, and our flag hoisted on shore to receive a twenty-one-gun salute? The damn fool!'

'Maybe Wilson won't let it get out of hand.' Yet Jim sounded pessimistic.

'A stupid incident like that could be contained,' Eric acknowledged. 'Mayo acted without consulting Washington. Wilson's down in White Sulphur Springs for a few days. I understand his wife is quite ill.' Eric consulted his watch.

'You're going to trial this morning,' Jim remembered.

'If I get out of here now, I will,' Eric conceded, grinning. 'Let's don't worry about this mess in Tampico until we have to.'

He arrived at court and settled himself beside his client. A change in the court calendar scheduled another case before his own.

'This won't take long,' he soothed the client. 'You'll be before the judge in an hour.'

Eric was restless, despite his appearance of outward calm. At recurrent intervals he chastised himself for not speaking his mind to Victor Adams that afternoon when Adams came into the library with Francis. Why had he retreated before that son of a bitch? What kind of man was he to allow his wife to lead him around like a puppet?

Francis was behaving better. But this talk about Francis' learning to read and write and handle figures – that was the sort of irresponsible encouragement that could hurt Caroline. Francis parroted; *he didn't comprehend.*

That Boston doctor was in love with Caroline. Couldn't she see that? Was she so wrapped up in Francis she didn't notice the way Adams looked at her? He was dying to take her to bed.

'Next case, *Ryan versus Corelli*.' The summons dispelled Eric's thoughts.

Two days later Eric walked into the reception room of his law firm after a morning session of the Legislature.

Their normally reserved secretary reported, in a flurry of excitement, that Jim had been on the phone with the Georgia party chief for twenty minutes.

'Thank you, Margaret.' Eric stalked into Jim's office.

Jim held up a hand to indicate that Eric was to remain silent while he listened to the voice at the other end.

'There'll be no problems, I assure you,' Jim said. 'We'll handle it with the necessary discretion. I'll tell Eric the situation as soon as he comes into the office.'

Eric sat across the desk from Jim and waited for the final amenities to be completed. What the hell did Jim mean by 'the necessary discretion'?

'What was that all about?' Eric asked, gearing himself for a battle.

'You'll have the nomination,' Jim told him. 'Now, don't blow up until you hear me out,' he ordered. 'The party wants a guarantee that you won't make any speeches for the peace movement between now and November. No articles in the newspapers. Field questions from the press – '

'Goddammit, Jim!' Eric exploded. 'I'm not a puppet! They can't tell me how to think!'

'You want to go to Congress. You're old enough and experienced enough to know you have to play games with these bastards.'

'I want to go to Congress to be there as a vote against war, if that arises.' Eric reiterated his stand. 'I don't want to compromise myself.'

Jim leaned forward, his face stern.

'You want to get into Congress for your own purpose. The only way to do it is to keep your mouth shut about peace.'

'What's happening in Washington?' Eric chafed at the restraints attached to his nomination, yet he realized Jim was right.

'I talked with Bolton at eight o'clock this morning. He said that Bryan briefed the President at White Sulphur Springs. Wilson wired back that Mayo couldn't have done otherwise. He instructed the matter be handled with extreme seriousness. And then he went back to finish his golf game with Secretary McAdoo.'

'The fucking ass!' Eric slammed one fist on the desk in frustration. 'Wilson is asking for war!'

'This morning Huerta's first formal reply came through. Huerta considers General Zaragoza's apology sufficient, along with the arrest of Colonel Hinojosa. He refuses the salute to the American flag. He pointed out that the United States was demanding a salute from a government it doesn't recognize.'

'Wilson has no sense of humour,' Eric reminded. 'He's forever the Princeton professor.'

'Let's go out for a good lunch,' Jim invited. 'My treat. You want to call Caroline before we go?'

'No,' Eric demurred. 'I'll tell Caroline tonight.'

En route home at the end of the day, Eric, on impulse, cut off Peachtree, where dogwoods bloomed in April splendour, to detour to Serena's house. He had been unable to reach her by phone all afternoon. It was careless to drive there in brilliant daylight, his mind rebuked; but he was impatient to share his news with her.

Serena had just arrived home. She was ecstatic that the nomination was virtually his, yet uneasy that he must cut back on his peace-movement activities.

'The compromises begin.' Her eyes were a challenge.

'Don't give this Machiavellian overtones,' he scolded.

'I'm sorry.' Her smile was wry. 'I just hate to see you have to capitulate.'

'I'm not capitulating!' he objected.

'Part of me realizes that,' she admitted. 'But to me you're still a modern-day Sir Lancelot, and I don't want to see your armour tarnished.' She reached out a hand to him. 'I don't suppose you could stay for dinner and a celebration?'

'Not tonight.' His eyes told her how much he would like that.

'Celebration?' she coaxed, a hand at his arm.

'How can I resist that?' he countered. Mattie could hold dinner.

Later, pulling out of Serena's driveway, he narrowly missed a collision with an ostentatious white Cadillac travelling twice the allowed speed.

'Damn these women drivers.' He scowled at the woman behind the wheel of the Cadillac.

Frightened by the near-accident, she had slowed down to a crawl. Pulling up beside her, prepared to deliver a lecture, he saw that the driver was Leonora Carlyle. For a moment their eyes clashed, then Eric moved ahead.

As soon as he walked into the house, Caroline ordered Mattie to serve dinner. He was almost an hour late in arriving home; the children had already been served in the breakfast room. He could hear their voices.

While they settled themselves at the dinner table, Eric told Caroline and Sophie that the nomination was sewed up. With party support the primary would be his. Caroline appeared delighted, yet he sensed her inner ambivalence. Dammit, she knew she had to go with him to Washington. She'd have long enough to get used to the idea. He'd take office next March, but there would be no real action until December unless the President called a special session.

They would rent one of those pleasant little four-storey row houses. It would be necessary to entertain once he was in Washington. With Francis settled on the top floor with Patience, Caroline and he could entertain at the necessary small dinners without fear of a tantrum disrupt-

181

ing the evening. The tantrums were less frequent, less vociferous; but they happened. At the top of a row house, the noise would be isolated.

For the past five days, since Leo Frank had been sentenced again to die, Atlanta had been a powder keg of emotions. Feelings had been exacerbated in the past two weeks by Tom Watson's scurrilous attacks in his weekly newspaper, *The Jeffersonian*.

Once the hope of the poverty-ridden farmers, Tom Watson had become a fanatic through the years, feeding on the ignorance, the fears, and the prejudices of the rural masses. He wrote diatribes against the Catholics, the pope, the Jews, and the industrialists and bankers of the North.

Leo Frank was scheduled to die by hanging on April 17. Tomorrow. Caroline dreaded coming home from the mill this afternoon. She walked slowly inside the house. In a matter of hours Leo Frank would hang from a rope until he was dead. Her city was about to be disgraced before the world.

She went into the library and sat in a stiff-backed chair behind the desk. Poor Liz. Poor David. More than anyone she knew outside Leo's family, those two would grieve the most. She would grieve, Caroline thought in angry defiance. She would grieve not only for Leo Frank but also for Atlanta.

'Caro!' She was startled by the sound of Eric's ringing tone in the hall. 'Caro, are you here?' She jumped to her feet, propelled by the urgency she heard in his voice.

'In the library, Eric.' She hurried to the door.

Eric strode towards her, his face elated.

'Caro, Leo's received a stay of execution.'

'Oh, Eric, thank God.' She flung herself into his arms. 'How did it happen?'

'I'm not sure. I suspect it's because of those affidavits about the two jurors, Henslee and Johenning. I wanted to come home and see Liz's face when I told her.'

'Eric, this means the Georgia Supreme Court will give him a new trial?' Caroline questioned.

'Not necessarily,' Eric admitted. 'It may be denied. But when I stopped by the store to discuss it with Noah, he said if that happens, the defence is going to take the case to the United States Supreme Court on a writ of error. Caro, you mustn't repeat this,' he exhorted. 'Not to anyone.'

'Of course not,' Caroline agreed. She listened to the sounds in the foyer. 'There's Liz. She's home from school.'

'I'll go tell her about the stay of execution.'

Over after-dinner coffee in the library, when the children had gone upstairs to their rooms, Eric brought Caroline and Sophie up-to-date on the situation in Mexico.

'Eric, you said there was a Cabinet meeting day before yesterday to deal with the situation,' Caroline reminded. 'What happened then?'

'The Cabinet backed Wilson's demands unanimously. He's ordered the Atlantic fleet to the east coast of Mexico.'

'Nobody wants to fight Mexico.' Caroline's mind hurtled back through the years. 'It's not like sixteen years ago in the Spanish-American War, when so many people were convinced we were fighting to free Cuba.'

The ringing of the telephone was a jarring note in the library.

'It's probably Jim,' Eric said, and crossed to the phone.

From the expression on his face, Caro knew this wasn't an ordinary call.

'When do you want me to leave?' Eric asked. He

listened, nodding in silent agreement. 'Yes, sir. I understand. I'll report directly to you as soon as I have concrete
information. Have a good trip back to Washington.'

'Senator Bolton?' Caroline asked.

'He's asked me to go to Veracruz on a private assignment for his committee. They want an inside view of
exactly what's happening. Wilson insists the salute must
be fired.' Exasperation crept into Eric's voice. 'Yesterday
Wilson had a meeting with the congressional foreign-
relations committees and said he was making tentative
plans to seize Veracruz and Tampico.'

'There's your great pacifist,' Caroline flared. And then
alarm for Eric's safety assaulted her. 'If he's sending the
Navy to take Veracruz and Tampico, why shouldn't you
be there?'

'Before any shooting starts, Wilson will have to ask
Congress for authority to use military force. Bolton and
his committee want ammunition to fight against this.'
Eric paused. 'I'll have to leave for Veracruz tomorrow
morning.'

16

Eric sat alone in the breakfast room, lingering over a second cup of coffee. Caroline and Sophie had left for the mill more than two hours ago; Liz and Josh were already at school. He glanced out the window at the persistent drizzle that had been falling since last night. A dreary day for his departure.

Within ten minutes Eric was hurrying through the drizzle into the waiting taxicab. Caroline was at a meeting at the mill, the children at school. Consulting his watch, he leaned forward to instruct the driver to take him first to Serena's house. When the taxicab approached the house, Eric spied the lights on in the kitchen. She was home. She would drive him to the train. He dismissed the taxi.

He could hear the clatter of Serena's Baby Louis heels as she hurried down the hall in answer to the summons of the doorbell.

'Eric!' Her smile effervescent, she pulled him inside the foyer. 'Indiscreet of you, but I'm delighted.' Now she noticed the suitcase he carried. 'Are you moving in?' She laughed.

'Off to Veracruz,' he explained. 'Bolton called me last night. I'm going down on a private mission.'

'Come out to the kitchen and we'll talk over coffee.'

'No more than ten minutes,' he cautioned. 'I don't want to miss this morning's train.'

'Would you like company to Veracruz?' Her eyes were adventurous.

'Serena, I have to leave this morning – '

'I could pack in twenty minutes,' Serena told him. 'I have this crazy habit of keeping money under my mattress – I won't even have to stop at the bank.' Independent woman. She wanted him to know she expected to pay her own way. 'With all that's happening in Mexico, I should have no trouble picking up an assignment. I'll cable from a stop along the route.' Her eyes were laughing. 'How many women will go down to Mexico to cover a possible war? One of the women's magazines will snap at it.'

'Pack,' Eric ordered, intrigued at the prospect of Serena's company. 'Fast.'

'Close all the windows for me,' Serena ordered, darting towards the bedroom. 'Make sure all the lights are off . . . and check the gas stove. It'll be hot in Veracruz this time of year, won't it?' she called over one shoulder.

'Hot,' he confirmed. 'The city is built on a low tropical beach.'

Eric moved about the small house, checking windows, pulling down shades. They would be gone at least eight or ten days, he reckoned. Serena was incredible, to be able to act with such decisiveness. Such speed. He went into the bedroom. Serena was throwing clothes into a large open suitcase resting on the bed.

'I phoned for a taxicab,' Eric said, and grinned. 'Did I ever tell you you're a remarkable lady?'

'Don't tell me now,' she warned, 'or we'll be sure to miss the train.'

Fifteen minutes later, with Eric acutely aware of the passing time, they sprinted through the rain and into the waiting taxicab. Eric instructed the driver to take them to Terminal Station and leaned back, groping for Serena's hand.

Half a block before the taxicab would turn in at the station, Eric spied a white Cadillac approaching from the opposite direction. The car slowed down to avoid hitting a dog. Leonora was at the wheel. He saw her mouth a profanity. Then, perhaps under the weight of his uneasy scrutiny, her gaze swung to the taxi. For a fleeting moment their eyes grazed; then the taxi moved on.

Clutching their two suitcases, Eric followed Serena, walking with quick small steps in her fashionably narrow skirt, to the ticket window. Serena bought her railway ticket, which was complicated by the change of railway lines and sleeper requirements.

Eric asked for his own similar accommodations, ignoring the clerk's covert interest. How many Atlantans were leaving this morning for Veracruz, Mexico?

'I'd like to make that train.' Eric was caustic, his politeness by the clerk's lackadaisical efforts. He kept seeing Leonora behind the wheel of the white Cadillac. Had she noticed Serena sitting beside him?

'Takes time making out your Pullman reservations.' The clerk was unperturbed. 'But the train won't leave without you,' he placated, his eyes appraising Serena. 'The conductor didn't go aboard yet.'

His ticket secured, Eric picked up their two suitcases; Serena and he hurried towards the tracks. They boarded the train, settled themselves in the ornately upholstered but decidedly hard seats, and waited for the train to pull out of the shed. Eric stared about at unfamiliar faces. No one aboard that he knew.

'Eric . . .' Serena leaned towards him. 'Have you ever made love in a lower berth?'

'I'm willing to give it a try.' He chuckled. 'Maybe when we change to the Southern Pacific at New Orleans, I can do something about getting us a compartment.'

'You Southern aristocrats,' she mocked. 'Just can't give up your comforts.'

They made a point of keeping their conversation political, veering from the trouble in Mexico to Colonel

187

House's efforts, on behalf of the President, to bring about peace in Europe. While the train waited in the station at Birmingham, Eric remembered that this was the day Leo Frank had been scheduled to hang. Thank God for the stay of execution.

Late that evening – tired, tense, and uncomfortably warm – they changed to the Southern Pacific Pullman train. Eric had contrived to switch their reservations from lower and upper berths to the privacy and comfort of a compartment.

'Eric, lock the door,' Serena instructed when the conductor had arrived to check their tickets and left them in the mirrored, wood-panelled opulence of a Pullman compartment.

Eric was jarred by Serena's admonition, seeing himself take this same action on endless nights at Hampton House, a precaution against an intrusion by one of the children while Caro and he were making love.

'Eric, lock the door,' Serena repeated. 'I don't want to have the railroad porter walk in while I stand here in my camisole washing my face.'

'You're not in your camisole,' he pointed out, his smile a debonair invitation.

'By the time you lock the door, I will be,' she told him. 'I've just discovered that trains make me terribly passionate.'

While the train swayed along the night-dark tracks in a sudden downpour, Eric helped Serena into the narrow lower berth. It was an automatic reaction, normally, for him to become aroused at the touch of her body beneath his. Tonight Caro intruded. Did she let that son-of-a-bitching Victor Adams make love to her?

'You're tired,' Serena said after a few minutes. 'It's been a long, hot day.'

In moments Eric pushed her hand away to bring

188

himself to her. Briefly he had been self-conscious about his lack of response. He never completely forgot that he was fifteen years older than Serena. But as much a man as he was at twenty, he told himself, thrusting himself within her. While the rain pounded at the window and the Pullman lurched in its own erotic rhythm, Eric moved with Serena.

'Oh, Caro, Caro . . .' He closed his eyes in exquisite relief.

'I'm Serena,' she corrected while they clung together, savouring the pleasure of this shared satisfaction.

'Honey, I'm sorry,' he apologized, dismayed by his slip.

'Don't go away. It's a long trip to Houston.'

Caro had a crazy way of intruding into his thoughts at unexpected moments. Because the situation in Mexico kept pushing him back into memories of the rotten weeks he'd spent in Cuba during the Spanish-American War, he rationalized. He had been so damned frustrated then – locked in marriage to Tina, loving Caro. Knowing she loved him.

Atlanta was caught in an early hot spell. Caroline sat on the veranda with Sophie in the evening while Josh darted about the lawn to catch 'lightning bugs', to be captured briefly, put into a jar, and shown to Francis.

'That breeze from the river feels fine tonight.' Sophie smiled in gratitude.

'This heat won't last,' Caroline guessed. 'Maybe another day or two and it'll be pleasant again.' Her mind roved to business again, as so often happened when she sat down to relax. 'I've been thinking about taking some of our brighter spinners and putting them into an evening training group to teach them to be weavers. We're always running short of experienced weavers.'

189

'Next you'll be sending them up North to those fancy textile schools,' Sophie bristled.

The side door opened and Roland appeared.

'Miss Caroline, phone call. Miss Leonora Carlyle askin' fo' you.'

'Thank you, Roland.'

Caroline rose to her feet and went into the house. What was Leonora phoning her about? Probably some charity ball.

'Hello.' Caroline contrived to sound gracious.

'Hello, Caroline. This is Leonora. How are you all?'

'We're fine, Leonora. How's your mother?'

'We're both recuperating after wandering all over Europe. It was fascinating, but we're just worn out. Did Eric tell you about our running into Chad in Paris?'

'No, he didn't.' Caroline's politeness was wearing thin.

'Chad's become so Parisian,' Leonora gushed. 'And he was just so sweet to Mama and me. But I know you must be exhausted from your long day at the mill, so I won't waste your time. I'm having a garden party on the first of May and I wondered if you'd be able to come?'

'Thank you, but I'll be tied up at the mill.' Caroline offered her usual response to daytime invitations.

'What about that cousin of yours who's staying at Grace Lamont's house out on Piedmont Road? I assume she's one of your English cousins,' Leonora gushed. 'Grace is over there in London, and she's come here to Grace's house. She's quite pretty. I happened to see her in a taxicab with Eric a couple of days ago –'

'Leonora, I have no English cousins,' Caroline interrupted firmly. 'Whoever's staying at Grace Lamont's house is a stranger to me.'

'Oh, I am sorry, Caroline.' Leonora pretended confusion. 'Please forgive me, honey.'

'There's nothing to forgive, Leonora.' She would not

190

give Leonora the satisfaction of thinking she was disturbed. Leonora had probably made up that business of seeing Eric in a taxicab with a pretty girl. Women like Leonora Carlyle had too much empty time on their hands.

At Houston Eric and Serena left the Southern Pacific to wait for the dreary, ancient train that was to carry them into Mexico. They would change to another train for the last stretch to Veracruz. Serena, as always, was stimulated by the prospect of newness, though she never for a moment discounted the seriousness of the situation between the United States and Mexico.

They left the train at the Veracruz railroad station, located close enough to the docks for them to smell the scent of the bay. The humid midafternoon heat was oppressive, but Eric and Serena were mesmerized by the exquisite blue of the sky, the emerald green of the sea. At the harbour stood the ancient fortress. San Juan de Ulúa, flanked by massive whitewashed seawalls. Gulls and pelicans flew above the broad waves, at intervals nose-diving into the water for fish.

'I want a bath,' Serena said. 'Eric, let's find a hotel.'

After consultation with a taxi driver, which required Serena's fluent Spanish, they were driven through narrow cobbled streets to the Hotel Diligencias, a favourite of tourists, situated on the central square called the Plaza Constitución.

The commercial and governmental buildings, as well as the hotels, markets, small shops, and boardinghouses, were close to the waterfront, Eric realized. The buildings were often garish in hue – brilliant blues, greens, and reds – alternating with delicate pastels.

When they had bathed and changed into fresh clothes, Eric suggested they seek out a restaurant. He preferred not to eat at the hotel, surrounded by other foreigners. His mission was unofficial; he was on orders to listen to what was said in Veracruz, to read the local newspapers, and to cable his reactions, in prearranged code, to Senator Bolton.

'Let's walk about before we go to the restaurant,' Serena suggested when they were outside the hotel.

Veracruz wore the aura of a Spanish colonial city. Its brick or adobe buildings, with flat parapet roofs, were not more than two or three storeys high. Only the lighthouse and the church towers soared higher. Coconut palms grew in abundance about the public plazas. Children played in the streets. Beggars approached with outstretched hands.

Beyond the business area, nestled in low, lush green hills, Eric and Serena saw the homes of the more affluent residents – the older houses constructed of white coral brought from reefs outside the harbour, the newer ones of concrete, brick, or granite. Many of the houses were adorned with wooden wrought-iron-railed balconies. From the patios in the centre of the houses rose tall coconut palms.

Most of the houses, Serena pointed out, had heavy, woodcarved, studded doors that seemed to warn against intrusion.

'The lower windows are all barred,' she noted in astonishment.

'A precaution against thieves,' Eric surmised. 'Of which Mexico has many.' He reached for her elbow. 'Enough sightseeing. I'm famished.'

They found a table at an outdoor restaurant on the Plaza Constitución. In the centre of the plaza was a bandstand flanked by shrubs. Stone benches were provided for those who came to hear the evening concerts. Eric was conscious of an air of casual good spirits among those who sat at the tables. Mexicans talked amiably with Americans. No sense of rampant hostility here, at least.

'We're seeing the fancy side of Veracruz,' Eric warned Serena. 'What the government likes to show to tourists.' He gazed in appreciation at the snowcapped Mount Orizaba. 'That's the highest mountain in Mexico. The colours all around us are enchanting. But move about the city and we'll encounter the poverty and the filth and the stench. Garbage everywhere. Dead animals rotting in the sun. The municipal dump is a disgrace, never burned clean.'

'How do you know?' Serena challenged.

Eric smiled.

'My law partner – Jim – spent a foul three weeks in Veracruz on a newspaper story years ago. It hasn't changed. I'll show you tomorrow,' he promised.

All day Saturday and Sunday Eric and Serena moved about the city, listening to those about them. They visited the fringes of the city where the poverty-ridden – and they were many – lived in wood or thatched huts. They saw the throngs of foul-smelling vultures that haunted the waterfront and fed on the piles of garbage thrown carelessly into the streets, and the packs of perpetually hungry dogs that prowled the streets in search of food, fighting over dead carcasses. Everywhere they travelled, they listened. In the evening Eric cabled the senator his reactions. The Mexican people showed no disrespect towards the United States.

Little was spoken among the common people of Veracruz about the strained relations with the United States. Obviously American, Eric and Serena were treated with cordiality wherever they travelled.

In the evening, sitting on the plaza sipping wine and fending off flies, Eric and Serena talked with a couple at the next table. The man, in his early thirties, spoke English as well as he spoke Spanish. His companion – his wife, they later learned – was English. At an invitation from Eric, they deserted their table to join his.

'The President of the United States cannot conceive of the importance of honour to the Mexican,' their Mexican guest told Eric and Serena, and the English girl nodded in vigorous agreement. 'Remember, we are not yet a great country. We have won no wars. We have only dead heroes. But we have a great feeling of *patria*. For Mexico to humble itself before the world . . .' He gestured eloquently. 'This would be impossible. Even those who have no love for Huerta prefer him to foreign invaders. Mexico belongs to the Mexicans.'

They talked late into the evening, returning to the hotel to find a note from the office of the American consul, warning of possible hostilities.

A coded cable from Senator Bolton arrived on Monday morning, warning Eric that Veracruz could expect an imminent takeover. The senator urged Eric to leave Veracruz immediately. Eric cabled back that the Mexicans would not accept this without a fight. There would be bloodshed.

Eric urged Serena to go up to Galveston, where American soldiers were on the alert, and wait out the next forty-eight hours. She refused. She would not be paid to report from the safety of Galveston.

On Monday morning Wilson returned to Washington from White Sulphur Springs. He met with his cabinet and with congressional leaders before addressing the two houses of Congress in joint session. He asked Congress for authority to use force in Mexico. He emphasized that whatever action would be taken would be against Huerta, not against the Mexican people. American honour, he emphasized, must be restored.

Rebel yells expressed the majority approval. At the conclusion of Wilson's speech, he received a standing ovation. The spirit of war was in the air. A resolution authorizing the President to use force against Huerta was passed in the House by a vote of 337 to 37. The Senate adjourned without taking action. The matter would be considered the next day. But before the Senate could act, Wilson issued orders to the Navy to seize Veracruz.

Anticipating trouble, though not knowing for sure when it would rise, Eric and Serena arose early on Monday morning. The sky was overcast with dark clouds. Strong winds rode in from the north. The sea was choppy. A storm was imminent.

Eric and Serena left the hotel and found a shaded table at the plaza, where they ordered coffee. A long procession of whale boats was coming in to Pier 4. Eric glanced about him. None of the locals gathered in the plaza seemed concerned. Only the scattering of Americans present realized what was happening. At the seawall a crowd – curious rather than apprehensive – was gathering to watch.

A total of 787 officers and men, including 502 marines, came ashore. The Mexicans were impressed by the khaki fatigues, the broad-brimmed hats, and the knapsacks carried by the marines. Marines and white-garbed sailors alike carried long-barrelled bolt-action Spring .03s.

All at once the *Veracruzanos* realized what was happening. The crowd of onlookers at the seawall moved back in apprehension to watch from adjacent streets. Mothers summoned their children from play. Iron grilles came down over shop windows. Market vendors folded their cloth awnings, packed up their vegetables or fruits, and hurried towards their homes. The city was ominously quiet.

'Let's go to the cable station.' Eric was anxious to send word to the senator.

At the cable station, crowded with American civilians and newspaper reporters, the Mexican office refused to put through any messages. A few minutes after Eric and Serena arrived, an armed marine corporal with several men entered the cable station and took possession. There was no indication of trouble, yet Eric was uneasy.

'Let's get back to the hotel,' he decided.

Eric and Serena hurried through the strangely quiet streets, disturbed only by the tread of boots. Under the *portales* at the Hotel Diligencias, Mexican soldiers – rifles in hand – waited. As Eric prodded Serena into the hotel, they heard the first shot fired.

'Stay away from the windows,' Eric ordered Serena when they were inside their rooms. They knew that Mexicans were firing on American sailors from the roof of their hotel.

At the end of the day, with the ships in the harbour beaming their lights on the city to discourage snipers, Eric was cursing himself for not insisting that Serena listen to Consul Canada's advice to board the *Mexico* or the *Esperanza* before the landing. He realized now that most of the Mexican forces were in their hotel or on the hotel roof.

With nightfall, firing all but ceased. An occasional machine-gun burst was heard, a shot from a sniper. Convicts had escaped from La Galera and roamed the streets, looting the stores, growing drunk on rum. Eric made a covert inspection of the lighted streets. Bodies lay in crumpled heaps. So much for Wilson's bloodless seizure.

'I'm starving,' Serena announced. 'I'm going downstairs and see if we can rustle up some food.'

'Are you crazy? With Mexican soldiers roaming through the halls?' Eric turned away from the window in alarm.

'They're all on the roof,' Serena said. 'That's where all the shots are coming from now.' She pulled herself to her feet. 'Let's go down to a lower floor. I'd like to put more distance between them and us.'

'I feel so damn useless,' Eric grumbled.

He knew no power on earth could make him lift a gun against the Mexicans. After Kettle Hill, he had vowed never to take a gun in hand again. Not even to hunt. He remembered Caro talking about her father, who had fled Atlanta on the eve of the War Between the States. *'How could I take up arms against my classmates at Princeton, my cousins in the North? My soul rebelled.'* He felt that way now.

'Eric, the Mexicans don't have a chance.' Serena's smile was shaky but determined. 'The Americans will take the hotel within hours.'

'Let's go to a lower floor,' Eric capitulated. All of the action would come from the roof when daylight arrived. A lower floor would be safer.

Eric and Serena were startled to discover about forty American women on the lower floor. Trapped in the hotel – to leave was to be caught in the crossfire – they had organized themselves into a nursing corps. They were caring for the Mexican wounded.

Eric remembered Cuba and his efforts to help the medical corps in the field hospital when he was recovering from his wound. He remembered the days and nights in the yellow-fever camp, when the hard-fighting soldiers of the all-black Twenty-fourth Infantry had volunteered for duty and cared for the stricken soldiers with the tenderness these women were showing the Mexicans.

'Eric, what a tremendous story!' Serena glowed as she turned away from him to assist one of the women.

Eric sought out the kitchen, boiled water, made himself useful to the volunteer nurses and their patients. How many men would die before this unnecessary incident was over?

Two mornings later a company led by the ensign son of the commander of the Atlantic Fleet took the Diligencias. Serena and Eric left the hotel at the heels of the advancing Americans.

Eric and Serena were startled to discover the Mexican women had taken up arms. Terrified of guns, some of them had nevertheless tried to help hold their city. Now the Americans were making a house-to-house search, with every man caught taken prisoner.

Veracruz was in the hands of the American forces. The *Veracruzanos* were too terrified to leave their homes. American marines and sailors began to bury the dead, already putrefying in the tropical dampness.

Correspondents were arriving. Jack London came to write for *Collier*'s magazine. Richard Harding Davis showed up in an immaculate white linen suit, carrying a portable bathtub and evening clothes.

The casualties totalled up to nineteen Americans dead and forty-seven wounded. There was no accurate accounting of the Mexican dead, estimated at perhaps two hundred, with another three hundred wounded. Some of them were women and children. Eric breathed a deep sigh of relief when, at last, Serena and he boarded the Mexican train and headed north to Houston for the first stretch towards home.

* * *

When at last they arrived in Atlanta, Eric took Serena home.

'I'm going to soak in a tub until my skin is all puckered, and then I'm going to sleep for twenty-four hours,' she told him while he deposited her valise inside her door. On the long ride to Atlanta, she had written her story. Now she had only to type it and mail it to the magazine.

'I'll call you,' Eric promised, and charged back to the waiting taxi.

Eric saw the relief on Roland's face when he walked into the foyer at Hampton House. Now he realized how much the family must have worried about him. They'd had no word. They knew only what they read in the newspapers.

'Roland, I want something to eat and a pitcher of ice-cold lemonade,' he said. 'Bring it into the library.'

In the library he phoned Caroline at the mill.

'Eric!' Her voice was shrill with excitement. 'When did you arrive?'

'I came into the house two minutes ago.' Right now he wanted to make love to his wife. He was tired and hungry and passionate. It had been a long time since he had felt such a need to hold his wife in his arms. Not just a woman. Caro. 'Come home and sit with me while I have something to eat.'

'Eric I can't,' Caroline apologized. 'Ed Swift and Tim Bullock are due in the office any minute. You're all right?' she asked with fresh anxiety. 'I've been so worried.'

'I'm fine.' Nothing had changed between Caro and him. The mill still came first with her. *His* needs meant nothing. His voice was cool. 'I'll see you at dinner.'

17

Frowning in annoyance. Maureen cleared her desk and covered her typewriter. She had dawdled in hopes that Andrew would drop by her office and invite her to go somewhere with him this evening. But he lingered in conversation with Caroline. Now that the machinery was quiet for the night, she could hear their voices.

'Yesterday morning the marines who died at Veracruz were buried,' Caroline said bitterly, 'and in the evening President Wilson went to the circus.'

Maureen walked past the office slowly, willing Andrew to follow her; but he was too engrossed in conversation. Did Caroline know that she was seeing Andrew outside the mill? Caroline didn't like her. Most women didn't.

It wasn't any of Caroline's business if she was seeing Andrew, she reminded herself, walking out into the early evening. She sniffed the fresh, balmy outdoor air in relief. Her eyes inspected the sky. Not a star in view. The moon hidden by clumps of dark clouds. It would rain within the hour, she surmised in distaste. She hated rain; it was so depressing.

Her thoughts returned to Andrew. She kept telling herself she was making progress. Andrew took her to the theatre, to the opera, to concerts. If they went somewhere on a work evening, he always asked her to have dinner at his cottage. He made it clear he enjoyed her company. He was sweet and attentive – and he never made a move even to hold her hand.

A light rain began to fall. She stood alone in the darkening evening, straining her eyes along the tracks, impatient for the shelter of a streetcar. She saw the headlights of an automobile moving in her direction. A Cadillac, she recognized in respect.

The black Cadillac stopped close by. A man leaned forward. Even in the meagre light she could see he was good-looking.

'This is no night to wait for a streetcar.' His voice was deep and sensuous. His accent told Maureen he wasn't a Southerner. 'May I drive you home?'

He owned a Cadillac; he must be rich.

'My mother would kill me if she found out I accepted a ride from a stranger.' She feigned hesitation. 'But it's such an awful night.'

'We won't tell your mother,' he promised, leaning forward to open the door for her. 'Where shall I deliver you?'

Maureen gave him her address. Why did she have to live in such a dreadful neighbourhood? she fumed in silence.

'I just arrived recently from New Orleans,' she fabricated. 'My mother knew the lady who runs this boarding-house. She would only let me come to Atlanta if I promised to stay at Mrs Ryan's.'

'I'm from Massachusetts,' he told her. 'Before that, Chicago and other points west. My name's Todd Murdoch.'

'Maureen Vauban,' she said.

'French and Irish,' he mused. 'Fascinating combination.'

'Do you like living in Atlanta?' What had brought him all the way down here? Business?

'I find Atlanta pleasant enough.' He shrugged. 'When I divorced my wife, I thought a change of locale would be interesting.' He was telling her he was not married, Maureen noted in rising excitement. 'An offer to buy a textile mill down here came up. I know textiles. I bought the mill. Not as big as the Hampton Mill,' he said with a sidewise glance at her. 'But I aim to make it bigger.'

He suspected she worked at the mill. She'd have to let him know she wasn't an operator. Couldn't he tell that from her clothes? Every cent that didn't go to Mrs Ryan for board and room was hoarded for dresses and shoes.

'I'm secretary to Caroline Hampton, who runs the Hampton Mill,' Maureen told him. 'My mother thinks I work in a law office. I wouldn't dare tell her about the mill.'

'Do you like being Caroline Hampton's secretary?'

'I hate the noise and the dampness in the mill.' She decided on candour. She wasn't pretending to be a member of the Atlanta Debutante Club. 'But Caroline Hampton pays the best wages in Atlanta for the kind of work I can do.' Being a secretary was respectable. Girls from decent families were flocking into offices.

'Well then,' Todd Murdoch said expansively, 'since we're both in the same business, may I ask you to have dinner with me tomorrow evening? At the Georgian Terrace. I'm sure your mother would approve.' For an instant she was guarded. Was he making fun of her? 'I'll tell you about my mill, and you can tell me about yours. Among other things,' he stipulated. His eyes told her she was beautiful; Maureen was jubilant. Maybe she'd found somebody richer than Andrew Hampton – and far less hard to nail.

At seven the next evening Murdoch arrived at the boardinghouse. Maureen was glad she had been insanely extravagant last week and bought the black crepe restaurant dress at Rich's. Todd Murdoch would not be ashamed of her when they walked into the fancy restaurant at the Georgian Terrace.

His hand at her elbow, Todd Murdoch guided her to

the waiting Cadillac. Maureen was sure that Mrs Ryan hovered at a window, watching their departure.

'Do you know the Georgian Terrace?' Todd asked, his eyes appraising her frock. He seemed pleased with her appearance. His own attire, Maureen suspected, was expensive. He was the kind of man who demanded the best.

'I've never been to the Georgian Terrace,' she conceded. 'I hear it's beautiful.'

'Probably Atlanta's finest hotel,' Todd said. 'It cost half a million dollars. It was just completed in 1911.'

Maureen was content to listen to Todd Murdoch talk while they drove to the hotel. She was impressed by his obvious wealth, his self-confidence in his future in Atlanta.

She enjoyed his sureness when they were shown to their table in Todd's favourite restaurant in the ten-storey Georgian Terrace Hotel. The waiters knew him. The hotel, as he had boasted, was magnificent. The elegant white walls, marble columns, dramatic murals, brilliantly coloured wall hangings, all impressed her.

Everybody around them was looking at Todd and her. The men looked because she was young and beautiful; the women were envious of her because she was with Todd Murdoch.

Todd's knee grazed hers beneath the table. She felt an unexpected flicker of excitement. All at once her face felt hot. Just because she worked in a mill, that didn't mean she was easy. But he hadn't done that deliberately, Maureen soothed herself. It was just an accident when he leaned forward that way to pour a glass of wine for her.

Though there were folks back in New Orleans who would never believe it, she had never let any man touch her. The price for taking Maureen Vauban was marriage. She would never be stupid like Mama.

What happened between a man and a woman was no secret to her. Once Mama knew she couldn't beat her twelve-year-old daughter, she decided the child had become a woman. Every time Mama drank too much wine at dinner, she would talk about what happened in the bedroom between Papa and her. She boasted there was nothing they wouldn't do. It sounded ugly and disgusting.

A waiter stood by them now, in consultation with Todd. She was relieved when Todd suggested ordering for both of them.

'There'll be music,' Todd promised when the waiter left them. 'And the food is the best.' Again she thought: Todd Murdoch will never settle for less than the best. A faint unease infiltrated her. What would Todd Murdoch demand of a wife?

Early in May Atlantans geared themselves for the National Shriners' Convention, which was scheduled to open on Sunday, May 10, and continue for three event-packed days. For almost a year the city had been working to make the Shriners' Convention the big event of 1914.

For months the Atlanta hotels had been besieged with requests for rooms. Every restaurant in the city had stocked up on food to accommodate the welcome invasion. Local Shriners were busy with plans for balls, dinners, garden parties, races, exhibition drills, dances. Every building in the city must be decorated.

On Sunday morning trainloads of Shriners, many of them in brilliant uniforms began to pour into Atlanta. They came from every corner of the United States and from Canada. Bands met them at the railroad stations and led them to their hotels, then returned to the railroad stations to greet fresh arrivals.

Liz and Josh clamoured to be taken to the big parade

on Tuesday morning. All of Atlanta would turn out for the event. Worn down by their pleas, Caroline agreed; she would take the morning off from the mill.

By 8:30 A.M. sharp Caroline and the children had deserted jammed Peachtree and discovered an area for themselves at the curb of a less crowded street, though already onlookers were filling in the area behind them. Liz and Josh would be disappointed, she knew, unless they saw every marcher, every band, every float in what promised to be a spectacular four-mile march.

Every office window was dotted with faces, every roof packed with spectators. Caroline was relieved that they had found places on the shady side of the street. Already the day was blistering hot in the sun.

Slightly past nine o'clock the roar of the crowd on the street above them, the sound in the distance of a band playing 'Dixie', told them the parade was approaching. Liz and Josh watched eagerly. First came the mounted police. Then the grand marshal and chief of staff, followed by Atlanta's own – the drum corps of the Yaarab Temple, 150 strong in crimson coats and white pants, with a tiny bugler from the Boy Scouts in the centre of the formation.

'Look at him!' Liz crowed, fascinated by the young baton-twirling drum major. 'Isn't he wonderful?'

'Look at the camel coming!' Josh yelled.

On they marched, Shriners in an Oriental procession that was like a tale from the Arabian Nights. Crimson bedouin uniforms with yellow satin trimmings. Zouave uniforms of red bloomers, black vests trimmed with yellow. An El Paso, Texas, patrol in old gold trousers, purple jackets, and sashes. A bagpipe band of Scottish Highlanders in kilts playing 'My Old Kentucky Home.'

All at once Caroline's face brightened in recognition. There was Eric on the other side of the street. He didn't see them yet; he was watching the parade. She raised a hand, hoping to capture his attention.

'Josh . . . Liz . . .' She meant to alert them to the presence of their father, but further words froze on her lips. There was the girl Leonora had talked about, Caroline thought in a flash of insight. The one Leonora said she saw in a taxicab with Eric. The pretty dark-haired girl at Eric's side, who was talking to him with such vivacity. She saw Eric's arm protectively about the girl's waist.

'Josh, Liz, we're leaving,' she said peremptorily.

'Mama!' Josh was outraged.

'Come along, both of you.' She reached for a hand of each. 'We'll hurry over to the Lyric Theatre, where the parade will wind up,' she mollified. She mustn't deprive the children of the pleasure of seeing the rest of the parade. 'You'll see everything better there.'

Three hours later Caroline sat in Ellen's Victorian parlour, cluttered with the furniture of her husband's previous marriage, and spoke with the openness that was possible only with Ellen.

'I told myself Leonora Carlyle was trying to cause trouble between Eric and me. I couldn't – I *wouldn't* – believe that Eric was having an affair. And then I saw them together that way. I'm furious. And I'm hurt.'

'Of course you are,' Ellen sympathized. 'But don't – '

'I won't divorce him,' Caroline interrupted. 'I couldn't expose the children to that. But Eric's killed everything we've ever had.' She spread her hands in despair. 'I don't know how I'm going to face him tonight.'

'You'll be sweet and charming,' Ellen told her. 'You won't let on that you know a thing about that girl. So Eric's having a fling for a few weeks. You've had a lot of good years between you. There'll be more.'

'Will there be?'

'A whole lifetime.' Ellen covered Caroline's hand with hers. 'Honey, you can ride this out.'

Caroline was obsessed by the realization that Eric was involved with another woman. Night after night she lay sleepless until dawn, visualizing Eric in bed with the girl she had seen the day of the parade.

Sophie worried because she looked tired and drawn.

'Eric and you ought to go away for a few days,' Sophie said one sweltering afternoon in the mill. 'Francis will be all right.'

'I couldn't relax away from him,' Caroline hedged. It would be a travesty to pretend to go on a vacation with Eric. 'It's just this heat wave that's been dragging me down,' she fabricated.

The following day Caroline left the mill in midmorning, ostensibly to go downtown to Rich's to do some shopping. En route she sought out Grace Lamont's house. Three times she encircled the block, watching for a sight of Grace Lamont's tenant. Then in the distance she saw a Pierce Arrow approaching. Even though she realized it wasn't Eric's car, she felt near-panic because he might have caught her here.

As prearranged, she met Ellen for lunch and they shopped together. 'I've joined a suffragist group,' Ellen volunteered. 'Come with me to the meeting tonight.'

Caroline was on the point of turning down the invitation. Why not go to the meeting with Ellen? she thought in sudden defiance. More evenings than not, Eric left the house after dinner. Supposedly to meet with Jim and other politicians, or on peace business. She suspected he detoured to visit the house on Piedmont Road.

'What time is the meeting?' Caroline asked. 'I'll drive by and pick you up.'

* * *

When Caroline and Ellen arrived at the meeting, they found the room filled almost to capacity with Atlanta suffragists. Not one male was present. The rap of a gavel at the podium summoned them to their seats. Caroline's eyes roamed about the assemblage.

The first two speakers were earnest but hardly contributed any substance to the meeting, Caroline thought in disappointment. Then the third speaker came forward to stand at the podium. Young, pretty, obviously enthusiastic about the subject she was about to discuss. A cold wave swept over Caroline despite the warmth of the room, which kept palmetto fans in constant motion. Her hand moved to Ellen's arm.

'That's the girl,' Caroline whispered, her face drained of colour. 'The one I told you about.'

Trying to thrust aside the trembling that seized her, Caroline listened to Serena Mayo talk about the suffragists in London and in New York. She talked about her involvement in the peace movement. *That was how Eric met her*.

Did this girl know that Eric was married, that he had three children? Would she care? No, Caroline decided in anger. This was the twentieth century. The New Young Women brushed aside such conventionalities when it was to their convenience to do so.

Serena Mayo was pretty and bright. Why should she settle for a clandestine affair with a man fifteen years older than herself? But many women found Eric attractive. In the years Eric and she had been married, she had known that there were women who extended blatant invitations. Including Leonora Carlyle. She had been sure he refused. Had she been wrong?

Caroline compelled herself to listen to the speech. Serena Mayo was articulate, enthusiastic, and bright. Under other circumstances, despite the difference in their ages, they could be friends. Would Eric tire of this girl? Right now Serena Mayo was more Eric's wife than she. He went to Serena Mayo's bed. He never came to hers.

This year Eric made no suggestion about going to Hampton Court for the hot months, though he planned some occasional weekends at the plantation with Liz and Josh. Ostensibly the campaign was keeping him in town, though Caroline suspected Serena Mayo was the real reason.

Late in June Eric told Caroline that Jim and he would expect her to campaign in the final weeks before the primary.

'I'm sorry, Eric.' She was polite and controlled. 'I can't do it this year.'

'But you always campaign.' Eric stared at her, baffled by her refusal.

'Not this year,' she emphasized, her eyes avoiding his. 'I'm too tied up with the mill. I couldn't take that much time away from the office.' Let him ask his mistress to campaign for him, Caroline told herself with the bitterness that was constantly just beneath the surface.

'I'll tell Jim not to count on you.' Caroline saw his face tighten. His eyes were furious. 'For a moment I forgot your dedication to the mill.'

Eric left the house to drive to a meeting at his office. What the hell had got into Caroline that she was refusing to campaign for him? She had been part of every campaign he had ever waged for public office. This time around, with some doubts about the outcome of the primary, it was urgent to utilize every advantage. Caro was a distinct asset.

He slid behind the wheel of the Pierce Arrow and drove away from the house. He should have argued with Caro about campaigning. Dammit, Sophie and Andrew could carry on at the mill without her for a few days at a time. That was all he asked of her. Two or three days a week for the last few weeks of the campaign.

She couldn't know about Serena. He dwelt on this disquieting possibility. No, he rejected. The only times Serena and he were together in public were at the peace-movement office and at meetings. *Nobody suspected*. They were alone at the Shriners' parade for about ten minutes, he pinpointed, when they happened to meet on the street. But what would that mean? They knew each other from the peace movement, they happened to meet during the parade.

He would never have allowed Serena into his life if Caro had not relegated him to such a minor role in her own. Serena made him feel like a man again. Both Serena and he understood this was a temporary situation. Yet he dreaded the day that Serena would decide to leave Atlanta.

At the office he told Jim about Caroline's refusal to campaign before the primary.

'Didn't you explain to Caroline that it was important?' Jim, too, was thrown by this unexpected rejection.

'She bit off too much with this new addition at the mill,' Eric alibied. Why was he lying to Jim? 'I don't want to push her into this.'

Would it matter what he said to her? He used to be proud of Caroline's strength. Now he couldn't cope with it.

Maureen

18

With the heat of summer settling down on Atlanta, Maureen awoke each morning with a reluctance to go into the mill, knowing that within an hour of arriving at the office her frock would be drenched with perspiration, her hair limp and moist. The ceiling fans in the office did little more than circulate hot air.

For over a month she had been seeing Todd two or three evenings a week, fretting that her wardrobe was inadequate for such a social life, though Todd seemed unperturbed. Todd enjoyed the way people stared at them in restaurants or at the theatre. Even though he was almost twice her age, she was intrigued by his sensuous good looks, his aura of wealth and power. More than she had ever wished for anything, she wished to become Todd Murdoch's wife.

Twice since Todd had begun to pursue her, Andrew asked her to go out with him. Each time she had turned him down. 'My cousin from New Orleans is visiting' had been her alibi. He wouldn't allow himself a third rejection.

Maureen sat on the streetcar this morning, touching her moist forehead with her handkerchief at regular intervals. When was Todd going to propose? He mentally undressed her every time they were together. So far he limited himself to a chaste good-night kiss in the car before he deposited her on Mrs Ryan's veranda.

She would ask Caroline if she could leave the office two hours early today. She had worked late twice last week; Caroline knew that. With her tiny emergency fund and part of today's pay she would go to Rich's and buy a dress to wear tonight. Todd was taking her to dinner at the Georgian Terrace again. How many times could she go there in the same dress?

Just before Caroline left for the house, Maureen approached her about leaving early.

'That'll be all right, Maureen. Just make sure the letters are ready to go out by noon tomorrow,' Caroline exhorted.

'Thank you. I do appreciate it.' Maureen exuded demure gratitude.

She hated having to ask Caroline for anything. She had hated being a nobody back in New Orleans. Only once did she feel special, when Mama sent her to Miss Anita's School of the Dance in New Orleans every Wednesday afternoon for four months. Mama wanted to show off to the ladies she sewed for that her daughter could go to the same dancing school as their daughters.

She was fourteen that year. Phillipe Alphand had been in her class. The others giggled and whispered that he was wild about her. He couldn't keep his eyes off her. She had adored Phillipe. He was so handsome and well-mannered. She waited impatiently for dance-class afternoons to arrive. But when Miss Anita gave a party at the end of the term for her dance class, Phillipe had asked to escort Mary Beth Keyes. That way he could be sure Mary Beth would invite him to her next party. Not one of the rich young men in that class had asked to escort Maureen Vauban. After that she hated everyone in the class.

Promptly at four o'clock Maureen left the mill and took the streetcar downtown to Rich's.

Maureen knew, when she saw Todd's eyes on her, that the dress had been a smart investment.

'You look beautiful, Maureen.' There was an extra

214

pressure on his hand at her elbow tonight when he guided her to the waiting Cadillac.

Maureen relished the attention she and Todd received at the restaurant. Being with Todd made her feel important. Everybody knew he was a mill owner. That he was rich.

'It was hot in the mills today,' Todd said when the waiter had left them. 'I thought about you in that stuffy office.'

'I hate the mill any time of year,' Maureen admitted. 'In the summer it's unbearable.'

'Caroline scratching to find enough workers?' Todd asked. For a moment Maureen was startled by his air of familiarity. Of course, he knew Caroline; that uppity bunch all knew one another.

'Right now we have no shortage. Not with all the cutbacks on orders.' Todd smiled. That pleased him. His mill must have had cutbacks, too. Andrew said the whole textile industry was being hit that way. 'Caroline's talking about taking some of the spinners and training them as weavers.'

'I hear the Hampton Mill runs on a higher profit than a lot of mills in the South,' Todd said curiously. 'You know anything about that?'

'I don't see the financial figures often enough to know what they mean.' Maureen was suddenly suspicious. Was Todd trying to use her to discover inside information about the Hampton Mill?

'Of course, some of the Southern mills have all new equipment,' Todd pursued. 'I brought down a lot of old machinery from New England and set it up here. I don't suppose Caroline economizes on machinery?'

'She's ordered the best for the annexe. Miss Sophie and Andrew think she's lost her mind, the way she's spending.' Maureen debated for a moment. Maybe it would be smart to show Todd she wasn't stupid about what went on inside a cotton mill. 'The looms at the Hampton Mill are all automatic Northern looms. This cuts labour costs in weaving way down.' Andrew had explained this to her. 'And the mill is equipped with ring spindles. They can be handled by women. Their wages are lower than men's.'

Todd whistled under his breath. 'That would give them a definite advantage on setting prices,' he gauged. 'But why are we wasting time talking shop?'

Todd devoted the next two hours to amusing Maureen with colourful stories of his boyhood in Chicago, adventures with his brother and father in Alaska. At intervals his knee grazed hers beneath the table. She knew this was deliberate. His eyes lingered often on the daring décolletage of her new frock.

'My mother's birthday is two weeks from now. I'm giving her a diamond necklace.' His smile was deprecating. 'I don't know a damn about jewellery. I hope I chose well.' He paused. 'Maureen, why don't you come over to the house and let me show it to you?' He felt her instant guardedness. 'Sugar, we'll be chaperoned by five servants. Your mother would not disapprove.' His gaze settled on the curve of her breasts, visible above the neckline of her dress. 'Though I'm not so sure how she'd feel about that dress.'

'It's very fashionable,' Maureen retaliated, stung by his inference.

'I know.' He grinned. 'But I can't say in polite society what it does to me.'

Todd's gaze held hers. All at once her heart was pounding. Listening to Mama talk about what happened between a man and a woman in bed, she had always been disgusted. Now she could imagine being in bed with Todd. Her face grew hot.

'I'd love to see the necklace you bought for your mother.' It would be a chance to see Todd's house. *Five* servants, he'd said; the house must be a mansion.

Maureen and Todd left the Georgian Terrace restaurant and drove out on Peachtree Street to an impressive granite Romanesque Revival house, which Todd told her was a replica of a Rhineland castle. A genial houseman admitted them.

'Orlando, bring champagne to the rear parlour,' Todd instructed, and led Maureen down a long high-ceilinged corridor covered with small Oriental rugs.

The real parlour was large, square, furnished with a collection of fine antiques. Maureen sat on an elaborately carved red-damask-covered settee while Todd crossed to an ornate cabinet painted with chinoiserie. A sense of exhilaration spilled over her. She could envision herself as mistress of this mansion with five servants at her disposal.

Todd removed a black velvet box from a drawer of the cabinet and brought it to the sofa.

'This cost a fortune,' Todd said while he opened the velvet box. 'But my mother loves diamonds.'

'It's beautiful.' Maureen's eyes clung to the display of diamonds.

'Would you like to try it on?' Todd offered.

'May I?' Her face was incandescent.

'Let me help you.' Todd scooped up the necklace with a carelessness that sent shivers through her, then leaned forward to fasten it about her throat. 'Now, go inspect yourself in the mirror,' he ordered as Orlando walked into the room, and she crossed to the gilt-framed mirror that hung above a lacquered commode. 'Orlando, leave the champagne on the table. That'll be all.'

'Good night, sir,' Orlando said politely. 'Good night,

miss,' he said when Maureen whirled about from the mirror.

'Good night.' Maureen's smile lost some of its spontaneity. Todd had dismissed Orlando. Where were the five servants that were chaperoning them?

'This is the most expensive champagne to be had today,' Todd told her. 'Come try it.'

'I am not a connoisseur,' Maureen admitted, borrowing the word her mother considered so elegant. She'd only tasted champagne once. That was a night that would remain in her mind forever. She had gone with Mama to help with last-minute alterations on a wedding gown that was so magnificent she had been breathless. Mama and she had watched the ceremony from the top of the stairs. With the servants. Among the guests she spied her half-sisters, neither of whom had ever acknowledged her. Champagne had been sent up to the servants. Two extra glasses for Mama and her. How galling! *To be grouped with the servants when her two half-sisters were guests at the wedding.* Maureen reached for the clasp of the necklace, released it. 'You'd better put this away.' All at once she was uneasy with Todd. His eyes were devouring her. Instinct told her this wasn't the look of a man about to propose marriage.

'I'll put it away in a few minutes.' Todd accepted the necklace and tossed it to the table, where the velvet box waited. 'Let's have some champagne.'

Maureen stood beside the table while Todd poured the pale liquid into a pair of delicate crystal goblets. The door to the parlour remained open. He wouldn't try to make love to her with the door open, she reasoned. Yet perversely she wanted him to make love to her.

'I've never seen you look so beautiful.' He handed one goblet to Maureen, lifted the other in a gesture of insouciant appreciation. 'To you.'

'Thank you.' He had never seen so much of her. She had hoped to bait him into a proposal. Hadn't she made it clear she wasn't the kind of girl he could have at a snap of his fingers?

Maureen sipped the champagne, aware that Todd's eyes were staring at her breasts. She was conscious, again, of unfamiliar arousal. The servants had retired to their quarters. Todd and she might as well be alone in the house.

'I shouldn't be here,' she said. 'Where are those five servants that were to chaperon us?'

'They've been up since dawn,' Todd chided. 'You wouldn't want to keep them awake.' *He was so good-looking*. 'Don't you like the champagne?' he reproached, and drained his own glass.

'It's delicious.' Did he think she'd never had champagne before? Deliberately she finished her champagne. She was aware of a strange lightheadedness as Todd reached for the bottle to refill their glasses. 'I can't stay here,' she said with a calmness she didn't feel.

'Mama might not approve?' His eyes were amused.

'She would be furious.' Maureen's face felt hot.

Todd took the glass from her hand and deposited it on the table.

'You're an exciting young lady.' With a sudden move he swept her to him. She could feel the hardness between his thighs. No man was going to do *that* with her unless they were married. That was the price tag.

'Please let me go.' Her voice was uneven.

'Honey, let's be grown-up,' he chided. 'I'll make love to you the way nobody has ever made love to you before.'

'Nobody has ever made love to me.' Her voice was unnaturally high. He froze in astonishment.

'Nobody?' His smile was quizzical.

'Nobody.' Every man who looked at her thought she was easy. 'Nobody will except my husband.'

'One marriage was enough for me.' Todd reached to pull her to him again. 'But, honey, we can make love – and you can go to your husband intact. I know ways to send you jumping right out of your skin, and no man will ever know.' His mouth burrowed at her ear.

'No,' she rejected. She knew what Todd meant. Mama had been most descriptive. 'No, Todd.' She was firm. 'I'm scared . . .'

'You don't need to be,' he insisted. 'Nobody will ever know.' His hand moved past the low neckline of her dress to fondle her breast. *She mustn't stay here.*

'Todd, take me home.' She was peremptory. Yet she made no move to draw away from him. She had never felt this way before.

'Wait here.' He left her to close the door to the rear parlour. He turned the key and returned to her. 'You mean it? About never having been with a man?'

'I mean it.' She was trembling. 'Todd, I can't. Not until I'm married.'

'We won't,' he soothed. 'I told you. There are ways to satisfy ourselves.'

Todd brought her face to his. His mouth was gentle at first, then probing. Her arms closed in about his shoulders. He fumbled with the hooks at the back of her dress.

'Let me,' she whispered when his tongue withdrew from her mouth. This dress cost too much to damage.

She manipulated the hooks. Todd thrust the dress from her shoulders, pushed down her camisole. His hands forming a cup for one lush breast, he brought his mouth down to its huge dark nipple. She cried out faintly when his teeth nipped.

He lifted himself erect and began to remove his jacket.

'Take off your clothes,' he ordered. She hesitated. 'Honey, take off your clothes.'

In a moment Maureen stood before him, nude and passionate. She had never seen a man naked before.

'Todd, you promised . . . we can't . . .' she stammered, her eyes holding his.

'Maureen, relax. You'll leave here technically a virgin. Your husband will never know about tonight.'

Why couldn't he say, 'Maureen, let's get married'? Then they could do everything. She clenched her hands while he prodded her towards the ornate red settee. She lay back against the settee while Todd went to switch off the lamps. Now the room lay in darkness.

She felt Todd's hands at her thighs. His warm, moist mouth at her breasts. She abandoned herself to the new feelings that invaded her. Todd's mouth left her breasts to move down the length of her. His mouth invaded her.

She cried out, her hands reaching to cradle Todd's head. In moments he was moving himself above her. She felt his hardness between her thighs. She stiffened.

'Todd, no!'

'Honey,' he rebuked. 'How can you say that now?'

'I can say it!' Her eyes smouldered. 'You promised.' She sat up abruptly. All her passion now turned to anger. 'If you force yourself on me, I'll make sure every textile operator in Atlanta hears about it,' she warned. 'Southern men don't take lightly to Northerners messing with their women.'

For a moment Todd's eyes narrowed in appraisal. Then he swore under his breath. 'Dammit, I believe you would. We'll play it your way,' he capitulated, his voice thick with passion.

Maureen waited until he left the settee and turned on the lamp before she rose to her feet. She walked to the chair where she had placed her clothes. Todd was redressing with angry swiftness.

'I'll drive you home. Orlando's gone to bed.' He was furious with her.

Her face hot, her head high, she walked with Todd down the long corridor to the door and out to the car. Todd would never marry her. He had been sure, once she was on her back, he could do whatever he wished with her. And he had been using her to learn what he could about the Hampton Mill.

Somehow, she had to make up with Andrew. If she ever manipulated Andrew into taking her to bed, he would marry her. He was too much of a gentleman to do otherwise. She couldn't afford to fail with Andrew. He was her only chance to marry well in Atlanta.

19

To Caroline, no summer in Atlanta had seemed so uncomfortable as the present one. All three children were fretful and restless. Liz and Josh squabbled constantly. Francis, whose progress had been heartwarmingly steady, regressed, though Victor refused to be discouraged by this. Caroline wished that Eric would take Liz and Josh to Hampton Court for two or three weeks, but she knew his campaigning made this unrealistic.

Eric said nothing about his political activities except on those occasions when he announced he would be away from Atlanta overnight. About once a week Jim would appear at Hampton House, along with party chieftains, for long late-evening conferences in the library. Caroline made no effort to join them, as she had done in the past, nor did Eric invite her to do so. She knew that Jim was puzzled by her behaviour. As close as he was to Eric, didn't he know about Serena Mayo?

In July Huerta relinquished his claim to the presidency of Mexico. It was expected that Carranza, who took control of the government, would hold new elections, and that the Mexican people would acquire a democratic government. But developments in Europe pulled the spotlight away from Mexico.

By late July newspaper headlines warned that Europe 'trembles on the brink of war'. On Saturday morning, August 1, Caroline was walking down the hall to the breakfast room when she heard Eric in agitated conversation on the library phone.

'Good Lord, Jim! All Kaiser Wilhelm's bluster about

building a huge army and navy to preserve the peace was a crock of shit.'

Caroline peered into the library. Eric beckoned her to join him. He was listening in grim intensity to what Jim had to report – the Kaiser had thrust Europe into war.

'If the New York Stock Exchange closed late yesterday, what about the New Orleans Cotton Exchange?' Eric demanded. He winced at Jim's reply.

Caroline dropped on to the edge of a chair. If the New Orleans Cotton Exchange was closed, then the others would follow suit. She grappled with the portent of closed cotton exchanges. The whole South would be in chaos. Not only would the cotton growers and the textile operators be affected, but almost every economic interest in the South.

Since 1897, despite the uneasy voices of those few – including Eric – who warned against a one-crop economy, Southern farmers had continued to devote every acre possible to cotton. The demands seemed insatiable. Nine million bales a year were shipped abroad. What would happen to the South with export markets closed by war?

Eric put down the phone. His face was drained of colour.

'All that fine talk at The Hague!' Eric was racked by rage. 'We accomplished nothing. Germany has declared war on Russia.'

Within the next few days the nation was assaulted by headlines. 'GERMANY INVADES FRANCE.' 'RUSSIA INVADES GERMANY.' 'GERMANY STRIKES FRANCE WITHOUT EVEN A DECLARATION OF WAR.' 'GREAT BRITAIN ARMED AND READY TO HIT GERMANY.'

The *Constitution* quoted the London *Times* as calling this 'the most terrible war since the fall of Rome'. Four great powers of Europe – Austria-Hungary, Russia, France, and Germany – were engaged in fighting.

Shock over the outbreak of war was superseded in the South by disruption of its major industry. Senator Bolton, brought home from Washington by the seriousness of the situation, summoned Eric to dinner, with instructions to make sure Caroline came with him. At the helm of one of the state's largest cotton mills, she understood the situation probably better than Eric or himself.

They sat at the dinner table, hardly tasting the sumptuous meal being served to them.

'John Sharp Williams told the Senate on Tuesday that in New Orleans and in Memphis and in Galveston, people are losing their heads,' Senator Bolton reported.

'It's no better in Atlanta,' Caroline confirmed. 'The farmers are in panic. With the cotton exchanges closed, there's no way of setting prices. Senator, when do you think the exchanges will reopen?'

'God only knows.' The senator was apprehensive. 'Though Secretary of Navy Daniels wants to ship cotton aboard in United States Navy vessels. Of course, Congress must approve it.'

'Harvey, Congress would never allow that,' Marian declared. 'A United States Navy vessel transporting cotton would run a heavy risk of being attacked – and we'd be sucked right into the war.'

'The farmers begin to pick cotton this month.' Caroline was more anxious at the moment about the plights of the farmers than the problems that were sure to arise in the mills with the continuance of the war. 'The South expects the largest crop in history. More than sixteen million bales. What'll happen if the export markets are closed?'

'The farmers can't ship.' Eric voiced her fears. 'What's cotton selling for now?'

'A week ago it was thirteen and a half cents a pound for middling cotton,' Caroline told him. 'With the exchanges closed, there's no price established.'

'It'll drop,' Eric warned. 'Probably to half of that.'

'The farmers will go bankrupt. They're all in debt to the banks until they sell their cotton.' Caroline was pale. 'The Legislature will have to take steps to help them.'

'It would mean calling a special legislative session. But even if we did, the Legislature would never pass any such bill,' Eric rejected. 'The farmers will have to be helped on a federal level.'

'You know how long that could take.' The senator was brusque in his concern. 'The bill would get buried in committee. The farmers could starve before we passed a measure to help them.'

'What can be done?' Caroline demanded. 'We can't sit by without taking action.'

'The Chamber of Commerce has called for an emergency meeting tomorrow,' the senator told them. 'Local bankers will be sitting on it. We'll have to start there. Caroline, do you expect to stockpile cotton? Do you think the other mills will do that? With prices dropping, it could be a smart move.'

'I don't know about the other mills, but I'm going to buy cotton with every dollar I can raise,' Caroline vowed. She ignored Eric's frown of disapproval. 'The equipment for the annexe is scheduled to arrive any day now, and that's going to tax our available cash; but the bank should be happy to lend me money. I have the collateral.'

'It could be dangerous,' Eric objected. 'God knows how long this war will continue. You could be eaten up with interest charges.'

'Cotton prices will collapse,' Caroline said slowly. 'We all know that. But they'll rise again, far beyond what they've ever been. Europe will be hungry for our products. We'll find a way to ship,' she said with conviction. 'The farmers are desperate to sell, and we have to help them. And we'll profit by buying now.'

'Enough of business talk,' Marian Bolton commanded when the maid arrived with dessert. 'The senator and I are going back to Washington tomorrow. I'd like us to have one evening of relaxation before we return to that madness.' Her eyes rested tenderly on her husband before returning to Caroline. 'Victor tells me he's mighty pleased with Francis' progress. His mother said he absolutely refused to come up to Boston this summer because he's so wrapped up in his work down here.'

'I thank God every night for Victor,' Caroline relinquished her soberness. 'He's even brought Liz and Josh close to Francis. You know how impatient Liz always was with Francis. Now she spends time with him every evening before we sit down to dinner.'

Eric said nothing, but Caroline intercepted his furtive glances at the grandfather clock that sat in one corner of the dining room. Was he impatient to run to his mistress?

In the midst of world chaos President Wilson's wife died. On August 10, shortly before noon, the funeral train carrying her body to Rome to lie beside that of her mother stopped briefly in Atlanta's Terminal Station. The State Legislature had adjourned. Flags at public buildings were at half-mast. Business was suspended as the funeral train passed through the city. Accompanying the body were President Wilson and members of his family. The nation – and particularly Georgia – mourned with the President.

Night after night now Caroline sat in the library after dinner and listened while Eric and Jim – and often David and Noah in these crucial days – dissected what was happening to the world.

'There's no real political leadership in Germany, Russia, or Austria-Hungary,' David said sombrely.

'Let's pray for level heads in Washington.' Noah was

thinking of his older son, who in a few years would be old enough to go to war, Caroline guessed. As she thought of Josh. *May he never have to fight a war.* 'We're going to need that sorely.'

'No matter how we complain about Wilson's efforts in Mexico,' Jim reminded, 'we know he'll fight to keep us out of the mess in Europe.' Unexpectedly he grinned. 'And soon we'll have another pacifist voice in Washington.' Despite problems, Jim was convinced Eric would win the primary.

On the primary day Caroline awoke with the familiar annoyance that, as a woman, she could not vote. Women would vote in New Zealand, in Finland, in Norway, and in Australia. How could the United States be so backward?

Walking down the stairs this morning, she heard the front door shut. Eric meant to avoid her. This was a day they should be sharing. If Eric won today – and indications were strong that he would – he would be moving up into national politics. The first major step towards the White House.

Eric had ceased to talk about her going with him to Washington. Did he plan on taking Serena Mayo with him? She would fit well into that scene. *Was Eric serious about Serena Mayo?* This might be more than a fling. He had been willing to divorce Tina for her, before Tina fled to Paris and died in a fire. Was he considering divorce again? No, she forced herself to be realistic. Eric couldn't afford a divorce. He would never be elected to another public office, and that was the driving force in his life.

Late in the evening Eric telephoned to say that the primary victory was his. He was remaining downtown on party business. Caroline heard the constraint in his voice.

He knew he would be going to Washington; he didn't know if his wife would be going with him.

Atlantans plunged into the effort to ease the cotton crisis. On September 1 the 'Buy a Bale of Cotton' movement was launched. The *Journal* urged everyone to buy cotton at ten cents a pound. 'We will buy from the farmer only. We will store our cotton in warehouses, garages, barns, on our porches – we will not sell it for a year.'

Despite her tight financial situation, Caroline began to buy cotton beyond the needs of the mill, buying first from Hampton Court's tenant farmers. She applied to the bank for a loan, bought cotton with a lavishness that unnerved Sophie.

'Caroline, where are you going to put this cotton?' Sophie challenged, sitting in Caroline's office late one afternoon after learning from Andrew that a new delivery was expected in the morning. 'We'll soon run out of space in the mill!'

'I'm renting warehouse space wherever I can find it. Sophie, the cotton must be bought. And we'll use it.' The price was down to six cents a pound, with no sign of the cotton exchanges' reopening. 'Sophie, even with bank interest and warehouse-rental costs, we're in a position to make a fortune on cotton. The prices are sure to rise.'

'God told you this?' Sophie was sarcastic in her nervousness.

'Instinct tells us this.' Caroline refused to be dissuaded.

'Instinct tells me you're going to lose everything Josiah spent a lifetime in building.' Sophie's voice soared to rare shrillness. 'You can't save every farmer in the South personally.' The farmers were desperate, many of them unable to move their cotton at any price. They stopped mortgage sales with shotguns.

'Sophie, I'm buying cotton not only because it's necessary to save the farmers' — Caroline struggled to sound matter-of-fact — 'but also because it's a healthy business move. Five and six cents a pound, when it was thirteen and a half cents a month ago. Before this war is over, I'll wager it goes to twenty-five or thirty cents a pound. I'm buying. I'm buying every bale I can raise the cash to pay for.'

'Talk to Eric about this,' Sophie pleaded. 'You're moving too hastily, Caroline.'

'I don't need Eric's advice,' Caroline's eyes were cold. 'Let him concern himself with his election. I run the mill.'

On October 18 Coca-Cola millionaire Asa Candler brought relief to the harassed cotton farmers of the South. That Sunday morning the newspapers heralded Candler's plan to lend thirty million dollars on cotton on the basis of six cents a pound. The loans would run until July 1915. In addition to pledging the resources of the bank to this effort, Mr Candler pledged his personal fortune.

With cotton at six cents a pound, Caroline made a fresh effort to buy, canvassing Atlanta for warehouse space. Even Andrew tried to quell this obsession. Caroline would listen to no one. She knew that an unforeseen turn of events could wipe out the Hampton fortune, yet she could not believe that cotton would not soar in price.

Ever since the primaries, Caroline had grasped at the business crisis that faced the South to blot from her mind the confrontation that must arrive when Eric was officially voted in as the new congressman from this district. On this first Tuesday in November Caroline sat at her desk and struggled to cope with the backlog of correspondence that required her attention, but today's election intruded. By tonight the Republican candidates would concede a Democratic landslide. While Eric would take office on

March 4, he would not attend a session of Congress until December of next year, when the Sixty-fourth Congress convened. Unless the President called a special session in this crucial period.

In a sudden need for privacy, Caroline rose from behind her desk and crossed to close her office door. Even if there should be no special session of Congress called, how could she commit herself to go to Washington in thirteen months? Earlier, her mind threatened. A suitable house must be located in Washington. Eric would need to arrange for a staff for his office.

These next months would be crucial to the mill's financial stability. Even if Francis should be well enough to take with them to Washington – and his rate of improvement was bringing joy to her – she had to remain here in Atlanta at the helm of the mill. Sophie and Andrew were indispensable, but final decisions were hers.

Caroline reached for the telephone. She could delay no longer. She had been avoiding the call to chef Michel Marat in New Orleans for the last two weeks. On every major occasion in their lives since the Peace Jubilee dinner in December of '98, Monsieur Marat came to Atlanta to supervise the banquet. No one in Atlanta provided the French flair that intrigued Caroline. To arrange for a banquet to celebrate Eric's victory was to accept that he would be moving to Washington.

At ten o'clock, while Caroline was fighting to ship Liz and Josh off to bed, she heard Eric's voice in the foyer.

'Papa's home,' Liz was triumphant. 'We have to welcome our new congressman.' She darted from the library and down the hall. 'Papa, Papa!'

Caroline was conscious of Josh's scrutiny. What was he thinking with such intensity?

'Josh, go greet the new congressman.' Caroline

231

struggled to sound convivial. With a dazzling smile he raced from the room. He had been waiting for her to release him. How sensitive Josh was. He realized that tonight was a traumatic occasion for her.

'Roland, bring a bottle of Dom Perignon and five glasses into the library,' Eric instructed ebulliently.

A moment later Eric appeared in the doorway, an arm encircling each child.

'It's official now?' Caroline asked. Her throat was tight. This should be a moment of exquisite pleasure.

'It's official,' Eric confirmed.

'Eric, we're so proud of you!' Sophie rushed to embrace him. 'Josiah would have been so pleased.'

'Aunt Sophie, nobody else had a chance with Papa in the race.' Liz glowed. 'David said he was sure to win.'

'Sugar, any Democrat who was running would win today.' Eric chuckled. 'The election was settled in the primaries.' His eyes moved across the room to Caroline. Questioning. He had expected her to run to him with her usual exuberance at such moments. Tonight she was asking herself if he had gone to Serena Mayo before coming home to his family.

Smiling broadly, Roland came into the library with the bottle of champagne and goblets. Eric popped the cork and poured. There was a brief celebratory atmosphere in the room while Sophie offered a toast and they drank.

'All right, off to bed,' Caroline commanded when Liz and Josh had consumed the minute amount of champagne allotted to each of them. 'Tomorrow's a schoolday.'

'Papa just got home,' Liz wheedled. 'Let us stay up another half-hour.'

'You heard your mother.' Eric leaned forward to kiss Liz, then pulled Josh to him. 'To bed.'

'I should be in bed already,' Sophie complained good-humouredly while Liz and Josh complied with orders.

'But I wasn't going upstairs until the congressman-elect was home.' Her face reflected the depth of her love.

'Sophie, wait a moment.' Caroline's heart was pounding. *Don't leave me alone with Eric.* 'Eric, have you heard anything about the cotton exchanges' reopening? There's a rumour that the New Orleans Cotton Exchange may open in a week or two.'

'There've been rumours since a week after they closed,' Sophie dismissed this.

'I've heard nothing.' Eric was serious. 'Are you still buying cotton, Caro?'

'I'm buying.' Her voice was defiant. 'It's necessary, and it's going to be profitable.'

'You hope.' Sophie was dubious.

'You could be putting the mill in jeopardy if you keep this up, Caro,' Eric warned. 'Nobody knows when this damned war is going to end. It's not Cuba.'

'I know what I'm doing.' Colour outlined Caroline's cheek-bones. 'Congress adjourned in October without doing a thing to bail out the cotton farmers. And I suspect that when they return December 3, they'll do little more. If the cotton farmers go under, so will the rest of the country.'

'Caroline, you can't save every cotton farmer in the South,' Sophie rejected. 'You've done more than your share already.'

'It's late.' Caroline's smile was polite but impersonal. 'I'm going up to bed.'

Between preparations for the victory banquet on Saturday and mill business, Caroline's waking hours were crammed with obligations. She was grateful that there was not a moment alone with Eric, though too often she felt his eyes on her. Thursday afternoon, with Liz insistent that nothing within her wardrobe was fine enough for

233

such an occasion, she deserted her post in the library during Victor's time with Francis to go with Liz to Rich's to choose a dress for the dinner. Liz clamoured for a charming turquoise-blue chiffon. The flared skirt was finished at the bottom with two bands of ribbon velvet, and there was a rose at the bodice.

'Liz, it's too old for you,' Caroline resisted.

'Mama, I'm practically fourteen!' Liz was outraged. 'I'm going to try it on.'

'All right.' Caroline was too exhausted for battle.

When Liz emerged from the dressing room ecstatic at her image, Caroline capitulated. Liz looked beautiful in the turquoise-blue chiffon. She appeared sufficiently grown-up to be a member of the Debutante Club, Caroline thought uneasily. Why must Liz always rush the years?

The evening of the banquet arrived with startling swiftness. Since Thursday the house had been permeated by tantalizing aromas from the kitchen as Michel Marat and his assistants baked and roasted and prepared for Saturday evening's festivities. This afternoon the florist had devised floral arrangements throughout the lower floor.

Caroline started at the knock on her door. She tensed, expecting Eric.

'Come in.'

The door opened. Liz hurled herself into the room. 'Mama, Josh said you're letting him come down to the dinner tonight,' she accused.

'That's right,' Caroline confirmed. 'Don't you think he should be there?' Her voice was a gentle reproach.

'He's such a baby,' Liz scoffed.

'He'll be fine,' Caroline reproved. Not one word about Francis, she realized with pleasure. Not even Liz expected Francis to embarrass them by throwing a tantrum upstairs in his room in the course of the evening. When Francis went into a tantrum these days, he was quickly calmed. Victor had accomplished that.

'Mama, is this dress all right?' Liz scrutinized her reflection in the mirror.

'The dress is exquisite, Liz. Didn't you show it to Janet?' Of late, no longer fearful of Francis' mortifying her, Liz had been bringing friends into the house at regular intervals. Caroline was glad that Liz and Ellen's daughter had become fast friends.

'Janet says it's gorgeous.' Liz was mollified. 'Can I sit next to her at dinner?'

'That's exactly where you're to sit,' Caroline assured her.

'And next to David?' Liz persisted.

'Next to David,' Caroline concurred. It was to David that Liz ran for help with her maths, which seemed incomprehensible to her.

'Did you put Victor next to Janet, like I asked you?' Liz persisted. 'She thinks he's so good-looking.'

'I told you I would,' Caroline reminded. She was sure Eric wouldn't object to his presence tonight.

'Victor likes you,' Liz remarked, her eyes too wise for her age.

Caroline refused to recognize Liz's soft insinuation. 'I'm very fond of him. We all should be, considering what he's doing for Francis.'

'I'm going downstairs. I want to check the place cards,' Liz decided. 'You look beautiful, Mama.'

'Thank you, darling.' Caroline reached to pull Liz close. Liz was chary with compliments. 'So do you.'

Alone, Caroline withdrew the jewellery box that she had brought up from the safe earlier. Tonight she would wear her grandmother's emerald-and-diamond necklace. Inevitably she wore this on important occasions.

When she went downstairs, Caroline could hear Liz and Josh talking with Sophie in the parlour. For once the two of them were not fighting.

Caroline went into the huge formal dining room. The table was laid with the Wedgwood china and Waterford crystal. Seth was inspecting the silver.

'Seth, I'm so pleased you came tonight.' She smiled in rich affection.

'Miss Caroline, you knowed I wouldn't miss tonight. Our Mist' Eric entertainin' as congressman. My, the General would have been proud!'

While she talked with Seth, Caroline heard the first cars pull up. She hurried to the foyer to be there with Eric as Roland admitted their guests.

'You look beautiful, Caro.' Eric smiled with the familiar Eric Hampton charm. He used to say that to her and mean it, Caroline thought. Tonight it was an automatic greeting.

'You'll be the most handsome congressman in Washington,' Caroline said unwarily, and felt colour rush to her face. She saw the inevitable question in his eyes. *Would the children and she be going to Washington with him?* He needed them as part of the picture. The handsome, still-young congressman, with his wife and family. Would the congressman have his mistress tucked way in a convenient apartment?

Appearing radiant, Caroline stood beside Eric and received their guests. She caught his quick intake of breath at sight of Victor. Tonight, however, he was cordial. It was Victor who appeared uneasy.

Before the soup course – a superb cream of artichoke – had been finished, Caroline knew tonight's dinner would be a success. Conversation was animated, at times provocative, which Eric appreciated. He glowed, Caroline thought. Josh's eyes rested regularly on his father.

Only now did Caroline realize how proud Josh was that his father had become a congressman.

Caroline's gaze travelled to Liz, absorbed in conversation with David.

'But when Leo's case comes before the United States Supreme Court,' Liz said earnestly, 'he'll be cleared, won't he? I mean, Justice Holmes said he doubted that Leo received due process of law.' How glib Liz had become in legal terms, Caroline thought tenderly.

'We'll know early next month.' David was grave. 'But, yes, Leo's new counsel is optimistic.'

During the past few weeks the efforts to have Leo Frank's sentence commuted had accelerated interest in the case. Georgia justice was being attacked in every section of the country except the Deep South. Editors in Baltimore vowed their faith in the jury system was shaken. Newspapers in Pittsburgh and Duluth and dozens of other cities accused Georgia courts of being ruled by racial prejudice and mob passions.

Towards the end of dinner a sombreness fell over the assemblage. The table at large was engulfed in discussion of the war in Europe. The terrible suffering of the Belgian people. The growing casualty lists among the troops. Food was becoming scarce in some areas, prices soaring.

'Let anyone who believes there is glory in war go to Belgium,' Eric said grimly. 'Let them come face to face with calculated brutality and mass hatred. We should go to bed every night and thank God that Wilson is a man dedicated to peace.'

'What about Italy?' Liz's voice was refreshing in the midst of such gloom. 'Victor, will there be fighting in Italy, too?'

'My grandmother writes that she expects no trouble. She refuses to leave Rome to come to this country to live with my mother. But the Italians are sympathetic with the Allies,' Victor said soberly.

'They won't be able to remain out of the war for long,' Eric warned. Tonight Caroline sensed a genuine communication between Eric and Victor. She was pleased. 'If my grandmother was in Rome, I'd fight like hell to get her over here.'

'My mother keeps trying. But my grandmother is a stubborn old lady.' Victor's smile was wry. 'She's probably nurturing ideas about joining the Red Cross, to help nurse the wounded.'

When the last guest finally left, Caroline sat down on a chair in the library, exhausted. Sophie had already retired. But despite the lateness of the hour, Liz and Josh were reluctant to go up to bed.

'Let's have hot chocolate,' Josh stalled.

'After all you've eaten?' Caroline protested.

'We'll have hot chocolate,' Eric decided. 'Josh, go out to the kitchen and tell Mattie to send hot chocolate into the library.' He paused. 'And if there're more of those petits fours, send in a plate of them, too.'

'Why can't Liz do it?' Josh balked.

'Because *you* asked for it,' Caroline told him.

'Papa, why did the war start?' Liz asked with disconcerting seriousness.

'Come over here and I'll tell you.' Eric patted a place beside him on the sofa.

Caroline recoiled from more talk of war. Yet she was drawn to the portrait of Eric and Liz, their heads almost touching as he leaned over her, explaining how the precarious balance of power in Europe had been disrupted, bringing on the worst war the world had ever known.

Josh bounced into the room with the exuberance of childhood.

'Mattie says we'll have hot chocolate and petits fours in a few minutes,' he announced. 'Papa, now that you're a Congressman, we'll live in Washington, won't we?' His face glowed in anticipation.

'Josh, I won't take office until next March.' Eric was not looking at her, but Caroline felt the tension in him. 'It'll be months before Congress convenes.'

'When Congress convenes, then we'll live in Washington,' Josh persisted. Caroline fought to hold on to her composure. *Why couldn't Josh shut up?* 'A Congressman has to live in Washington.'

'*We* can't go to Washington, silly.' Liz glared at Josh. 'We go to school here.'

'They've got schools in Washington,' Josh shot back. 'We'll go to school there.'

'No!' Liz shrieked. 'I won't leave Atlanta. I won't go to Washington! I won't! I won't!'

'Stop screaming, Liz.' Caroline flinched at her shrillness. 'We can't think about going to Washington with Papa. I can't leave the mill when business conditions are in such chaos . . .'

Caroline stopped short. She felt the rage that charged behind Eric's impassive stare. All right, he had his answer. She would remain in Atlanta with the children. He would go alone to Washington.

20

Maureen left the streetcar in the still-dark December morning and walked towards the mill. What had been a light snow when she left her rooming house had become a bone-chilling sleet. Tonight the path to the mill would be a sheet of ice.

Maureen drew her coat collar more snugly about her throat. The blue serge coat had been warm enough in New Orleans. It was too light for the more severe Atlanta winters. But to buy a new one on her wages was unthinkable this year.

The aroma of fresh coffee brewing drifted into the dank air from Andrew's cottage nearby. How stupid she had been to brush off Andrew in favour of Todd Murdoch. She must do something to win back Andrew. Sometimes she glanced up and saw him looking at her. Polite as he was, she knew he was dying to take her to bed. If he ever laid a hand on her, he'd feel obliged to marry her.

Christmas was breathing down her neck. She hated all the holidays. She was always alone, nothing to do. Her second Christmas in Atlanta, and what had she accomplished? Mama complained she gave herself airs since she learned typing and stenography. She was a good secretary, she thought with satisfaction. She had Papa's brains if not his money. But being a good secretary wouldn't buy her a mansion, Paris clothes, and a Cadillac.

She didn't meet anybody. Only the mill lintheads and Mrs Ryan's boarders. For a little while, going out with

Andrew and then with Todd, she had been glad she came to Atlanta.

Now all she did on Sundays was lie in bed and read the magazines Mrs Ryan lent her. That and eating chocolates was all she did the whole bloody day. She'd buy a box of Huyler's out of one pay envelope and make it last four weeks. Mama used to say she'd get fat, the way she was always wanting chocolates. She wasn't, was she? All at once she was nervous. She couldn't afford to lose her looks. That was all she had to take her out of the mill.

I can't go back to New Orleans. Mama didn't even bother to write to thank me for the Christmas present last year. I hate working in the mill, but I earn more here than I can anywhere else in Atlanta.

Maureen walked into the mill, welcoming its overheated, damp atmosphere this morning. She pulled off her coat while she walked down the long corridor to her small office, situated between Caroline's and Sophie's.

She heard Andrew's voice as she neared Sophie's office. 'Phoebe's leaving this afternoon for a family wedding down in Americus,' he was saying to Sophie. 'I told her I'll drive her to Terminal Station. I don't want her climbing on the streetcar with a suitcase in this weather.'

'You spoil Phoebe.' Sophie chuckled. 'But she spoils you rotten, too! Nobody – not even Mattie – cooks like Phoebe.'

Maureen hung away her coat and settled herself at her desk to finish up the report that Caroline had dictated yesterday afternoon. Her mind was racing. Pheobe was leaving for Americus this afternoon. Andrew would be alone in his cottage this evening.

All through the day Maureen searched her mind for a way to get herself into Andrew's cottage at the end of the working day. He would never invite her inside without

241

Phoebe to chaperone them. He was too much the gentleman for that. But this was a chance she couldn't afford to miss.

Maureen contrived to work late that night. She waited until she heard Andrew leave before she began the routine of closing up her office for the night. Give him plenty of time to get into the cottage, she exhorted herself. He wouldn't be going anywhere on a night like this.

Only Sophie remained in the mill, along with the night watchman, when Maureen walked out into the cold night. The temperature had dropped. She walked on a bed of ice. Ostensibly she was headed for the streetcar. Just past the pathway parallel to Andrew's cottage, she made a pretence of falling on the ice. This must be staged exactly right. If anyone, including Andrew, should happen to see, it must look as though she had slipped.

Gingerly Maureen picked herself up, pantomimed pain when she attempted to put weight on her foot. She glanced about her. Nobody was in sight. In Andrew's cottage lights were on in the parlour and in the kitchen. Andrew must be heating up the dinner that Phoebe was sure to have left for him on the kitchen stove.

Maureen limped along the path to Andrew's cottage, made her way up to the small veranda, and rang the doorbell. In a moment a light glowed in the foyer. Andrew pulled the door wide.

'Andrew, will it be all right if I rest for a few minutes on your veranda?' Her voice was appealingly apologetic. 'I fell on the ice and turned my ankle. I'm sure it'll be all right in a few minutes if I – '

'Come inside out of the cold, Maureen.' His eyes solicitous, he helped her into the house. 'Sit down in the parlour and rest your foot on a stool.'

Appearing brave despite her pain, Maureen allowed

Andrew to settle her into a comfortable chair. He moved across the room to bring her a footstool, helped her lift her foot on to it.

'Your shoes are all wet.' Andrew was hesitant for an instant, then decisive. 'Take off your shoe, Maureen. That ankle should be packed in ice to prevent its swelling.' With delicacy he averted his head as she bent forward demurely to remove her shoe. 'I'll bring the ice.'

While she put aside her shoe and, after a moment of deliberation, removed the lisle stocking, Maureen could hear Andrew hacking with the ice pick. In a few moments he returned, the chopped ice wrapped in a towel.

'This is going to be cold,' he warned. Maureen winced as the cold wet towel touched her ankle. 'But it'll stop the swelling.'

'I'm sure it'll be all right if I just sit still for a few minutes.'

'I'll put a log on the fire. You must be chilled to the bone. This is the worst night of the winter.'

'I'm sorry I disturbed you this way.' Maureen's eyes pleaded prettily for reassurance.

'You're not disturbing me. I was just going to spend the evening listening to records.' Delicious aromas were emanating from the kitchen. 'Phoebe went down to Americus for a wedding,' Andrew explained, all at once self-conscious at being alone in the cottage with Maureen. 'She left a potful of beef stew. Why don't we have dinner together here by the fire?' He hesitated. 'Or is your cousin expecting you home?'

'Oh, Peggy went back to New Orleans weeks ago. She missed her family. She's not really my cousin. We just always say that because we grew up together.' Maureen contrived to appear wistful. 'I have no family. Only my mother. And we've never been close. After my father died – when I was six – she kind of drew within herself.'

243

'You sit there and warm up,' Andrew told her. 'I'll bring in dinner for us.'

'It's so sweet of you to go to all this trouble on my account, Andrew.'

'No trouble at all.' He walked to the Victrola, put on a record. 'You'll have some music while I'm busy in the kitchen.'

Satisfaction brought a glow to her eyes while she leaned back in the chair and listened to the magnificent voice of Enrico Caruso fill the room. Andrew and she would have dinner by the romantic light of the fireplace. Afterwards he would make love to her. *She must see that he did.*

Andrew returned to the parlour and drew a walnut table on cabriole legs into position between the two chairs that flanked the fireplace, taking care to fit it over the footstool on which Maureen's foot rested. He placed a protective board across the table, cut to fit it precisely, and covered this with a white damask cloth. Andrew often dined here by the fireplace, Maureen interpreted. Alone.

'What a beautiful table.' She knew little of fine furniture, but instinct told her that every piece of furniture in this charming room was of great value.

'It's an early-eighteenth-century gaming table.' Andrew was gratified by her interest. 'I've been collecting antiques for twenty-five years. Each piece in this room is special to me.'

'It's all so beautiful.' Admiration shone from her eyes as she glanced about the parlour.

'I'll bring in the stew.' He was delighted to have her here, yet she sensed his discomfort. He was unaccustomed to entertaining young ladies alone.

Andrew returned with a tray laden with two plates of steaming stew, an assortment of silver, a plate of cornbread cut in squares.

'Oh, it smells so good!' She leaned forward to help Andrew dispense the silver.

'I'll bring in the tea.'

Moments later they were eating Phoebe's savoury stew with gusto. How diferent from the food served by Mrs Ryan! At the rooming house, stew was a concoction of potatoes, vegetables, gravy, and an occasional piece of beef.

'Tell me about that wonderful cabinet.' Maureen focused on an ornate, colourful cabinet on a sculptural stand.

Andrew beamed. 'That was supposed to have been made at the royal French furniture factory, identical to one presented to Charles II of England by Louis XIV of France.' He rose to his feet and crossed to open a large central door that was flanked by small drawers on each side. 'The marquetry is exquisite, and inside here there's a view of Versailles.' He stood aside to allow her to gaze within the cabinet.

Maureen was an appreciative audience. Andrew was relaxing now, pleased that his prized possessions were being so well received. It was easy to talk to Andrew. But she had not arranged this encounter for the purpose of talking.

'I'll bring in more stew,' Andrew said.

'I couldn't eat another bite,' Maureen protested. 'It was just delicious.' When Mama was in the mood, she was a wonderful cook. She had not been in the mood often.

'Phoebe left a full cookie jar, even though she'll be gone only four days. We'll have some with our tea.'

Nobody would guess, from the outside of the cottage, that it was so large within. All these fine antiques. The beautiful rugs. Even the dishes were special. She frowned in distaste, visualizing the cracked, stained dishes that

245

graced Mrs Ryan's table. Andrew had never lived the way she did. Without money, you were nobody.

Andrew came back into the room with a hand-painted plate piled high with pecan-plump cookies. Maureen leaned forward to pour tea for Andrew and her from the Meissen teapot, knowing what an enticing image she presented to him.

'I think the ice was just what my ankle needed,' Maureen confided. 'It isn't throbbing at all any more.'

'I'm so glad.' His smile was shy yet warm.

While Andrew cleared away the table, Maureen pulled on her stocking, which had dried by the fire. She tested her shoe. It, too, was dry and warm. She ought to have boots, she thought; but there was no money for boots, nor the fine silk stockings she coveted. Caroline always wore silk stockings. If she married Andrew, she would never wear a pair of lisle stockings again.

Andrew returned to the parlour. In a minute he would say something about driving her home, she warned herself in sudden panic.

'Andrew, who is the lady in the group of miniatures on the wall there?' She clutched at any delay.

'That was my mother.' Andrew turned to gaze at the cluster of six enamel miniatures that hung above a small lacquered table. 'She died when I was sixteen. My father died two years earlier. General Hampton – Caroline's grandfather – was my cousin. He brought me here to live with him. He wanted to send me to college, but I was fascinated by the mill.' His eyes lit as he talked. 'I persuaded him to let me work there and learn everything I could about machinery.'

'I heard Miss Sophie tell somebody once that nobody in the state knew as much about mill equipment as you do.'

'It's been my life.' For an instant Andrew's eyes held

hers; then he averted them in confusion. But Maureen recognized what she saw there. Many men had looked at her in that fashion. Now. If she couldn't persuade Andrew to make love to her now, it would never happen.

Maureen leaned forward in her chair. Her soft, full mouth parted in her intensity, she concentrated on the miniatures of Andrew's mother.

'You loved your mother very much.'

'Yes.' It was like a benediction. 'She was warm and lovely and compassionate. It was a tragedy that she died so young.'

'And a mother like mine survives,' Maureen said bitterly, then gasped in confusion. 'Andrew, please forget what I said . . .'

'Of course.' He was reassuring, but Maureen sensed his curiosity.

'I shouldn't talk about Mama. I've never told anyone. *Not ever*. I left New Orleans because I couldn't bear to stay in the house with her. Oh, Mama didn't lay a hand on me since I was twelve,' Maureen said conscientiously. 'But you don't forget the kind of childhood I had.'

'She . . . beat you?' The words were wrung from Andrew. He started at Maureen in disbelief.

'I still have marks from her.' Tears welled involuntarily in her eyes. She rolled up the sleeve of her dress to reveal a hairline scar that extended for four inches along her forearm. 'She beat me into unconsciousness once with her boot. I was eight then. Every time she was upset, she would beat me.' Maureen's voice broke. She was wrapped up in the ugliness of those years. Reliving the pain of being beaten and unloved.

'She ought to have been horsewhipped!' Andrew rose from his chair in a need for action.

'I don't know why I'm talking like this tonight.' Maureen apologized. He was unnerved. Sympathetic.

'I've never talked this way to anybody. But you've been so sweet. I'm not used to that.' She lifted her eyes to him. Limpid and adoring.

'Maureen, that's all over.' He stood beside her, reached for her hand.

'Sometimes I dream about those times. Once I woke up screaming. My landlady came running. I told her I'd had a nightmare. I was remembering the night Mama hit me across my back with a leather thong until she laid the skin bare. I couldn't go to school for a week. She told the teacher I'd been down with a fever.'

'Maureen, it'll never happen again,' he comforted. She lifted her face to his.

'Andrew, you're so understanding. I've never known anybody like you.' Her eyes willed him to kiss her. He was mesmerized, she thought in triumph. *He's going to make love to me.*

His mouth was gentle on hers. Eager yet timorous. She reached up to fold her arms about his shoulders. She felt the shudder of passion that racked him as her mouth responded to his. Without releasing her mouth, he fumbled to lift her into his arms. He carried her from the parlour into the darkened bedroom.

Andrew deposited her on the patchwork comforter that covered the four-poster bed. He sat beside her and sought her mouth again. Her arms told him that she was as eager as he for this union.

'Maureen . . .' His voice was tortured, doubtful.

'Andrew, yes,' she whispered, and reached to unfasten the bodice of her dress.

With a strangled groan he helped her. His hands fondled the voluptuous spill of her breasts. She reached to pull her dress down about her hips. Was he thinking she had done this with other men? But in a little while he would know. Nobody before him. He had taken advantage of a virgin. *He would marry her.*

Andrew undressed her with the tenderness of a man unused to such tasks. He deposited her clothes on a chair near the bed, her shoes beside it.

'You're beautiful.' He stood beside the bed inspecting her nakedness in the faint light that invaded the bedroom from the hall. 'I knew you would be.' *He had thought about her like this.*

'I'm wicked,' she decried. 'But I don't care.' An arousing defiance lit her eyes. She held her arms up to him. He had slept with other women, she assumed. Women in brothels, where he paid for what he took. He was going to pay for tonight. The price was higher than he had ever encountered.

Andrew undressed beside the bed in impatient swiftness, then lowered himself above her.

'You're an exquisite porcelain statue,' he whispered, separating her legs with one of his while his hands fondled her breasts. 'I've never known anyone so lovely.'

She felt the heaviness of him upon her, the first thrust within her. Her arms tightened about him. Pretend this was Todd Murdoch. Only, tonight they didn't have to play games. *This was the moment.* The moment that was going to make her Andrew Hampton's wife!

He was thrusting within her with growing excitement. A sudden, expected pain elicited a cry from her. He stiffened.

'It's all right,' she whispered, in simulated passion. 'I love you, Andrew.' And then simulation became real. The body pushing within her was Todd's. The hands moving about her belonged to Todd. She had never expected it could be this way.

'Oh, God!' He clutched her in convulsive pleasure,

then resolutely withdrew, spilling his passion on one naked, sculptured thigh.

They lay motionless for a few moments; then Andrew was pulling away from her.

'Lie still,' he ordered, and crossed the room to open a commode. He pulled forth a towel and returned to cleanse her.

'Andrew,' she whispered in a display of sudden alarm. 'I won't get pregnant?'

'No,' he soothed.

She saw shock in his eyes as he rose from the bed and reached for his clothes. In a gesture of contrived confusion she darted from the bed to retrieve her own clothes. In pained silence they both dressed. Maureen's sprained ankle was forgotten.

'Maureen, I don't know what possessed me.' His voice was anguished. 'To take advantage of you when you came to me for help.'

'It was wrong of me to come here.' She lowered her eyes before his tormented gaze. 'You must think I'm awful.' She managed a break in her voice.

'Maureen, no.' His own voice was unsteady. 'It was unforgivable of me.'

'Andrew . . .' She raised her eyes to his. 'Andrew, I'm so scared. Are you sure I won't get pregnant?'

'Sure,' he reiterated.

'I'm so ashamed. But I . . . I never even let a man kiss me before tonight,' she said with a show of shaky bravado. 'You know that. Don't you, Andrew?'

'I know,' he soothed. He hesitated a moment. 'Maureen, I want you to marry me.'

'Oh, Andrew.' Her voice was hushed. Her eyes glistened tenderly. Then she allowed wistfulness to wash away her pleasure. 'No. You're saying that tonight, but you may be sorry tomorrow . . .'

'I won't be sorry.' Elation coloured his voice. 'I love you, Maureen. Will you marry me?'

Everything was working as she had planned.

'When? When, Andrew?'

'In the spring,' he said, with decision. 'April. To give the family a chance to get used to the idea. Honey, I'm so much older than you.'

'I love you, Andrew. It doesn't matter. We'll be married in April,' she agreed. 'Oh, Andrew, I've never been so happy in my whole life.'

21

Caroline sat behind her desk, striving not to lose patience with Sophie and Andrew.

'Caroline, you're buying cotton as though it was never going to be planted again,' Sophie remonstrated. 'Maybe some farmers will hold down next year's crops, but there'll be others who'll go on planting cotton like always.'

'The New York and New Orleans cotton exchanges both reopened in the middle of last month,' Caroline reminded. 'Prices are up already from five to seven and a half cents. They're going to soar.'

'You'll have to spend more to erect the sheds to protect the cotton than you anticipated.' Andrew was worried. 'I've got some figures here.' He spread several columned sheets across her desk. 'Construction costs are going sky-high. They'll eat up our profits.'

'We'll come out ahead,' Caroline insisted. 'If we need more money for the sheds, then I'll borrow again.'

'If you put yourself in further bondage to the banks, they'll dictate orders,' Sophie warned. 'They're already convinced that you coddle your workers.'

'They won't dictate to me,' Caroline was confident. 'I run this mill with Andrew and you. Not with the banks. They know that.'

'It's useless to talk to you.' Sophie shook her head in defeat. 'You're as stubborn as your grandfather.'

Caroline's face softened. 'The General would see exactly what I'm working for. He'd approve.'

'I have some personal news.' Andrew cleared his throat

nervously. Colour flushed his face. 'I'm going to be married in April.'

Caroline gaped at him in shock. *Maureen?* Sophie said Andrew had stopped seeing her.

'Somebody we know?' Sophie asked, her eyes opaque.

'Maureen.' Andrew forced a smile. 'I know she's quite a bit younger than me, but that doesn't bother either of us. It'll be a quiet wedding. We won't even go away. Maureen understands I can't leave the mill with a war going on in Europe.'

'Andrew, I hope you'll be very happy.' Sophie's voice was gentle. 'I won't deny that I'm astonished.'

'We both want to see you happy, Andrew,' Caroline hastened to add. *She couldn't believe he meant this.* 'I know you don't make any decision without giving serious thought.' Yet instinct told her he had given this little consideration. What had happened to Andrew?

'Maureen will continue to work until the week before the wedding.' Andrew sounded simultaneously elated and uneasy. He was forty-four years old, Caroline thought in anguish. Maureen was nineteen. How had she managed to trap him?

'Mr Andrew . . .' One of the foremen hovered in the open doorway. 'We got trouble with two spindles.'

'I'll be right there.' Andrew was relieved to have an excuse to get away from them, Caroline thought.

She waited until Andrew was down the hall, then went to close the door to her office.

'Sophie, he's out of his mind!'

'That was my first reaction,' Sophie acknowledged. 'But maybe it'll be good for him.'

'Why is Andrew marrying that girl? What do we know about her, except that her mother sews for Marian's niece?'

'Maybe that's enough for Andrew.' Sophie was cryptic.

'I'm afraid he's going to be hurt. What does he have in common with Maureen?'

'He's a man and she's a woman,' Sophie said drily. 'Maybe Andrew wants a woman in his bed.'

Caroline was taken aback. 'After all these years, Sophie?'

'Maybe he's tired of crumbs from your table,' Sophie said, and Caroline recoiled. 'Honey, you know Andrew has always idolized you. Now he'll have a woman of his own.'

'I just don't want him to be hurt,' Caroline reiterated, guilty that she was aware of a sense of loss. Andrew was always there to take her to a concert or the theatre or the opera when Eric was unavailable. Now he would have a wife.

'Andrew's always been too much of a recluse. Marriage will pull him out of that,' Sophie surmised. 'Maureen isn't stupid.' All at once cynicism undercoated her voice. 'A stupid woman could never have prodded Andrew into a marriage proposal.'

'I can't believe this is happening.' They should have been aware, Caroline chastised herself. Protected Andrew. 'I'm going to ask Marian to talk to her niece about Maureen's background. What sent her running to Atlanta?'

'You leave them alone, Caroline.' Sophie was sharp. 'Let Andrew handle his life himself.'

'I'll have to ask her to dinner.' Caroline retreated. 'If Maureen is going to marry Andrew, she'll be a Hampton.'

Maureen stood before the mottled mirror in her room and inspected her reflection. She had discarded the black dress from Rich's as being too daring to wear to Hampton House tonight. She wore instead a demure blue crepe that Mama had made two years ago for a customer who

254

abandoned it in a fit of pique. With alterations it fitted her well enough, but it wasn't fashionable this year. Pleasure lent a glow to her eyes. After the wedding she would buy herself the kind of clothes Caroline wore.

Caroline and Sophie must have been shocked out of their minds when Andrew told them he was marrying her. They knew she was marrying him for what he could give her. They never figured maybe there was something she could give him that he never had.

'Maureen,' Mrs Ryan called up the stairs. 'Your gentleman friend is waitin' for you.'

Maureen hurried downstairs to join Andrew, knowing Mrs Ryan and the roomers sitting around the parlour were consumed with curiosity. They'd learn about the wedding when she was ready to tell them.

'I didn't mean to keep you waiting,' Maureen apologized. She made a point of being downstairs when Andrew arrived. She knew he was uncomfortable in the presence of her fellow roomers.

Maureen was abnormally quiet on the drive to the house. She was nervous about meeting the Hampton family on a social level. Not that she didn't know how to handle herself, she bolstered her ebbing self-confidence. Even Mama, who complained she gave herself airs, admitted she could play the tenderly raised young lady as well as her half-sisters.

With Andrew's hand at her elbow, Maureen walked up the stairs and across the wide veranda to the door of Hampton House. Tonight she was a guest. Tonight was a landmark in her life. A fixed smile on her face, she waited with Andrew for the door to be opened.

'Good evenin', Mist' Andrew. Good evenin', miss.' Roland smiled politely.

'This is Miss Maureen, Roland,' Andrew introduced

her. Tonight he seemed to have acquired a new assurance. 'She's going to be my wife.'

'Mist' Andrew, now ain't that somethin'!' Roland beamed. 'She is sure one pretty young lady.'

Roland ushered them into the parlour, where the family was gathering before dinner. Liz was at the piano playing something by Chopin. She stopped playing at their entrance to smile in lively curiosity. Caroline and Sophie were polite in their greeting, as was Eric; but Maureen sensed the women's disapproval. Only with Liz did she feel at ease. She could accept Liz's curiosity.

'Welcome to the family.' Eric's warmth seemed genuine. Again Maureen wondered that Caroline could allow him to go off to Washington alone. There would always be women eager for Eric Hampton's affections.

'Thank you.' She sounded scared. Maureen rebuked herself.

'Where are you going to be married?' Liz had abandoned the piano. She seemed enthralled by the prospect of a wedding in the family.

'I . . . we haven't decided yet.' Maureen turned questioningly to Andrew.

'At the cottage, I think.' Andrew's colour was high. He was uncomfortable, Maureen thought. Had Caroline and Sophie told him they were against his marrying her? 'There'll just be family.' Andrew was struggling to sound relaxed.

'Maureen, can I be a bridesmaid?' Liz asked enthusiastically. 'I'm fourteen.'

'Liz! Don't be impertinent,' Caroline reprimanded.

'I'd love to have you as my bridesmaid, Liz. My maid of honour,' Maureen corrected. 'Nobody else.'

Roland appeared in the parlour doorway to tell Caroline that dinner was to be served. With Andrew's hand at her elbow, Maureen walked with the others into the dining room.

'Will your family be coming to Atlanta for the wedding?' Caroline asked her at a lull in the table conversation.

'I have no family except my mother,' Maureen explained, exuding deferential sweetness. 'If she can manage to leave her shop for a week, then of course she'll come.' Caroline was dying to know more about her. She never would. Mama would not come to the wedding; she would not be invited.

'I hear that many of the Metropolitan Opera singers are marooned in Europe,' Andrew reported while Roland and Elvira appeared with platters of roast beef and braised sweetbreads. Mrs Ryan, complaining about prices, served spaghetti and meatballs or a meat-spare stew as the meat meal of the week. 'Several tenors are in the German Army. Both Toscanini and Caruso are in Italy and members of the reservists.'

'Let's hope Italy manages to stay out.' Eric's eyes were serious.

'Eric, let's not talk about the war at dinner.' Caroline frowned in rejection.

'There's little good to talk about.' Eric's smile was wry. 'Food prices are soaring beyond belief. I won't accept the packers' explanations. I'm convinced they're using the war as an excuse to increase profits.'

Despite her air of enjoyment, the evening was a trial for Maureen. She was going to be a Hampton. She mustn't make any mistakes, say anything that could cause Andrew to reconsider his proposal. But he wouldn't do that. No matter what Caroline or Sophie said, she promised herself, Andrew was going to marry her this coming April.

* * *

Christmas this year was robbed of much of its joy by the presence of war in Europe. The casualties were heavy. By the end of 1914 France estimated her dead at 380,000; another 600,000 were reported wounded, prisoners of war, or missing in action. Germany's losses were slightly less; they had the advantage of better training in defence. No figures were offered for the Russian casualties at Tannenberg, but they were said to be staggering. The defeated Russian General Samsonov committed suicide.

Throughout the United States, women were involved in sewing for the war refugees. By early 1915 the South began to relax; European cotton purchases were stabilizing. The price of cotton was slowly rising. But the crisis was not over. In February the Germans began their submarine blockade of Britain. Britain reciprocated with a blockade of Germany. Russia refused to pilot cotton ships through mines in the Baltic Sea. The British halted shipments to Germany. Again the South experienced panic.

Late in February Caroline looked up from her desk to see Todd Murdoch standing in the door of her office.

'I didn't call for an appointment because I figured you might not see me,' he drawled, striding uninvited into the office and dropping his tall, muscular frame into a chair that flanked her desk. 'You've been buying up a lot of cotton.'

'How does that affect you?' she retaliated. Todd Murdoch had a way of looking at a woman that made her feel naked, Caroline thought in anger.

'You've got a hell of a lot of your funds tied up in cotton, and now there's this rotten business with the German subs. Prices are going to plummet. Cotton will be a glut on the market. You're going to have a struggle selling your merchandise.'

'Mr Murdoch, worry about your mill.' Caroline was

terse. 'I can handle mine. Now, if you'll excuse me, I'm very busy.'

'My people are willing to buy you out at an impressive price.' He was talking business, but his eyes carried on a much more personal conversation. Todd Murdoch couldn't conceive of a woman running a big business, Caroline recognized in irritation. To him a woman was a plaything. Because she was successful in a man's world, he was intrigued. 'Sell now, before you feel the pinch and the offer goes down.'

'Mr Murdoch, I don't feel a pinch. My mill is in a healthy condition. We've just doubled out capacity. I don't want to discuss this further. I don't even want to discuss it again.'

'You will.' His arrogance infuriated her. 'I'm going to own the Hampton Mill within the next six months.'

'Get out of here!' Her colour high, Caroline rose to her feet. 'Get out before I call a foreman to escort you out!'

Todd rose to his feet with a low chuckle, bowed in extravagant politeness, and sauntered from the office.

In the next office Maureen sat frowning before her typewriter. She had been eavesdropping and was disturbed. If Todd took over the mill, Andrew might be in trouble. *Her future was involved.*

'Well, look who's here.' Todd grinned at her from the doorway of her office. 'Still working for Caroline Hampton.'

'For now.' Maureen caught herself from telling him that she was to be married. What had Todd meant when he told Caroline that he could own the Hampton Mill in six months?

'Call me when you feel like having dinner with me again,' Todd said casually. He hadn't bothered to call her once since that night in his house. 'I'm in the phone book.'

Todd Murdoch expected her to jump at his invitation. She was out of her mind over Todd for a while, but not so much that she'd let him have his way with her. She was proud that she had made him play by her rules that night in his big, fancy house.

When Todd moved on, Maureen tried to concentrate on the bills to be typed for Caroline. Her mind refused to cooperate. *What had Todd meant when he said he'd own the Hampton Mill in six months?* Andrew owned part of this mill. What would it mean to Andrew and her if Todd took over?

In a burst of impatience she left her office to seek out Andrew. She found him in the weaving room, repairing a piece of equipment.

'Andrew, can I talk to you for a few minutes?' The urgency in her voice communicated with him.

'Of course, Maureen.' Andrew laid aside his tools and walked with her in silence to his office. 'Honey, what's bothering you?' he asked, closing the door behind him.

'Todd Murdoch was here,' she told him, and gave him a full account of what was said. 'Andrew, I went out with Todd a few times. I was lonely, and he was persuasive. I stopped because he was hard to keep in line. But I'm worried about what Todd said. He'll try anything if he wants this mill.'

'I don't know what he means to do.' Andrew was troubled. 'Murdoch has no business ethics.'

'I could have dinner with him,' Maureen offered. 'He loves to brag about how smart he is in business.' She refrained from telling Andrew how Todd had pumped her for information about the Hampton Mill. 'I might find out something important.'

'Maureen, I won't expose you to that,' Andrew rejected.

'Andrew, we have to know what Todd's planning. That's the only way to fight him.'

'No.' Andrew's voice was firm. 'I won't allow you to put yourself in that position.'

'I'll go with him to the Georgian Terrace for dinner, the way we did before. And then he'll drive me home.' Maureen tried to sound matter-of-fact. 'Andrew, I'll find out why he's so sure he can buy the Hampton Mill.' She felt he was wavering. 'Honey, we can't let Todd Murdoch take over the mill.' Her eyes went limpid in persuasion. She didn't care what happened to Caroline. But this was *her* future at stake. *She was going to be a Hampton.*

'Maureen, I'm touched that you'd do this for us.' Andrew's face was suffused with tenderness. 'But I can't allow it.' He was resolute. 'I'll talk to Caroline. We'll check out the syndicate behind him. Don't worry about this, honey. Todd Murdoch won't take over the Hampton Mill.'

Maureen fretted the remainder of the afternoon. Todd must not be allowed to take over the mill. It would give her pleasure to stop him.

When she heard Andrew talking with Caroline about a Friday-night conference with the mill's accountant, she knew what she would do. Once a month the accountant came into the office. Andrew and Caroline had their dinner on a tray from Hampton House and spent the rest of the evening with the accountant.

Before she left the mill, Maureen phoned Todd. He was elated to hear from her. Yes, he'd be pleased to take her to dinner on Friday. Was he planning to invite her to the house again? It wouldn't matter what happened now, Maureen realized. She could do anything she wanted with Todd. But she wouldn't. He wouldn't have that pleasure.

Friday evening Todd's black Cadillac appeared before Mrs Ryan's rooming house. Maureen had been watching for its arrival. Almost before Todd was out of the car, she was charging through the front door of the house. She knew Mrs Ryan was peeking through the curtains. Inquisitive old witch.

'It's been a long time,' Todd commented, helping her into the car.

He had not bothered to call her, Maureen was on the point of retorting; she decided this would be undiplomatic. Mama used to hold her tongue with the ladies who came to her for sewing and then let loose with shrill denunciations when they left.

'Todd, what were you doing at the Hampton Mill?' Maureen made a show of curiosity. 'I couldn't believe it when I looked up and saw you there.'

'Business.' Todd's eyes were guarded. 'I thought you'd be long gone by now.' His turn to be curious.

'I told you. Caroline pays better than anybody in Atlanta. I got a raise.'

'Did she raise the workers, too?' His interest heightened.

'No,' Maureen lied. 'Though everybody's complaining about how high food is these days.' Caroline had given the workers a raise, even though Sophie carried on against it, fearing if she didn't they'd have a strike on their hands. They couldn't afford a strike, with all that cotton piled up in warehouses and orders pouring in for textile goods. 'Did your mother like the diamond necklace?'

'She loved it.' Todd sounded amused. 'When she found out what it cost, she nearly had a stroke.'

'Where are we having dinner?' Maureen asked.

'Georgian Terrace. You like that, don't you?'

'Oh, yes.'

'That's a beautiful dress you're wearing,' he told her. It was the same black dress she wore the last time Todd took her out. 'Beautiful girl inside that dress.' His voice was a sensuous caress.

'Thank you.' And the beautiful girl was *staying* inside this dress, Maureen promised herself. But sitting beside Todd this way, his thigh pressing against hers, she was reliving that evening at his house. She was remembering the feelings she had never expected to experience. But she was not going to start up again with Todd. *She was going to marry Andrew Hampton.*

At the restaurant Todd and she were greeted with the cordial warmth she remembered. She saw his pleased awareness of the glances they were garnering. He was making a point of being charming. After dinner, she surmised, he was going to invite her to his house again.

Tonight Todd wasn't talking business. How was she going to get him to talk about the Hampton Mill? By the time dessert arrived – a dramatic flaring concoction that enraptured everybody around them – Maureen knew she would have to move quickly.

'You know, Todd . . .' She made a pretence of hesitancy. 'I really shouldn't talk like this before I tell Caroline. I'm going to quit in another month. I hate working in a mill.' She grimaced in distaste. 'I can't stand Caroline.'

'You won't have any trouble finding a job,' Todd reassured her. Under the table his knee found hers. 'How would you like to work for me? Oh, but you don't like working in a mill,' he chided before she could reply.

'I don't like working in the Hampton Mill,' she said. 'I don't like working for Caroline. I wouldn't like working for any woman,' she added with unexpected candour, and Todd chuckled.

263

'Honey, you and Caroline are just natural-born enemies.'

'Todd, I heard you tell Caroline you'll own the Hampton Mill in six months. Is she going to sell to you?'

'She doesn't know it yet, but she will. I made up my mind to own the Hampton Mill the first month I was in Atlanta. If you've got the money, you find a way to buy what you want. Why don't you hang on at the mill. When I buy, you'll be my secretary. There'll be lots of night work,' he warned, his invitation blatant.

'Todd, are you serious?' Maureen made a pretence of being enthralled at this prospect. The bastard. He'd underpay her as his secretary and have her in his bed for nothing. She'd die before she'd let any man use her that way. 'No, you're teasing me,' she scolded. 'Caroline won't ever sell. That rotten mill means more to her than anything else in the world.'

'Even Caroline Hampton can be brought to heel.' For a moment he looked as though he had a personal vendetta against Caroline, she thought. No, she corrected herself in astonishment. He was wishing he could throw Caroline Hampton on her back, the way he did every other woman who took his fancy. 'You'll see, Maureen.' Todd was smug. 'I'll own the Hampton Mill.'

'Nobody's going to make Caroline sell that mill,' Maureen said airily. 'Not even Todd Murdoch.'

'Todd Murdoch and his money syndicate,' he stipulated. 'Caroline's out of her mind, the way she's been buying up cotton on top of building that huge annexe. She's in to the bank for a fortune.'

'That doesn't seem to bother her,' Maureen retaliated.

'It will.' Todd's eyes glistened. 'We've just negotiated for a controlling interest in the bank. I'm calling in her notes in sixty days. No renewals. Caroline Hampton won't have a pot to piss in. Excuse me,' he said with exaggerated politeness. 'In sixty days Caroline Hampton won't have a mill to run. The bank will own the mill. I'll run it.'

22

Caroline sat in the library, her coffee growing cold while she listened to Andrew. Elvira had been dispatched upstairs to fetch Sophie, who had retired to her room.

'I was against Maureen's pursuing this, but she was insistent,' Andrew explained. 'Thank God, she did. As soon as Murdoch took her to her rooming house, she phoned me. Caroline, the man means to take over the mill.'

'He won't,' Caroline promised.

'Has something happened?' Sophie strode into the library.

'Andrew's been briefing me on Todd Murdoch's plans for the Hampton Mill.' She had said nothing to either Sophie or Andrew about Todd's visit to the mill. She had assumed he was trying to bluff her into selling. Now she gave Sophie a full report.

'When are the notes due?' Sophie was apprehensive.

'The first batch in two weeks,' Caroline admitted. 'The bulk in sixty days. I'd planned on an automatic renewal.'

'Todd Murdoch won't allow that,' Andrew pointed out. 'That doesn't give you much time to make a deal with another bank.'

'Time enough.' Caroline forced an optimistic smile. 'The Atlanta banks are in good shape. I'll put up everything I can lay my hands on as collateral. Even Hampton Court. We'll pay those notes. Todd Murdoch and his syndicate won't take over the Hampton Mill.' Caroline prodded herself to say what she knew was required of her. 'I must thank Maureen for giving us this warning. We'd have been hard-pressed without notice.'

'We'll be hard-pressed *with* notice.' Sophie was upset at the prospect of Hampton Court's being mortgaged.

'Sophie, nobody's taking over the mill,' Caroline vowed. 'I'll be at the banks tomorrow morning.' Her mind was devising an approach. 'I'll take loans at three separate banks. I'll raise the money to pay off those notes. Trust me, Sophie.'

What other banks were under Todd Murdoch's control? Caroline conjectured. Before she approached any bank, she must make sure who held the majority shares. Only then could she negotiate. Within sixty days the transactions must be consummated.

Senator Bolton called Eric from Washington, urging him to be in the city for the final days of the Sixty-third Congress, in session for an unprecedented nineteen months. The senator considered it a propitious time to introduce Eric to key figures who would be returning to the Sixty-fourth Congress. One of the senator's favourite sayings was that 'it helps to play poker with the Speaker of the House'.

'You'll stay with Marian and me, of course,' the senator wound up his phone call. 'Plan on being in Washington for at least four or five weeks. We have work to do.'

Late that evening Eric sat in Serena's parlour in the rented house on Piedmont Road and told her he would be leaving for Washington the next day. He had thought much about Serena and himself these past weeks. He knew that there were congressmen who enjoyed illicit affairs in Washington. He knew how infrequently they remained secret. Serena said nothing about travelling with him to Washington, yet he knew she had considered this.

'With Senator Bolton pushing you, you'll be properly launched, Congressman,' Serena told him while she poured the espresso she had learned to make in Italy and taught Eric to enjoy. 'In a dozen years you may be moving into the White House.' Her voice was convivial, unlike her eyes.

'If the winds are right.' Eric shrugged. He was going to Washington without Caro and the children. To be deprived of Serena would be painful. He could hire Serena to be part of his official staff in Washington. He contemplated the possibility briefly.

'Eric, I'm accepting a job offer in San Francisco.'

'When did you decide this?' Eric was shaken.

'I think I decided it back in Veracruz.' Serena was candid. 'The night you made love to me and called me "Caro".'

'Honey,' Eric expostulated, 'that was an old habit.'

'Eric, we've had a wonderful interlude. But that's all it can ever be. I'm second best,' she pinpointed, her eyes serious. 'Fine enough for an interlude, but I'd like to find a man for the long-term deal. Somebody with whom I won't be second-string.'

'Serena, I can't imagine not having you close by. You've become important in my life.' Yet he knew Serena was right. No matter how furious he was at Caro's behaviour, her refusal to recognize his needs, he knew that Caro remained the one woman in his life whom he would ever love completely.

'You stick to your guns there in Washington,' Serena ordered with mock ferociousness. 'All this talk of preparedness scares the hell out of me. You be the vote in Congress that fights for peace.'

'You know I will,' Eric chided. 'That's the driving force that sends me to Washington. I think of Josh. He's twelve years old. If this insanity in Europe continues and we're drawn into it, Josh could be in the army in six years.'

'Wilson won't let it happen,' Serena insisted, but Eric saw the doubt in her eyes. She was thinking about Teddy Roosevelt and Henry Cabot Lodge. 'Too many people in this country want to keep us out of the war.'

He could talk with such contempt about nations that refused to allow the world to live in peace. He ranted against the recurrence of war in every generation; but not even within his own family, Eric jeered at himself, he could not maintain the peace. In his own household there was war. Caro and he in silent battle.

The following day Eric left for Washington. Rain assaulted the Eastern Seaboard, continuing through the night and into the following morning. Since leaving Atlanta, the Pullman in which Eric rode had seemed isolated from civilization except for those minutes when it paused to disgorge or accept passengers. Its phalanx of windows was opaque from the relentless downpour, but from habit Eric sat with his eyes on the window.

In five days he would take office as congressman from his district. Already the wheels were in motion for his Atlanta office, which Jim would head in his absences. Arriving in Washington as congressman-elect should be a memorable occasion. He felt cheated of the joy that should be his.

Caro had said not one word to him about the trouble facing her with the bank because of Todd Murdoch and his syndicate. Sophie told him. Caro seemed optimistic about consummating a deal with another bank, before Murdoch could call in her notes. Still, these were tricky times. She was in a precarious position.

The conductor moved through the cars, alerting passengers to the imminent arrival in Union Station. Eric reached for his luggage. This was a hell of a time for him

269

to be in Washington; Caro was gambling with the family fortune.

Caroline sat in a comfortable leather-upholstered armchair in the wood-panelled office of the president of the Fifth National Bank and explained her financial requirements.

'Mrs Hampton, you're asking for an enormous loan.' He was disquieted by her request.

'I'm asking you to provide one-third of my needs,' Caroline stipulated. 'I'm approaching two other banks for equal amounts. I realize the situation at this time, but my assets would comfortably cover fifty such loans.' She must dispel his doubts. If the Fifth National approved one loan, the other two would be simple to acquire.

'In normal times, yes,' he conceded. 'We don't know what'll happen to the cotton market in the next forty-eight hours.'

'Mr Bullock, I own more cotton at this moment than any other mill in the state. I'm not concerned that the price is going to drop. We're in the midst of a war that's consuming gunpowder in horrifying quantities. And gunpowder consists mainly of cotton. The *Queen Elizabeth* uses a bale of cotton each time one of her fifteen-inch guns is fired. Every great nation in the world is after Southern cotton to convert into smokeless powder. Can you possibly worry that the price could drop?'

'With the price of cotton up to nine cents already, and knowing how much you have warehoused, I'm surprised that you won't sell.' The banker was curious. 'You'd save interest charges.'

'I won't sell a bale until the price rises to twenty-five cents.' Caroline smiled at Bullock's astonishment. 'It'll reach at least twenty-five cents. Possibly thirty. But the day it goes to twenty-five cents a pound, I'll sell what we won't require for our own manufacture for the next year.'

'Mrs Hampton, you never cease to amaze me. Beauty and brains, plus an uncanny business sense,' Bullock said in a surge of gallantry. 'How many times does a man encounter all these qualities in one dainty lady?'

'Mr Bullock, what about my loan?'

'Mrs Hampton, it's yours. I'll have my secretary draw up the papers. They'll be delivered to you by hand.'

Encouraged by her success at the first bank, Caroline tackled the next two on her list. Both admitted to heavy commitments, yet agreed to consider the substantial loans she requested. They requested extensive information, which under normal circumstances Caroline would have considered an outrage. She realized they were delaying tactics until the banks could negotiate their internal business to accommodate her.

Leaving the third bank, Caroline decided to go home for lunch instead of returning directly to the mill. Only now did she realize how exhausted she was from the morning's efforts. And she was tense in the realization that the loans must come through within the next sixty days if she was to save the mill from Todd Murdoch's conniving hands.

Driving up before the house, Caroline heard someone at the piano. Not Liz, she realized. Liz played beautifully. What she heard was a one-finger rendition of 'Twinkle, Twinkle, Little Star'. Puzzled, she left the car and went into the house.

'Roland, who's at the piano?'

'I 'spect it's Miss Liz,' Roland said.

'She home from school today,' Elvira said.

'Thank you, Roland.'

Caroline paused at the entrance to the parlour. Liz sat

271

at the piano bench with Francis beside her. *Francis was playing the piano.*

'Mama, don't be mad,' Liz pleaded, striving to appear wan and wistful. 'I stayed home because I've got cramps. Elvira brought me hot tea and a hot-water bottle, and it's all right now. I'll go to school tomorrow,' she cajoled.

'Yes, you'll go tomorrow.' Though part of her mind was overwhelmed by what she observed, she was firm. Liz had early discovered the ability to skip school one day a month on the basis, of 'Mama, I've got such awful cramps.'

Francis looked up from the piano with a beatific smile. 'Liz teached me, Mama. Listen.'

Caroline stood beside the piano while Francis played again for her the brief melody he had learned. How happy he was in this accomplishment, she thought tenderly. Victor once told her that children like Francis sometimes learned to play a musical instrument. Most of them loved music.

Patience came into the room.

'Time for your lunch, Francis.' Patience took him by the hand without protest and led him off to the breakfast room.

Liz joined Caroline in the library for a tray luncheon. She was delighted for this company, Caroline sensed, and was pleased.

'Mama, when will we know about the Supreme Court's decision on Mr Frank?' Liz was all at once serious. 'Why is it taking so long?'

'The Supreme Court has many cases to handle, Liz. I'm sure there'll be word soon.' Caroline strove to appear optimistic. 'But let's not think about that now. We have to talk with Maureen about your dress for the wedding. We can't wait until the last minute to have it made.'

Liz's face lit up. She was enthralled at the prospect of being Maureen's maid of honour.

'Mama, do you suppose she'll let me wear pink? I want to wear pink,' Liz said dreamily. 'And carry a bouquet of pink rosebuds.'

Eric had promised to be back from Washington for the wedding. He had been calling home every Sunday evening. Each time, she heard the constraint in his voice. She had felt a terrible loneliness when he was in The Hague and again when he went down to Mexico for the senator; but there was a special pain in this separation.

Eric arrived from Washington the day before the wedding, warning the family that he would have to return to Washington the day after. He was engrossed in Capital activities.

'I'm up at seven sharp,' he told Caroline and Sophie while they sat on the veranda in the balmy night air. 'Downstairs at breakfast with the senator by seven-thirty. We sit there at the table reading the Washington *Post*, the New York *Times*, and the Atlanta papers the senator has delivered regularly. By nine o'clock we're off and running.' All at once Eric was serious. 'I understand why the senator was so insistent on my being in Washington at this time. He's introducing me to all the powerful Democrats. The party faces problems this coming session.'

'Is the Washington social life as hectic as Marian claims?' Sophie asked, ever curious about the customs of other places.

'Sophie, it never stops.' Eric shook his head in bafflement. 'Unbelievable.' Particularly for an unattached man, Caroline thought in fresh comprehension. A lone congressman would be invited everywhere.

'How much longer will you be in Washington?' Sophie voiced the question Caroline could not bring herself to ask. 'I mean, before you have to go for the opening of Congress.'

'I'll go back for just another two weeks,' Eric said appeasingly. 'The senator has some meetings set up.'

Perhaps Eric was going back for just two weeks, Caroline assessed. But Washington was already his life. For fifteen years they had shared everything. She would have no part in the existence Eric would shape for himself in the Capital.

Standing the next afternoon in Andrew's parlour while he waited at the improvised altar with Eric as his best man, Caroline visualized her own wedding. She had gone to Eric with such love. With a conviction that nothing save death would ever separate them. Now she was letting him go alone to Washington.

Smiling broadly, Phoebe appeared in the doorway to indicate that the bride was ready. Miss Emily, the tall angular harpist who presided at many Atlanta weddings, plucked at the strings. The poignant strains of 'Oh, Promise Me' filtered across the parlour. Miss Emily had played 'Oh, Promise Me' when she married Eric.

Liz appeared at the doorway. Exquisite in delicate pink pussy-willow silk and carrying pink rosebuds she walked down the improvised aisle to the altar. Caroline's eyes involuntarily moved to Eric. He was gazing not at Liz but at her. Disconcerted, her smile tremulous, Caroline swung her eyes to the doorway.

Pale and composed, Maureen followed Liz down the aisle. Her wedding gown had been ordered through *Harper's Bazaar*'s personal shopping service in New York City. She wore old point lace draped in a single flounce over a foundation of cloth of silver. Her court train of silver cloth held sprays of orange blossoms. The tulle veil was held in place by a bandeau of pearls, forming a becoming frame for her face.

Phoebe, Mattie, and Elvira hovered in the doorway while the minister read the service. Josh squirmed in restlessness. Her smile fixed, Sophie was an attentive guest. Caroline felt an unexpected compunction at the sparse attendance. How sad that Maureen's mother had been unable to come to Atlanta for the wedding.

After the ceremony, Phoebe, with the help of Mattie and Elvira, served an elaborate wedding dinner. Maureen's colour was high, her eyes triumphant when she cut the wedding cake. The seamstress' daughter had married into one of the first families of Atlanta.

Caroline sat in the library and fidgeted. When would Victor return to the house with Francis? He had said nothing to her about taking Francis on an outing. Only when she came in from the mill this afternoon did she learn from Patience that Victor had arrived earlier than normal and had taken Francis to visit somewhere.

Since the family had stopped going together to Hampton Court for the summer, Francis had not travelled beyond the front lawns of Hampton House. It upset him to face unfamiliar surroundings, strangers.

'Miss Caroline, Francis be fine with Dr Victor,' Patience soothed, bringing her a cup of tea.

'I know he will.' Caroline smiled, yet she strained to know what was happening. 'You said they left the house before two?'

'Yes'm. And Francis, he was so excited.' Though Patience made a show of confidence, Caroline knew that she, too, was anxious. This was an enormous step forward for Francis.

Ten minutes later Caroline heard a car arrive in front of

the house. She put aside her cup and leaped to her feet. Patience was running down the hall to the front door.

'I went to school!' Francis crowed, his eyes brilliant in his excitement. He spied his mother. 'Mama, I went to school! I played with a boy. We painted!'

'Francis, how lovely.' Caroline's heart was pounding. 'What else did you do?'

'Some things.' Francis' exuberance was waning. He yawned.

'You go upstairs and take a nap,' Caroline encouraged, giving Patience a meaningful glance. 'You're tired from going to school.'

'Wanna sleep.' Francis yawned again. Patience reached down to pick him up, and without a protest started up the stairs.

Caroline stood at the foot of the stairs, watching Patience's progress.

'Were you worried?' Victor was solicitous.

'He was with you,' Caroline said. 'Why would I worry? Come into the library and let's have tea.'

'I wasn't sure until this morning that I could arrange to have Francis be a visitor at the private kindergarten,' Victor explained while they walked to the library. 'I didn't want to disappoint you if they refused.'

'And he wasn't frightened? He was willing to stay?'

'He was scared to death at first,' Victor admitted. 'But intrigued by the other children. A couple of times I expected him to bolt. But he remained in the classroom for twenty minutes. That's a beginning, Caro.'

'He went willingly in the car?' Caroline questioned.

'I assumed he would.' Victor's matter-of-factness was reassuring. 'If I had let him suspect otherwise, he might have balked.'

'He used to sit on my lap in the car and hide his face

276

against my shoulder,' Caroline reminisced. 'He was terrified.'

'We're through the worst. I'll take him to the kindergarten twice a week, stretching out the period each time. We don't know that Francis won't resist,' Victor warned. 'But we'll try.'

On April 19 the United States Supreme Court rejected Leo Frank's plea for a writ of habeas corpus. He was scheduled to die on June 22. The governor and the prison commission were bombarded with letters and petitions pleading for commutation of Frank's sentence. They came from every state in the union, from Canada and Mexico. From governors, congressmen, financiers. The president of the University of Chicago and the dean of Yale College.

Mass meetings were held throughout the nation. This was a plea for commutation on a scale never known in this country. Leo Frank himself was receiving more than fifteen hundred letters daily. Thousands of petitions were gathered together, containing over a million signatures.

Each night at dinner Liz reported on her own efforts. Janet and she were helping add names to the petition being circulated by David and other friends of Leo Frank.

'We've got a lot of teachers in our schools,' Liz reported. 'But some won't sign.' Her face was unhappy. 'They believe Mr Frank killed Mary Phagan.'

'I know, darling.' How could she tell Liz that many Georgians were determined to see Leo hanged? Caroline asked herself. They were blind to the overwhelming evidence against Jim Conley. They ignored Judge Roan's statements that he was uncertain of Frank's guilt, that he had shown 'undue deference to the opinion of the jury'. Tom Watson was responsible for much of that. Watson was building new power for himself by crusading against the 'jewpervert'.

'When will the governor commute Mr Frank's sentence?' Liz refused to consider that this might not happen.

'The prison commission meets at the end of May to consider it.'

'Mama, this isn't even the end of April,' Liz said in exasperation.

'We'll have to wait. Papa's coming home in a few days,' Caroline reminded, hoping to lift Liz's spirits. 'Perhaps we can go up to Hampton Court for a weekend.'

'You won't take Francis to Hampton Court.' Liz was sceptical.

'I think he's ready for that.' Pleasure warmed her. 'I'll talk to Victor about it tomorrow.' Perhaps Victor would come with them. It would be beautiful this time of year. She would enjoy showing Hampton Court to Victor.

Early next morning, shortly after her arrival at the mill, Eric telephoned Caroline from Washington. He never called her at the mill. In inchoate unease she searched her mind for a reason for this call, while Eric made perfunctory inquiries about the children and she responded.

'Caro, I have to go to Europe on an assignment for the senator.' He was speaking guardedly now. 'The senator would like it to appear that I'm going to Liverpool and then on to London on business for the mill. If any questions arise, cover me on this.'

'Of course,' she agreed automatically, then stopped short. 'Eric, how can you go to Europe at a time like this? The seas are infested with German U-boats!'

'I'm going on a ship that can outrun any submarine.' Eric chuckled.

'Eric, this sounds dangerous.'

'Not at all. Senator Bolton's committee just wants

278

some answers. Beyond what Colonel House is sending back.'

For several minutes they delved into this situation, and then again Caroline revealed her anxiety about his trip. 'Eric, you'll come home before you leave?'

'I can't. The senator already has a booking for me. I sail on May 1 from New York.'

'What ship?'

'The *Lusitania*. She's been sailing between Liverpool and New York regularly with no problems. I'll call you when we arrive in Liverpool,' Eric promised.

23

Valise in hand, Eric walked into the south entrance of the monumental white Vermont granite Union Station. He went into the huge colonnaded waiting room with its barrel-vaulted ceiling ninety-five feet above the floor and sat on one of the high-backed benches. Sunlight filtered into the room through the semicircular windows above the five massive archways that led to the concourse.

A pretty young woman with a small child sat down beside him on the bench. She reminded him of Caroline, not only in appearance but in her warmth towards the little boy whom she was cajoling into good humour. Caroline had sounded disappointed that he was not coming home before going to England.

Now he wondered: What did it matter if he came home or not? Caroline had little room in her life for him. From habit she worried about him. The way she worried about the children. Damn, that was not the relationship he expected of his wife!

Sitting on the hard waiting-room bench, impatient for his train to be announced, Eric was conscious of physical desire. On endless nights, lying in his bed in one of the Boltons' elegant guest rooms, tired but too keyed up from the day's activities to fall immediately to sleep, he asked himself what he could have done to save his marriage.

For a while Serena had assuaged his physical needs. More than that, he conceded in honesty. Serena had been a replacement for Caro. But even Serena had realized that Caro was the woman he would always love. At last the departure of the New York-bound train was announced. Eric hurried through the immense concourse and boarded his train.

In New York Eric spent the night at the new Ritz Carlton Hotel on Madison Avenue. Over an early breakfast the next morning he scanned the pages of the New York *Sun*. An advertisement on the shipping page brought him to a halt:

NOTICE! TRAVELLERS intending to embark on the Atlantic voyage are reminded that a state of war exists between Germany and her allies and Great Britain and her allies; that the zone of war includes the waters adjacent to the British Isles; that, in accordance with formal notice given by the Imperial German government, vessels flying the flag of Great Britain or any of her allies are liable to destruction in those waters and that travellers sailing in the war zone on ships of Great Britain or her allies do so at their own risk. IMPERIAL GERMAN EMBASSY, WASHINGTON, DC, APRIL 22, 1915.

Eric scowled. What was the German government trying to pull off? Capable of twenty-six knots an hour, the *Lusitania*, though a British ship, could hardly be in danger; it could outrun any submarine in existence. He had no intention of cancelling his booking to sail on the antiquated *New York*.

Arriving at the Cunard Line's Pier 54 almost two hours before the noon sailing time, Eric inspected the four-funnelled 45,000-ton ship before boarding. God, she was huge. A floating six-storey hotel. A stroll about her promenade deck would probably come to a quarter of a mile.

Nobody would be unduly alarmed by the advertisement. Probably some prankster placed it in the *Sun*. The *Lusitania* was a noncombatant ship, operating within the law of nations, which stated that no ship might be sunk without prior warning and evacuation of civilian passengers. For ten months ships had been sailing, despite the hostilities, without incident.

Heading towards the ship, Eric noticed a cluster of reporters and a movie newsreel team at the foot of the gangplank, gathered around a couple with two small children, who were about to aboard the *Lusitania*. Eric stared in curiosity.

'Aren't you afraid to sail under these conditions?' a reporter demanded of the young man as Eric approached. 'You saw this, didn't you?' The reporter held up a folded back page of a newspaper.

'Oh, my God!' The man blanched. 'No, we didn't see it.'

'It's probably a bad joke,' the young woman with him decided in annoyance. 'Of course, we'll sail.'

'What about you, sir?' Another reporter pounced on Eric, and the others deserted their earlier quarry to join him. 'Did you know about this?'

'I saw it at breakfast,' Eric acknowledged. 'It seems unrealistic that any U-boat on the seas could catch up with the *Lusitania*.' He paused. 'However, I'm travelling alone. I wouldn't dare take the responsibility of travelling with my family.'

On board, Eric realized that many of the passengers had not seen the warning in the morning newspapers. The word was racing about the ship now. The usual 'bon voyage' spirit was missing. Passengers gathered in small, anxious groups. How many were fighting to muster up the courage to cancel before the ship sailed?

'A dozen passengers have asked me not to unpack for them,' Eric heard one steward whisper to another. 'They're scared to death.'

Shortly after noon the *Lusitania* sailed. Flags were

hoisted to signal the British cruisers blockading the three-mile limit that she was approaching. All afternoon Eric fought to brush away a feeling of impending disaster.

At dinner Eric admired the first-class dining saloon, elegant in its Louis XVI white-and-gold decor, the predominating colour a restful *vieux* rose. He smiled in agreement as passengers exclaimed at the splendour of the gilt-ornamented mahogany sideboard, the magnificent lofty dome with its Boucher-like painted panels. The food and service were superb.

After dinner Eric retired to the Late Georgian Lounge, adorned with inlaid mahogany panels, marble mantelpieces, and a dome ceiling. He was conscious of the stark difference between this first night on board and his first night on board the *Rotterdam* slightly less than two years ago. He had travelled to The Hague with such hopes for world peace. He had met Serena that first night aboard the *Rotterdam*.

Usually on board ship Eric was able to disassociate himself from worry. Time at sea was for him – on previous occasions – a respite from reality. Now he discovered enforced idleness was a trap. The situation between Caro and himself haunted him.

Scheduled activities on board ship included daily deck sports and evening entertainments. However, passengers were tense and watchful.

On the third day aboard ship a few more outspoken passengers approached Captain Turner to request a boat drill among the passengers, in the event the published warning was not a bluff.

Captain Turner rejected this, pointing out that a U-boat travelled at around nine knots submerged. Even on the surface, the best of them could not do more than fifteen knots. The *Lusitania* could outdistance any German U-boat that approached. However, the captain did not tell them that because of the sharp rise in the price of coal and falloff in passengers the Cunard board had decided to cut overheads. The engine-room crew was decreased by eighty-three men, and thus the use of one of the boiler rooms was eliminated. As a result, maximum speed was dropped from twenty-six knots to twenty-one, and the cruising speed from twenty-four knots to eighteen.

Tension on board increased as the days moved past. By Thursday morning most passengers knew the *Lusitania* was approaching the war zone. Eric arose early to take a brisk walk on deck before breakfast. He realized the ship's speed had been diminished. He saw members of the crew swinging out the lifeboats and removing their tarpaulin covers.

The *Lusitania* carried forty-eight, his mind tallied. Twenty-two were conventional wooden boats suspended from davits. Twenty-six were collapsibles with wood bases and canvas sides and could be set up on board or in the water. The capacity of each boat ranged from fifty to seventy.

Eric saw that double lookouts had been posted. Later in the day the stewards were ordered to black out the cabin port-holes. The captain requested that the gentlemen refrain from lighting their after-dinner cigars on deck.

In the first-class smoking room that evening Captain Turner responded to the nervous questioning of some of the passengers.

'We've received a submarine warning. We're taking routine precautions.' Captain Turner spoke with commendable British calm. 'In the morning we'll welcome a cruiser alongside to guide us into Liverpool. On entering the war zone tomorrow, we shall be securely in the care of the Royal Navy.'

Eric slept little that night. He awoke to an early morning drenched in fog. When he dressed and went on deck, he estimated visibility at no more than ninety feet. The ship had slowed down to fifteen knots. The foghorn blared an eerie symphony.

Eric saw no cruiser alongside. He worried that they had missed it in the fog.

Later in the morning the fog lifted. The sun rose, full and strong. The sea was calm. Passengers were aware of a faint blur on the horizon that the crew identified as the coast of Ireland. Speed was increased to eighteen knots. By the time lunch was served, the spirits of the passengers soared. The Irish coast was in clear sight. The *Lusitania* was heading for shore.

After lunch Eric settled himself at the rail to watch the progress of the ship. In the distance, high on a bluff, he saw what he guessed was a lighthouse. That would be Old Head of Kinsale. For two thousand years the Old Head of Kinsale had been a landmark to ships at sea.

Captain Turner was navigating into Queenstown without pilot or tugs. Fortunately this channel was said to be swept daily for mines, Eric recalled.

'How far are we from land?' a middle-aged nursemaid, clutching a restless tow-headed toddler in her arms, paused beside Eric to inquire.

'I imagine no more than a dozen miles,' Eric told her, then turned cold with shock. About six hundred feet beyond, he spied the periscope of a submarine.

'What is that?' The nursemaid's voice was shrill with terror as her eyes fastened, along with Eric's, on a streak of white foam heading towards the ship. 'Is it a torpedo?' Her face was ashen.

The German warning had not been a bluff. A twelve-foot-long torpedo travelled about three feet below the surface. Eric propelled himself into action.

'Go to your stateroom for your life belt,' he ordered the woman. 'Fast!'

'The baby!' the nursemaid shrieked, and darted off towards the nursery on the shelter deck.

Eric heard shouts from a trio of passengers down the deck who had also spied the torpedo. Seconds later an explosion rocked the ship, thrusting it into a fifteen-degree list to starboard. A tremendous column of water and debris shot up to the bridge deck. Steam enveloped the iron forepart of the vessel. Eric was flung to the deck.

Recovering his equilibrium, Eric staggered to his feet. The hull of the ship had been blown open. He saw a gaping hole probably forty feet wide and fifteen feet high.

A second explosion came. My God, Eric thought, we're carrying ammunition! Moments later an order ricocheted about the ship.

'*Lower the boats and abandon ship.*'

The list of the ship was growing worse. The foredeck was swept totally under water. The sea was pushing through the forward hatches, over the bulkheads. Water poured into the open portholes on the lower deck. Eric knew that countless passengers must be trapped below. There was nothing he – anyone – could do to save them.

The decks were swarming with confused, frightened people. Like other male passengers, Eric hurried to help the crew with the lifeboats. It would be difficult to lower them, he saw in alarm. Because of the list, they swung in across the deck. They would have to be pushed over the side.

'Don't lower the boats!' a crew member called out. 'Captain's orders!' He turned to Eric and the men working with him. 'The captain says we've got to clear the decks.'

But the frantic passengers had not waited. They had piled into unprepared boats until there was not an inch of unoccupied space, and pleaded to be lowered over the side.

'Push the boat out from the side!' a male voice yelled, and hands rushed to comply.

The boat, loaded mainly with women and children, crashed against the side of the ship and dumped its occupants screaming into the sea. Sickened by the carnage, Eric was compelled to witness one boat after another crash against the side of the ship and splinter, occupants crushed to death or thrown, injured, into the sea. The sounds of their agonized screams blended with the clamour of passengers fighting for places in the remaining boats.

Eric pushed his way through the chaos on deck to his stateroom. He grabbed his life jacket and put it on. The starboard list was now at twenty-five degrees. The port boat deck seethed with terrified humanity. People were jumping into the sea. Eric stared down at the maze of wreckage. Deck chairs, boxes, rubble, bodies, floated in the water. Passengers were struggling to swim to empty, overturned lifeboats that had been swept into the sea.

'My baby! My baby!' a woman screamed, pushing through the panic-gripped horde.

In the big entrance hall a cluster of passengers were tying life jackets on to the baskets in which many of the babies aboard had been sleeping before the torpedo struck. Eric threw himself into this effort.

Suddenly the bow of the *Lusitania* was plunging downward. A rush of water swept into the hall. Eric felt himself carried out on to the deck, over the rail, and into the sea. He was conscious of a devastating pain at the back of his head. In his right ankle.

The water was cold and green. Numb with shock, Eric saw hundreds of heads bobbing between islands of debris. Dead bodies floating – men, women, children, infants. A hundred yards beyond, he spied a boat, and then another and another. Six in all. Hands were reaching from the boats to pull in survivors.

Quickly the boats were crammed with humanity. No space remained for myriad others – like himself – who depended upon life jackets or a floating deck chair or a piece of lumber to keep afloat. The *Lusitania* had disappeared.

Beside him a small body in a life jacket floated face down. Fighting a wave of sickness, he reached for the child, hoping that a wisp of life remained. Eric held the dead body in his arms for a few minutes before releasing it to the sea. Twenty minutes ago the tiny boy had been in the arms of the nursemaid who stood beside him at the rail.

Suddenly Eric heard voices raised in song. 'Nearer My God to Thee.' They belonged to members of a professional group who had entertained last night in the smoking room.

A life-jacketed man a few feet from him began to scream hysterically, his arms flailing the air. Despite his pain, Eric managed to swim to the man, stretched a hand to slap him hard across one cheek. He shrieked, then subsided into sobs.

'Hold on, old man,' Eric gasped. 'Hold on.'

'We're going to die,' the man beside Eric moaned. 'We're going to die.'

'Boats will come,' Eric promised, extending a hand in comfort.

As Eric leaned towards the man beside him, he realized his wallet was slipping from his jacket pocket. He reached in one convulsive movement, but the wallet was beyond his grasp. The contents floated clear of the wallet.

Eric spied a photograph. *Caro*. His lungs bursting, one leg useless, he pulled his hand free from his companion to swim towards the scrap of paper that carried the image of his wife. Absurd relief welled within him when he brought the photograph close to his eyes. Caro was with him. The one woman in his life he had ever truly loved.

24

Caroline sat at her desk struggling to focus on the sales figures before her. The sunny May morning had given way to a humid, overcast afternoon. In another forty minutes she would leave for the house. Why was she so restless today?

The loans had come through. Todd Murdoch was no threat to the mill. Already the nation was beginning to feel a developing prosperity, though cotton farmers complained that this was only for the munitions and steel manufacturers.

Her eyes settled on the calendar. May 7. Tomorrow Eric would be in Liverpool. At recurrent intervals she worried about his travelling in Europe. But he would be in Liverpool and London, she rationalized – not on a battlefield. She hoped he had taken along a light coat. London could be cool in May.

She left the mill at three sharp, as always. Today Victor was taking Francis to be a guest at the private school again. On the last visit Francis had stayed for an hour without asking to be brought home. Wistfully she wished she could share these small triumphs with Eric. He was so determined to make himself accept Francis' condition as 'God's will' that he couldn't see the parade of small improvements that brought such joy to her.

Caroline settled herself in the library, still fighting restlessness. Elvira brought her tea and the English biscuits she liked. How much longer would these tea biscuits be coming over from London? Food was being rationed in England. She remembered that Liz and Josh were remaining at school this afternoon for a fair. With this threatening weather the fair would be held indoors, she guessed. At the sound of a car pulling up before the house, she was on her feet, ever anxious when Francis was visiting the school.

She pulled the door wide, a smile in readiness for Francis.

'I think we're just ahead of the storm.' Victor's voice was casual, yet Caroline sensed a current of excitement in him. Sometimes she felt closer to Victor than anyone else alive. They shared Francis; they shared a dream.

Caroline reached down to bring Francis to her for the usual affectionate hug. She could remember when she would not have dared hug or kiss Francis. Now he courted these indications of love.

'Did you have fun at the school?'

'Un-hunh.' His small arms tightened about her neck.

Instantly she was concerned. Had Francis been frightened, and ashamed to tell Victor? Her eyes searched his face.

No, she decided in relief. He was fine. He would not have a nightmare tonight.

'Here comes Patience,' Caroline turned towards the stairs. 'You go out to the breakfast room and have some fruit and milk.'

'Not yet, Mama,' Francis rejected with a new air of assurance.

'Francis has something to ask you,' Victor explained, his demeanour serious, but Caroline felt his inner exhilaration. 'Go ahead, Francis,' he encouraged.

'Mama, I want to go to school. Not just a little bit.' He was stammering in his excitement. '*The whole time*. Can I, Mama?' His eyes pleaded with her.

'But the school year is almost over.' Now it was Caroline who was stammering. 'I don't know if they'll let you.' *Francis was asking to go to school. He wasn't afraid.* The miracle she had prayed for was happening. 'Victor?' She looked up at him for advice.

'The school will be happy to allow him to attend,' Victor told her. 'I spoke to the principal before we left.'

'Then you'll go, Francis.' Caroline smiled, but tears threatened to flood her eyes. When had she last experienced such happiness? *Francis was coming into his own.*

'Patience, did you hear? Francis is going to school for the whole day.'

'Yes'm.' Patience was ecstatic at this victory. 'Come along, Francis. If you're going to school, you gotta drink lots of milk and eat plenty of fruit. And you tell me what you do in school, you hear?' she exhorted, taking him by the hand.

'Wanna tell Liz,' Francis said, a gleam of triumph in his eyes.

'You tell Liz and Josh later,' Patience decreed. 'They's stayin' at school late for a party. Come on, now.'

'Victor, I can't believe it,' Caroline whispered, walking beside him to the library, where Elvira was setting down the tea tray.

'I knew we were close, but not this close,' Victor acknowledged. He seemed to be in inner debate.

'Victor, you're afraid he's going to regress,' Caroline accused, her earlier joy ebbing away. 'Is that what bothers you?'

'No,' he denied. 'Francis won't regress. I've watched him closely these last weeks. I just want to make sure you understand his limitations.' Victor waited until Elvira left the library, then went to close the door. He returned to sit beside Caroline on the sofa. 'Francis will be able to start first grade in September. He's a year behind, but that doesn't matter. He'll be able to function in a normal world. But, Caro, you must not put pressure on him,'

292

Victor emphasized. 'Don't expect him to become a lawyer or a scientist or a politician. He'll find a place for himself, with encouragement. Just understand, Caro. Don't make demands he'll be incapable of fulfilling.'

'Victor, I understand.' Her face was radiant. 'This is a miracle. To know that he can go to school. He'll learn a trade – he'll be useful. Only because of you, Victor. Nobody else could have accomplished this.' Caroline reached to cover his hand with hers. 'No one ever had your patience. Your dedication.'

'We did it together, Caro.' Victor's voice was uneven.

'You never let me become discouraged. You comforted me, Victor.' She was conscious of thunder overhead. Lightning zigzagging across the library rug. 'You gave me a reason for living.'

'Caro . . .' His face moved close to hers. 'I swore I would do this for you.'

'On that first day, I knew you were going to help Francis.'

All at once Victor's mouth was on hers. His arms about her. For one instant Caroline was startled. Then she responded with an ardour that matched his. The parade of empty nights that had haunted her converted into one unspoken incessant demand. *Love me, Victor. Please love me.*

'Wait,' he exhorted, pulling away for a moment, and walked over to lock the library door.

Caroline sat immobile, encased in emotions too long left locked within her. Feeling herself lifted on to a velvet plateau isolated from the world.

She trembled at the touch of Victor's arms about her. His mouth on hers. His body demanding. She lay back across the sofa, matching passion with passion while the storm played a tumultuous symphony outside.

At last they lay limp and exhausted. For a moment

neither spoke. Then Victor pulled himself to his feet and turned away while Caroline restored her attire to presentability.

'Caro, how could I have let this happen?' His eyes were agonized. His rage at himself thickened his voice. 'I had no right. What can I say?'

'Victor, we both let it happen.' Caroline was remembering another storm. A barn at Hampton Court, where Eric and she had taken refuge that afternoon when they had struggled together to stop a lynching. Eric and she, keyed up from the trauma of what had happened. Alone together in the barn, Eric and she had made love. Before they were married. 'We'll wash this afternoon from our minds, Victor.' Caroline was resolute.

'Caro, I couldn't bear to lose your friendship.'

'How could that ever be?' she asked tenderly. 'This afternoon never happened,' she repeated. 'You'll always be my dear friend, Victor.'

They both started at the sound of the telephone. 'Hello,' Caroline's voice struggled to sound natural.

'Caroline, I wanted to catch you before the evening papers come out. Everything's all right,' Senator Bolton soothed. 'Everybody on board was saved. But Eric's ship, the *Lusitania*, was attacked by a submarine and sank off the Irish coast.'

'Are you sure everybody was saved?' Caroline was cold and shaking. 'How do they know?'

'A cable was received in Washington,' the senator explained. 'There'll probably be extras on the streets tonight. Caroline, you are not to worry,' the senator insisted. 'The cable was specific. Everyone on board is safe.'

'Thank God,' Caroline gasped. 'I'm sure we'll have a cable from Eric as soon as that's possible.'

'There's a war going on in Europe,' the senator reminded. 'Don't be upset if the cable's delayed.'

'Thank you for letting me know, Senator.' Caroline struggled to retain her composure.

Caroline and Victor were talking in low, worried tones about the attack on the *Lusitania* and its possible repercussions for the United States when Liz and Josh came into the house. Both children charged into the library, eager to report on the school fair.

Caroline listened for a few moments, then interrupted to tell them about the sinking of the *Lusitania*.

'Nobody was hurt,' she assured Liz and Josh. 'We'll probably be hearing from Papa in the morning.'

Caroline was determinedly cheerful. Let the children believe this was an adventure. She dreaded to read tomorrow's newspapers. Too many Americans would take it for granted that this country would enter the war.

Caroline thrust about in bed until dawn, falling into a heavy dream-racked slumber. She awoke with a start at the hour long ingrained in her. While she dressed, she heard a sharp ring of the doorbell. Who was calling at this hour?

She was already at the head of the stairs when Roland admitted their caller, Jim.

'I have to talk with Miss Caroline immediately,' he told Roland.

'Jim, what's happened?' She rushed down the stairs. He was grim and ashen.

'Let's go into the library.'

Silently they walked down the hall and into the library.

'Caroline, Senator Bolton called me from Washington. He asked me to come to the house and tell you. That first cable about the *Lusitania* . . .' He paused. 'It was a mistake. The ship sank. There were heavy casualties. Washington is waiting to hear from the American consul about Americans who were saved.'

'Oh, my God!' Caroline stared in disbelief.

'The senator is standing by for the news. The minute there's word of Eric, he'll telephone.'

'Eric's all right,' Caroline insisted. *She would not believe that Eric had not survived. How could she believe that and live?* 'I'm going to New York,' she decided. 'The Cunard office will have the latest information.'

'No later than Washington,' Jim protested. 'Caroline, it'll accomplish nothing for you to go running to New York.'

'I have to go,' Caroline insisted. 'If Eric's hurt, I'll go to England and bring him home.'

'Caroline, that's dangerous. Eric wouldn't want you to take chances.' Neither of them would face the premise that Eric might not have survived. 'I'll call Washington again,' he compromised.

'Call,' Caroline agreed. 'And try the Cunard office in New York. I'm going upstairs to pack. It'll only take me ten minutes. We'll have breakfast together.' She started from the library, calling as she headed for the staircase. 'Elvira! Elvira, tell Mattie to prepare breakfast for two.'

In her room Caroline packed in haste, her agile mind checking off what would be required.

She would go to the Cunard office in New York and learn what she could before she tried to book passage. Ships were sailing to Europe, despite the sinking of the *Lusitania*. If there was no passenger ship leaving immediately, then she must travel on a merchant ship. Thank God, she had connections in the shipping trade.

Downstairs again, forcing herself to eat a breakfast that had no taste for either Jim or her, Caroline scheduled her day. Much must be done before she boarded the New York-bound train.

'Caroline, it's absurd for you to go dashing off to New York,' Sophie objected. 'We have telephone and cable lines.'

'I have to go, Sophie,' Caroline insisted.

'What about Francis?' Sophie threw out in desperation.

'Francis will be fine. I'll phone Victor and explain what's happened. I won't be gone any longer than necessary,' she promised. 'As soon as there's news, I'll wire you.'

'Have you told Liz and Josh?' Sophie asked. Her hands trembled as she reached for a cup of coffee.

'I'll tell them when they come downstairs.'

For a moment Caroline was uneasy when she explained to Francis that she had to go away for a few days.

'Will Patience be here?' he demanded. 'And Victor and Liz and Josh and Aunt Sophie?'

'All of them,' she promised, drawing him to her.

'Will you bring me a present?' He was accepting her absence.

Jim, Sophie, and the two older children accompanied her to Terminal Station. The children were unfamiliarly silent. They knew that if she were to go to England, she would be away from Hampton House for more than a few days. Travelling time alone would be at least nine or ten days each way. Caroline saw fear for their father's safety in their eyes, felt it in the fervour of their embraces before she climbed aboard the train.

Caroline had brought newspapers and magazines aboard the train with her. They lay unopened on the seat. If Eric's name was on the list of Americans saved and the Cunard people could assure her he was unharmed, then she would wait in New York for his return. If there was any doubt about Eric's welfare, then she would manage to acquire passage to Queenstown. Jim said most of those who had been saved were taken to Queenstown, in County Cork.

As planned, Senator Bolton was at Union Station in Washington to deliver the hastily acquired special passport. She was grateful he made no further effort to dissuade her from a possible journey to Queenstown.

When the train arrived in Pennsylvania Station in New York, Caroline checked her luggage and took a taxi directly to the Cunard office. The office was jammed with people seeking information. Hundreds more crowded on to the sidewalk the length of the block, waiting to go inside the office. Desperate-faced men and women, some with children in their arms. Many in tears.

'Is there any news?' Caroline asked a matronly woman who stood beside her in stoic calm that belied the anguish in her eyes.

'The names of the survivors have come in. A man came out to tell us a while ago,' she said. 'When we get inside, we'll see the lists. It's going to be a long wait,' she cautioned.

'I know.' Caroline managed a shaky smile of gratitude.

For close to two hours Caroline waited among the crowd on the sidewalk, pushing closer as those inside left the office, the ones on the sidewalk watching the faces of those emerging as though seeking reassurance. Some faces mirrored relief, joy; others seemed numb, disbelieving, struggling to cope with death. A woman screamed hysterically as she stumbled through the door, supported on each side by a sombre-faced relative.

At last Caroline was inside the Cunard office. Placards lined the walls and the counters. A man patiently explained at intervals that those names with checks beside them were accounted for, though he could not vouch for their conditions. As soon as word was received, this would be posted. According to word from Queenstown, there were survivors, some of them Americans.

Caroline searched the passenger lists. Terror welled in her when she discovered Eric's name with no check beside it. Eric was unaccounted for, her mind registered. Then she must go to Queenstown.

Passenger ships would continue to travel to Liverpool, she discovered; but there was no departure scheduled for three days. She searched her mind for New York men with whom she carried on business. One of them would help her acquire passage on a merchant ship.

With her passage assured, Caroline made another trip to the Cunard offices. She waited on the sidewalk again until she could acquire admittance. Again she sought out Eric's name. Again, no check beside his name. One of the harried men answering question of those besieging the office told her, his voice compassionate, that all Americans known to survive had now been posted on the passenger list.

By nightfall Caroline was a passenger on an American merchant ship headed for Liverpool. Its first port of call would be Queenstown.

'It's dangerous,' the captain warned her for the third time minutes before they were to sail. 'You know about the *Lusitania*.'

'I know.' Her face was grim.

'We'll be in a blackout every night. That American flag flying overhead may not mean a thing if we run into a German U-boat.'

'I have to go to Queenstown,' Caroline insisted. 'I'll take the risk.'

The only woman on board ship, Caroline spent most of her time in her small, cramped cabin. The captain had pointed out to her that they carried cotton. No munitions, no contraband. Still, they must travel through water populated by German U-boats.

The trip across the Atlantic was slow and laborious. In the long, dark nights Caroline re-examined her life and her marriage. When this nightmare was over, she would take the children and be with Eric much of the time he would be in Washington. At intervals she'd return to Atlanta to consult with Sophie and Andrew on the management of the mill. Major decisions could remain in her hands.

In Washington I won't allow myself to become just another congressman's wife. I'll be Caroline Hampton, useful to my husband in a way that extends beyond attending endless luncheons and teas. I'll make Eric understand that the mill is important to me, but I'll adjust my life to accommodate his needs. Above all else, I want to share Eric's life.

And constantly Caroline prayed that Eric was alive.

With the morning sun rising warm in the sky, the ship approached the Irish coast.

Her suitcase in tow, Caroline disembarked and headed, on the advice of the captain, for the Queens Hotel, the largest in town, with forty-three rooms. The town itself sat in a half-circle overlooking the harbour.

Her suitcase left, still packed, on the neat, clean bed, Caroline left the Queens Hotel to seek out Consul Frost. Passing the shop windows, she read the pitiable signs posted in windows, pleading for information that might lead to a lost child, a missing husband or wife, sister or brother, mother or father. It seemed to Caroline that the town was in mourning.

She found Consul Frost's second-floor office above a bar. The office was dingy, depressing. The consul himself was off on the ghoulish task of viewing bodies still being

300

washed ashore, on the premise that some might be those of Americans.

A young woman in that office assured Caroline there had been no cables delivered for her in the care of the consul. She gave directions to the hospital, hotels, and rooming houses where some of the survivors still remained – either too ill to be removed or too terrified as yet of taking another ship to continue their journey.

At the hospital a young blue-eyed, black-haired nurse inspected the photograph of Eric that Caroline carried in her purse.

'I don't remember seeing him come in here,' the nurse told her after an intensive study of Eric's features. 'And there's no one like him in the hospital now. But that night was so awful.' Her features, pretty and pert, seemed to sharpen in recall. 'The injured were brought in here, till every bed was filled. Every hotel, every rooming house, was filled. Folks in town opened their houses. They came from the sea – some of them – with their clothes washed from them, wrapped in blankets or whatever could be found. We knew we'd lose some of them.' Her eyes filled. 'Not one survivor was picked up before being in the water for at least two hours. The boats were still bringing them in when night fell.'

'I'll try the hotels.' Caroline struggled to hold on to her composure.

She moved from the Westbourne Hotel to the Rob Roy, from one rooming house to another.

'It was a living nightmare, it was,' a portly rooming house owner told her. 'Little ones alone. Only the dear Lord knew what had become of their families. Women running in search of their husbands. I had a little tyke here, no more than four. She was brought in wearing only a thin little petticoat and holding on to a doll. That

301

was all she had left in the world. The sisters from Liverpool are caring for her now.'

'You're certain you haven't seen this man?' Caroline interrupted.

'I'm sorry, ma'am. He hasn't been here.'

Sick with fear, Caroline emerged from the last of the boardinghouses. The nurse at the hospital said that folks in Queenstown had opened their homes to the survivors. She must canvas every house in town.

She approached a small, neatly painted white frame house with a tiny garden. She felt weak and faint. She should have stopped for tea, she reproached herself. Shaky but determined, she knocked on the door of the house.

A young woman with a high-spirited toddler hanging to her skirt opened the door. Caroline's eyes settled on the tiny boy. His was the first happy face she had seen in Queenstown. He was too young to be part of the trauma that had overtaken the town.

'You do look pale, miss,' the young woman said solicitously.

'I'm looking for someone . . .' Caroline's voice trailed off.

'We'll talk about that later.' The young woman drew Caroline into the tiny parlour. 'First you'll be having a cup of hot tea and a scone.'

'You're very kind.' Caroline had no strength left with which to protest.

The young woman deposited Caroline in a chair, with the ebullient toddler left to entertain her. All at once, lonely for her own brood, Caroline leaned foward to hug him and was engulfed in a sticky embrace that was bittersweet. Was Francis all right?

'The scones are fresh-made and the tea as well,' the young woman said, setting a dainty cup and saucer and a matching plate of scones on a tiny table beside the chair. 'I'll bring you milk and sugar for your tea.'

'No need,' Caroline said quickly. 'I drink it plain. Just like this.' Not true, but she was impatient to ask questions.

'Are you English?' The young woman seemed perplexed.

'American,' Caroline told her. 'But my mother was English. I was born in London and lived there until I was eighteen.'

'Drink your tea and eat your scones,' the young woman ordered. 'When I see some colour in your cheeks, then you can talk.'

Caroline obeyed. Her hostess must know she was searching for a missing passenger. Her eyes showed her sympathy.

'Like most folks in town, we had some of the survivors staying here in the house. We put all but the last one on the boat train for Kingston two days ago.'

'You have a survivor in the house?' Caroline set down her teacup. 'A gentleman?'

'A delightful gentleman,' the young woman said with a lilt in her voice. 'He spends hours telling my little one stories.'

Then the survivor was not Eric, Caroline told herself in disappointment. If Eric was well enough to tell stories to a youngster, he would have cabled her.

'We're quite certain he's an American,' the young woman continued. 'He speaks in the American fashion.'

'Doesn't he say?' Caroline was bewildered.

'Oh, the poor sweet man,' she murmured. 'He's recovering as fine as you please from his fractured ankle, but he has no memory. There was a bad blow on the head that took it away, the doctor told us.'

Caroline's hands trembled when she opened her purse

to draw out the much-handled photograph from her purse. Her heart pounding, she extended the photograph to her hostess.

'Would you look at this, please? Is this the man?' It wouldn't matter if Eric had amnesia. She would take him home. She would nurse him back to reality. 'It's an old photograph,' Caroline stammered. 'It was taken almost ten years ago.'

'It's difficult to say,' the woman apologized. 'Please come with me.'

The young woman opened the door to a tiny, sun-drenched room. In a wicker chair by the window sat a man – his back to them – watching a bird eating from an improvised tray on the sill. His hair was dark, with a small, neat bandage covering an area at the back of his skull. His right leg was in a cast.

'There's a lady here who would like to talk to you,' she said persuasively.

The man in the chair turned to face them. A kind of joy she had never yet experienced washed over Caroline. The man in the chair was Eric.

'Eric,' she said softly, remembering that he had lost his memory. 'Eric, I've come to take you home.'

He turned around, wary at first. And then, while Caroline and the young woman hovered before him in a pregnant silence, Caroline saw the machinery of his mind click into place again.

'Caro. Oh, my God, Caro!'

Enveloped in each other's arms, they heard the door close quietly behind them.

25

Maureen led Liz into the main café at the Piedmont Hotel. The luncheon rush hour was ebbing away. To Maureen's satisfaction they were shown to a choice table. She was conscious of the eyes that followed Liz and her. Wearing expensive, beautiful clothes gave her a self-confidence that was new and exhilarating. It irked her that opportunities to show off her fashionable wardrobe were so limited.

For a few moments Liz and she concentrated on ordering their luncheon; then Maureen leaned back in her chair, reached into her Mark Cross purse, and drew out a small silver cigarette case. Liz's eyes widened in astonishment when she pulled out one gold-tipped cigarette, brought it to her lips, and lit it.

'Don't tell Andrew I was smoking in the café.' Maureen laughed. Everybody was staring at their table. She wished she could blow smoke rings. That would shock the hell out of them. 'He doesn't mind if I smoke at home, but he'd be upset if he knew I did it on the outside.'

'I won't say a word,' Liz promised, loving being Maureen's confidante. Wouldn't Caroline be furious if she knew that Liz was spending so much time with *her* now that school was over!

'Don't you adore those white silk stockings diamonded in black that I bought at Chamberlin-Johnson-DuBose?' Maureen asked.

'I liked everything.' Liz's smile was ebullient. 'The fleshtinted *crêpe-de-Chine* slumber robe and two *crêpe-de-Chine* dressing gowns. And those beautiful blue satin mules! Wear the mules with that silk and embroidered albatross negligée and you'll look like Theda Bara.' Liz rhapsodized.

Caroline was rotten not to have given Andrew and her a wedding at Hampton House. At least Caroline ought to give a party for them. That way she would be introduced to Atlanta society. Nobody invited them anywhere. Everybody remembered that Andrew never accepted social invitations.

But Andrew was married now, she thought plaintively. Everybody in the city must have seen that picture of her in her wedding dress, and the announcement of the marriage of Maureen Bienville Vauban to Andrew Carter Hampton.

Her father's mother had been a Bienville. For the purpose of the wedding announcement Maureen had borrowed the name. Twice she had seen her grandmother. Once from the gallery of the St Charles Theatre and once as the bitter, arrogant Mrs Beauchamp stepped from her carriage on Chartres Street.

'Are we going somewhere after lunch?' Liz inquired.

'Shopping again,' Maureen decided. 'I want to buy a little present for Andrew.'

The taxicab drew up before Hampton House. Caroline's face was suffused with tenderness as she inspected the familiar structure. She had been away slightly more than three weeks; it seemed interminably long. She was hungry for sight of the children. 'Eric, be careful getting out of the car,' Caroline cautioned. While the doctor in Queens-town had removed the cast on Eric's ankle and pro-nounced himself pleased with the way the ankle was mending, Eric was still dependent on the use of a cane.

While Eric paid the driver, Elvira appeared at the door. Her face creased in a broad smile of welcome, she hurried down the stairs to relieve Caroline of the valise she had brought out from the taxicab.

'Miss Caroline, Mist' Eric, sho is fine to see you both home!'

'Thank you, Elvira. It's wonderful to be home.' She hugged Elvira, conscious of how much Hampton House and all those who were part of it meant to her. 'Where are the children?'

'Francis, he home,' Elvira reported. 'Josh, he went swimmin' with his Boy Scout troop. Liz went downtown with Miss Maureen – Roland drove them.'

Caroline frowned. Why had Liz gone downtown with Maureen? Immediately she felt guilty. Maureen was Andrew's wife, and they had to make the best of it. Still, the image of Liz becoming close to Maureen was irritating.

'Who's playing the piano?' Eric asked when they walked into the reception hall.

'Francis.' She laughed at Eric's bewilderment. 'Eric, I told you. Francis is quite musical.'

'He played with one finger, last I knew,' Eric recalled.

'Liz has been teaching him,' Caroline explained, rushing across the reception hall and towards the parlour. All at once she couldn't wait to hold Francis in her arms again.

The folding door to the parlour was open. Francis sat at the piano. His back to her. Victor hovered over Francis, murmuring encouragement. The last time she had seen Victor before going to Queenstown was on the errant afternoon when he made love to her. The afternoon the *Lusitania* sank.

'Mama!' Francis spied her. 'Mama, Mama!' He hurled himself across the room into her arms.

'What about your father?' Eric chided humorously while Francis plied Caroline with kisses.

'Papa, did you get very wet when the ship sank?' Francis wanted to know, while Eric swept him off his feet in a warm embrace.

'Very wet,' Eric assured him.

'Victor, how nice to see you.' She moved forward impulsively to him because he seemed rooted to the spot. *He must put out of his mind what had happened between them.* 'I wouldn't have dared to go to Queenstown if I hadn't known you were standing by.' She lifted herself on her toes to bestow a sisterly kiss on his cheek.

'Thanks, Victor.' Eric's show of gratitude was spare, yet both Victor and Caroline were aware of sincerity.

Victor had been fearful of this first meeting, Caroline thought. He was trying to appear natural.

'You must have been through a dreadful experience,' Victor commiserated.

'Nobody on the *Lusitania* on May 7, 1915, will ever forget it.' Eric's face was taut in recall. 'After the first hour in the water, we saw smoke from a ship that seemed to be coming towards us. Then, with the ship's funnel clearly in view, it retreated.' The frustration he felt then echoed in his voice. 'It was the *Juno*, the cruiser that was supposed to have been our escort. She was coming to our rescue when Lord Fisher – Admiral Lord Fisher,' he corrected himself in bitter humour, 'ordered the *Juno* recalled. He didn't want her to run the risk of being torpedoed. We were in the water for over two hours when boats began to arrive. Anything that could float was sent out.'

'You know Italy declared war on May 23,' Victor said soberly.

Eric nodded. 'We heard.'

'I've been waiting for your return before going to Italy. My mother asked me to go there and bring my grandmother to Boston.' His eyes crinkled in momentary amusement. 'By force if necessary.'

'Victor, be careful,' Caroline urged. 'You're very special to this family.'

Maureen and Liz emerged from Davison-Paxon-Stokes, each clutching a box. Maureen was pleased with the dressing robe she had bought for Andrew. She knew that Liz was ecstatic over the *crêpe-de-Chine* and chiffon petticoat that Maureen dubbed a belated Christmas gift to her.

'Let's go over to the John M. Smith Company and look at cars,' Maureen told Liz.

'Maureen, are you buying a car?' Liz was awe-struck.

'No, silly.' Maureen laughed. 'At least, not now.' But it piqued her that Andrew, who was sweet in every other aspect, refused to teach her to drive their Pierce Arrow. She suspected Andrew felt driving was a man's prerogative. If he persisted in that, then he would have to hire a chauffeur. To ride the streetcar now that she was Mrs Andrew Hampton was unthinkable.

In a continuing mood of conviviality Maureen and Liz went into the Smith store. Maureen knew exactly what car she wanted to see. The Chalmers limousine, as advertised in *Harper's Bazaar*.

A salesman immediately led them to the sleek grey Chalmers limousine that had enchanted Maureen for months. She visualized herself exquisitely dressed, being handed into its plush interior by a respectful liveried chauffeur.

'Maureen, it's beautiful.' Liz was enthusiastic as her eyes moved over the impressive limousine.

The salesman beamed.

'It has the French-type aluminium body,' he explained, throwing open the rear door. 'And notice the silk grab cords, speaking tubes and armrest. The dome, shoulder, and step lights. Upholstery is of imported cloth. You choose between blue German Walfine cloth or brown English Bedford cord. Of course, the carpet and cushions will match.'

'What about the engine?' Maureen asked. She was eager to appear knowledgeable, as though she had owned cars.

'A powerful six-cylinder engine,' the salesman told her with pride. 'It's a six-thousand-dollar limousine available for only thirty-two hundred.'

'I adore it,' Maureen admitted. 'I'll have to talk to my husband, of course.'

'Of course,' the salesman acknowledged, smiling.

When they drove back to Hampton House, Liz insisted that Maureen come in with her. Lovingly she clutched the parcel from Davison-Paxon-Stokes.

'You won't have dinner for two hours yet,' Liz coaxed. 'Let's play cards. Roland will drive you home with the packages.'

'I'll stay for a little bit,' Maureen capitulated.

'Mama and Papa are home! Come on, Maureen.' Liz darted towards the library. Reluctantly Maureen followed. 'Mama, when did you get home? Why didn't you send a telegram?' Liz chided.

'Liz, honey! Oh, I've missed you all!'

'Where's Papa?'

'I insisted he go upstairs and take a nap. He's been through an awful time, and the ankle still isn't entirely well.'

'He'll be downstairs for dinner?' Liz prodded, and Caroline nodded in reassurance.

'Welcome home, Caroline.' Maureen hesitated in the doorway. Caroline had been unaware of her presence until this moment.

310

'Thank you, Maureen.'

'Mama, Maureen and I had the most wonderful day. We shopped and had lunch at the Piedmont Hotel, and look . . .' Liz was busy unwrapping the parcel from Davison-Paxon-Stokes. 'Isn't this breathtaking?' She borrowed Maureen favourite word of late. 'Maureen says it's my late Christmas present.' She held aloft the petticoat.

Caroline frowned. 'Maureen, you shouldn't have bought Liz such an expensive gift.'

'It was on sale,' Maureen defended herself, relieved that the saleswoman had removed the price tag at her request. 'And Liz liked it so much.' Caroline was thinking she was wasting Andrew's money.

The sound of steps in the hall interrupted their conversation.

'Papa!' Liz cried out jubilantly, and raced across the room to kiss her father. 'Papa, we were so scared when we heard about the ship sinking. I want to hear about every little minute, from the time the torpedo hit the *Lusitania* until you were on land. Your ankle's still hurt!' She spied the cane in Eric's hand.

'I don't use this thing often.' He brushed aside any dependency on the cane. 'How are you, Maureen?' Eric was always warm.

'Fine, thank you. Andrew and I were so relieved when Caroline cabled that you were all right. I'd better get home now and see what Phoebe's doing about dinner.'

'Roland's waiting to drive you home,' Liz reminded, and giggled. 'You'd never make it home with all those packages.'

'No.' Maureen smiled. So Caroline knew she had shopped madly today. 'It's good to see you both back at Hampton House.' She contrived to be demure and sweet.

'I'll walk with you to the door. Papa, you stay right

311

there,' Liz ordered, darting to hang on to Maureen in her departure.

Caroline crossed to open a window. A faint breeze from the river drifted in to alleviate the June heat.

'You look upset,' Eric said.

'No,' Caroline denied. 'Just tired from the train trip.' How could she tell Eric she was annoyed to see Liz drawn to Maureen? Men never understood those things. Eric would think she was jealous because Maureen was young and beautiful.

'I ought to call Jim and let him know we're back,' Eric decided.

'Ask him over for dinner tonight,' Caroline encouraged as Eric walked to the phone. 'Our first night home, Mattie's sure to prepare a feast.'

'Wear yellow for dinner,' Eric instructed, his eyes making love to her. His first objective on coming home had been to move himself back into the master bedroom. Every night on board ship he had made love to her, as though to compensate for the parade of lost nights.

'If you'll come up and help me dress,' Caroline stipulated, conscious of arousal. With them passion had never been solely a nighttime interlude.

'I'll be right upstairs,' Eric promised, and turned to give the operator the number of the office phone.

Eric would come up to their bedroom and find her naked beneath the coverlet, Caroline plotted. Eric was never one for reticence in bed. She felt like his mistress in moments like this. And then she remembered Serena Mayo. For a moment her happiness was clouded. Only for a moment. Her husband had come home to her.

Lying on the bed beneath a silken coverlet, her hair fanned about the pillow, Caroline waited for Eric. She heard Liz's laughter filter up the stairs. How long would she detain her father? *Liz, darling, go phone Janet again.*

312

Caroline was conscious of how much she wanted Eric. Making love unexpectedly this way could be doubly sweet. Then she heard the piano. Liz had gone into the parlour to play. These days Liz found a release in playing the music she had learned two years ago under protest. That was because David was fond of the classics.

A smile touched her lips when Eric opened the door, came into the room, and turned around to lock the door.

'You took so long,' she rebuked, pleasure lighting her face. She wanted to lie in Eric's arms. She wanted to be filled with him.

'Not much longer,' he promised, stripping beside the bed. Still one of the most handsome men in Atlanta, Caroline thought with pride. Still with that special appeal for women. If the women got the vote, Eric would never have to worry about winning an election.

Caroline's eyes trailed over Eric's tall, lean, firm body. She cleared her throat in anticipation when he walked to the bed. With a dazzling smile he tossed aside the coverlet in one swift gesture.

'You are a delectable woman, Caroline Hampton.'

'Show me,' she commanded. He was ready to make love. These days all he had to do was look at her like this, and he was ready.

She held her arms out to him, murmuring in pleasure when she felt the weight of him above her. Felt the sweet intrusion that would be frenetic in a moment.

'Oh, Eric, honey!' her arms and legs imprisoned him and they thrust in oneness.

'Sssh,' he whispered in the familiar caution. 'We don't have to let the whole house know.'

Dinner was to be a festive occasion. Caroline confirmed on consultation with Mattie, who had chosen each course with Eric's favourites in mind.

Eric came downstairs to the library shortly after Caroline. He appeared relaxed and refreshed. He was always like that after making love.

'You look beautiful in that dress, Caro. Is it new?'

'Yes,' she lied. He had never noticed it before.

'Would you like a glass of wine before dinner?'

'Tonight champagne,' she said in heady pleasure, then laughed. 'Mattie is chilling it.'

Eric had scolded her for making the trip to Queenstown, but she knew what joy the effort had instilled in him. He knew his wife loved him enough to risk her life to search for him.

Eric listened to the sound of a car coming up the driveway.

'That must be Jim. Have Elvira bring in the champagne glasses.' Eric hurried from the library and down the hall to greet Jim.

Caroline was conscious of a sharpness in Eric's voice while he talked with Jim in the hall. Was there bad news about the war in Europe? It was sinful for her to feel such happiness, she reproached herself, when this minute soldiers were dying in Europe.

'That son of a bitch Watson never lets up on Frank,' Jim harangued. 'He's using his vendetta against Frank to build up his rotten *Watson's* magazine and *The Jeffersonian*; and by God, it's working.'

'Are you serious about starting up the magazine again?' Eric asked.

'You're damn right I'm serious, with Watson stirring up mass meetings in Atlanta.'

'Jim, what mass meetings are you talking about?' Caroline inquired in astonishment as Eric and he walked into the library.

'They're rallies to convince the governor and the prison commission that the citizens of Georgia won't accept a commutation of Frank's sentence from death by hanging to life imprisonment. There's a meeting going on right now on the grounds of the state capitol. A mob of thousands down there, bloodthirsty as hell.'

'What's going to happen, Jim?' In Queenstown and on the ship coming back to New York, she had been so caught up in Eric's brush with death that her concern for Leo Frank had retreated to a remote cavern of her mind.

'Nobody knows, Caroline. But Frank's chances are better with Governor Slaton than with Harris. The new governor is Watson's man.'

'What about the prison commission?' Caroline asked. 'They consider the appeal for commutation first, don't they?'

'I just told Eric. The prison commission turned him down. By a vote of two to one. It's up to the governor now.'

'And he's got problems,' Eric reminded. 'He just lost his race for the Senate. If he runs again, he needs Tom Watson's support. If he refuses commutation, he'll be sure of it.'

'Let's don't talk about the case now,' Caroline said hurriedly. She could hear Liz and Josh in the hall. 'What's happening with the Secretary of State in this *Lusitania* mess?'

Conversation focused on Bryan's pacifism efforts in the face of American rage at the sinking of the *Lusitania*. Jim reported that Colonel House, being entertained at an embassy dinner the night of the sinking, had announced to the guests that he expected the United States to be at war with Germany within a month.

'There's going to be a rush towards preparedness, whatever,' Eric guessed. 'But dammit, those who're demanding war don't represent the people. I'd lay odds that the average farmer, the typical worker, the smaller businessman don't want us involved in a European war.'

'Wilson hasn't called Congress in special session yet,' Jim pointed out. 'Though everybody expects it to happen any time.'

'I phoned Senator Bolton from New York,' Eric said while Liz settled herself on the arm of his chair. 'I'm expected to report to the President on my experiences.'

'Papa, you can't go to Washington now,' Liz was outraged.

'He has to tell the President about what happened with the ship,' Josh reprimanded.

'I won't go for at least a week,' Eric promised. He turned to Caroline. 'Washington is impossible in the summer. I don't expect you to join me there with the children until it's absolutely necessary.'

'We ought to start looking for a house early next month,' Caroline said. Why was Liz staring at her that way?

'Mama, you said we couldn't go to Washington. You said you couldn't leave the mill with war going on in Europe,' Liz accused.

'I'll come down to Atlanta at regular intervals,' Caroline explained. 'Andrew and Aunt Sophie will manage when I'm not here.' Josh was elated at the realization he would be living in Washington. Why was Liz so agitated?

'We'll have to look into schools in Washington,' Eric reminded. 'Marian will have some suggestions.'

'I won't leave Atlanta!' Liz interrupted. 'I won't leave my school and my friends! I can stay here at home with Aunt Sophie. Can't I stay here with you, Aunt Sophie? I won't be any trouble. I swear I won't.'

Sophie's face brightened. Only now did Caroline realize how Sophie dreaded the impending separation.

Sophie would love having Liz at Hampton House with her while the rest of them were in Washington.

'Liz, that's up to your mother and father.' Sophie might spoil the children on occasion, but she was scrupulous about not siding with them against Caroline.

'School's a long time off,' Caroline stalled.

'No, it isn't,' Liz objected. 'And I don't want to go to Washington. I want to stay home with Aunt Sophie.' Her face was set in that bulldog determination Caroline knew.

'Caro, maybe we should let Liz stay here,' Eric said slowly. 'So she can graduate with her class. We'll be coming home for all the holidays. You'll be home a few days each month to sit in on what's happening at the mill.'

'I don't like it.' Caroline swung her eyes from Eric to Liz.

'Mama, it'll be fine.' Liz threw herself on Caroline, knowing she had won.

'I'll keep a sharp eye on her,' Sophie promised. 'You won't get away with one little thing,' she warned Liz with mock severity. 'I'll be stricter than your mother.'

But Caroline was unhappy. She would not have a truly restful moment in Washington with Liz remaining in Atlanta.

Liz

26

In deference to the hot weather, Caroline decreed that Sophie and she would go with the children to Hampton Court for long weekends until the family made the move to Washington. Eric would join them on these weekends as soon as he returned from the Capital. Liz asked to be allowed to invite Janet to go up with them on the first weekend, and Caroline was delighted.

On Sunday afternoon, June 20, Caroline and Sophie returned with the children to Atlanta. Eric had arrived from Washington earlier in the afternoon.

'I had to be here tomorrow,' Eric said, holding Caroline close to him. 'It's the last chance for Governor Slaton to save this state from moral disaster.' On the morning of June 22 Leo Frank was scheduled to be hanged.

On Monday morning Caroline came down to breakfast early as usual. She sat down at the table with Sophie.

'I'll be in to the office later,' she told Sophie. 'I want to spend the morning with Eric.'

While they were waiting for Mattie to send in breakfast, Eric came downstairs.

'I thought you'd sleep all morning,' Caroline reproached. He had been restless last night, muttering in his sleep at intervals.

'I'm waiting for the morning papers,' he admitted.

Over breakfast they struggled to avoid discussion of what most concerned them. While they lingered over a second cup of coffee, Liz – appearing pale and wan – walked into the breakfast room.

'Did you hear anything yet?' she demanded. It wasn't necessary to be more explicit.

'No word so far.' Eric's face was troubled.

'Call Uncle Jim,' Liz prodded. 'He always knows everything before anybody else.'

'When something happens, he'll call,' Caroline insisted.

The governor had listened to both the defence and prosecuting attorneys. He had even visited the factory where Mary Phagan was murdered. Now he was reading the exhaustive reports of the court hearings and the various judicial decisions.

Caroline knew the governor had been bombarded with letters, both friendly and hostile towards Leo Frank. Eric and she had written. Rumours claimed that more than a thousand writers had theatened to kill Governor Slaton and his wife if he commuted Leo Frank's sentence. It would take courage and a tremendous dedication to justice to allow Leo to live.

It was going to be a hot, humid day, Caroline thought in distaste. Already, despite the ceiling fan, the breakfast room was uncomfortable.

'Let's go out and sit on the veranda,' Eric said. 'In the shade. There might be a breeze from the river.'

While they settled themselves on the veranda, the phone rang. All three hurried to the library. Jim was calling.

'Thank God,' Eric said, and Liz threw her arms ecstatically about her mother. Caroline felt tears well in her eyes while she waited for Eric to finish the phone conversation.

'Governor Slaton commuted the sentence.' Eric confirmed what they knew. 'Last night he ordered Leo moved from the jail to the state prison farm at Milledgeville. While reporters watched a car with its motor running that had been planted in front of the jail, the sheriff and six deputies spirited Leo out through a rear exit. The governor said, "Feeling as I do about this case, I would be a murderer if I let that man hang."

'I'm going to call David,' Liz insisted jubilantly, and reached for the telephone.

'Governor Slaton has cut his throat politically,' Eric said. 'But he's the tallest man in Atlanta today.'

The Atlanta *Constitution* and the Atlanta *Journal* praised Governor Slaton for his decision. Some of the rural Georgia press concurred, though many denounced him. Throughout the country the newspapers and the public rejoiced that Leo Frank would not hang.

But there were angry mobs throughout the state who demonstrated against the governor's decision, burning him in effigy. Georgians turned against Jewish neighbours. In Canton all Jews were warned to be out of the city within twenty-four hours.

In downtown Atlanta mobs congregated to demonstrate. An entire battalion of state militia was ordered out to guard the governor's estate with bared bayonets. They surrounded the area with barbed wire and declared martial law within half a mile of the governor's residence.

That evening David had been invited to dinner. He arrived early, shaken by the mood of the city.

'The sheriff was afraid of a mob invasion of the Southside area.' This was where many of the local Jews maintained their residences. 'He even authorized some of the Jewish men to carry guns.'

'But it didn't happen,' Liz encouraged. 'That crazy mob went out to the governor's mansion.'

Over dinner David was eloquent about the feelings of the Jewish community in Atlanta. He expressed their fears of Tom Watson, crusading against 'the capitalists of

Big Money who're refusing justice to a poor man's daughter.'

Liz was absorbing every word David uttered, Caroline thought anxiously. David saw Liz as a cherished younger sister. He knew she wasn't yet fifteen. But Caroline sensed that Liz, mature beyond her years, was developing a woman's love for David.

Eric decreed that the family would delay leaving for Hampton Court this weekend until after the inauguration of Governor-elect Harris on Saturday. Thursday afternoon Caroline and he were sitting on the veranda sipping from ice-islanded glasses of lemonade when David's Ford drew up before the house.

'Sit down and cool off, David,' Caroline urged after their greeting. 'Elvira will bring you a glass of lemonade.' But from David's face, pale beneath its tan, she knew this was not a casual visit.

'I just left my brother Noah's store,' David told them. 'You know he has a branch in Marietta . . .'

'Yes.' Eric leaned forward, anticipating ugliness.

'The Marietta Vigilance Committee delivered a leaflet to the store. All Jewish merchants are ordered to leave by Saturday night. Or take the "punishment the committee may see fit to deal out to you".'

'How dare they!' Caroline flinched.

'I hope Noah will take the precaution of closing for a week or two,' Eric said quietly. 'This insanity will die down.'

'Read this.' David handed a card to Eric. 'They're being given out to people in Marietta, warning them not to buy from Jewish merchants.'

'David, Eric's right. Noah must close the store in Marietta until this horror dies down.'

'He will,' David promised. 'Rae has told him she doesn't want a dead rebel for a husband.'

On Saturday Eric escorted Caroline and the two older children to the inaugural ceremonies. He was concerned, Caroline knew, about former Governor Slaton's presence; but Slaton was bound by tradition to attend the inauguration.

After the ceremony Caroline and Eric became separated from Liz and Josh.

All at once, as Slaton and Harris walked down the steps of the capital, boos filled the air.

'Lynch him! Lynch him!' yelled some on the fringes of the crowd. The former governor's guards closed in about him, escorting him to his car.

'Eric, there's Liz!'

Liz and Josh stood at the edge of the crowd. She was shouting at a cluster of rural workers seething to do violence.

'How can you be so stupid?' Liz reviled. 'Governor Slaton saved the Georgia courts from making a shameful mistake. Leo Frank is innocent! He didn't kill Mary Phagan!'

Eric shouldered his way through the crowd to pull Liz away. But Caroline saw the pride in his eyes as he marched Josh and Liz to where she waited for them.

'Like mother, like daughter.' Eric grinned. 'Now, let's get the hell out of here.'

That weekend at Hampton Court Eric wrote an article for Jim's resurrected bimonthly magazine. Liz was entranced by the attack on Tom Watson as a racist demagogue. She was outraged when her father told the family three nights later that Jim insisted on publishing the article under a pseudonym.

'Why?' Liz demanded. 'Are you ashamed of it? What's the matter with Uncle Jim?'

'He's concerned about my being reelected to Congress.' Eric was candid.

'But because you're a congressman, that article means more,' Liz protested. 'Mama, tell him.'

'Honey, your father isn't compromising his principles,' Caroline insisted. 'He'll be running for reelection next year. It would be unwise to bait a . . . a fairly large segment of the voters.'

'Oh, I hate that attitude!' Liz retorted.

'Spoken with the ideals of fourteen,' Eric twitted, but his eyes were understanding.

'Papa, I'm almost fifteen. And what's wrong with fighting for your ideals?'

'You have to grow into the realization that sometimes it's important to sidestep confrontations. Look ahead, Liz. See what's at stake. I want to go back to Congress. We've got people in this country who're raring to push us into the war. I want to be in Congress to fight against war if it comes to a vote.'

'I think it's awful.' Liz sulked. 'This is supposed to be a free country.'

In mid-July Caroline and Eric went up to Washington to house-hunt, leaving the children in Atlanta. Liz was delighted by the aura of freedom elicited by her parents' absence. Sophie was ever eager to please with such treats as a freezer of ice cream on a hot night or permission for Janet to stay for dinner and the night at Hampton House.

Days were casual and unstructured. Either Janet came to spend the day at Hampton House, or Liz went to Janet's house. Twice, to Liz's rapture, Maureen took Liz and Janet – in her gleaming new Chalmers – for an afternoon in Druid Hills Park.

Today Liz waited impatiently by the roadside for Janet to arrive on the streetcar.

326

'Janet!' She hurried forward in exuberant welcome.

The two girls linked arms and walked towards Hampton House.

'There're two dogs.' Janet – an animal lover, like Liz – pointed to a pair of mongrels romping ahead of them.

All at once the larger, shaggy mutt was mounting the smaller, short-haired dog. The two girls giggled self-consciously.

'We were walking with our biology teacher in the school garden one day – he was going to talk to us about plants – and all of a sudden there were these two dogs. Doing *that*,' Janet said in remembered discomfort. 'We all nearly died. It was so embarrassing.'

'It's natural,' Liz said, striving to sound adult.

'I know, silly. But there was our whole class and the teacher. Some of the boys got all red in the face.'

'What about the girls?' Liz prodded.

'They pretended to look the other way.' Janet was silent for a moment. 'I know we wouldn't be here if our folks hadn't done it. But it seems so . . . so disgusting.'

'No,' Liz rejected. 'Not if you love each other.'

'Mama told me when I was thirteen what happened between folks when they got married. Did your mother tell you, Liz?'

'Sort of,' Liz acknowledged. She was excited that Janet and she were talking this way. It meant they were both growing up. 'She didn't exactly draw any pictures.' Liz laughed. 'She was glad when it was over. But I learned everything from one of Papa's law books,' she confided. 'There was this report on a rape case. It told everything. You want to see it?'

'You mean it's right there on your library shelf?' Janet stared in astonishment.

'It's a case history. *Smith versus Hendricks*. We'll take

it up to my room and read it,' Liz decided with relish. 'We'll lock the door if you're scared.'

'Did you ever wonder how it feels? I mean, a boy sticking that in you.' Liz felt a shiver of pleasure in the contemplation.

'I'd be ashamed,' Janet admitted.

'Not if you were married,' Liz insisted. She threw her arms about Janet. 'I can't kiss David, so I'll kiss you!'

'Liz, you are silly,' Janet squealed.

Liz and Janet went out to the kitchen, where Mattie provided them with tall, frosty glasses of lemonade and a plate of cookies. They detoured into the library, and Liz immediately reached among the shelves that held law books to pull down the one she wished.

'This is it,' she whispered in conspiratorial satisfaction. 'Let's go upstairs to my room.'

In Liz's pretty pink-and-white bedroom, the drapes closed against the early-afternoon sun, the two girls sprawled across the canopied bed and read the court record of a rape case.

'They talked like that in court?' Janet was awed. '"He put his penis in my vagina." Couldn't you just die?'

'Let's put the book back in the library. Then we'll go for a walk along the river. It's awful hot in the house.'

At shortly past four Janet announced she had to leave for home. She had promised her mother to be home early to help with preparations for her stepfather's birthday party.

Liz walked with Janet to the streetcar, waited until it arrived and Janet was on board. Now she left and headed down the narrow honeysuckle-flanked road that led back to Hampton House. The air was fragrant with summer flowers, the heat less oppressive as the day waned.

Liz moved to one side of the road at the sound of an approaching car. She stared in curiosity. Was it somebody coming to Hampton House? Now she recognized the car as one that had been sitting down a piece from the streetcar stop. Janet and she figured the three men in it, all of them reading newspapers, had been waiting for a friend on the streetcar.

The black Chevrolet drew to a jerky stop a few yards ahead of her. One of the men jumped from the backseat. All at once Liz was scared. Her instinct was to run. The honeysuckle bushes towered above her head. Nobody could see them. She turned to run back to the streetcar stop.

A second man emerged from the car. They sandwiched her between them. One man clamped a hand across her mouth before she could voice more than one terrified shriek. She kicked at them with her feet in frenzy.

The third man left the car.

'Let's get the hell out of here quick!' he ordered, and pushed a gag into her mouth when, at his signal, the restraining hand was removed. 'Hold her feet still, for God's sake, before she kicks me in the balls!'

Two of the men carried her, still struggling, to the car. They bound her hands and feet with rope. What were they going to do to her? She remembered Mary Phagan. Mary had been all cut up before she was choked to death. Some folks were sure she had been raped.

'Biff, we better use the chloroform,' one of the men said. 'She's kicking up a storm.'

27

At a few minutes past five Sophie left the mill. With Caroline and Eric in Washington she felt an obligation to spend more time with the children. Today she was relieved to put the mill behind her. The heat had been intolerable. No rain had fallen in almost three weeks.

At the house she went directly up to her room. She would soak in a tepid tub. She had instructed Mattie to serve dinner earlier these nights when Caroline and Eric were away. The children liked that.

By five minutes to six Sophie was downstairs in the library, cooling herself under the ceiling fan. She could hear Josh and Francis playing catch out on the west lawn. It was too hot to play ball, she fretted. But at least they were in the shade. Where was Liz?

At six Elvira came into the library to say that Mattie was ready to serve dinner.

'Thank you, Elvira. Will you please call the boys to the table? And where's Liz?'

'I ain't seen her since she went to walk her friend to the streetcar,' Elvira said. 'That musta been close to five. I'll just go up and see if she's in her room, Miss Sophie.'

Josh and Francis, perspiring but ebullient, came into the dining room and were shipped off to wash up. Elvira returned downstairs to report that Liz was not in her room.

'Maybe she over at Mist' Andrew's house, visitin' with Miss Maureen,' Elvira suggested. 'I 'spect she just forgot the time.'

'You're sure she didn't go home with Miss Janet?' Sophie probed.

'No, ma'am, she wasn't goin' home with her.' Elvira was emphatic. 'Miss Liz was just walkin' her to the streetcar.'

'Tell Mattie to hold dinner.' Sophie's voice was sharp in anxiety.

She went to the telephone and asked for Andrew's number.

'Hello,' Maureen answered on the second ring. Exuding the cloying sweetness of honeysuckle.

'Maureen, this is Sophie. Is Liz there with you?'

'No, I haven't seen Liz all day.' Maureen hesitated, sensing Sophie's concern. 'She's probably with Janet.'

'Janet was here all afternoon. Elvira said she walked Janet to the streetcar stop around five.'

'Then maybe she's visiting with David over at the Kahns' house. You know how upset she's been about that convict slashing Leo Frank's throat. The doctors still aren't sure he won't die of blood poisoning. She may have gone over to talk with David about it, and just forgot the time.'

'Probably,' Sophie agreed, fighting against panic. 'I'll call over there.'

She called the Kahn house and spoke to Rae, who had not seen Liz for the past three days. Sophie put down the phone, trying to decide where to call next. It wasn't like Liz to be away from the house without telling one of the servants where she was going. That was Caroline's firm rule.

'I'm hungry, Aunt Sophie.' Josh appeared in the library with Francis trailing behind him. 'When are we going to eat?'

'Right away,' Sophie soothed. 'Liz will have to eat alone.'

331

'Where is she?' Sophie's anxiety was transferred to Josh. 'She knows she has to be home for dinner.'

'Maybe she went for a walk and lost sight of time,' Sophie fabricated. 'Go out to the kitchen and tell Mattie we're ready for dinner.'

Sophie forced herself to eat, lest she frighten the children. She alternated between fear for Liz's safety and anger at Liz's thoughtlessness.

They were rising from the dinner table when she heard a car draw up before the house. Relief flooded Sophie. Liz had been visiting a school friend and forgot the time. She walked towards the hall, words of reproach forming in her mind. How could Liz frighten her this way?

Roland was at the door, kept wide in deference to the summer heat. David stood behind the screen door, staring at an envelope in his hand.

'Good evening, suh,' Roland greeted him with warmth, pushing the screen door open. 'Hot weather we're havin'.'

'Yes, it is, Roland.' David walked into the house. 'Has Liz come home?'

'No, she hasn't, David.' Sophie strode down the hall towards him. 'I'm worried to death.'

David extended the envelope.

'I found this stuck in the screen door. It's addressed to "The Hampton Family".' He sounded oddly concerned.

Sophie accepted the envelope and frowned at the awkward block letters. 'Why didn't they ring the doorbell?'

'Miss Sophie, I think you ought to open it.' David's face was impassive, yet she knew he was alarmed.

'I'm a Hampton in everything except name,' Sophie conceded, and ripped open the envelope. She stared in disbelief at the words printed across the sheet of cheap notepaper. 'Oh, my God!' Her face drained of colour,

332

Sophie handed the sheet of paper to David. 'They warn us not to call the police.'

'Phone Eric and Caroline,' David instructed. 'Immediately.'

'David, what will they do to her?' The words of the message ricocheted in her brain: '*Don't call the police or Elizabeth Hampton will be murdered in the same way as Mary Phagan. In seventy-two hours a letter from the congressman must be printed on the front page of the* Constitution. *It must say that Congressman Hampton is convinced Leo Frank murdered Mary Phagan, and he's sorry for taking the part of the infamous murderer and despoiler of young girls. If the letter doesn't appear, Elizabeth dies.*'

'We'll find Liz,' David was holding on to his tenuous calm for her sake, Sophie realized. 'Call Washington.'

Sophie phoned the Bolton house in Washington. Only the servants were home. Numb, she put down the phone. This wasn't happening; she was having a nightmare.

'There's nobody at the house. We may have to wait hours till Caroline and Eric come back.' Her voice was uneven.

'The servants might know where they are,' David persisted.

'I didn't think to ask,' Sophie admitted. 'I'm too upset to think clearly.' Knowing something terrible had happened but fearful of asking questions, Elvira had coaxed the two boys out on to the back porch with the bribe of ice cream.

'Give me the phone,' David said gently. 'I'll see what I can find out.'

With prodding the maid at the Bolton house remembered the Boltons, along with Caroline and Eric, had gone to a dinner for the new Secretary of State, the

333

dignified and tough-minded Robert Lansing. David elicited the name of their host and phoned.

Sophie listened, clasping her hands in agitation, while David – as succinctly and gently as possible – told Eric that Liz had been kidnapped.

'It has to be a bunch of rabble-rousing agitators.' David was straining to sound matter-of-fact. 'They warn against calling the police,' he reiterated. 'Do you think we should risk it?' He listened for a moment, then shook his head to pass on the decision to Sophie. 'I plan to do that,' David acknowledged. 'We'll expect you home tomorrow. Hopefully Liz will be back by then.' David put down the phone, his eyes contemplative.

'How could this have happened in broad daylight?' Sophie felt sick.

'Eric and Caroline are leaving the party immediately. They'll be home by tomorrow.'

'They've missed the last train leaving today for Atlanta,' Sophie reminded.

'They'll come on a freight train if need be. One way or another, Eric and Caroline will be here tomorrow. Eric wants me to call Jim. We'll get a few men together and start a private search. No police,' he emphasized. 'We can't take that chance.'

'Call Jim,' Sophie urged, but before David could do this, the phone rang. Sophie went to pick it up, almost fearfully. 'Hello.'

'Sophie, has Liz come home yet? Maureen was worried.'

'Andrew, I can't talk on the phone.' Sophie was wary of someone intercepting the call. 'Will you come right over?'

Twenty minutes later Sophie sat on the library sofa with Maureen at her side while the three men grappled with the ugly situation.

'Eric can't write that letter,' Jim said with finality, and Sophie stared at him in disbelief.

'Jim, how can you say that?'

'Do you know how damaging a letter like that would be to Leo?'

'Eric will write a retraction as soon as Liz is released,' Sophie said.

'It'll be too late,' Jim rejected. 'People will have read that first letter, right on the front page as those bastards ordered . . .' Jim paused. 'Excuse me,' he apologized. 'But all people will remember is that first letter. Eric can't write it.'

'Jim, this is his daughter's life at stake!'

'I called Janet,' David told Jim and Andrew. 'Liz walked with her to the streetcar stop at about five. Janet saw her turn down into the shortcut road that leads back to the house. She thought Liz might call her later, but she didn't.' David's voice deepened in alarm. 'She was kidnapped on that narrow stretch of road.'

'It sounds like the work of the Knights of Mary Phagan,' Jim pinpointed. Two weeks after Leo Frank's sentence was commuted, a group of a hundred and fifty men made a secret pilgrimage to Mary Phagan's grave, where they pledged themselves to avenge her death. 'I have some names. If we have to, we'll track down every man among them.'

'That's going to take time,' Andrew reminded. 'We have seventy-two hours.'

'Let's set up two teams,' David volunteered. 'I'll phone Noah. He'll go out with me.'

'I'll make calls,' Jim said, moving towards the phone. 'Andrew, you come with me.'

'Poor Liz . . .' Sophie's voice thickened. 'She must be frightened to death.

* * *

335

Liz awoke to a hazy awareness of hunger. She made a move to stretch and realized her wrists were bound together. All at once she remembered being grabbed on the road and carried to the car. She remembered the cloth over her nose and the nasty odour.

Her eyes swept about the tiny whitewashed room. Its one window was covered with a stretch of black cloth, but moonlight seeped through the sides, allowing her to inspect her surroundings. The furnishings in addition to the cot were one cane chair and a paint-peeling dresser.

The gag was off her mouth. In a burst of determination she sat up, swung her feet – tied at the ankles – to the floor. She manoeuvered herself to the window, open except for the black cloth tacked in place, took a deep breath, and began to scream.

'Help! Help! Help!'

The door flung wide. A greying, scrawny woman and a husky middle-aged man clutching a kerosene lamp rushed into the room.

'Stop that screeching, honey,' the man ordered, setting the lamp on the floor. 'Way out here, nobody's gonna hear you. You behave yourself, and your folks do like we say, you ain't gonna get hurt.'

'What do you want?' Liz asked with shaky bravado.

'Justice.' The woman began to chew a chunk of tobacco. 'Somethin' your papa don't care too much about.'

'He cares more about justice than anybody I know.' Liz's eyes blazed.

'Rich folks' justice,' the woman said in contempt. 'He better do what we say, or he's gonna be sorry.'

'You're talking too much,' the man warned her.

'I think you're all crazy,' the woman retaliated. 'An eye for an eye, like it says in the Bible. Her for Mary Phagan. It ain't enough he writes that letter.'

'You shut up, you hear?' her companion ordered. 'We stay here with the girl till that letter shows in the *Constitution*.' He turned to Liz. 'You hungry?'

'Yes,' Liz admitted. Why was Papa supposed to write a letter to the *Constitution*?

'Bring her some food, Mae,' he ordered. 'I'll sit here and keep her company till I gotta go to the meetin'.' His eyes clung to her breasts.

'You keep your hands off her, George,' the woman flung at him. 'Biff, he'll be real mean he finds out you been foolin' around with her.'

'Go get the food,' George reiterated. 'I can look if I want to. She sure got a pair of boobs on her.'

'If Biff had any sense, he'd let us give her to the Knights of Mary Phagan. They'd know what to do with her.'

'You leave them out of it,' George said nastily. 'They didn't ast us to join up with them. We do this our way. Go on and git her somethin' to eat, Mae.'

Liz inched her way back to the cot and sat down, uncomfortable in the way George's eyes devoured her. She remembered the rape case in the law book she had read with Janet this afternoon. He wouldn't try to do that with her, would he? She'd rather die.

Mae came back into the room with a plate of cabbage flanked by a few strips of fatty bacon. Liz felt sick. The newspapers said Mary Phagan ate a plate of cabbage not long before she was murdered.

'Ain't it good enough for you?' Mae demanded. 'That's what we eat here on the farm. We ain't rich like the Hamptons.'

'I can't eat unless you untie my wrists,' Liz pointed out.

With her wrists free Liz took the plate and began to

eat. She couldn't try anything now. Later, she promised herself. When George went to his meeting.

Maureen gazed up at the rain-heavy clouds. The moonlight that had bathed the veranda earlier was gone. Sophie and she had been sitting out here on the screened-in section of the veranda since Francis and Josh had been sent up to bed. That was four hours ago.

'It's going to pour,' she said to Sophie. 'The mosquitoes are out in droves.'

'Maureen, do you think they've hurt her?' Sophie's eyes searched hers.

'No,' Maureen soothed. 'They're using Liz to get that letter in the *Constitution*. Suppose Eric asks to speak to her on the phone to make sure she's all right. They don't dare hurt her,' Maureen insisted with more optimism that she felt.

'I didn't think we had to watch the children every minute. Not out here.'

'I'll go in and make us some coffee.' Maureen rose to her feet. 'We may be up all night.'

'I wish Eric was here,' Sophie said impatiently.

'The men are out searching.'

'Eric doesn't have much respect for the Atlanta police, but I'd feel better if they were looking for Liz, too.'

'That would be dangerous,' Maureen reminded. 'I'll put up the coffee.' She wanted Caroline to suffer, but not this way, Maureen thought defensively. She didn't want anything to happen to Liz.

Maureen felt strange going to the Hampton House kitchen to make coffee. For the first time she felt like one of the family. She stopped dead at the end of the hall. The kitchen was lighted, Mattie, a kimono over her nightgown, was making cornbread. Coffee was brewing.

'The menfolks didn't come back yet?' Mattie's dark eyes were fearful.

'Not yet. I came out for coffee for Miss Sophie and me.'

'I thought maybe the menfolks would be hungry when they come. I'm makin' some cornbread and biscuits.' Her voice broke. 'Miss Maureen, I don't want to think about what's happenin' to our beautiful baby.'

'Liz is going to be fine,' Maureen insisted, but sickening visions haunted her. They'd all heard too much about what happened to Mary Phagan two years ago.

As the first grey streaks of dawn brushed the sky, Maureen and Sophie saw David's Ford approaching the house. From the sombre faces of the three men when they emerged from the car, Maureen guessed they had no word of Liz.

'The other men went home to catch a few hours' sleep,' Jim reported. 'We'll go out again at six A.M. Every one of the leaders of the Knights of Mary Phagan will be followed. If they're holding Liz, we'll know in the morning.'

'Suppose it's somebody else?' Sophie asked. 'What do we do then?'

'Eric and Caroline will be home in the morning.' Jim was unfamiliarly gentle. 'It's their decision if the police are to be called in.'

'Mattie has cornbread and biscuits and hot coffee waiting,' Maureen said. 'If you'd like that.'

Andrew smiled.

'None of us had dinner. We'd like it.'

'If you're starting out again at six A.M., stay here,' Sophie urged. 'There're bedrooms enough.'

'That makes sense,' Jim accepted. He knew that Sophie felt better with them in the house, Maureen thought. But

339

they were no closer to finding Liz than they were when Sophie received that note.

David lay fully dressed across the bed in a Hampton House guest room. Exhausted as he was, sleep refused to come. Perhaps, he surmised, because he was so drained. He remembered the horror of Mary Phagan's murder. Would that never be put to rest in Atlanta?

Logic told him that the Knights of Mary Phagan were responsible for Liz's kidnapping. Yet were they wasting precious time pursuing this? What other lead did they have? he asked himself in soaring frustration. Liz was so dynamic, so outspoken. Would she be wise enough not to put herself in further jeopardy by baiting her captors?

With the pinkness of the sky warning him that this would be another scorcher, David splashed cold water on his face, ran a comb through his unruly hair, and hurried downstairs. Reaching the reception hall, he heard voices outside. Andrew and Jim were sitting on the veranda drinking coffee.

Within twenty minutes the five men enlisted to help them were arriving, each chosen for the dual attribute of loyalty to Congressman Hampton and the possession of a car. The searchers were tired but determined.

Jim had broken down the list of prime suspects from the known members of the Knights of Mary Phagan. Each of the men at Hampton House was to trail the man assigned to him.

'Sometime in the course of the day,' Jim predicted, 'one of them will lead us to where Liz is being held. Don't take any action alone. Phone the house. We'll all check in every hour to see if anybody's come up with information. I talked with people at the *Constitution*. They know nothing about this.'

'They won't print a story?' Andrew was alarmed. 'That would be the same as calling in the police.'

'I have their word,' Jim assured. 'Nothing will hit the newspapers.'

'Let's move.' David was restless.

The cars formed a forbidding parade, to detour shortly into various directions. David searched his mind for the shortest route to the house of the man he was to follow. He would have to be careful not to show his hand, David cautioned himself. If this man was involved in the kidnapping, he would be very wary.

In his mind David went over the brief physical description they had managed to assemble of this member of the Knights of Mary Phagan. About five-foot-nine, dark hair, walked with a slight limp. A salesman.

David drove up to within a hundred feet of the house on Peters Street and waited for his quarry. At twenty minutes before eight o'clock a man carrying a small suitcase emerged from the modest frame house and began to walk towards the streetcar line. David noticed the slight limp.

David drove past the streetcar stop. A streetcar bound for downtown was picking up passengers. His man. David managed to follow. The man disembarked from the streetcar and walked briskly west. He was going to Union Terminal, David realized. Seeing him enter the station, David parked and hurried inside.

He frowned in irritation. Where was his man? Had he suspected he was being followed? A knot tightened in David's stomach. Was the man with the limp one of the monsters who seized Liz in retaliation for Mary Phagan's death? They knew that more than one man must be involved.

David leaned forward intently. There was the man, buying a ticket. He was leaving the city. This was not one of Liz's kidnappers, David conceded in defeat. They would not be leaving Atlanta.

He walked back to the car. The seventy-two-hour deadline haunted him. Go over and talk to Janet. Maybe she could be pushed into remembering something useful.

Janet herself, her eyes red and swollen, opened the door to him. He heard her mother calling to her. After what happened to Liz, Mrs Hammond was nervous.

'It's David, Mama,' Janet called over her shoulder while she pushed the screen door wide for him to enter.

'Have they found Liz?' Janet's mother was pale and fearful.

'Not yet,' David acknowledged. 'But I'd like to talk to Janet if I may. She might just remember something helpful if we talk about what happened there at the streetcar stop.'

Janet and he sat down on the sofa in the parlour while her mother went off to bring him coffee. He persuaded Janet to repeat what she had told Jim earlier.

'Janet, think hard,' David pleaded. 'Was there anybody there at the streetcar stop? Anybody at all?'

'Just Liz and me . . .' Janet faltered and then sat up straight. 'There was something . . .'

'What, Janet?' David leaned forward, willing her to remember.

'A car. A brand-new black Chevrolet. It was down a piece from us. I figured they were waiting for someone getting off the streetcar . . .'

'They?' David pushed.

'Three men. They just sat there and read newspapers,' Janet explained.

'Did you know them?'

'No,' Janet said.

'But you're certain the car was a new black Chevrolet?' David pursued.

342

Janet nodded.

'It was just like the one Uncle Charlie took us to see at the store. Remember, Mama?' Janet appealed to her mother, who had returned with coffee for David. 'He's hoping to buy one this winter.' Her eyes searched David's face. 'Will that help, David?'

'It just may.'

'But there's so many cars in Atlanta now.' Ellen's frown was pessimistic. 'The last I read, somebody claimed six thousands cars in the city.'

'But only some of them are new black Chevrolets.' David's mind raced. Only five years ago the State Legislature had passed an act providing that all cars had to be registered in the office of the secretary of state, where for a two-dollar fee a number plate would be given. The number plate had to be displayed on the car. 'Janet, you may have pointed the way to Liz.'

'Is Caroline back from Washington yet?' Ellen asked.

'She's expected any time.' David abandoned the coffee and rose to his feet. 'I want to go check out that black Chevrolet,' he excused himself.

'Poor Caroline.' Ellen's eyes were troubled. 'She must be out of her mind with worry.'

David raced to the office of the secretary of state. Impressing a clerk with the urgency of the situation, he was able to acquire a list of Chevrolets registered with the office. Only four were both the current year's model and black. The owners of two were personally known to David. He rejected them without wasting a moment. The third was a local doctor. The fourth man lived on a farm just outside of town.

En route to the farm, David paused at his house long enough to order his sister-in-law to relay what happened to Sophie and Maureen, who were standing by at the telephone at Hampton House.

'David, you can't go there alone!' Rae protested, following him to the door.

'I can't wait,' David insisted. 'How can we know what they'll do to Liz? *Call the house.*'

David drove away at a rate of speed that brought a screech from Rae. His sole thought was to arrive at the farm before harm could come to Liz. He refused to allow himself to believe that she had been murdered. Illogical, he told himself. The kidnappers needed Liz as a bargaining agent.

He left the city behind and drove into rural country. The only car on the roads. Few farmers had extended themselves to buy even Mr Ford's Model-T. On either side of the road, fields of cotton spread in every direction. Any day the farmers would begin to pick cotton, but right now nobody was in sight.

David squinted in thought, striving to get his bearings. This must be George Martin's farm. He parked. No use drawing attention to his presence. He left the car and began to walk along the side of the road. He saw a rundown farmhouse on his right. A coon dog slept on the decaying veranda.

David moved into the path between the cotton that towered above his head. Arriving close to the house, striving to silence his advance lest the dog awaken, he heard a woman and a man quarrelling inside. He moved around to the rear, inspecting the broken windowpanes.

At the sight of a black length of cloth covering an unglazed window at the back of the house, David stopped short. The window was close enough to the ground for him to push aside the cloth and look inside.

His eyes searched the tiny room. A rumpled cot sat against one wall. A ramshackle chair and a decrepit dresser. Disappointment flooded him. He had been sure he would find Liz here.

He turned away in dejection, and then focused his attention again on that window. With one sweep of his hand he shoved aside the tacked-up black cloth and pulled himself up into the window frame. Then he saw her. Liz, hands and ankles bound with rope, lay huddled on the floor beneath him, as though sleeping after an exhausted effort to escape through the open window.

Striving to move in silence, he dropped himself into the room. Fearful of alerting the quarrelling couple. Scared that Liz would see him and react aloud. He dropped to his knees beside her and covered her mouth with one hand lest she cry out.

'Liz,' he whispered. 'Be quiet. It's David. David,' he repeated, feeling her stiffen into awareness.

'Oh, David!' she mouthed the words rather than spoke them. Her eyes eloquent with relief.

David untied the rope at her wrists. The rope at her ankles. In silence he helped her to her feet and prodded her to the window.

'It's just a short drop,' he murmured in her ear, and she nodded.

David lifted Liz up to the window frame, waited till she had jumped to the rain-thirsty earth below, then leapt down beside. Her hand in his, they darted through the cotton field towards the car.

All at once the coon dog was barking. They heard the woman shrieking inside the house.

'Run!' David ordered Liz, releasing her hand for the sake of speed. 'To the car!'

The coon dog was pushing through the tall cotton. The man and woman appeared, rushing behind him, handi-capped by age and weight. His breathing heavy from exertion, David raced protectively at Liz's heels through the narrow path between the cotton. The dog caught up with them, nipped at David's trousers.

'Go way,' David gasped, fighting for breath. 'Liz, run to the car,' he ordered while he tried to free himself from the tenacious small dog. He could feel teeth clamping at his ankle now. 'Liz, go on . . .' Panting but frantic, their pursuers were gaining on them.

'You stop 'em,' Mae yelled. 'Biff'll kill us if we let 'em get away!'

Liz turned around to tug at the dog's tail. He released David's ankle to snarl at her.

'Liz, you've got to get out of here!' As he spoke, he was aware of the sound of a car close by. And then another. But nobody could see them here among the cotton.

The man threw himself at David. Twenty years older but sixty pounds heavier. They scuffled while the woman's scrawny arms reached out for Liz. With one frenzied effort Liz pushed her to the ground and moved to help David. The dog barked vociferously, at the same time trying to attack David.

'Liz, yell!' David called out, on his back on the ground beneath flailing fists. 'I hear cars!'

'Help! Help!' Liz's voice was lusty and clear. 'Over here!' Raising herself on tiptoe, she lifted a hand above the cotton, waving for attention. With one foot she shoved Mae, struggling to rise to her feet, to the ground again. 'Over here!'

Several men were pushing through the cotton towards them.

'Papa,' Liz shrieked, and threw herself at him while Noah and Jim pulled George from David. 'Oh, Papa, I was so scared.'

28

One week after Liz's rescue from the kidnappers, Eric returned to Washington to wind up meetings scheduled with congressional Democrats and to arrange for the rental of the furnished house Caroline had decided would satisfy their needs.

Early in September Caroline would leave for Washington with Josh and Francis. It unnerved her to remember that Liz would remain in Atlanta.

Francis was doing well, but now she would be anxious about Liz when they went up to Washington. Was there ever a time in life when anxiety didn't intrude?

She would spend one week out of each month in Atlanta, Caroline tried to reassure herself. She would be in phone contact with Sophie and Andrew. Neither Liz nor the mill would suffer because she was in Washington.

Leaving the office, Caroline looked forward to seeing Victor again at dinner tonight. They had survived the first difficult encounters after the one afternoon when friendship had escalated into passion.

In the library at Hampton House Caroline found Liz and Victor engrossed with Francis in a box of Montessori toys Victor had brought with him from Boston. The mood was warm and relaxed. When Victor accompanied Francis upstairs, Caroline went out to the kitchen to instruct Roland to set up a picnic table on the screened-in section of the veranda.

'Why are we having dinner outdoors?' Liz asked. 'Is it a celebration?'

'I celebrate every night because you're safe at home.'

347

Caroline saw the pleasure that suffused Liz at this admission. How did you make your children understand how deeply they were loved?

They were having dessert when they heard a car pull up in front of the house.

'That's Janet.' Liz jumped to her feet. 'Please excuse me, everybody.'

'Mama, can Josh and I go chase after lightning bugs?' Francis asked.

'That doesn't seem very kind,' Caroline rebuked.

'We let them out of the jar in a few minutes,' Josh was conciliatory. 'Francis likes to see them blink close up.'

'All right,' Caroline capitulated. 'But stay where we can see you.'

'I never thought the day would come when Francis would behave so well.' Sophie's face radiated pleasure.

'I hope to bring all my work together in a book in a year or two. Using Francis' progress as the basis. I won't mention him by name,' Victor promised, 'but I want to share what we were able to accomplish with other parents and doctors.'

'Victor, you must,' Caroline approved.

'I have another proposal,' Victor hesitated.

'Victor, tell us,' Caroline prodded.

'I'd like to offer my services as a physician in a once-weekly clinic to be set up in Hamptonville. It would cost the mill only the salary for a nurse. I'm sure you can find a place to be used.'

'Oh, Victor, yes!' Caroline glowed. 'How soon can we set it up?'

It was almost eleven o'clock, but Liz and Janet were reluctant to go to sleep. They lay across Janet's double bed in her small, modest bedroom and talked about the kidnapping.

'I wake up at night sometimes and remember how those men grabbed me. Mama tried to find out if it still bothers me. I won't talk about it,' Liz admitted. 'Only with Maureen and you.' A guilty delight surged in her. 'It was worth going through all that, to be rescued that way by David. It was like a movie, Janet. Like I was Pauline in *The Perils of Pauline*, and David was Harry.'

'Liz, he's so much older than you,' Janet was doubtful about Liz's romantic fantasy.

'It doesn't matter, Janet,' Liz insisted. 'In some ways David's as young as I am. All he thinks about is how well his research is going and the mail he gets from those scientist friends of his all over the world. I'll bet he's never kissed a girl.'

'Liz!' Janet was shocked.

'We're best friends. We can talk about anything.' Liz was nonchalant.

'Liz, weren't you scared?' Janet asked. A hundred times they had played this game, yet both still relished it.

'I knew I'd be rescued.' Liz brushed from her mind the memory of her sick fear of what might happen to her. 'The worse part was when I had to go to the outhouse with that old witch. The man stood right outside the door. He could hear,' Liz said in fresh outrage. 'And she sat there and watched me. All they had was old newspapers, ripped into small pieces.'

'Liz, did you know that for two days your picture was on the front pages of every newspaper in Atlanta?'

'Queen of the outhouses,' Liz mocked. 'But you know what I keep remembering?' Liz became serious, her eyes introspective. 'That old woman shoving that plate of cabbage in front of me – and she got insulted when I kind of made a face when I saw it. Afterward, talking to Papa about everything, I realized that was all they had to eat. I understand why she was so mad.'

'Liz, most people don't live like the Hamptons. You're rich.'

'Rich or poor, now I know how Leo Frank must feel.' Liz's face clouded. 'Do you realize he's been in jail for more than two years – for something he didn't do? I know how the Russian serfs feel. Papa says they live like prisoners.'

A rap on the door was followed by Janet's mother's voice.

'I expect to see those lights out in five minutes,' she said briskly. 'It's eleven o'clock already.'

By August Georgia farmers were picking the first cotton. Prices had risen to ten cents a pound and were expected to climb higher. The mills were working at full capacity. The South seemed destined for unprecedented prosperity, though there were some Americans bitter about cotton that was moving through neutral ports into German hands. Americans were strongly pro-Allies now. Those with sympathy for the German cause had defected when the German air raids killed civilians and Germans began to experiment with poison gas.

British nurse Edith Cavell was arrested and imprisoned by the Germans. She was awaiting court-martial and faced a probable firing squad. Reading about it in the morning's *Constitution*, Liz fretted all day.

'She was in charge of the Red Cross hospital in Brussels,' Liz said when Caroline lifted her troubled eyes from the newspaper. 'She took care of lots of wounded German soldiers.' Liz was incensed.

'And she helped care for and hide two hundred wounded and fugitive British and French soldiers,' Caroline reminded. 'Until they could reach the German border. It was dangerous and courageous.'

'Will the Germans kill her?'

'I'm sure there'll be tremendous efforts to save her,' Caroline consoled.

'Mama, when will Victor start running the clinic in Hamptonville?' Liz asked.

'He expects it to be in operation in about three weeks,' Caroline told her.

'I want to help,' Liz said. 'And don't say I'm too young,' she warned.

'We'll talk to Victor about it.' Liz was taken aback by her mother's matter-of-fact acceptance. She had not anticipated such an easy victory. 'Tomorrow,' Caroline promised.

Liz spent most of her time with Janet and Maureen. She had been thrilled when Maureen taught Janet and her to 'rag'. Maureen took them to the chautauqua and to the movies and for drives through Piedmont Park. Every time she went over to the Kahn house, expecting to see David, he was closeted in his laboratory and never came downstairs to sit with Rae and her out in the tiny summerhouse. Liz always told Rae she came over to see the baby.

On this sultry mid-August morning Liz lay wide-awake in bed, listening to the early-morning sounds. Mama and Sophie were going down to breakfast; in a little while they would leave for the mill. From out behind the house she heard Mattie calling to Patience to bring in some peppermint from the herb garden.

In sudden impulse Liz kicked off the sheet and sat up at the side of the bed. She would have breakfast, then have Roland drive her over to the Kahn house. She would take Rae some peppermint. Rae loved peppermint in her tea.

Exhilarated by her decision, Liz dressed and headed downstairs for breakfast. Josh and Francis slept till noon

351

on hot days like this. She ate breakfast alone with Elvira, fussing because Liz just picked at her food.

'Tell Roland I want to go over to the Kahns' house,' Liz said to Elvira.

'At seven-thirty in the morning?' Elvira was scandalized. 'Your mama won't like that one bit.'

'Mama won't care,' Liz dismissed this. 'They all get up at five. Mr Kahn opens his store at six-thirty. And I promised to bring Mrs Kahn some of our peppermint. She says yours is the best she ever tasted,' Liz cajoled. 'After that I'm going over to visit with Janet.'

'I'll go pick some peppermint. Then I'll tell Roland to bring the car out front. But you wear a hat when you go outdoors, young lady,' Elvira said firmly. 'In this kinda weather you can get sunstroke.'

Twenty minutes later Liz left the car and walked up the steps to the Kahns' front door. She rang the bell and waited. She could hear the hum of voices from somewhere in the rear of the house. This morning the clamour of the children was missing.

The front door opened. Rae stood there, ashen, her eyes not seeming to recognize Liz.

'Rae, are you all right?' Alarm chilled Liz.

'Liz, you don't know what's happened.' Her voice broke. 'Come out to the kitchen.'

The two boys sat at the table, ignoring the breakfast growing cold before them. Their young faces frightened but uncomprehending. David stood behind them. Like Rae, he seemed in shock.

'You heard, Liz?' The words were wrung from him. All at once he seemed decisive. 'Rae, I'm going over there.'

'David, no. It's dangerous,' she warned.

'David, what's happened? I just came over to visit. I

'. . . I haven't seen you in a week,' Liz stammered, afraid of what David would tell her.

'It's Leo. He's been lynched.' Liz flinched at David's words.

'I don't believe it.' Liz's voice was barely audible. 'When?'

'Around dawn. The word just came through. Noah called from the store a few minutes ago.' He turned to his sister-in-law. 'I'm going over there.'

'All the way to Milledgeville?' Liz asked.

'It happened out in Marietta,' Rae told her. 'They took Leo from the prison farm in Milledgeville and drove all night through the back roads.'

'David, I'm going with you.' Liz's face tightened in determination. 'I want to see where it happened.'

'Liz, you can't go there!' Rae was outraged.

'*I have to go there.* I want to remember this day forever. David, let me drive with you. I'll send Roland home.'

'That's no place for a young girl.' Rae turned to David. 'David, tell her.'

'I'm going,' Liz insisted. 'If David won't take me, I'll find another way.'

David hesitated. 'I'll take Liz with me, Rae,' he resolved. 'She's been part of the fight to save Leo. She was kidnapped, because her father spoke out for him. She has a right.'

'Let's go.' Liz reached out to tug at his arm. Leo Frank was dead. Lynched. *How had God let it happen?*

'David, Caroline will be furious,' Rae called after them, but they hurried down the hall and out of the house.

They drove in silence for a few minutes, each numbed by the sudden tragedy. Then Liz turned to David.

'How did it happen?'

'A bunch of men appeared at the prison farm with

353

guns. They took Leo. They cut the telephone and telegraph wires in the area. But they missed one wire, and the news was flashed to Augusta. Georgia sheriffs were alerted to stop them, but they never made it. At dawn they lynched Leo.'

'They're murderers. Stupid scum!' Liz lashed in contempt.

'Murderers, yes,' David agreed in cold rage. 'But neither stupid nor scum. Noah said the twenty-five men who kidnapped and lynched Leo include two former Supreme Court judges, a minister, and a former sheriff. The leader is one of the most respected men in the community.'

'If the police know who they are, then they'll be thrown in jail and tried,' Liz asserted. 'They're all murderers.'

'They'll never be brought to trial,' David predicted. 'No jury in the state of Georgia would convict them.'

Soon the road that lead them to their destination became cluttered with cars and horse-drawn carriages. The drivers reckless in their haste.

'They're all running to see Leo's body hanging from a tree,' David guessed, his eyes pained.

'You think he's still there?' Liz recoiled from the vision that assaulted her. She had embarked on this pilgrimage without much thought. She was going to see the place where Leo died, to keep the memory forever with her. Now she felt sick.

David's eyes left the road for a moment. 'Liz, shall I take you home?' he asked gently.

'No.' She lifted her head in determination. 'I want to see whatever there is to see. David, how did we let this happen?' It was the anguished accusation of a city.

'There was no stopping them, Liz.'

The road was so congested it was difficult to move. David pulled off into a field and parked, like other drivers around him. Hand in hand, Liz and he moved towards the noisy crowd that seemed to surround a towering oak tree. Liz shuddered at the faces of the men and women – some of the women with babies in their arms – who were avid to see the site of the lynching.

'Now we've got you!' A male voice edged in hysteria seeped above the ominous mutterings of the onlookers. 'You won't murder any more little innocent girls! We've got you now! We've got you now!'

Liz clutched at David's arm as other voices yelled in agreement rising to a staggering crescendo. She shivered at the sight of a little boy, scarcely as old as Josh, darting forward with a camera.

'David, I want to go closer.' She prodded him forward in the surging crowd. Leo was hanging from that tree. These insane people were behaving as though it were a circus.

'Liz, don't look!' His voice thick with grief, David tried to shield her from the sight just ahead of them.

'I will!' she insisted, and a wild-eyed woman beside her, misunderstanding her motive, poked David in the ribs in reproach.

'Let her look! It mighta been her next!'

Liz's gaze was riveted to the dead body of Leo Frank that swung from an oak tree. The rope about his neck had ripped open his throat wound, which was gaping red against the white of the handkerchief that covered his face and the white of his pyjama jacket.

'Oh, God!' The words seemed wrung from David. He was staring at the men and women who were trying to tear bits of cloth from the sleeve of Leo's pyjama jacket. Others were pulling forth knives to snip bits of the rope that had swung Leo to the tree. *Souvenir hunters.*

'We don't want him havin' no decent burial!' the fanatic

who had been screeching at intervals bellowed. 'Let's cut him down and stomp on him! Then we'll burn him!'

'No!' The word rose in rage from David's throat as he geared himself to push towards the body. Suddenly alarmed for David's safety, Liz threw her weight to hold him back. 'Damn you, no!'

David's voice was drowned by that of a new arrival.

'It's Judge Morris!' a woman said excitedly. 'Somebody musta.told him what happened. But he can't stop nothin'. It's done.'

Liz clung to David while they listened to Judge Morris plead with the crowd to allow the undertaker to take away Leo Frank's body.

'Let his parents have the comfort of giving him a decent burial,' the judge harangued. 'Don't deny them that.'

Slowly the crowd became subdued. While the judge gestured to the undertakers to come forward, someone cut the rope and Leo's body dropped to the ground. Liz buried her face against David's chest when the maniac who had urged the crowd to violence moved forward to stamp upon Leo's face and grind his heel, over and over, into the corpse. The crunching sound etched itself on to the minds of the shocked-into-silence onlookers. Somewhere at the side of the mob a man retched.

The crowd parted to allow Leo Frank's body to be removed to the undertaker's wagon. David seemed in shock. Liz clung to his arm.

'David, let's go home.'

29

Atlanta was an obsessed city in the days that followed the lynching of Leo Frank. Thousands besieged the funeral parlour to which Frank's body had been taken, clamouring to be admitted. After much indecision the police capitulated and allowed the body to be viewed before it would be shipped to New York for burial. A police guard of fifty men was present as fifteen thousand morbidly curious residents filed past the bier.

The crowds were noisy, shoving and jostling in their avidity to gaze at the corpse. The atmosphere was that of a Fourth of July celebration.

On the sidewalk hordes waiting for their turn to be admitted bought souvenir photographs of Leo Frank's body hanging from the tree and pieces of rope purported to be from that used in the lynching. Horrified, the Atlanta City Council passed an ordinance against selling photographs of the body of an illegally killed victim.

Liz was inconsolable, travelling constantly to the Kahn house. For days David abandoned his research to mourn, spending hours in the tiny summerhouse in the humid August weather, talking with Liz and Rae about the outrage.

The early-September day was as hot as mid-July. Caroline walked out of the house on to the veranda, with Liz clinging to her arm. Patience was prodding the two boys into the waiting Pierce Arrow.

'Janet's coming to the station to see you off, too,' Liz reported. 'She's going to spend the day with me. Aunt

Sophie said it was all right for her to stay for dinner and sleep over.'

'That'll be fun,' Caroline approved, yet already she felt a sense of loss at leaving Liz behind in Atlanta.

They found Janet waiting for them in the train shed. Liz and Janet kissed the departing party good-bye and watched while they climbed into the Pullman car. Glancing backward at the two girls for an instant, Caroline felt the wrench of separation with its full brutality. Her convivial smile wavered.

She was leaving Hampton House, the mill, Atlanta, behind her except for those weeks when she would be able to escape from Washington. She must depend upon the telephone and the mail to stay in touch with Liz and Sophie. For more than fifteen years the mill had monopolized many of her waking hours. Now she must fit herself into the pattern of the congressman's wife.

'Mama, can I have ice cream for dinner on the train?' Francis asked, a look of bravado in his eyes.

'I'm sure they'll have ice cream on the menu,' Caroline said, leading the way to their drawing room. Victor and she had laboured to prepare Francis for the new life that lay ahead of him, but it was natural that he should feel some insecurity. Even Josh, so delighted at the prospect of living in Washington, was awestruck now that the day of departure was here.

Caroline checked the number on a drawing-room door. 'Here we are.' She thrust open the door and ushered them inside.

'There's Liz!' Francis threw himself at the window and waved excitedly. This was a familiar sight.

Liz and Janet remained while the train began its slow chug from the station. Francis continued to wave until the girls were out of sight. Patience commanded his attention with a new game brought along for diversion, before he could give himself up to alarm.

Despite Caroline's tense watchfulness, the trip offered no problems. Eric met them at Union Station with the senator's car and drove them to the tall, narrow town house on the Hill that everybody said they were so lucky to have been able to rent.

Soon cartons would arrive from Hampton House, Caroline reminded herself. She would sprinkle her private belongings among the furnishings of the rented house, and it would have the look of home.

Though the social season was not officially open, Caroline was aghast at the way Eric and she were swept up into socializing. Luncheons and teas with other congressional wives, nightly dinners with other congressional couples. Meeting Marian Bolton before being taken to yet another luncheon, Caroline confessed over a cup of tea that she was exhausted.

'Honey, you must learn to relax,' Marian urged. 'The summer in Washington is deadly, of course. No opera, no theatre, just the awful city heat.' Marian turned to inspect the seventeenth-century bracket clock that graced her parlour mantel. 'We'll have to leave in about ten minutes. At least, these hot-weather affairs are less formal than winter entertaining. But, Caroline, it *is* important for Eric that you're here in Washington. A wife can often arrange – through another wife – a meeting that just doesn't come off except in a social route. And when a congressman's wife, is young, beautiful, and intelligent, she's a real asset.'

Despite mushrooming social engagements, Caroline wedged in time to spend with the children each day. She took them to the zoo, to the historical sights that lured classes of high-school children to the Capital in increasing volume. She took Josh to the new National Museum on the Mall. To her delight, Francis has taken easily to his new school.

In mid-October Caroline returned to Atlanta for two weeks. Now she made a point of leaving the mill at three in order to be at Hampton House when Liz arrived from school. These hours were precious to her. In the evening Sophie and she involved themselves in mill business.

Cotton was up to twelve cents a pound. Not only had the British bought 275,000 bales – not a particularly impressive amount – during the late summer and early fall, but Dr Heinrich Albert, head of the German Purchasing Commission, had personally purchased one million bales. What had seemed in August to be a cotton crisis had been weathered comfortably.

Caroline and Eric returned to Hampton House, along with the boys and Patience, on the Tuesday prior to Thanksgiving.

Late in the afternoon, Josh asked permission to have Roland drive him to a former classmate's home. 'Fred says I'm invited to spend the night.' Josh was hopeful, yet unsure of approval.

'All right, Josh,' Caroline agreed. 'Pack what you'll need overnight and tell Roland I'd like him to drive you to Fred's house. Dress warmly. It's bitter cold out.'

Francis was delighted to share an early supper in the breakfast room with Liz and Janet, who were eager to escape to the privacy of Liz's room for the rest of the evening. Before supper was finished, he was yawning. Patience took him up to his room when the two girls went upstairs.

How empty the house seemed with the children all out of sight, Caroline mused while Eric, Sophie, and she settled themselves before a blazing fire in the library, where shortly they would dine from trays. Sophie was enjoying their presence at Hampton House.

Shortly before ten Fred's mother phoned, full of apologies because Josh would be driven home shortly.

'I'm so embarrassed,' she gushed. 'And Fred's terribly disappointed. But I didn't know Fred's father had made special plans for the evening. A father-and-son occasion. But we certainly hope Josh can come over and spend the night tomorrow.'

'If Josh has nothing else planned, I'm sure he'll be delighted.' Caroline was polite but annoyed. But her annoyance turned to something much deeper when Josh returned.

'Fred wasn't supposed to tell me where he was going, but he figured I ought to know why I had to go home. His father wants him to see what's happening on the top of Stone Mountain tonight.' Josh bristled with excitement.

'What's happening on the top of Stone Mountain?' Eric laid aside the *Literary Digest* he had been reading.

'Fred wasn't supposed to tell me,' Josh reminded conscientiously. 'He's not even sure he'll be allowed to watch, but his father hopes he can sit in the car nearby. Fred's father and thirty-two friends of his are going up there to Stone Mountain to burn a cross at midnight. They're going through some secret rites that'll bring back the knights of the Ku Klux Klan.'

'Good Lord!' Eric jumped to his feet, his magazine forgotten. 'That's been dead since the early 1870s! Where did they get the nerve to bring it back now?'

'Fred's father says they're doing it to drive the Catholics, Jews, and niggers from this country,' Josh said.

Eric's hand swung out and smacked Josh across one cheek. Josh stood there, pale and frightened, the imprint of Eric's fingers red against the whiteness of his face.

361

Frozen into immobility, Caroline gaped in disbelief. Eric had never laid a hand on any of the children. Instantly Eric reached out to draw the trembling boy into his arms.

'Josh, I'm sorry. You shocked me. I've never heard such a sentiment expressed in this house. I never want to hear it again.' Eric's contrition was replaced by stern exhortation.

'I'm . . . I'm sorry, Papa,' Josh stammered.

'The Ku Klux Klan is an evil organization that should be banned from the face of the earth. Sit down here with me, Josh,' Eric ordered. 'I want to talk about this.'

'Yes, sir.' Josh's voice was unsteady.

'Eric, wouldn't they have to get a charter from the state to start up the Klan?' Caroline asked.

'They have it,' Sophie surmised, her mouth set in a grim line. 'Or they will have soon enough.'

'Josh, I want you to remember as long as you live: it doesn't matter what a person's religious beliefs are, what the colour of his skin is, where his parents or grandparents were born. In this country everybody is free and equal. It was promised in our Constitution when this country was founded. At intervals some people forget. It's our obligation to make them remember. You are never to talk that way again. How would you feel if Mattie or Elvira or the other servants heard you talk like that?'

'I'd feel awful.' Josh's voice was low. 'Papa, I'm sorry.'

Only now did Caroline realize that Liz and Janet stood in the doorway, absorbing what was being said. Their faces were sombre.

'Liz, did I tell you?' Caroline said in an effort to relieve the tension that hung over the library. 'We'll be home again ten days before Christmas. We have to be here for your birthday. We'll have a party,' she decided effervescently. 'You make up a list of girls you'd like to invite, and I'll – '

'I'd rather have a grown-up dinner party,' Liz interrupted. 'Family and the Kahns and Victor and Janet. May I, Mama?' How guileless and lovely she looked, but Caroline saw beyond this.

'If that's what you'd like, of course,' Caroline approved after a moment's hesitation. In another year Liz would go away to college. Probably to Randolph-Macon up in Virginia. All this would change.

30

Caroline awoke on the crisp, cold first Monday in December with an immediate awareness that this was a landmark day in her life. Today the Sixty-fourth Congress would commence its first session. At noon the new House would be called to order. Eric would be sworn in as congressman from Georgia.

Pride stirring in her, she turned to Eric. He was sleeping soundly. On this morning he would eschew all business until the time arrived to go to the Capital. Marian and she would be in the gallery for the opening session, though Marian warned that only new congressional wives were apt to put in an appearance. Eric had been a congressman for thirteen months, but only now would he feel himself part of the body that guided the nation.

Caroline slid from the bed, careful not to disturb Eric, and walked to the marble-faced fireplace. Enjoying the ritual, she laid three small birch logs in the grate, added kindling wood, crumpled paper and stuffed it beneath the grate. She lit the paper and watched orange-red flames leap upward, igniting the oil-rich kindling. In moments the scent of birch would fill the room.

She walked to the door and turned the lock, though she had cautioned Patience that this morning Eric and she would not be at the breakfast table with the boys. Last night they had attended one of the first official functions of the winter season, returning home shockingly late.

Caroline returned to the bed and pulled the frilly but

practical nightgown over her head and dropped it to the floor. For a moment she flinched in the morning coolness; the fire would not send warmth across the room for a while yet. A smile touched her mouth. How long had it been since she had taken the initiative in lovemaking?

Beneath the comforter Caroline flung one leg across Eric's, burrowed her mouth at his ear. Almost immediately she felt him move into wakefulness. Her hand sought him. Passion surged in her. Times like this, she felt almost wanton.

'Are you going to sleep all morning, Congressman?' she murmured, relishing his sudden awareness of the situation.

His hands reached for her beneath the comforter, discovering her nakedness.

'Is this a ruse to make me miss the opening session?' he demanded in mock reproach.

'We don't have to leave for the Capitol for hours.' Her eyes made love to him while his hands roamed.

After all the years of being together Eric knew every little area that increased her arousal, as she knew his. How had she survived that period without Eric in her bed?

'The fire's sending out heat,' he said after a few minutes of their explorations, and tossed aside the comforter. 'I may never go to the Capitol,' he warned, feasting his eyes on her. 'At your age it's indecent to be so seductive.' It was a favourite reproach of his.

'I saw all those women lusting after you last night,' she clucked. 'The most handsome man in Congress.'

'You'll be in the gallery when I'm sworn in?' One hand moved between her thighs.

'I'll be in the gallery if you hurry up and make love to me.' All at once it was unbearable not to have him within her. 'Eric, now.' Her hand reached to him, knowing he was ready.

He lifted himself above her, and in a remembered symphony they moved together. Subconsciously she was aware of Francis' voice in the hall, and then Josh's. Patience was taking them to school.

'Sugar, you are marvellous,' Eric gasped while they rocked in perfect union. 'Nobody like you, ever.'

She could forgive him for Serena Mayo, Caroline realized in a new awareness while she rested in the curve of his arm. Yet instinct still told her she must be silent about the one afternoon with Victor. Perhaps he would forgive her; she would not allow herself to gamble.

'I wish the children could be in the House today,' she said wistfully.

'There'll be other times,' Eric promised. 'They'll be there.'

At a few minutes before twelve Caroline entered the House gallery with Marian Bolton. Excitement spiralled in her at her first view of the impressive House chamber. Her gaze sought to encompass everything.

'There's Eric,' Marian pointed. 'Now, of course, the representatives seat themselves on a first-come, first-served basis. Until two years ago each representative had a permanent seat with a desk. Then they were removed and replaced with those benches.'

Caroline and Marian seated themselves, exchanging greetings with several ladies among the spectators in the gallery. Caroline remembered the high turnover among the members of the House. The senator had said last night that the average length of service was less than six years. When would there be *women* sitting in Congress?

Caroline's eyes swept from the thronelike marble dais on which the Speaker would sit, past the mahogany tables midway back along the aisle that divided the majority party from the minority. She knew that these were the 'leadership tables', occupied by the powerful men of each party. She saw the small, arched area before the Speaker's dais, known as the Well of the House, where members stood to deliver their speeches. She inspected the panelled skylight adorned with medallions representing the coats of arms of the forty-eight states.

Excitement rippled through the gallery as, sharply at noon, the clerk of the preceding House – according to procedure – rapped for order. The chaplain took his place and the members and spectators rose and bowed their heads while he briefly prayed. The clerk began to call the roll.

Caroline listened attentively while the Speaker was selected and escorted by a committee of three to his desk on the dais. The Speaker took his oath and in turn began to administer the oath to the new representatives, called by state to take their places before his desk. Caroline's heart pounded while she watched Eric being sworn in. *At last he was here*. How proud the General would have been to witness this.

Caroline felt a thrill of pride while she watched the sergeant at arms lift the historic mace of the United States House of Representatives – thirteen ebony rods banded in silver and topped by a silver globe on which perches a massive eagle with widespread wings – and place it on a malachite pedestal at the Speaker's right. The signal that the House of Representatives was officially in session.

On December 16, two days before President Wilson was to marry Mrs Galt in a quiet ceremony in her Washington house, Caroline and Eric left for Atlanta with the boys and Patience. From Washington she had arranged Liz's fifteenth birthday dinner.

Sophie had relayed Liz's plea that the evening's festivities include attendance at the new movie. Despite the high admission of two dollars per person, *The Birth of a Nation* was playing to packed houses at every matinee and every evening performance. Eager to please Liz, Caroline asked Sophie to make arrangements for the dinner party to attend the film.

The birthday dinner was going well, Caroline congratulated herself when the beautifully decorated two-tiered birthday cake was brought to the table by Roland to the accompaniment of admiring comments.

Liz gave no indication of missing them, Caroline rationalized. She was happy in Atlanta. David was here. Though Liz had grown four inches in the past year and appeared a nubile eighteen-year-old, Caroline knew she could depend upon David to dismiss any romantic overtures Liz might make. To David – like Eric – Liz was still a little girl, to be protected and cherished. David didn't see that he had become Liz's knight in shining armour by rescuing her from the kidnappers.

In high spirits tonight, Liz reminded everyone of the necessity to be at the Atlanta Theatre by eight-thirty. Birthday cake and coffee were consumed without delay. Alerted to the imminent departure, Elvira and Patience were waiting in the reception hall to dispense coats.

'Andrew,' Liz said with the appealing quality in her voice that no male seemed able to resist, 'may David and Janet and I ride in the Chalmers? David says he can't believe any car can ride as smoothly as we told him your Chalmers does.'

'My pleasure,' Andrew agreed, beaming.

The Pierce Arrow and the Chalmers deposited their occupants on Exchange Place, in front of the Atlanta Theatre, which on most occasions was devoted to the finest in stage productions. Noah and the others in the

Ford would join them as soon as Noah found a parking spot.

'Mama, they won't be long, will they?' Liz was eager to be inside the theatre.

'They're coming now,' Caroline said, clinging to Josh.

'Did you know that this is the only fireproof theatre building in the South?' Eric asked while they joined the convivial hordes walking into what the *Journal* had called 'the best-appointed and probably the handsomest playhouse in the South' when it opened four years ago.

'That may be necessary tonight,' David said cryptically.

With Eric's hand at her elbow, Caroline walked behind Liz and Janet, who were plotting to sit with David. She tried to concentrate on the elegance of the theatre, its green-and-gold decor, the high-domed ceiling with its sunburst of gold leaf, the colourful fresco of the proscenium arch. There were four huge boxes and two balconies, reached via marble staircases.

'They must be making a fortune on this film,' Eric guessed, surveying the rapidly filling house. 'Seventeen hundred seats at two dollars each, two showings a day.'

She had been right in her assumption, Caroline noted. Liz and Janet contrived to sit with David between them. Eric and she seated themselves in the two remaining seats alloted to their party.

'My brother saw the picture with his wife last night,' a man behind them said expectantly to a neighbour. 'They can't stop talking about it! You never saw so many big actors and actresses in one picture before. And the story will just knock you over.'

Almost immediately Caroline realized the power of the picture, which opened with young Confederate soldiers marching off to war while a band played 'Dixie'. Her hand reached out for Eric's. Soon the Battle of Atlanta was recreated before them. She was remembering her father's two young brothers who died in the Battle of Atlanta. She was remembering the General, who had fought in this battle. In the balcony a woman cried out in anguish. Somewhere behind them another woman sobbed. A man emitted a rebel yell.

On the field of battle a Northern boy hovered with bayonet in hand above the body of a Southern friend, only to fall before Confederate bullets. He died, an arm about his Southern buddy, and the man sitting behind Caroline cried. She felt wetness on her own cheeks. Papa had fled to England to avoid meeting his Princeton friends on a battlefield.

For three hours the anguish of the South, during the war and Reconstruction, smote the audience without relief. Caroline cringed – and heard Eric curse beneath his breath – as the movie showed the lynching of Negroes and the rise of the Klan. An orchestra of twenty provided music dramatically adapted to the story, ranging from a plaintive lullaby in one scene to a crescendo of battle in the next. Wild, barbaric music, and music that brought the audience to tears. How ironic that on Thanksgiving evening – just three weeks ago – the Ku Klux Klan had risen again, on the top of Stone Mountain.

Seeing that Eric and David were deep in sombre talk about the movie's portent, Caroline invited David to return to the house with them.

'Come back and let's talk more,' Eric urged. 'Roland will drive you home later.' Eric grinned. 'He's happiest when he's behind the wheel of the car. I'll phone Jim and ask him to come over, too.'

'Eric, it'll be almost midnight by the time we get home,' Caroline rebuked.

'Jim won't mind. He never goes to bed before two. Four hours of sleep and he's raring to go again.'

Andrew and Maureen had driven directly home.

Sophie went upstairs to her room on arrival at Hampton House. Josh was shipped off amid protests because Liz and Janet, who had been invited to sleep over, were stalling on going upstairs to bed.

'Liz gets away with everything,' Josh grumbled. 'Just because she's two years older than me.'

Caroline went out to the kitchen to prepare a pot of coffee, since Mattie and Elvira had retired. She placed slices of birthday cake on a hand-painted tray, mindful of Eric's affection for sweets. Only on special occasions did she cater to this. She returned with the tray just as Jim arrived at the house. Eric was greeting him at the door.

'You mean to say you went to see that damn-fool movie?' Jim demanded in scepticism.

'Liz wanted to see it,' Eric explained. 'I'm glad we went. God, the racial prejudice in it! The heroic portrayal of the Ku Klux Klan!' He flinched in distaste.

'Eric has no respect for your time,' Caroline said in indulgent apology. 'This was an unconscionable hour to call.'

'We're seeing unconscionable things in Atlanta.' David appeared in the doorway and relieved Caroline of the tray. 'First some evidence that the Ku Klux Klan is reborn. Now the whole country is bombarded by this epic to intolerance.' His eyes were furious. 'It's an insult to the nation.'

'D. W. Griffith's father was a Confederate colonel,' Jim reported drily.

'That doesn't mean he has to act like he approves of lynchings and the Ku Klux Klan.' Liz's face was stormy.

They settled themselves in the library over cake and coffee. It was inevitable that the conversation focused on politics.

'It seems so weird that Eric will have to start campaigning for reelection in a few months,' Caroline mused.

'When is Congress going to do something about these insane waits before a congressman actively serves?'

'It'll come,' Eric promised. 'Nothing happens fast in Congress.'

'The President won't have an easy time next November,' Jim warned. 'It's going to be a close election in 1916.'

'He has one thing in his favour,' Eric said. 'Some voters will be reluctant to change horses in midstream.'

'Is it true what we hear about Dorsey running for governor?' David asked.

'He'll come out soon with the announcement,' Jim predicted, unhappy at the prospect.

'The man who crucified Leo Frank to be governor of this state.' David grimaced. 'I can't believe it.'

'He won't win,' Liz said quickly.

'He'll win,' David said. 'Hugh Dorsey was campaigning the moment he set foot in that courtroom and prepared to convict Leo.'

'That's right,' Jim agreed. 'Why do you think Dorsey worked so damned hard on the case? He knew that convicting Frank would buy him a hell of a lot of votes.'

'Tom Watson will fight for Dorsey,' Eric pointed out. 'Watson's still picking our governors.' He paused. 'I'll fight against Dorsey, for what it's worth. But I'm not running for re-election next November.'

'What the hell are you talking about?' Jim demanded, vocalizing the shock of the others.

'I'm a maverick. I'm swimming upstream. Sitting there in the theatre, I realized that. I don't think I can win in the next election.'

'What's so different between 1914 and 1916?' Jim challenged. 'Of course you'll win.'

'Papa, run for governor,' Liz said, her eyes brilliant.

'This is where you belong. Here at home.' She did miss them, Caroline thought tenderly.

'Honey, if I thought I had any chance at all, I'd run for governor. I'd like to clean up this state and make our people able to hold up their heads again. But I haven't a chance with feelings what they are in the rural areas and with Tom Watson beating the drums for all the wrong things.'

'Georgia needs you in Washington,' Caroline insisted. Eric couldn't mean what he said. The movie had upset him.

'I'm forty-one years old. I've got a lot of good years ahead of me, and I intend to use them well. I want to devote the rest of my life to pacifism.'

'Papa, you can be a pacifist *and* a congressman,' Liz said, capitulating on the governorship.

'No, Liz. I'm going back to Washington and I'm going to talk out loud and hard against preparing ourselves for war. I don't believe for one moment that the German Army is going to cross the Atlantic Ocean to murder Americans. This whole business of preparedness is running amok.'

'Eric, this isn't a new situation to you.' A vein throbbed in Jim's temple. 'How many peace speeches did you eliminate from your schedule when you were campaigning for this term? The circumstances are the same. *Play down your feelings about preparedness.* We need a voice like yours in Congress to talk loud and eloquently at the right time. *After* you're reelected,' he emphasized.

'But until November I'm to be quiet?' Eric asked in sardonic humour. 'Dammit, Jim, you know how I feel.'

'You're a freshman congressman. Bolton's told you that you can't afford to talk too much – the old-line congressmen resent it. They'll farm you out to ineffectual committees. Sit back and listen, Eric. Talk when you're

373

on safe ground and when you can be effective. When the issue is important to Georgia.'

'I ran for Congress to be a voice against war,' Eric said, his face taut. 'You want me to do nothing.'

'Don't be so all-fired impatient,' Jim scolded. 'In ten months you'll have a second term under your belt if you play the game right. Then you can talk.'

'But now, when any German lieutenant can catapult us into war, I'm supposed to be silent,' Eric said derisively. But Caroline sensed he was considering the situation.

'Wilson is fighting to keep us out of the war,' Caroline reminded. 'You said yourself that he'll campaign on the issue that he's kept us out so far. You can wait till November.'

'I'm afraid the day'll come when Congress must vote for or against involvement in the war,' Eric said tiredly. 'I want to be there. You're right as always, Jim. I'll have to play the game.'

'Papa, that's dishonest!' Liz was outraged. 'How can you turn your back on what you believe?'

'Twenty years ago I would have refused,' Eric admitted. 'But I've learned through the years. Sometimes compromise is necessary. In Congress I'll fight every inch of the way against our involvement in this war – or any war. But no speeches against preparedness. I'm starting right now to campaign for re-election.'

'I think it's terrible,' Liz stared at her father as though she had never truly seen him before. 'You're acting just like all other politicians. I thought you were different. Come on, Janet. Let's go up to my room.'

Caroline stared unhappily while Liz stormed from the library, an apologetic Janet at her heels. Eric turned to David, knowing he, too, was upset by this acceptance of political rules.

'David, it's still unofficial . . . and I know you won't

repeat it outside of this room. In January a new Supreme Court judge will be appointed. I'm quite certain it'll be Louis Brandeis. The first Jew on the Supreme Court. There'll be a fight,' Eric guessed, 'but I'll vote for the confirmation. Senator Smith will keep silent until the last minute, but I know for a fact that he'll vote, too, to confirm the appointment. Don't lose your faith in this country, David. There *are* clear heads in Washington.'

Immediately after New Year's Liz saw her parents and brothers off for Washington. She refused to relinquish her rage that her father was playing politics to retain his seat in Congress. She felt betrayed.

As always, she saw much of Maureen, who had become one of the New Young Women, shortening her skirts, smoking, drinking cocktails. Liz was enthralled at being Maureen's confidante. Only to her did Maureen admit that Andrew was upset by her activities.

Liz was delighted when Maureen brought her into the suffrage movement. Nobody guessed she was fifteen. They thought she was Maureen's contemporary. The women in the movement, Maureen pointed out, cared nothing about her family background. Liz knew now about Maureen's father, and the half-sisters and half-brothers who never acknowledged the relationship. To her Maureen had become a romantic figure.

Over tea in the Georgian Terrace restaurant Maureen told Liz that she was pregnant.

'Is Andrew excited?' Liz felt grown-up, to be taken into Maureen's confidence on such an important subject. Someday she'd be pregnant. She'd have David's baby.

'I haven't told Andrew. I'm telling him tonight,' Maureen explained. 'I saw the doctor this morning.'

'Aren't *you* excited?' Liz pressed.

'I'm scared a little,' Maureen admitted. But she looked

375

pleased. 'It's going to be awful to walk around with an ugly fat stomach. I won't be able to wear any of my beautiful clothes.'

Maureen dressed with special care for dinner tonight. Instinct told her Andrew would be delighted at the prospect of parenthood. Giving Andrew a child would make her marriage forever secure. She would never have to worry again.

It annoyed her that Andrew and she lived so close to the mill, but now with a child coming she would persuade Andrew to build them a fine house some distance away. With the car it would take Andrew only a few minutes to drive to the mill. *She wished for a home as fine as Hampton House.*

Phoebe seemed to sense that tonight was an occasion. She sang joyously in her rich, melodic voice while she moved about the kitchen concocting culinary master-pieces. Did Phoebe know she was pregnant? Maureen asked herself. Sometimes Andrew laughed and said Phoebe had supernatural abilities.

Not until they had finished dinner and were sitting in the parlour with their coffee, listening to Geraldine Farrar sing the big aria from *Madame Butterfly*, did Maureen allow herself to tell Andrew of her pregnancy.

'Andrew, I went to the doctor today,' she said in the soft, breathy fashion to which she resorted in tense moments.

'Maureen, aren't you feeling well?' Instantly he was solicitous.

'I feel wonderful, Andrew. I'm pregnant.'

The bone-china cup rattled against the saucer he held. He reached to clutch it with his other hand.

'Maureen, you're sure?' He appeared stunned by her announcement.

376

'Quite sure.' she was stricken. Andrew was upset. 'I
. . . I thought you'd be pleased.'

'Honey, I'm delighted,' he stammered. 'I was sure I
was past the age to . . .' Colour suffused him. 'To become
a father.'

'Andrew, how could you think that?' she chided.
'You're like a very young man when we make love.' It
was true. It astonished her that she found such pleasure
in bed with Andrew.

'Maureen . . .' He put aside the cup and saucer and
reached for her.

'Andrew, let's go into the bedroom.' She felt so
powerful.

'Is it all right now?' he stammered. 'I mean, for the
baby?'

Maureen laughed with heady pleasure. 'It'll be all right
for months yet.'

Maureen revelled in her pregnancy. For the first time in
her life she felt important. Loved. Andrew hovered in
solicitude every moment he was in her presence. Gilbert,
their chauffeur, was given strict instructions to drive
carefully.

Liz was in and out of the cottage. Liz felt closer to her
than to Caroline, Maureen told herself with satisfaction.
Both Liz and Janet adored being with her, running
around Atlanta in the Chalmers. Their presence helped
her ignore her lack of social life.

The society pages of the Atlanta newspapers had
carried reports of her engagement and marriage to
Andrew. But Caroline should have given a formal dinner
to introduce Andrew's wife to the fine old Atlanta
families. To Atlanta society, Andrew and she did not
exist.

She could not attempt to give a party in their cottage.

Not in a cottage at the edge of the mill village. Only Hampton House could escape the stigma of being at the edge of Hamptonville.

She must make Andrew understand that it was important for them to have a new house now that the baby was coming. He never talked about how much money he had, but he must be rich. He owned stock in the mill. When everybody was buying cotton, he'd bought, too – and the price for cotton kept going up. Caroline said it would hit thirty cents a pound.

Saying nothing to Andrew yet about her determination to move into a fine house in a prestigious neighbourhood before the baby was born, Maureen began to search for a suitable home. Liz was with her when a real-estate salesman showed her a handsome red-brick house on a two-acre tract in one of Atlanta's exclusive new residential areas.

'Liz, isn't it beautiful?' she whispered while the salesman crossed to throw open the French doors that led to a balcony off an upstairs bedroom.

'Tell Andrew you want it,' Liz urged.

The salesman returned, smiling in anticipation of a sale.

'I'll talk to my husband about it.' Maureen forced herself to appear doubtful. 'He may feel it's too expensive.'

'We'd be happy to discuss it with Mr Hampton,' the salesman assured. 'It's a fine house, and the neighbourhood is superb.' He knew she was bargaining, and he respected her for it. Liz looked shocked. Liz grew up in a world where people bought without looking at price tags.

'Thank you for showing us the house.' Maureen knew the salesman had seen the Chalmers. He was aware that

378

her clothes were expensive. 'I'll phone you when I've discussed the house with Mr Hampton.'

Maureen and Liz returned to the cottage, caught up in pleasurable intrigue. Tonight, Maureen confided to Liz, she would try to persuade Andrew to buy the house.

'Liz, you'll be the baby's godmother,' Maureen decided impulsively, and Liz threw her arms about Maureen with a screech of delight.

Suddenly a sharp, searing pain attacked Maureen. She tensed, clutching at her stomach. Her face was drained of colour. Seconds later a second pain. She was barely in her fourth month. She couldn't be going into labour.

'Maureen?' Liz was scared. 'Are you all right?'

'I think I'd better lie down,' she gasped.

Liz protectively at her side, Maureen stumbled into the bedroom. Gritting her teeth against the recurrent pains, her forehead beaded with perspiration, she allowed Liz to help her to lie on the bed.

'Should I call Phoebe?' Liz asked while she removed Maureen's white duck pumps.

'Call the doctor,' Maureen ordered. She could feel the warm wetness between her thighs. *She was losing the baby*. 'Call him quickly, Liz. Dr Desmond. Then tell Phoebe to come to me.'

In moments Phoebe was in the room, murmuring consolation, changing Maureen into a nightgown.

'Miss Liz, this ain't no place for you,' Phoebe scolded, but Liz refused to leave.

'Let her stay, Phoebe.' Maureen reached for Liz's hand. Liz was her first real friend.

'Does it hurt, Maureen?' Liz was distraught.

'I don't care about that. But I'm losing the baby, Liz.' Everything depended upon her giving Andrew a child. What had she done to make this happen?

Dr Desmond arrived and ousted Liz from the bedroom.

Maureen abandoned herself to pain and disappointment. When Phoebe had changed her into yet another fresh nightgown, and a fresh sheet had been slipped beneath her, Dr Desmond sat beside the bed and took her hand in his.

'You're going to be all right, Mrs Hampton,' Dr Desmond soothed. 'But I must warn you. You must never conceive again.'

'But why?' Maureen stared at him in bewilderment. 'Dr Desmond, I want to have a baby!'

'It could mean your life.'

'You said nothing about that before,' she protested.

'I was fearful when you came to me. Just looking at you – before the examination – I knew your narrow bone structure would put you through a most difficult delivery. Mrs Hampton, don't gamble with your life.' His eyes were compassionate. 'If you like, I'll explain to Mr Hampton.'

'No,' Maureen said quickly. 'I'll tell him.' Knowing she would not.

31

While the war in Europe continued unabated, the United States in the first six months of 1916 was caught in a ferment of national discontent. The country was plagued by strikes and lockouts. At a time when a segment of the poor was beginning to enjoy unprecedented affluence, militant voices rose in strident demands for woman suffrage, prohibition, birth control, rights for blacks, better education. A million socialists were alarming the populace with their vociferous clamour for the overthrow of capitalism.

In Washington Caroline and Eric were disturbed by the preparedness wave. In January and February, President Wilson, so strong for peace, had toured the Midwest on behalf of preparedness.

In mid-1916 Atlanta was in crisis. Grady Hospital was in poor shape, as Victor deplored at regular intervals. Streets were in desperate need of repairs and paving. Schools were low on funds. Money to pay city officials was running so low, some suspected they'd soon be serving without salary.

In Atlanta Maureen learned from Liz that the story of her illegitimacy was being whispered about at ladies' luncheons and tea dances and garden-club meetings. Two ladies from New Orleans who employed Maureen's mother as a seamstress were spreading the story of her illegitimate birth. At school Liz, proud of her beautiful, rebellious young cousin who dared to smoke in public and enjoyed afternoon cocktails, had talked about

Maureen constantly until one classmate repeated the gossip. To Liz this only added to Maureen's allure.

Maureen had told Andrew about her mother. She was terrified that he would learn the truth about her father. At least, Atlanta society was aware of her existence. She *was* a Hampton now.

Late in June Maureen suspected that she was again pregnant. She delayed going to Dr Desmond, knowing he would chastise her for gambling with her life. But she told Liz.

'You'll have to be careful,' Liz told her, mindful of her miscarriage and solemn at being taken into Maureen's confidence even before Andrew was told. 'Do exactly what the doctor tells you.' In a burst of exuberance Liz flung her arms about Maureen. 'Am I still going to be the baby's godmother?'

'I wouldn't consider anybody else. Shall we drive downtown this afternoon?' Maureen was suddenly restless. She tried to tell herself she wasn't afraid of being pregnant again, but at errant moments Dr Desmond's face flashed across her mind. He had been so serious.

'Do you think you should, in all this heat?' Liz worried.

'Sugar, the heat doesn't bother me one bit. At least not yet.'

'Could we stop by Rae Kahn's house so I can give her some peppermint from the garden? She loves it.' Liz appeared so guileless, Maureen laughed.

'You can think of more excuses to try to see David.'

'He still keeps treating me like a little sister,' Liz fretted, 'but in December I'll be sixteen. He won't have to be afraid to admit he's in love with me.'

'Has he ever said anything, Liz?' Maureen was uncomfortable when they talked about David.

'No. But when I'm sixteen he will. Did you know that Rae was only fifteen when she married Noah?'

'No.' She frowned. She didn't understand the Hamptons' closeness to the Kahn family. 'Let me call Gilbert and tell him to drive us downtown.'

Two weeks later Maureen told Andrew that she was again pregnant. He was simultaneously exhilarated and fearful. As soon as she was into her fourth month with no problems, she promised herself, she'd take Andrew to see the red-brick house the real-estate man had shown her the day of her miscarriage. He'd buy the house for them.

Dr Desmond confirmed her pregnancy. He was unhappy. 'Mrs Hampton, I thought I made it clear that it would be dangerous for you to have a child. How could your husband subject you to this?'

'I didn't tell him.' Her eyes met his in faint defiance. 'It's important to both of us to have a baby.'

He sighed. 'I presume you don't want him to know now?'

'No.' Her voice was involuntarily sharp.

'I'll respect that,' Dr Desmond promised.

Telling herself that her activities about town would soon be curtailed – and to escape from her fears that she might be one of those wives who miscarry time after time – Maureen took Liz and Janet to the first matinee at the fine new Criterion Theatre at 43 Peachtree. They would see Alice Brady in the movie version of *La Bohème*. For a little while she would have no time to worry that she would again disappoint Andrew.

The doctor seemed to have no concern about another miscarriage. He was worried about delivery. But she wouldn't think about that until she went into labour, Maureen promised herself. She must give Andrew a child. Only then would she know her marriage was on solid ground.

* * *

Early in June the National Defence Act was passed, authorizing an army of nearly a quarter million. The National Guard was mobilized, and across the country society ladies met arriving trains of guardsmen with sandwiches, coffee, and ice cream. In July a German U-boat showed up on the East Coast, causing minor hysteria.

The South was entering a boom period. The war in Europe, earlier appearing to be a disaster to the South, had become its salvation. Andrew was delighted by the soaring price of cotton. He confessed he had bought heavily out of respect for Caroline's judgement.

'Caroline has a feel for the cotton market,' Andrew told Maureen. 'Like the General.'

Maureen abandoned her trips downtown now that her pregnancy was obvious. She hated the loss of her slimness. Late in August, well into her fourth month of pregnancy, she persuaded Andrew that they must move into a more suitable house for the sake of the baby. Everything must be right for him from the day he was born.

Uneasy at the expenditure but determined to do what was right for the child he had never expected, Andrew allowed himself to be prodded into buying the red-brick house. At a yet-to-be-settled date in October Maureen and Andrew would move into their new residence.

Congress had closed its session on September 8. Eric was rushing home for last-minute campaigning and to vote in the primaries on September 12. Liz tried to fabricate an excuse not to go to Terminal Station with her mother and brothers.

'You're coming with us, Liz.' Her mother was adamant. Couldn't Mama understand how uncomfortable she was with Papa since he sold out to the politicians?

'I'm supposed to be at the clinic with Victor this afternoon,' Liz resisted.

'Victor knows Papa's due in Atlanta. I told him,' Caroline said. 'He doesn't expect you this afternoon.'

'I'll have to call him and ask,' Liz insisted, though she recognized defeat.

An hour later she stood with her mother and the two boys while the train chugged into the shed. For a few minutes she allowed herself to be caught up in the excitement that the arrival of the crack Washington–New York train generated.

'There's Papa!' Josh spied him and rushed forward with the new growth he was finding difficult to handle with grace. Josh was taller than she was, Liz thought in recurrent astonishment.

'Papa, Papa!' Francis, too, darted forward. As ever, following Josh's lead.

Eric hugged the two boys, and with an arm about each moved towards his wife and daughter. Liz felt strangely self-conscious at the sight of her parents in such a warm embrace.

Dutifully Liz kissed her father. That didn't mean she wasn't angry with him, she reassured herself. She could feel his awareness of their strained relationship.

'I brought you a book,' Eric cajoled when they were settled in the car. 'That new best-seller by Booth Tarkington. It's called *Seventeen*.'

'Thank you, Papa.' Liz could not resist a reproach. 'But just because it's on the best-seller list doesn't mean it's good.'

'When does school open?' Eric pretended to ignore her coolness.

'In ten days,' Liz told them. Right after the primaries, Papa and Mama and the boys would be going back to

385

Washington. They had to be there for the beginning of school.

'I had a long talk with Jim last night,' Caroline told Eric. 'Whatever problems you might have faced earlier, you're sure to win the primary.'

'Unless there's an upset,' Eric stipulated.

'Jim says even the opposition conceded you'll be sent back to Washington for a second term.' Caroline's face was tender. *She* wanted Papa to win, Liz told herself guiltily. Only, not this way. He ought to be true to his convictions.

On election afternoon Liz went with Josh to a birthday party for Rae and Noah's older son. When Roland came with the car to take them home, she sent Josh alone. She had contrived to invite herself to remain for supper, hopeful of seeing David.

'It's all right, Roland,' Liz insisted when he hesitated. 'I'll phone Mama and explain.'

'Yes, ma'am,' Roland accepted reluctantly. 'But if she say she wants you home, I'll come right back.'

Liz and Rae were alone in the house with the children. David was downtown.

'He went to vote early and said he'd stay at the store with Noah until they heard about the elections. He was too upset to work on his research,' Rae told Liz.

'You don't think Mr Dorsey's going to win?' Everybody was saying he would, but that would be terrible.

'He won the election in the courtroom, Liz,' Rae said. 'The man who told the jury that the Jews "rise to heights sublime, but they also sink to the lowest depths of degradation" will be elected governor of Georgia.'

Earlier than either Liz or Rae expected him, David appeared at the Kahn house.

'I was just distracting Noah's attention from business,'

David's smile was wry. 'And he said not to hold supper for him. He'll be late tonight.'

'That means he'll want delicatessen,' Rae surmised. 'And I have none in the house.'

Liz laughed at Rae's crestfallen expression.

'Phone and have them send it out,' she said.

'Sugar, where I buy on Decatur Street they don't deliver.' Rae chuckled.

'I'll drive down and get it for you, Rae,' David offered. 'Noah insisted I take the car. He'll come home on the streetcar.'

'David, I don't want to send you back downtown again,' Rae fretted.

'I don't mind,' David said, and Liz sensed his restlessness. He was upset about the elections.

'David, let me go with you,' Liz said on impulse. 'I've never seen Decatur Street.' She knew it was a section of the city where Noah had his store, and where the coloured folks did all their shopping.

David and Rae exchanged indulgent glances. At moments like this Liz sensed the protectiveness of her life, her isolation from the mainstream of Atlanta. Even Janet went to Decatur sometimes with her mother.

'Come along and be educated,' David teased. 'To live in Atlanta without knowing Decatur Street is like living in New Orleans without knowing Canal Street, or Paris without knowing the Champs-Elysées.'

With instructions about what to buy, David prodded Liz from the house into Noah's Tin Lizzie. Liz was exuberant at this special treat. So rarely could she contrive to be alone with David.

'David, what are folks saying about the election?' Liz asked as they approached the downtown section. 'Do they know anything yet?'

'It's too early to tell.' His face was sombre.

387

'I don't believe Mr Dorsey will win,' Liz said defiantly.

'We won't think about it until later,' David decreed. 'How would you like some ice cream on Decatur Street? But don't tell Rae,' he warned. 'She'll be furious with me for killing your appetite before dinner.'

'I'd love ice cream.' Liz's smile was dazzling.

'Decatur Street really starts east of Pryor,' David said. 'The real Decatur Street,' he emphasized.

Liz leaned forward, intent on seeing everything at once. Decatur Street became alive with unfamiliar sounds and smells. Fried fish, chile con carne, near-beer, steaming clothes and cheap cologne. Cars inched along, though most folks walked, Liz noticed. Behind them a car honked, its raucous sound blending with a peanut vendor's whistle.

'We'll stop down the street for ice cream.' David was craning his neck to spot a parking area. 'This little Greek man makes the best ice cream you ever tasted,' he boasted.

'We mustn't forget Noah's delicatessen,' Liz reminded, feeling totally grown-up.

'We won't.' David spied a precious wedge of parking space and manoeuvered the car against the curb.

His arm at Liz's waist, never guessing the pleasure this small gesture elicited in her, David guided her through the maze of shoppers. A fat coloured woman with a broad smile was arguing price with a shopkeeper, her laughter trailing out on to the sidewalk. Immigrants new to Atlanta mingled with mountaineers, and a white-haired Confederate veteran told a Yankee tourist about the two blocks of shoe stores just ahead. Yankee accents mingled with Yiddish and Irish, and most noticeable of all were the melodious Southern voices of the coloured folks.

Liz and David walked into the delicatessen shop

favoured by Rae, and Liz sniffed hungrily at the appetizing aromas that filled every corner.

'This is where the Italian chorus men from the Metropolitan Opera eat all their meals when they're in town,' David told her. 'Everybody calls them "Caruso's Band".'

With the delicatessen purchased, Liz and David left the shop to walk farther along Decatur Street. They paused at the fish market, where later whatever fish was left of the morning's catch would be auctioned. They saw the pawn shops and the near-beer places and the poolrooms. A street photographer snapped their picture. With mock seriousness David paid the man and presented the tintype, available in moments, to Liz. Her eyes shone. *She would treasure the tintype forever.*

After dinner Liz sat beside David on the front seat of the Tin Lizzie as he drove her home. This had been a day she would treasure. She was conscious of the tintype of David and her that was stashed away in her Mark Cross envelope purse, which she had teased Mama into giving her. She couldn't wait to show the tintype to Janet and Maureen.

They drove in a comfortable silence, which Liz considered grown-up, until David pulled up before the house.

'Did you enjoy your sightseeing trip?' David asked, a hand on the car door.

'David, it was such fun.'

With seeming impulsiveness Liz reached to kiss him in gratitude, her arms closing in about his shoulders. All at once she discovered herself in a passionate embrace, David's mouth on hers. She could feel his heart pounding. Then, in disappointing suddenness, he was pulling away.

'You've had a busy day for a little girl.' David struggled

to sound like an indulgent uncle. 'I hope you don't have any homework to do before you go to sleep.'

'I did it all at school,' Liz said offhandedly.

She wasn't a little girl. But she wouldn't press the point. She knew now. David was hers. The time would come when she'd make him admit it. In December she would be sixteen. A respectable age to talk about getting married.

32

Maureen lay across the parlour sofa with several pillows beneath her head while she listened to Liz, curled up in Andrew's favourite wing chair. Andrew had returned to the mill after dinner to check on activities of the second shift. Phoebe had retired for the night to her cabin behind the house. Maureen and Liz were alone.

'Maureen, I know David loves me.' Liz's face was suffused with triumph. 'He gave himself away, though afterwards he tried to pretend it was nothing. Like I was a little girl and he was my big brother. But he didn't kiss me like he thought I was a little girl.'

'He had no right,' Maureen objected. The vindictive pleasure she had felt earlier in winning Liz's friendship had been replaced by genuine affection. Liz truly liked her. Now she worried that Liz would be hurt. 'David's taking advantage of your family's friendship.' Her voice was angry.

'Maureen, you won't tell anybody?' Liz sat up straight.

'Liz, you know I won't,' Maureen scolded. 'But you're not even sixteen.'

'I kissed him first,' Liz confessed. 'I've been wanting to do that forever.' Liz closed her eyes in an aura of ecstasy. 'It was wonderful. I wanted to do everything with him.' Her eyes met Maureen's in disconcerting candour.

Colour outlined Maureen's cheekbones. Tonight it embarrassed her to talk this way with Liz. She felt a maternal protectiveness that astonished her.

'Liz, don't let him kiss you again,' Maureen ordered.

'Maureen, I'd let him do anything he wanted,' Liz

admitted. 'I know you're not supposed to do it until you're married; but if we did it, I'd feel married. And if we did,' Liz concluded with a beatific smile, 'then David would have to marry me.'

'Liz, you don't want to get married when you're so young. You'll meet lots of men.' When Liz and she were going about Atlanta, both of them attracted men like flies. Nobody realized that Liz was so young. 'They'll be chasing after you in droves.'

'I don't want anybody but David. Not ever.'

'Liz, you might get pregnant.' Maureen grasped at this in frenzy. 'You don't want to be walking around like this.' She grimaced, circling her protruding belly with slender hands.

'I wouldn't care. Aren't you glad you're having Andrew's baby?' Liz challenged.

'Yes.' Sometimes it frightened her, the way she was beginning to feel about Andrew. She'd never allowed herself to love anybody. To love was to be hurt. Mama had hurt her. Papa had hurt her. 'But Andrew and I are married.'

'If I get pregnant, David will marry me,' Liz pointed out triumphantly.

'Liz, you mustn't let David touch you. Not until you're married. He . . . he won't respect you if you do.' If Liz threw herself at David again, what would happen? She ought to warn Caroline, yet how could she when Liz trusted her?

'I probably scared him to death last night.' Liz giggled reminiscently. 'I know David. He's going to avoid being alone with me like the plague.'

'He should,' Maureen insisted, relieved at this prediction. 'And you still have another year of high school. You can't get married until you graduate.'

'I have to go home.' Liz sighed. 'I told Aunt Sophie I'd just stay a little while.'

Maureen walked to the door with Liz, trying not to show her anxiety over the situation with David.

The night was becoming sticky. Earlier there had been a breeze from the river. Maureen went into the bedroom to change into a nightgown.

Feeling guilty because the doctor had ordered her not to smoke while she was pregnant, she foraged for her tiny silver cigarette case, hidden beneath a pile of lingerie in a dresser drawer, and pulled out a gold-tipped cigarette. The cigarette lit, she inhaled in gratified breaths, searching now for a magazine.

Maureen returned to her place on the sofa, the cigarette case and matches conveniently at hand. Tonight the fashion magazine held little interest for her. Her eyes heavy with sleep, she tried to concentrate on predictions for winter styles.

Maureen's eyes fluttered shut. *Harper's Bazaar* slipped from her fingers to the floor. The lighted cigarette fell upon the open magazine. In moments, edges of the magazine pages began to curl in a smouldering black border.

At the mill, Andrew cleared off his desk, preparing to return to the cottage. The night superintendent walked in to report a breakdown on several looms in the weaving room. Andrew frowned. He might be stuck here for another two hours.

'I'll be right in to look at them,' Andrew said, his eyes moving to the open window of his office. All at once he stiffened. In the spill of moonlight he saw flames at the windows of his parlour. *The cottage was on fire*. 'George, call the fire department!' He charged towards the door.

'Pull a dozen men off the machines and bring them to my cottage with buckets of water! My wife's there alone!'

Andrew raced from the mill and towards the cottage. He breathed in painful gasps, terror ripping at him as he ran.

'Maureen!' he yelled, praying that she was not caught in the house. 'Maureen!'

Only silence greeted him as he hurried up the steps to the veranda. He pulled open the door, only to be thrust back by the intense heat.

'Andrew!' Liz was running towards him, a Chinese kimono wrapped over her nightclothes. Her voice was shrill with fear. 'Where's Maureen?'

'I don't know . . .' Smoke poured from one parlour window. At another they saw flames devouring the lace curtains. 'I'll try to get in from the back.'

'I called the fire department.' Liz's voice followed him. 'Mama and Papa are out at a campaign rally.'

Andrew pulled open the kitchen door. Smoke was permeating the house. *He had to find Maureen.*

'Maureen,' he called, propelling himself into the smoke-filled house. 'Maureen . . .'

Andrew pulled a handkerchief from his pocket to cover his nose. Behind the house he heard Phoebe wailing. Liz was with her. He stumbled across the kitchen into the hall. The smoke was acrid, burning his eyes and throat.

'Maureen . . .' His voice was harsh from smoke irritation.

'Andrew . . .' A thin cry came to him.

'Where are you? Maureen?'

'Andrew . . .'

The bathroom, Andrew decided, and pushed himself through the thickening smoke. The flames were extending beyond the parlour with an intensity that was hardly bearable. The bathroom door was ajar. He heard the sound of running water.

Andrew thrust the door wide. Maureen lay huddled on the floor, her breathing laboured, her eyes closed. He scooped her into his arms and staggered into the hall, out towards the back door. He could hear Phoebe fighting with Liz.

'Missy, you can't go in there!' Phoebe wailed. 'You'll be kilt! Missy, you stay out here! The menfolks are fightin' to put it out.'

While Andrew struggled towards the back door, he heard the fire truck arriving out front. He had to get Maureen out into the fresh air. The flames had not touched her. *But how much smoke had she inhaled?* Andrew laid Maureen on the grass. His eyes clung to her ashen face. She was breathing. Thank God for that. Liz and Phoebe were dragging out a mattress. Phoebe had a fresh sheet tucked beneath one arm. She changed the sheet, and Andrew lifted Maureen on to the mattress.

'I'll git a blanket and a wet towel,' Phoebe said, darting back into the cabin.

'Andrew . . .' As though with great effort, Maureen opened her eyes.

'You're all right, honey,' Andrew reassured, reaching for her hand. 'I'm going to call for Dr Desmond.'

'Stay,' Maureen implored. 'Don't leave me.' Her hand moved to her swollen belly. 'Andrew, the baby,' she whimpered.

'The baby's fine,' he insisted.

'Shall I call Dr Desmond?' Liz asked Andrew.

'Tell one of the men from the mill to go back and phone,' Andrew instructed.

Phoebe returned with a blanket to cover Maureen. Andrew saw Sophie moving towards them with unfamiliar swiftness.

'I looked out the window and saw the flames.' Sophie's voice was husky from exertion. 'Andrew, what happened?'

'We don't know yet. I was at the mill.' His eyes clung to Maureen.

'Oh, Andrew,' Maureen gasped. 'I fell asleep. I must have dropped my cigarette.'

'Honey, don't talk. Just rest.' But relief surged through him. Colour was returning to her face.

'I told somebody to call for Dr Desmond,' Liz reported. 'The firemen have it under control. I heard one of them say they'll save the rear of the house.'

'The parlour?' Maureen asked weakly.

'Just cinders,' Liz admitted.

'Oh, Andrew, all your beautiful antiques.' Maureen shuddered.

'They don't matter,' Andrew told her. 'As long as you're safe.'

'But you loved them so,' Maureen whispered, her face stricken.

'I love my wife more,' Andrew said, and saw Maureen's eyes fill with tears.

'Andrew, nobody's ever cared about me that much.' Maureen reached for his hand and brought it to her lips. 'Andrew, I love you.'

Liz sat on the stair landing waiting for Dr Desmond to emerge from the guest room to which Andrew had carried Maureen. Sophie was downstairs in the kitchen making coffee. Even in Hampton House the aroma of the smouldering ruins of the cottage was heavy. The firemen still laboured to make sure every ember was dead.

Liz looked up when she heard a door open. Dr Desmond walked out, followed by Andrew. They were talking in quiet tones, but they didn't look worried, Liz decided.

'Liz, would you go in to Maureen?' Andrew asked, smiling. 'She wants to see you. But don't let her talk too long.'

'She'll sleep,' Dr Desmond promised, a humorous glint in his eyes. 'She'll be out in a few minutes.'

Liz hurried to Maureen. There was a serenity about her that was new. A softness that was new.

'Liz, did you hear Andrew?' Maureen asked, her eyes bright with pleasure. 'He didn't care about his antiques. He was only worried for me. *He put me first.*'

'He went in there to bring you out.' Liz was caught up in recall. 'The way David came into that awful place to bring me out when I was kidnapped. Oh, Maureen, aren't they both just beautiful?'

Maureen laughed shakily. 'That's not exactly the word I'd use. But for the first time in my life I *know* I'm first with somebody. Andrew treasured those antiques. He's collected them one by one over so many years. But all he thought about, when he came into the burning house, was me.' Her voice was ebbing away.

'Dr Desmond said you're to sleep.' Liz bent over to kiss Maureen. 'You sleep, you hear?' she admonished, but Maureen's eyes were already closed.

For a moment Liz allowed one hand to rest in affection on the mountainous bump that protruded beneath the coverlet. Maureen's baby. He was all right. And she was going to be the baby's godmother. When she had David's baby, Maureen would be his godmother.

Maureen was ordered by Dr Desmond to remain in bed at Hampton House for several days. Liz was in her room almost every moment she was home. Josh shyly brought her late-blooming roses. Caroline and Sophie visited each evening.

Andrew was able to arrange for them to move into the new house several days ahead of schedule. Maureen loved the new house with a passion. Yet her pleasure was diffused by growing fears of delivery. She was narrow, and she carried a large baby. She saw the anxiety in Dr Desmond's eyes at unguarded moments. *She didn't want to die in childbirth*. She wanted to live for Andrew and their baby.

33

Atlanta waited eagerly for the opening day of the South-eastern Fair on Monday, October 16. For a year and a half the Fair Association had been labouring to bring this event to fruition. The buildings at Lakewood Park were in readiness. The streetcar line had been extended into the fairgrounds. Seven southeastern states were participating.

In addition to livestock, agricultural, woman's work, art, and farm-machinery exhibits, there was to be an impressive programme of special events. An automobile show, a suffragette demonstration, grand-circuit horse-races, and a huge fireworks display. There were to be band concerts by the celebrated Webber's Band. A midway had been erected at a cost of several thousand dollars.

Hotel reservations poured into the city until there was not a hotel room to be had. The Chamber of Commerce appealed to residents to entertain in their homes one thousand boys and five hundred girls who were coming to Atlanta to participate in the fair.

Liz was ecstastic when Rae Kahn phoned, just as she was leaving the house for the clinic on Wednesday afternoon, to invite her to go to the fair on opening day with the boys and herself.

'Oh, Rae, I'd love it!' Liz accepted with enthusiasm. 'I've never been to a fair.'

On Monday afternoon – 'Atlanta Day' at the fair – Liz arrived at the Kahn household. She wore the uniform of the young, so becoming to her spectacular figure – a brilliant blue sweater and matching skirt – beneath her blue gabardine semimilitary coat. The two boys, Sam and Melvin, were impatient to leave. The baby – Bessie – would remain at home in care of the nurse.

'We have to wait for Uncle David,' Rae scolded. 'He's going to drive us.'

'David's going with us?' Liz sought to mask her delight.

'Noah thought it would be more comfortable to drive than to take the crowded streetcar,' Rae explained. 'We'll leave as soon as David comes home from the college. The newspaper this morning said at least thirty thousand people are expected at the fair today. They've sold that many "opening-day keys".'

Liz knew that entrance today was by 'key' only. For weeks they had been on sale in every office building, bank, retail store, hotel, and cigar stand in Atlanta.

'If Uncle David doesn't hurry, we'll miss the grand-circuit races,' Sam, the older of the two boys, warned plaintively.

'We'll be there on time,' Rae soothed, and at the same moment they heard the front door open. David had arrived.

Rae decided to sit on the rear seat of the Ford in order to referee in the event the boys began to fight. Liz sat up front with David. He talked to her about the war in Europe. His friend in Copenhagen was leaving for London to enlist in the British Air Force.

'Why is he doing that?' Liz asked, chilled.

'Henrik worries about freedom.' David's face was troubled. 'If Germany wins, no one will be free.'

'When Papa was home for the primaries, I heard him say he expects us to be in war within six months. David, do you believe that?'

'I don't like to think about it,' David admitted. 'But I don't see how we can stay out.'

400

Liz was enthralled with the diversion provided by the fair. She clung to David's arm while they followed Rae and the boys from one exhibit to another, pushing their way through the convivial hordes. They tried the merry-go-round, the toboggan slide, the 'old mill'. They ate ice cream and cotton candy and drank Coca-Cola. At nightfall Rae insisted they pause for solid food.

The hours raced past until David instructed them all to head for the grandstand to watch the fireworks. But the fireworks never overshadowed Liz's pleasure at being close to David. His arm protectively about her waist as the crowd jostled them. Rae and the two boys were directly in front of them. While the watchers waited in darkness for the next burst of colour, Liz lifted her face to David's.

'David . . .' she whispered, and he met her gaze in the faint spill of light afforded by the night sky. 'David, I love you.' She relished the matching ardour in his eyes. The involuntary pressure of his hand at her waist. Again he betrayed himself, she thought with joy.

'I love you.' The words seemed wrung from him, but immediately he sought to retreat. 'All the Kahns love you.'

The attention of the nation was focused on the imminent national elections. In the Hampton family there was the comfortable realization that Eric would be voted another term as congressman. Eric would vote by absentee ballot, since he was involved in congressional committee work in Washington. Caroline would spend election eve at home; she had no intention of sitting in a crowded auditorium while returns were flashed across the screen.

After dinner on election eve Roland drove Liz and Janet to the Kahn house. Liz had persuaded David to take them to the auditorium-armoury to watch the returns. He seemed relieved that she had brought Janet along, Liz decided. He remembered the night at the fair. Would Rae be upset if she married David? Janet said Jewish people didn't often marry out of their religion. Like Catholics.

Along with Rae, Noah, and David, Liz and Janet went in Noah's Ford to the auditorium-armoury. David placed himself between Liz and Janet to guide them inside. Liz was glad that the incoming crowds made it necessary to walk so close to David. She wished they were walking alone in the woods, David's arm about her. She'd stop and reach up to kiss him. It would be wonderful.

'We can sit in here,' Noah said, triumphant at finding five seats together.

Within fifteen minutes the auditorium was jammed to capacity. Hordes congregated outside. All at once organ music reverberated through the vast auditorium. An aura of drama emanated from those present. Everyone was excited about what promised to be a thrillingly close race.

'There must be ten thousand people here,' Noah judged, surveying the crowd.

'The police and firemen are turning them away in droves,' Rae said. Her face clouded. 'The betting is still twenty to seventeen against Wilson.'

Liz had contrived to sit between Janet and David. At irregular intervals Janet and she exchanged pregnant glances and suppressed giggles. Janet knew how she felt being with David. Sometimes Janet was shocked, the way she talked about him; but then, Janet didn't want to get married before she was twenty-five.

The organ music stopped to allow the early returns to be flashed on the big screen before the stage. Then the state election returns began to come in. When the congressional returns were shown and it was clear that Eric Hampton was reelected as expected, Liz squealed in delight, kissed Janet, turned and kiss David. Nobody could think anything of it, she told herself in satisfaction, while David's arms closed about her in reciprocation. It was natural to react this way to Papa's reelection.

The early presidential returns were disheartening to Atlantans. Indications were that Wilson was defeated. People left the auditorium in an aura of gloom. The South's own man would soon be vacating the White House. Late that evening the New York *Times* brought out extras declaring Hughes the president-elect.

On Wednesday morning newspapers across the country were proclaiming a Hughes victory. Only a few newspapers – including the Atlanta *Journal* – refused to concede the election to Hughes. The *Journal* insisted that the votes rolling in from the West would overcome the Republican lead.

On Wednesday it was clear that the election would hang on California, Minnesota, New Mexico, Oregon, and West Virginia. After dark, the Atlanta *Journal* carried election returns in front of its office on Forsyth Street. Sophie refused to allow Liz to go again to watch the returns. Later in the evening, when Liz was finished with her homework, she could call Jim and ask what was happening.

By the time Liz called Jim to ask about the election returns, he was able to tell her that the election would depend on the votes in California. Results in California would be announced tomorrow. Not until Friday morning was the nation sure that Woodrow Wilson would remain in the White House.

Two weeks before her sixteenth birthday, Liz received a phone call from her mother in Washington. She swept aside Caroline's suggestion of a predebutante dinner dance at the Piedmont Driving Club to celebrate the occasion.

'I wouldn't even walk into the Piedmont Driving Club,' Liz said with blistering disdain. 'Don't you remember what David told us? They don't allow Jews there.'

'I'd forgot,' Caroline apologized. 'We can have it at the Ansley.'

'I'd like a family dinner party again,' Liz said demurely. 'With Janet, Victor, and the Kahns included.' Mama didn't expect her to play at being a debutante, did she? No, Liz decided. Mama took it for granted she would go to college next year.

'I'll talk to Aunt Sophie, and we'll make all the arrangements,' Caroline agreed after a pregnant silence. 'We'll be home the day before your birthday. There'll be time to go over to Chamberlin-Johnson to buy you a new dress – '

'I won't need one,' Liz interrupted exuberantly. 'Andrew and Maureen are giving me a dress for my birthday. Maureen ordered it through the *Harper's Bazaar* shopping service in New York. It'll be here in time to have it altered if it doesn't fit just right. I'm so excited. It's a claret-coloured velvet by Lucile.'

'A designer dress is a terribly expensive gift.' Caroline was startled.

'Maureen said I'd be sixteen only once, and Andrew agreed.' Liz refused to be ruffled. Mama couldn't refuse to allow her to receive a birthday present from Maureen and Andrew. 'She said Andrew told her he was going to make a fortune on the cotton he bought because you were so sure the price would go up. He says cotton will be twenty-seven cents a pound by the first of the year.'

'I wish the farmers would think about saving some of that money that's rolling in,' Caroline said soberly. 'Instead of running out to spend every cent as soon as it comes into their hands. Liz, I have to go now,' Caroline said. 'Papa and I will be late for the embassy dinner.'

Liz was aware of the elaborate preparations for her birthday dinner. Champagne was to be served. She overheard Sophie arranging for a string quartet to play during dinner. Sophie ordered a loving cup of pink carnations for the centre-piece.

Maureen was horrified when Liz insisted she attend the birthday dinner despite her advanced pregnancy. At the last moment Maureen capitulated, won over by her eagerness to please Liz. The guest list had been expanded to include Senator and Maria Bolton, who were arriving in Atlanta for Christmas, and Jim.

Janet was invited to come over to Hampton House immediately after school on the day of Liz's birthday. Liz and she would dress together. To Liz today was the crowning event of her young life. She was sixteen.

'You look beautiful, Liz,' Janet said with just a touch of wistfulness when Liz stood before her in the claret velvet designed by Lady Duff-Gordon, known in the fashion world as Lucile.

'Do you think David will like it?' Liz's eyes focused anxiously on her reflection in the mirror.

'I think any man who saw you looking like that would go out of his mind for you,' Janet declared, subconsciously smoothing the lilac velvet frock that her mother had bought for her at Chamberlin-Johnson-DuBose, a store normally foreign to them.

'I told Mama to put us between David and Victor,' Liz reported. 'Don't you think Victor's handsome?'

'Stop being romantic,' Janet scolded. 'Victor's at least ten years older than me.'

'David's lots older than me by the calendar.' Liz's eyes were brilliant. 'But it doesn't matter to us.'

'Liz, is my dress all right?' All at once Janet was uneasy.

'You are so pretty I'm not sure I ought to allow you at my birthday party.' Liz laughed and reached forward to hug her – careful not to disarrange their coiffures. 'Janet, it's so exciting, being sixteen!' Janet had arrived at that exalted state five months ago.

The girls started at a brisk knock on the door.

'Liz, Janet . . .' Caroline called to them. 'It's time you two came downstairs.'

Liz revelled in the elegance of the dinner. Roland and Elvira were solemn as they circulated about the table, serving the gourmet dishes ordered for the occasion. The three-tiered cake was an artistic masterpiece. As she cut the first piece, the string quartet played 'So Sweet She Is'. All through the evening Liz was conscious of a tenderness in David's eyes that was more potent than the champagne she drank tonight.

Andrew and Maureen were the first to leave. Liz suspected Maureen had been upset when Mrs Bolton and Victor talked about New Orleans. Victor's college roommate apparently knew Mrs Bolton's niece in New Orleans. That city held unhappy memories for Maureen, Liz surmised with compassion.

Soon most of the guests left, yet David lingered. David seemed to be in an odd mood tonight, Liz thought while they sat down at the walnut gaming table across the room from her father and Jim. At dinner he had seemed so warm to her, yet he had spoken little. Now he seemed distracted.

'Shall we play whist?' Liz asked, determined to extend these minutes alone with David as long as possible.

'Whatever you like.' His eyes met hers. They were unfathomable.

'David, is something wrong?' Liz asked on impulse, propelled to probe by an inchoate alarm.

David hesitated. 'Not wrong, Liz. I've had to make a decision. Nobody knows yet. Not even Noah and Rae. Of course, I had to tell the college.'

'What kind of a decision?' Instinct warned her this would bear unhappiness for her.

'I'm arranging to join the Canadian Corps.' She gazed at him without comprehending. 'I'm going to fight with the Canadian Army.'

'David, no!' Her voice soared raggedly. Both David and she glanced about in apprehension, but the others were too involved in conversation to have noticed.

'I've thought about it for weeks. Even before Henrik wrote me about going to England. I have to do this, Liz.'

'David, why?' Anguish turned her cold. She was assaulted by terrible visions of David lying wounded on a battlefield. 'It's ridiculous,' she rebuked. 'Your research is important to the whole field of science. Noah and Papa both think you'll win a Nobel prize someday.' Liz leaned forward, her face drained of colour. 'What you do in your laboratory is lots more important than if you carry a gun against the Germany Army.'

'I hate war. I hate any kind of killing.' David frowned in distaste. 'You know that, Liz. But I look around here at home, and I know that what happens in Europe will ultimately affect us. Noah and I came out of the pogroms of Europe to freedom here. I have to fight to preserve that kind of freedom – because without that, life isn't worth living.'

'David, Germany isn't coming over to fight us.' Liz grasped at her father's oft-repeated pronouncement. 'Our democracy isn't being threatened.'

'It was threatened here in Atlanta,' David reminded. 'When Leo was tried for a murder he didn't commit.

407

When he was lynched. It's threatened again with Hugh Dorsey going into the governor's mansion next June. Still, we know that in this country democracy is alive – it'll fight what's happening in Atlanta, and we'll be able to hold our heads up again. But the war in Europe is a threat to the world. Liz, I couldn't respect myself if I didn't fight. I owe this country.'

This was unreal, like watching a movie. Mama had said David would never go to Europe because of his bad childhood memories. Mama was mistaken.

'I'm awaiting word from Canada about when and where I'm to report,' David said gently. 'I'll continue teaching until the Christmas recess.'

Tears filled Liz's eyes and spilled over unheeded. She awoke this morning with such joy at being sixteen. Life had seemed so beautiful.

34

For Liz the war was all at once intensely personal. She devoured every morsel of news, all the while praying that word would come from Canada denying David acceptance into the Canadian Corps.

On the pretext of writing a school paper about the Canadians in the war, Liz manoeuvered her way into the *Constitution*'s file room on back issues. She had been confident the newspaper would not turn away their congressman's daughter.

The Canadian Corps had been fighting in Europe since early in 1915. They'd fought beyond the call of duty, time after time, refusing to retreat even when far outnumbered. They'd endured shrapnel, rifle fire, high explosives, and gas attacks. Their casualties had been heavy.

Now the Canadians were preparing for a major offensive. They laboured on their trenches, repairing old fortifications and erecting new, laid miles of railway, and worked on roads. And all the while they preyed on the Germans in opposing trenches. They were taking German prisoners and equipment.

Three days before Christmas, David received his orders. He was to report to an area in Canada where new troops were being trained as replacements.

Liz spoke little at dinner that evening, though her mother strove to brighten her mood. The family had been told about David's imminent departure for Canada.

'Liz, would you like to drive over and see the Christmas tree on the lawn of the Capitol?' Caroline asked. 'I'm taking Josh and Francis.'

'I told Janet I'd come over after dinner to help her wrap presents. Later her mother's taking us to see the tree,' Liz fabricated in sudden decision. 'I may sleep over.' She tried to sound nonchalant. She might eventually arrive at Janet's house tonight, but she was plotting an earlier destination.

Liz was impatient for dinner to be finished. She heard not a word of the conversation around her. Why did Francis have to dawdle that way over dessert?

David would be alone except for the maid and the children tonight. Rae and Noah were going to a wedding. They must have gone already. She could get into the house without the maid's even hearing her. She would be upstairs with the children. Rae always kept a spare key above the doorframe downstairs. She could let herself in and go right upstairs to David's apartment. They'd be alone. Just the two of them.

As soon as the family arose from the table, Liz fled to her room for her coat. Her mother had already instructed Roland to drive her to Janet's house. She could walk from there in five minutes.

Roland was waiting before the house with the Pierce Arrow when she hurried out into the sharp cold of the night. She climbed into the car and huddled in one corner, simultaneously hot and cold. Roland deposited Liz before the Hammond house and waited to see her approach the door. Liz made a pretence of ringing the doorbell, her heart pounding lest her presence be discovered, and waved Roland on. Seeing the car roll away from the house, Liz darted down the stairs and hurried off in the dark.

She walked with compulsive swiftness, oblivious of the biting wind, the sharp drop in temperature in the last two hours, framing sentences in her mind. How could David desert his work, which could be so important to so many

410

people, to go off to fight another country's war? *He might die in that war*. If that happened to David, she wouldn't want to live.

Approaching the Kahn house, Liz saw the darkened lower floor. Only a small foyer light showed. There were lights upstairs in the boys' room and the little room where the maid slept.

At the door, Liz reached up for the key that was kept there, because David was absentminded about such things as keys. She brought it down, unlocked the door, and walked into the foyer. With plotted quietness she moved up the two flights of stairs to David's attic apartment. She could hear Alice ordering Sam and Melvin to turn out the lights in their rooms and go to sleep.

She knocked softly. She heard David coming to the door. She hadn't seen him since the night of her birthday dinner. He pulled the door wide. Her smile was incandescent.

'Liz . . .' He was startled by her presence.

'Rae told me you've received your orders.' Liz strode into the small sitting room. 'David, how can you go away and leave your research?' *How can you go away and leave me?*

'Liz, I explained it to you . . .' He left the door open. 'Haven't Rae and Noah left yet for the wedding? They should be gone.' He seemed bewildered.

'They've gone.' Liz moved to the door and closed it. 'I took the key from above the door and let myself in. David, you mustn't go to Canada!'

'Liz, it has to be.' His eyes strayed to the door. He was uneasy alone with her.

'David, stay here.' She took a step towards him. 'I told you. I love you. Doesn't that make any difference?'

'Liz, you shouldn't be here.' His voice was uneven.

'David, I'll die if anything happens to you.'

411

'Honey, nothing's going to happen . . .' He reached out to console her, and instantly she was in his arms.

'David, I can't think of anything but your going away. I can't sleep nights. Oh, David . . .' She lifted her mouth to his.

His mouth came down, bruising hard on hers. His arms folded her in against his tall, slender frame. She had waited so long for this.

'Liz, you can't stay here.' All at once he was releasing her, alarmed at the emotions that gripped them.

'I won't go, David.' She reached for his mouth again, heard the anguished sound deep in his throat. She could feel him growing hard against her. 'David, I love you. Please, love me.'

Her eyes held his, commanding him. She thrust her hips against his, recognizing his mounting passion.

'Liz, this is insane . . .' But he was wavering.

Liz pulled off her coat, dropped it to the floor. She reached at the sides of her sweater, pulled it above her head, and tossed it on to a chair. David's eyes clung to the voluptuous spill of her woman's body.

'David, don't you want to make love to me?' *If he did, he would never go to Europe.* He would stay here and marry her. With cold fingers she reached behind her to release the hooks of her brassiere. The lace fell free, releasing her milk-white breasts.

'Liz, we shouldn't . . .' He faltered.

'We have to,' she insisted.

Joy swept through her when David lifted her from her feet and carried her into the darkened tiny bedroom. She felt the firm mattress welcome her. Pausing to burrow his mouth in the valley between her breasts, he sought to free her from her skirt.

'Liz . . .' Hovering above her, David hesitated again.

'David, quickly,' she pleaded, her arms encircling him.

412

If he stopped to think, he'd make her put on her clothes and ship her right home. *There would never be a moment like this again in her whole life.* 'I'm not afraid,' she whispered. 'David, love me.'

For a moment she was still, waiting for him to free himself for her. Even if it hurt, she would not cry out. The first time, it was supposed to hurt. A beautiful hurt.

She felt the first tentative thrust between her thighs. She closed her eyes, impatient for what she had never known. His hands caressed her breasts while he manoeuvered himself within her. She stifled a faint cry and then relaxed to move with him to ultimate, ecstatic climax. Clinging to him afterwards, as he clung to her.

'Liz, I love you. But how could I have taken you this way? How can I ever face your parents again?'

'David, I came here to you,' she reminded, her face pressed against his. 'My fault more than yours. *I planned it.*'

'I've loved you since you were fourteen,' David said. 'I would never admit, even to myself. It seemed so wrong.'

'Why is it wrong?' Liz challenged.

'I'm twice as old as you,' he reminded.

'Not quite,' she contradicted. 'And that's now. It'll seem so much less when we're older. You won't be able to say, "I'm twice as old as you."' She laughed.

'Our religions are different. We come from different cultures.' His eyes were troubled.

'David, are you going to marry me?'

'Will your parents allow it?'

'I'm sixteen. I'm old enough to make that decision for myself.'

'We'll talk to them tomorrow,' he decided. 'Right now you get yourself dressed and I'll take you home.'

'Take me to Janet's,' she corrected. 'I'm supposed to be there,' she explained, and he flinched. 'David, it's all

413

right. We'll be married,' she soothed. 'The day after I graduate.'

'I'd like for us to be married before I leave for Canada. If your parents agree. Nobody has to know except family.'

She stared at him in disbelief, her body rigid in his arms.

'You're not going to Canada now?'

'Liz, I have to go. I couldn't live with myself if I didn't.'

'Suppose you're killed? David, no!' Her voice broke. 'David, don't leave me. Please don't leave me.'

He cradled her in his arms while she cried; but when she lifted her eyes to his again, she knew he would go to fight.

'We'll talk to Mama and Papa tomorrow,' she reminded. 'We'll be married before you go away.'

Liz spent the night with Janet, who was unnerved by the situation between Liz and David. In the morning Liz phoned David. They arranged to approach Liz's parents just before dinner, when both Caroline and Eric would be home.

'Liz, I feel so rotten,' David sighed while they waited in the library at Hampton House for Caroline and Eric to arrive.

'David, don't tell them we've slept together,' Liz admonished, in this situation feeling herself more mature than David. Papa wouldn't try to fight a duel – that went out years ago – but her parents would be outraged. They'd never understand. 'Just that we both realize we love each other, and we want to be married before you go away.' She still clung to the hope that David would change his mind and remain in Atlanta.

'They're going to hate me,' David warned.

414

'David, they could never hate you,' Liz objected tenderly.

'We should be honest with them,' David decided.

'No,' Liz refused. 'Why make them unhappy? What we did was beautiful. I want it to stay that way.'

'I should have sent you away before you set foot inside the apartment,' he reproached himself.

'David, I wouldn't have let you.' Her voice was triumphant. 'I'm a devious female. You didn't have a chance.'

'Liz, I love you.'

'We'll make Papa and Mama understand how important it is for us to be married. We won't let them stop us.'

'We'll talk to them,' David said. 'But, Liz, if they refuse, we'll have to accept. We'll have to wait until I return.'

If Mama and Papa knew she slept with David, they couldn't refuse. Suppose she was pregnant? She wished she was. It would be wonderful to carry David's baby. If she was pregnant, he'd have to ask the Canadian Army to release him.

While Elvira moved about in the dining room setting the table for dinner, Liz and David faced her parents. Haltingly David explained the situation. Feeling his despair, Liz reached for his hand and clung to it.

'David, she's only sixteen,' Caroline remonstrated, pale but composed. 'Not yet out of high school.'

'Mama, I'll finish high school,' Liz promised. 'But David's going away in less than two weeks. We want to be married before he leaves.' Truantly she thought: *How do I know he'll come back? David, don't go. Please, don't go.*

'Liz, it would be wrong for David and you to rush into marriage under the pressure of his going off to war.' Eric turned to David. 'David, you understand that.'

'I'd like to go away knowing Liz is my wife.' David was apologetic, distressed to be opposing Liz's parents.

'David, why don't you consider remaining in Atlanta?' Eric persuaded. 'It's not as though this country is at war. Your research is important – don't sell that short.' Papa was looking at her, trying to comprehend that his spoiled little girl was a young woman. He couldn't understand that she could have grown-up emotions.

'David, marrying Liz before you leave is out of the question,' Caroline said. Liz opened her mouth to refute this, but the pressure of David's hand on hers ordered her to be silent. 'When you return from Europe, if you both still feel that you wish to marry, then will be the time. Liz is caught up in the war hysteria. She's so young and so romantic.' Liz was astonished to see tears in her mother's eyes. 'David, you know how Eric and I feel about you. We'll be proud to have you in the family if Liz and you both are convinced that marriage is right for you.'

She could feel David's helplessness. He couldn't bring himself to fight Mama, yet he was afraid to go away and leave her, knowing she might be pregnant. If she was, Liz promised herself, David would find a way to come home.

Liz contrived to spend every moment possible with David in the following days. She was conscious of an unspoken pact between her parents and Rae to make sure David and she were never alone. Either she went to the Kahn house for dinner, or David came to Hampton House.

To provide an excuse to be in David's arms, she undertook the task of teaching him the Castle walk and the foxtrot. Unable to make love to her, David would sing 'So Sweet She Is' under his breath while they

416

pretended to play chess and their knees touched beneath the gaming table.

In her wretchedness, Liz asked herself if Rae and Noah were angry that David planned to marry out of his religion. Were Mama and Papa upset that David was Jewish? Would they have allowed David and her to marry now if David was a Baptist or a Presbyterian? She asked herself this endless times in simmering resentment, and each time was ashamed. Of all the people in Atlanta, her parents and David's brother and sister-in-law were the least intolerant.

The Christmas spirit this season was subdued. The Germans had made a peace overture, which President Wilson was asked to deliver to the Allied capitals. Wilson released his manifesto to the State Department on December 18. It reached the press on December 20.

Eric had deep respect for the President's desire for the formation of a 'league of nations to ensure peace and justice throughout the world', but he viewed with alarm Secretary of State Lansing's admission to the press that the President's manifesto was not an indication of peace. The nation hovered on the brink of war.

On New Year's Eve David, along with Rae and Noah, came to Hampton House for a small party, which included the Boltons, Janet, Victor, and Jim. The conversation inevitably focused on the war in Europe.

'American young men are rushing to enlist in the British and French armies,' Jim reminded, and Liz reached for David's hand. 'The overtures towards peace are not working. In a matter of a few weeks, a few months at the most, this country will be pushed into sending soldiers to fight with the Allies.'

'If this country joins the war, then it'll be over fast,' Liz predicted with bravado, and felt conscience-stricken.

She had grown up in an aura of pacifism, and now she talked about American boys going to fight.

'When will people realize that the Germans are not going to cross the Atlantic to attack us?' Caroline demanded. 'I can't understand this hysteria.'

At five minutes to midnight whistles began to blow all over the city. Automobile drivers leaned on their horns. People shouted 'Happy New Year' from open windows. All the hotels were scenes of partying, yet no one forgot for a moment how close the nation was to war.

New Year's Day Liz spent at the Kahn house. Rae mercifully allowed Liz and David moments alone in the Kahn parlour. In the face of his imminent departure, David and Liz clung in passionate embrace, hardly bothering to separate when Rae returned.

Noah's store, like all Atlanta businesses except for banks, was open today. The boys had been shipped off to ice-skate with friends. Little Bessie remained for much of the bitter cold day in the nursery with Alice. Rae was a shadow that moved in sympathetic chaperonage.

Despite Rae's efforts to make David's final dinner at home a festive occasion, gloom infested the dining room. Earlier than Liz wanted, David insisted on driving her home. From there he would go to the store to pick up Noah.

They drove in silence, Liz's head on David's shoulder, thighs touching.

'David, I'll come to you later when they're all asleep,' she whispered when he took her in his arms before the door of Hampton House. 'I can take a streetcar. Nobody'll know . . .'

'Liz, no,' David rejected gently. 'Not until you're my wife. And you're not to come to the train tomorrow. I want to remember you this way.'

'David!' She was aghast. 'Of course I'll see you off.'

418

'Nobody will see me off,' David insisted. 'I'm just going away for a little while,' he soothed. 'Once America comes into the war, it'll be over in a hurry. I want to remember the family at dinner tonight, and you standing here at the door this way. Not the rushed, impersonal scene at a railroad station.' His eyes were worried. 'I wish we knew already that . . .' He hesitated. 'That nothing happened that night. You'll write me?'

'I'll write you,' she promised. He'd be in Canada in training for a few weeks. If she was pregnant, he'd come home. *Oh, please, God, let me be pregnant.*

She stood, smiling as David instructed, while he returned to the car and drove away. Now she let herself into the house and walked up the stairs to her room, relieved that her mother and Sophie had not heard her come in. She couldn't talk to anybody. Not tonight.

Fighting tears, Liz prepared for bed. Hearing footsteps outside in the hall, she switched off the lamp beside the bed and slipped beneath the covers. She ignored the light knock on her door, feigning sleep.

'Liz?' her mother called, then opened the door to gaze inside.

Mama knew she was home. Mama would understand why she didn't come into the library to say good night. She turned to burrow her face in the pillow to silence the sobs that wrenched themselves from her being. David was leaving tomorrow.

Liz awoke shockingly late. She was conscious of a feeling of physical discomfort. In sudden realization she left the bed and hurried into the bathroom. Fresh grief invaded her. She wasn't pregnant. The hope she had nurtured that her pregnancy might bring David back from the camp in Canada was gone.

She ought to tell David she wasn't. Let him have that off his conscience.

She dressed in sudden decision, pulled a coat from the closet. She'd go down to the library to phone the Kahn house and ask when David's train was due to leave. She couldn't tell David this over the phone. No, she wouldn't call Rae, Liz decided while she darted down the stairs. Phone Terminal Station.

At the doorway to the Library Liz stopped dead. Her father was on the phone, listening in serious attentiveness to what was being said at the other end. Mama must be at the mill, Liz surmised. She'd call on Mama's phone.

As Liz turned to leave, her father beckoned her into the room. He was making monosyllabic comments that gave her no clue to what was being said. Concealing her impatience, Liz came into the room and sat at the edge of a chair. David was taking the same train Papa would be taking tomorrow. She strained to remember what time the family was leaving.

At last Eric was off the phone.

'That was the senator,' he explained to Liz. 'He just heard that General Wood is coming to Atlanta this week to look for a site for a cantonment. He's looking for a tract of at least eight hundred acres with place for a rifle range and an eight-mile artillery range. He's chief of staff of the army, Liz.' Eric's tone was ominous.

A chill brushed Liz.

'Uncle Jim said last night that we'd be in the war within weeks or months,' Liz remembered. Everything was so unreal. 'That confirms it, doesn't it?'

'It would indicate that the President and chief of staff expect war.' Eric sighed, then forced a smile. 'What are you doing with yourself this morning?'

'I told Maureen I'd come over,' Liz improvised. She couldn't talk to Papa about going to Terminal Station to see David off. Papa might decide to go along with her.

420

'Is it all right if Roland drives me over, or will you be needing him?'

'It's too far to walk in this cold. Tell Roland to drive you over and come right back. I have a meeting at the office in an hour.'

'See you at dinner, Papa.' She leaned forward to kiss him. All at once she regretted the coolness she had displayed towards her father. 'I'll miss you when you go back to Washington.'

'We miss you, Liz.' He hugged her with unexpected urgency. His eyes were sombre and brooding. It shocked him to realize she was old enough to want to be married, Liz thought, and felt tenderness replacing hostility.

Roland deposited Liz before the red-brick house. In these final weeks of her pregnancy Maureen alternated between despondency and high spirits. It was silly, the way Maureen was so scared of having the baby. *She* wouldn't have been afraid, Liz told herself, wistful at being denied this.

Liz walked up the steps and across the veranda to the front door, Phoebe, her face brightening at the sight of Liz, beckoned her inside.

'Miss Liz, I'm glad you's here. Miss Maureen, she so low in spirit.'

'Where is she, Phoebe?'

'In the sittin' room. You go on in there,' Phoebe encouraged. 'I'll bring some tea.'

She didn't want tea. She just wanted to phone and find out when the train would be leaving.

'Thank you, Phoebe.' She forced herself to seem casual.

Maureen sat in a lounge chair before a blazing fire, her feet propped on a needlepoint footstool.

'How're you feeling?' Liz asked solicitously.

'Rotten,' Maureen said. 'I can't sleep. I can't get

comfortable. And the baby never stops kicking,' she complained. Her eyes focused on Liz. 'How're you?'

'I've got cramps,' Liz admitted.

'Your folks don't have to worry that you're pregnant.' Maureen was flip in a manner that had gone into eclipse these last weeks. Liz felt guilty that she had not confided in Maureen. Only Janet knew that she might have been pregnant. 'Did David leave?' Her voice softened.

'He's leaving this afternoon. We said good-bye last night, but I can't let him go off alone. May I call Terminal Station and see when the train leaves?' Panic tied a knot in her throat. David mustn't leave without her there to see him off. She didn't care what he said last night. She belonged at the train when he left.

'Go call the station,' Maureen prodded, and Liz crossed to the phone which sat on a Chinese black-and-gold lacquered cabinet miraculously saved in the fire.

While she waited for someone to answer, Liz sensed Maureen's curiosity.

'I came to phone here because I didn't want Papa to offer to go to the station, too,' Liz said in candour. Maureen would understand. Someone had picked up at the other end of the line. 'Could you please tell me when the train leaves for New York?'

Her heart began to pound when the clerk gave her the departure time. Would she be able to reach the station before the train pulled out? Why had she slept so late?

'Maureen, is Gilbert busy?' she asked, self-conscious about asking for a ride into town.

'He can stop whatever he's doing and drive you to Terminal Station,' Maureen said, and tinkled the small bell that Andrew insisted she keep at her side in these final weeks of her pregnancy. 'He'll wait and bring you back.'

Liz sat on the back seat of the Chalmers, checking her watch – which Mama and Papa had given her on her sixteenth birthday – with the church clocks they passed en route to Terminal Station.

At the station Liz jumped from the car and hurried through the waiting room to the shed. A train was boarding.

'Is that the New York train?' she asked a porter.

'Yes, ma'am. She'll be leavin' in a few minutes.'

Liz's eyes surveyed the crowd, searching for David. People were saying last-minute farewells at the steps. Some travellers were already boarding. *Where was David?* Now she scanned the windows. Was he sitting on the other side of the aisle? she asked herself in panic.

'Liz!' David's voice swung her about to face him.

'Oh, David. I was afraid I'd missed you.' She flung herself into his arms, felt his heart pounding against hers. 'You don't have to worry,' she whispered in his ear. 'I'm not pregnant.' She had to be honest. She couldn't let him go away worrying about her.

A porter bumped into them with an armload of suit-cases and apologized profusely, but they were too absorbed in each other to bother to reply.

'All aboard that's going to board,' the conductor called out, and there was a rush for the steps.

'David, I love you.' Liz reluctantly released him.

David's eyes seemed to be memorizing her face. 'I love you, Liz. I'll write as soon as I reach camp. I'll keep writing,' David promised.

Liz stood before the train, her eyes searching for David at one of the windows. In a moment he leaned across someone to wave to her. He was seated across the aisle, but he was determined for this last sight of her.

Liz smiled brilliantly, waving to him as the train began

its slow chug from the station. She watched while tears formed an opaque window across her eyes. The train was out of the shed. Now she turned around and headed for the waiting car.

35

Liz waited impatiently for David's first letter, which arrived a week after his departure. He wrote about the beautiful Canadian scenery, the people he met, saying little about his training and imminent departure for action in Europe. The hours at school each day were torture to Liz. Bright enough to earn passing grades with little effort, she allowed her mind to conjure up images of David in camp. He must hate the army training. David, of all people to be going off to fight a war! She was sick with fear each time she read about fresh casualties.

In the afternoons Liz visited with Maureen or Janet. Friday evenings she went to dinner at the Kahns', as though their closeness would cloak David in protection. Much of each weekend was spent in Janet's company. Maureen was difficult in this last month of pregnancy, alternating between ebullient spirits at the prospect of delivery and alarming depression.

Sophie bought matinee tickets for Liz and Janet to *Peg o' My Heart*. Ellen took them to see Theda Bara in *The Darling of Paris*. When Alma Gluck came to Atlanta late in January, Sophie arranged to take the two girls to the opening performance.

Dressing for the concert, Liz rebuked herself for being so frivolous when David expected to leave momentarily for the war zone. He had written that he would join the Second Division of the Canadian Corps, which had suffered heavy losses and was now recuperating and waiting for replacements.

The following week Ellen arranged to take Janet and

her to see Sara Bernhardt, appearing in Atlanta for the first time in seven years. Mama was behind all this socializing, Liz surmised, and was impatient at being distracted from her anguish.

But Liz went with Janet and her mother to see Bernhardt, seventy-two years old and crippled, play the frail young Marguerite in *Camille*. Like the rest of the audience, she was spellbound by Bernhardt's genius. Janet and she cried during the last tragic scene. Few eyes were dry. She tried to remember every detail about the performance because Maureen would expect a full report tomorrow.

The following afternoon Liz sat with Maureen in the parlour of the new house and extolled Sarah Bernhardt's performance. Suddenly Maureen cried out and clutched at her stomach.

'Maureen?' Liz asked, all at once fearful.

'I think this is it.' Maureen was white, deep in concentration. 'Call Phoebe. Then phone Andrew and Dr Desmond.' Her hands poised above her swollen belly, she geared herself for the next pain.

Liz hurried to obey. Phoebe rushed to Maureen's side, murmuring reassurances. Andrew said he'd be home in minutes. Dr Desmond could not be reached, but his nurse gave instructions for Maureen to be driven to Grady Hospital. Dr Desmond insisted the delivery must be at the hospital.

'I don't know why I can't have the baby at home like other women,' Maureen rebelled, yet Liz saw stark terror in her eyes.

'Dr Desmond wants to be sure you're all right.' Liz flinched as Maureen reached for Liz's hand and held it in a painful grip as she coped with fresh pain.

'Liz, it hurts,' Maureen moaned.

'Phoebe, tell Gilbert to bring the car in front of the

house,' Liz ordered, feeling inadequate. Why didn't Andrew get home?

'Liz, stay with me,' Maureen pleaded, her face drenched in perspiration despite the chill in the parlour. 'I'm so scared.'

'Maureen, having a baby is natural,' Liz consoled. 'Think how wonderful it'll be afterwards.'

'Dr Desmond warned me,' Maureen gasped. 'He said I might die.'

Liz was ashen in shock. 'Does Andrew know?' Liz was sure he didn't.

'I didn't tell him. I was afraid he wouldn't let me have a baby. But, Liz, I have to tell somebody.' Her voice was unnaturally high.

'You're going to be all right, Maureen,' Liz insisted tenderly.

'Oh, my God!' Maureen's voice rose to a shrill wail. 'Why doesn't Andrew come home?'

Andrew arrived. He carried Maureen into the car. Maureen insisted that Liz go with them to the hospital. By the time they were there, Dr Desmond was waiting. From his grim face Liz knew that Maureen was in for trouble. Why had she taken this risk? But Liz knew Maureen was determined to give Andrew a child.

Maureen was wheeled away down a cold white corridor. Andrew and Liz sat down to wait for word.

For three hours Liz and Andrew waited in the reception room of Grady Hospital. When Dr Desmond appeared, both leapt hopefully to their feet.

'There's a problem,' Dr Desmond explained. 'She's narrow and she's carrying a large baby. There's no way she can deliver normally.' He hesitated. 'Mr Hampton, we'll need your permission to perform a Caesarean section.'

'Surgery?' Andrew gazed at Dr Desmond in disbelief. 'That's dangerous.'

'It's more dangerous to allow her to continue in labour,' Dr Desmond said bluntly. 'She's suffering terribly. Caesarean sections are being performed under these conditions with good results.'

'But to cut her?' Andrew recoiled.

'Andrew, it's necessary.' Now it was Liz who was calm. 'You have to give permission.' She turned to Dr Desmond. 'Will the baby be all right?'

'We hope so.' Dr Desmond was guarded.

'Forget about the baby,' Andrew said. 'Save my wife.'

'I've already taken the liberty of calling in a surgeon who's performed sections with much success,' Dr Desmond said gently. 'He's here in the hospital now. We'll proceed immediately.'

Dr Desmond left them. Andrew sank into a chair, his face contorted in pain.

'How could I let her go through with this? Why didn't the doctor warn us?' Rage brought colour to his face.

'He did. Maureen kept it to herself. She only told me while we waited for you to come home.'

'I never knew I could love anyone the way I love Maureen.' Andrew's voice broke. 'Liz, what have I done to her?'

'She's going to be all right,' Liz promised, and reached out for his hand. 'We'll wait here together.'

It seemed hours before Dr Desmond appeared. He looked tired but pleased. He extended a hand to Andrew.

'Congratulations, Mr Hampton. You're the father of a nine-pound son.'

'My wife?' Andrew's eyes clung to Dr Desmond's face. 'Is she all right?'

'She came through the surgery splendidly. She's sleeping now, but you can see the baby.'

'First I'd like to see my wife. Just to look at her,' Andrew placated the doctor. 'I have to see her.'

Together Andrew and Liz were allowed into Maureen's room. As Dr Desmond told them, she was asleep. She seemed strangely fragile lying there so flat beneath the sheet.

'You can come back later when she's awake,' Liz soothed.

'I'll stay here until she awakens. I want to be here when she opens her eyes,' Andrew insisted.

'Mr Hampton, don't you want to see your son?' A uniformed nurse stood in the doorway, holding a small bundle in her arms.

How tiny he was, Liz marvelled, inexplicably touched by the flailing hands, the heavy thatch of dark hair. Maureen and Andrew's child. Tears filled her eyes. How often she cried these days, she thought in impatience while she dabbed at her eyes with a wisp of linen. She never used to cry except in rage.

'Andrew Hampton Jr,' Andrew dubbed him with pride. 'He's the image of his mother.'

When Maureen came home with the baby, affectionately known now as Andy, Liz spent so much time at the red-brick house that Sophie scolded her for neglecting her school work. No one said a word to Liz about preparing for college next autumn. Liz suspected her mother had cautioned against this. Could anybody expect her to think about college when David was fighting a war?

Janet's mother had returned to work as a part-time secretary in a law office. Janet was ecstatic at this assurance that she would be able to attend Agnes Scott. She knew Liz's feelings about college and accepted this.

Not until mid-February did Liz hear from David. He was somewhere in France – censorship forbade his being specific – and on the move. He warned Liz she might not hear from him again for a while. That meant the Second Canadian Division was moving into action, she conjectured in alarm.

Each night before she went to bed, Liz reread David's letter that said so little of what she wished to hear about his daily activities, and much about his plans for them when he returned. Even in training as a soldier he was absorbed in the research project he had left behind.

For a while, after they were married, David wrote, they would live in Chicago so that he could continue his research at the University of Chicago, which was much excited with his progress. Later they would spend a year or two in Germany.

Only with Victor and Janet did Liz talk about David's career plans. Victor was fascinated by David's research. Whenever they had been together at Hampton House, Victor had plied David with questions. Janet was her closest friend. Maureen was so involved with Andy that anything else seemed an intrusion.

Victor was much worried about the progress of the war. Italy fought furiously on the Austro-Italian frontier, and he confided to Liz his fears for the safety of Italian cousins and friends. Long past clinic hours on last Wednesday afternoon Liz and Victor had talked about the perfidy of the Germans, who had reintroduced unrestricted submarine warfare at the end of January in the belief that victory would be theirs if they starved Great Britain.

This Wednesday Liz had arrived earlier than usual. Victor, too, came in ahead of his schedule. They sat together in the reception room, before patients began to appear; and Victor told her of his increasing sense of guilt. His mother's country was suffering badly. He was considering enlisting.

'Victor, you're doing important work here,' Liz said, chilled by the memory of saying these same words to David. 'And you've told me about how your parents have been working for Italian relief.' She recoiled from the prospect of Victor's enlisting in the Italian Army. Victor and the clinic had become a focal point of her life.

'And how are you feeling, Mrs Jones?' Victor said with a warm smile when the door opened to admit the first patient of the day, with Miss Miller – the nurse – at her heels. Clinic hours were about to commence.

Liz was drawn to some patients, rejected others, yet each became a part of a mosaic. Close at hand she saw the mill workers' poverty, and acquired fresh respect for her mother's efforts to improve conditions in Hamptonville. When she was younger she had resented her mother's being 'different' from the mothers of her classmates. These ladies spent their days in social activities or doing volunteer work. This was acceptable; operating a mill was not.

'Miss Caroline, she's good to her folks,' a scrawny, stooped-over woman in her sixties, suffering from pellagra, told Liz while she waited to be admitted to the doctor's office. 'You seen how she paved our streets. Even put in sidewalks. And there ain't a house in Hamptonville that ain't got indoor plumbin' and electricity.'

'But nobody wants the union in,' a young man suffering from a mill-orientated arm injury complained. 'Profits are going up to the sky, but we have to fight for every increase we get.'

'Don't you be talkin' like that,' the woman admonished, but was cut short by the appearance of the nurse in the doorway.

'You can go in now, Mrs Cooke,' Liz said gently, and returned to the typewriter.

She knew there were labour problems from time to time in the mill. She had heard Mama and Aunt Sophie talk about how troops had been called out last November to eject families of cotton mill strikers in Anderson, South Carolina.

All through dinner Liz fretted in silence about Victor's possible enlistment. After dinner she determined to take action. She called Washington, breathing a sigh of relief to find her mother home because she was familiar with her parents' heavy socializing in Washington. Caroline listened while Liz explained the situation.

'Mama, make Victor understand that he's needed here in Atlanta,' Liz commanded. 'At the mill clinic and as a practising physician.' With her family in Washington and David away, she clung to familiar faces. 'What about the children he's working with? Mama, will you write him?' she demanded with the old imperiousness.

'I'll phone him tonight at home,' Caroline promised. 'You're right. Victor's needed in Atlanta.'

Late that evening Victor phoned Liz. He spilled over with excitement as he reported on her mother's phone call. Caroline was laying out the funds for a special children's clinic in Atlanta, which Victor was to supervise.

Mama was so canny, Liz thought in satisfaction, though on other occasions her mother's astuteness irritated her. That was the one move that would guarantee Victor's remaining out of the war. He had long talked about his hopes for a children's clinic in the city.

'Victor, when school closes in May, may I come in to work full-time with you at the children's clinic?' She needed to fill every idle minute.

'We'll be starting in a primitive situation at first,' he warned. 'But I don't want to delay, because this is so necessary. Liz, your mother's a wonderful woman.'

'She's a very rich woman' – Liz laughed – 'with the way cotton prices keep going up.'

'You'll have to ask your mother if it's all right for you to work there,' Victor cautioned.

'I'll ask her,' Liz agreed. Mama wouldn't refuse. 'Victor, I'm so excited about it!'

The nation's headlines read: 'GERMAN PLOTS TO CONQUER US WITH THE AID OF JAPAN AND MEXICO REVEALED.' Hysteria rocked the nation. Caroline wrote home that mass meetings for peace were being held daily in New York and several other major cities, though newspapers – except for the New York *Evening Post* – ignored these happenings.

A mass meeting for peace had been held a few evenings ago at Washington's All Souls Church, Caroline reported. She had attended. Not Papa, Liz assumed in fresh bitterness.

In March headlines reported the revolt of the Russians. Czar Nicholas II was forced to abdicate. The Czar and his family had been imprisoned. On the first of April Liz received a letter from David. He was joyous at the overthrow of the Czar.

'No more pogroms, Liz,' he wrote in his difficult-to-decipher scrawl. 'No more starvation and repression. Dostoevsky and Tolstoy should have lived to see this!'

In Washington Caroline was disturbed that Eric and she found themselves frequently quarrelling, yet she realized this was only because both of them were distressed at the prospect of the United States' entry into the war. Even the clergy, with few exceptions, seemed war-mad.

On April 2, with gallery cards in hand, Caroline and Marian went to the Capitol for the convening of the special session of Congress called by the President. This

433

Congress held special appeal for both women because Jeannette Rankin was to be sworn in as congresswoman from Montana. Caroline wished wistfully that Liz could be here for such a memorable occasion; but to take her out of school for several days so close to graduation was unthinkable.

'Caroline, there's Carrie Chapman Catt,' Marian whispered. 'Of course, she'd be here today.'

'I've lost some of my enthusiasm for the lady,' Caroline said bluntly. 'Since she offered the Woman Suffrage party for military service if we're dragged into the war.'

Everyone in the gallery whispered about the new congresswoman. She was eliciting more interest than the election of the Speaker, though it was assumed that Champ Clark would be chosen.

'There's the congresswoman!' A pretty young girl who sat directly before Caroline and Marian leaned forward in excitement.

A composed, unaffected young woman escorted by an older congressman and carrying a bouquet of flowers had arrived. The purple and yellow flowers had been given to her at the suffrage breakfast this morning, Caroline guessed. She wore an attractive dark blue silk-and-chiffon suit, with white crepe collar and cuffs. All at once the men on the floor were applauding her appearance, cheering in good humour. This was Jeannette Rankin. The nation's first congresswoman.

Congresswoman Rankin headed for her seat, to the rear of the Republican side. Smiling colleagues moved forward to shake her hand. She should have invited Liz to come up, Caroline berated herself. This was a memorable occasion.

The proceedings followed the routine schedule, except that when Jeannette Rankin's name was called, the House rose and cheered. There was some conjecture about when the President was to arrive. At five o'clock, when the diplomatic and executive galleries emptied out, visitors followed suit. Out on the plaza a troop of cavalry waited to guard the President when he arrived.

At 7:30 P.M., with an ominous wind blowing up outdoors, Caroline and Marian returned for the joint session, astonished to find some of the Cabinet ladies attired in evening garb. Word circulated that the President would arrive at 8:30.

Ten minutes later than anticipated, President Wilson walked through the swinging doors of the House chamber. Speaker of the House Champ Clark brought down his gavel.

'Gentlemen, the President of the United States.'

'Gentlemen and lady,' Caroline whispered to Marian while everyone present arose.

When the clamour had subsided, the President, appearing gaunt and tired, began to read his address from the rostrum. His voice was low and husky. Only at intervals did he raise his eyes.

'Property can be paid for,' Wilson said. 'The lives of peaceful and innocent people cannot.' He explained the futility of armed neutrality, and then declared, 'There is one choice we cannot make, we are incapable of making; we will not choose the path of submission.'

A tall figure rose in the audience. Alarm shot through some of the listeners. Caroline involuntarily reached a hand to Marian's arm. She saw the Secret Service men move into alertness. But there would not be a repetition of what happened in the Ford Theatre all those years ago. The figure was that of Chief Justice White, who had fought with the Confederacy.

Justice White brought his hands together with a resounding clap. The galleries took this up, filling the chamber with applause. When they were silent again,

President Wilson continued his speech. In conclusion he made the pronouncement that many had feared they would hear today.

'The World must be made safe for democracy. Its peace must be planted upon the tested foundations of political liberty . . .' The President continued in quiet eloquence, in his final statement saying: 'To such a task we can dedicate our lives and our fortunes, everything that we are and everything that we have, with the pride of those who know that the day has come when America is privileged to spend her blood and her might for the principles that gave her birth and happiness and the peace which she has treasured. God helping her, she can do no other.'

When the President finished speaking, an utter silence greeted him for a moment. Then a thunderous response of approval reverberated through the House chamber. Caroline's eyes sought out Eric. The droop of his shoulders told her his feelings of overwhelming defeat.

That evening Caroline and Eric sat over endless cups of coffee in their comfortable rear parlour and discussed the consequences of the President's proclamation. Despite Eric's gloomy predictions, Caroline had forced herself to believe for months that this day would never arrive.

'Caro, we've been in the war for a long time,' Eric told her. He seemed drained, Caroline thought. A man torn asunder within himself. 'Wilson made the commitment months before his announcement last night.'

'When do you expect the House will vote?'

'By the end of the week,' Eric said after a moment of thought. 'But the vote is unimportant. We're at war, Caro.'

'It doesn't matter how you'll vote,' Caroline comforted.

436

'The House and the Senate will push through the resolution for war. President Wilson will sign it.'

Eric set down his coffee cup. He leaned forward, forcing himself to be honest.

'There'll be men in the House and the Senate, not enough to matter,' he conceded, 'who'll vote against war. Men who respect their principles. Caro, I have no respect for myself.'

'Eric, don't succumb to sentimentality. If you vote against war now, you'll be fighting the administration. You'll never be elected to another public office. Your usefulness in the House will be shattered.' She paused, feeling his agony. 'Call Jim. Talk to him about this.'

Eric straightened up in his chair. His mouth was taut.

'There's no need to call Jim. He'll say what you've said. I know you're both right. I'll have to vote for war.'

Caroline sat in the House gallery and watched Eric's agony when the vote on the war resolution was taken. She fought back tears when Jeannette Rankin, with a break in her voice, cast her vote.

'I love my country, but I cannot vote for war. I vote no.'

Of the 423 members voting, only 50 went on record as opposed to the resolution.

On Friday Caroline sat in the Senate gallery with Marian while the senators voted, with only six dissenters.

'No resolution ever passed so swiftly in the history of this country,' Eric pointed out later that evening while Caroline and he sat alone in the rear parlour. 'Congress acted with almost one voice. In committee rooms I argued, Caro. I fought with all my strength.'

'You – and the vocal dissenters – were too few.' After all their years together, Caroline could taste Eric's anguish. An anguish she shared. 'Before the votes were taken, it was clear where everybody stood. Eric, those against going into the war were helpless.'

'Liz will disown me,' Eric warned. 'Her respect for me will be even lower than my own.'

Caroline rose to her feet, her head high.

'In years to come, Liz will understand. I respect you, Eric. I love you.' She reached out a hand to Eric. Instantly he was on his feet, drawing her to him.

'Caro, I couldn't survive this without you.'

'It's late.' She pressed her face against his. 'Let's go upstairs to our room.'

36

Behind the Canadian front south of Neuville St Vaast, soldiers worked at building enormous dugouts suitable for receiving the wounded from what was planned as a major advance. By night they laboured to dig additional trenches to care for the attacking troops. Since early March this operation had been in effect. Its objective, the taking of the Vimy Ridge.

On March 20 the preliminary bombardment, in which the Second Divison participated, began. For almost two weeks the Germans were attacked, with field guns and mortars striking the barbed wire of the Germans' first and second lines. Howitzers and machine guns provided further damage. Now the Second Division had been withdrawn from the trenches for a brief rest period.

At intervals, bogged down in homesickness and distaste for war, David questioned his reasoning for enlisting. Yet each time he resolved that he had had no choice if he were to live with his conscience. The Russian revolt had lifted his spirits; here was an oppressed people fighting for their freedom.

On Easter Saturday word reached David's division that the United States had declared war. For an emotional moment David feared for the physical safety of those close to him. But the United States was across an ocean, logic reminded. It was unlikely that any civilian would taste war as it was known in Europe. David prayed that his country would never again experience war on home soil. Why else was he enduring everything that was contrary to his soul?

That evening David sequestered himself in a Second Division rest billet behind the lines with paper, pen, and a candle to provide proper illumination. The men knew that at any moment they would move out. David was eager to have a letter to Liz in the next batch of outgoing mail. No one knew when they might have a chance to write again.

Recurrently he was amazed at the change in his thinking that Liz had wrought. His life had revolved around his teaching, his research, and his family. His only socializing was at Hampton House and occasional faculty dinners. Liz taught him to laugh, to relax. To love.

For years Rae had tried to marry him off. He had balked at any emotional involvement. Liz said he had been waiting for her. He could believe that. His face softened while he remembered the night she had come to his apartment. So beautiful and loving. So desirable.

He had been afraid of moving beyond the tiny circle of Noah and Rae and the children. He had been convinced that all he needed of life was his work. Emotional involvement was dangerous. Even now he remembered the agony of returning to their small village near Riga with Noah – to find their family annihilated. He had been afraid to love a woman, until Liz pushed him past that fear.

In quiet embarrassment he had gone at intervals to a red-light district to purchase physical relief. Those clandestine encounters provided little pleasure. With Liz he was a boy again, finding first true love. First satisfied passion.

Noah and Rae were unhappy about his involvement with Liz. They saw her as a sweet, lovely child. Of another religion. But when this rotten war was over and Liz and he were married, they'd come to understand that this was as true a marriage as their own. God, he wished this frightful war was over. *He wished he were alone with Liz, holding her in his arms.*

'Hey, David,' a fellow soldier called to him. 'Mail's going out in an hour. Hurry it up.'

'Right away,' David agreed.

'You hear the word?' the soldier asked, and David looked up inquiringly. 'We begin to move early tomorrow morning. Easter Sunday. Can you beat that?'

At dawn, in sleet and snow and high winds, the Second Division began to march. All day they marched, gathering at a position in Bois des Alleux. They settled in the trenches to await daybreak. Long, formidable Vimy Ridge lay ahead. After a week of wretched weather, the ridge was sure to be a quagmire. But to take Vimy Ridge would be a major victory for the Allies.

At 5:30 A.M. sharp the machine-gun corps that was to assist the Second Division launched a fierce attack. The soldiers of the Second Division climbed out of the trenches and moved forward, bayonets fixed. Eighteen-pounders kept up an endless shrapnel fire. Field guns and machine guns rained death on the enemy.

Again the Canadians were hampered by sleet and snow and strong winds; but the Germans fared worse. Wind converted the snow and sleet into a horizontal attack weapon that blinded the Germans. Smoke from the shells intensified the curtain between the two forces.

Behind a wall of artillery the infantry moved forward in waves. The ground was treacherous, pitted with shell holes, laden with shot-down barbed wire. Collapsed trenches and destroyed dugouts were everywhere in evidence. And most of all the men of the Second Division were conscious of the deep mud through which they must struggle. The tanks that had been assigned to assist them were useless.

Moving ahead, the Second Division discovered the

wrecked defences of the enemy. German dead were strewn about the ground. In the underground tunnels they found hundreds of Germans, who surrendered with no resistance. Prisoners and Canadian wounded were routed to the rear.

By seven o'clock the following morning the attack continued. The machine-gunners moved into action. A reserve battalion of the Second Division prepared to accompany the Third Division towards the next objective while the rest of the Second Division remained behind.

In their impatience to see a victory at Vimy Ridge, David and a young Canadian poet with whom he had become close infiltrated the reserve battalion. David wanted this war to be over. He wanted to go home to Liz. To his family and his work. He hated being eternally cold and tired and afraid.

In thick fog and smoke the soldiers paraded at the heel of the barrage. Insecure, uncertain of the terrain, some moved forward incautiously. David froze in horror when he saw men on either side of him fall to the ground, though enemy fire had ceased. *They were being hit by their own shells.*

David manoeuvred away from the line of Canadian fire, but at that moment the few German machine guns that remained in action began to fire. David was conscious of a searing pain. He clutched at his chest as he fell. *Where were the medics? Would they find him in this fog?*

On the Sunday morning after Wilson's announcement of a state of war, army, navy, and marine recruiting offices throughout the country were inundated with young men eager to serve. Wilson's hopes that American participation in the war would be limited to supplying ships, munitions, and credit were swiftly shattered. The English and French demanded reinforcements as fast as these could be readied.

The President and the military were in agreement that conscription would be the effective way to recruit the necessary armed forces, but in the House a selective-service bill rain into opposition. Even before war had been declared, former President Roosevelt had contacted members of his old Rough Riders and was clamouring for permission to raise a voluntary division to fight in France under General Wood. Wilson, Secretary of War Baker, and General Pershing rejected this. They were waiting for Congress to pass a draft bill.

Not all Americans were happy about the nation's entry into the war. Many German-Americans and Irish-Americans, who still protested British rule in Ireland, were opposed to fighting on the side of the Allies. Some Progressives felt it was not their country's place to intrude on what they felt was a war between imperialistic nations. The pacifists were against all fighting. But the population in general was caught up in a surge of patriotism that held the seeds of a crusade.

In Atlanta, Police Chief Mayo ordered a campaign against loafers. Fort McPherson sprang into fresh activity. When company quarters proved inadequate to handle the rush of new recruits, tents were set up, beds installed in the gymnasium. White-uniformed German sailors, interned for the duration, occupied barricaded quarters.

On April 18 Atlantans learned that Fort McPherson had been chosen as one of the fourteen sites in the nation where future officers were to be trained. Within two days a thousand workmen were involved in building new barracks.

All over Atlanta – as throughout the nation – vacant lots were being converted into vegetable gardens. Food crops were urgently needed. Victor joined forces with

Grace and Henry Roberts to persuade the mill folks to clear out weed-infested land and plant vegetables. Liz was recruited to distribute seeds among the families and to keep a record of what was planted.

On the summer-hot first of May Caroline arrived from Washington. Roland met her at the station with the car. Caroline was disappointed that Liz was not there to greet her. She suspected that, deep within herself, Liz resented the family's absence from Atlanta, even while she refused to accompany them to Washington. Liz was punishing her by not coming to Terminal Station today.

Roland delivered a message from Sophie. She was to come immediately to the mill. Was there labour trouble? she worried. Right now, with governmental orders on their hands, they could not afford a strike.

Sophie and Andrew were watching for her arrival. As she had feared, a strike situation was imminent.

'We hear the undercurrents. We haven't been approached,' Sophie pinpointed.

'We'll announce an immediate five per cent raise,' Caroline decided. 'With another five per cent promised June 1918.' Sophie was about to protest. 'We can increase prices to cover the raise,' she soothed. 'And we'll cut back on village improvements.'

'Prices are bringing screams from customers right now,' Andrew warned.

'They'll scream and pay more,' Caroline said calmly. 'They need us. Make the announcements tomorrow. Tell the newspapers.' Other mill owners would be livid, but they'd follow suit. The increase would be passed along to their customers. Simple arithmetic.

Caroline left the mill for Hampton House. She was eager to see Liz. The servants welcomed her with customary warmth.

'Miss Liz, she over at Miss Maureen's,' Elvira reported. 'She jes' crazy about that baby.'

'Mr Andrew tells me he's thriving.' Caroline forced a smile. Liz knew she was coming in on this afternoon's train. She might at least have been here at the house.

Caroline settled herself in the library with a cup of tea. Roland had taken up her luggage, and Elvira would unpack for her. She must talk to Liz about college next fall. Liz was graduating on May 18. It was incredible to realize Eric and she had a daughter of college age.

Caroline leaned back in her chair, remembering how desperately she had wished to attend lectures at Oxford, though as a girl she would not have been eligible for full membership nor been allowed to take a degree. Liz could attend any one of a dozen fine colleges in the United States and study for any degree she chose.

Caroline heard a car pull up before the house. She straightened up, an anticipatory smile lighting her face. Liz's voice filtered to her through the open windows.

'Wait a minute, Gilbert,' Liz called. 'Take some of these roses back to Miss Maureen.'

Caroline put down her teacup and hurried down the hall and out on to the veranda. Liz was snapping off red roses from a bush near the steps.

'Liz!' Caroline walked down the steps with outstretched arms.

'Mama, I didn't realize you were coming home today.'

'Be careful of the thorns, darling.' Caroline leaned forward to kiss her. Liz *knew* she was coming home today. 'How've you been?' Liz never wrote. Sophie kept her posted.

'All right. How are Papa and the boys?' There was a synthetic gaiety about Liz. She was worried about David.

'Everybody's fine. Papa will come home with them a few days before your graduation.'

445

Caroline walked with Liz to the car and exchanged greetings with Gilbert while Liz deposited the roses on the front seat beside him.

Gilbert drove away. Caroline and Liz walked up to the veranda and sat down in comfortable high-backed rockers.

'Mama, I'm not going to bother going to those silly graduation exercises,' Liz said with a contrived air of amusement. 'They can mail me my diploma.'

Caroline gaped in disbelief. 'Liz, your father's looking forward to attending your graduation.' *She* had looked forward to it with unexpected sentimentality. Less and less she understood her daughter.

'It's not important,' Liz reiterated.

'Have you heard from David?' Caroline retreated from the subject of graduation. They would talk about this later.

'Not since his first week in France.' Liz was avoiding her eyes. 'He didn't say much about what was happening. I guess maybe he wasn't allowed to talk about that.'

'It must be difficult to write under war conditions,' Caroline placated. 'You'll hear soon.' She had seen this happening with Liz, Caroline berated herself. Why hadn't she done something to stop it? Yet she knew that Liz's feelings for David could not have been changed. She had been helpless.

All through dinner and later in the evening, sitting in the library with Liz and Sophie, Caroline was aware of Liz's aching loneliness. She was so young to be so hurt. She was growing up too quickly. Only when Caroline asked about Andy did Liz seem to come alive. She adored Maureen's young son.

'We'll have a dinner party when Papa arrives,' Caroline decided on impulse. Before graduation, she plotted. Liz couldn't say she was giving a graduation party without consulting her. 'Not just family,' Caroline stipulated. 'A real party. Andrew tells me Maureen and he seldom go out evenings since the baby was born. It's time they became involved in Atlanta social life.' It was time *Liz* moved beyond their tight, safe circle. In Washington she had first comprehended how limited their social life in Atlanta had become with the birth of Francis.

'Mama, how can you talk about giving a party now?' Liz was glaring at her. 'When everybody's trying so hard to economize because of the war!'

'We'll have a simple dinner.' Washington continued to give dinner parties, Caroline remembered with sardonic humour. It was fashionable for hostesses to boast about how thriftily they could entertain. All at once it was a compulsion with her to give this party. A gesture of goodwill towards Maureen, and an effort to divert Liz from her anxieties. 'Creamed oysters because they're plentiful,' Caroline planned. 'Chicken and duck, which we can bring down from Hampton Court, and vegetables that are growing right in our own garden. Mattie will bake her petits fours. Strawberries – also from the garden – drenched in champagne. That'll be our one extravagance,' Caroline compromised.

Maureen listened in delight to Liz's report about the proposed dinner party.

'Liz, it sounds exciting. Do you know how long it's been since I've been to a dinner party?' She had never been to a real party in Atlanta. Only small dinners at Hampton House. But Liz said this would be a party with at least forty guests.

'It seems awful to be giving a party in the middle of the war.' Liz clung to her sombre mood.

'Sugar, read the society pages of the Atlanta papers,' Maureen teased, in high spirits at the prospect of the dinner. 'People give parties all the time.' Maybe now Andrew and she would be invited to some of those parties reported in the newspapers. Maybe she'd be invited to luncheons and tea dances.

'Mama plans on having it outdoors, with tables set up on the lawn. And the string quartet that played at my sixteenth birthday.' All at once Liz's eyes were tortured. Maureen knew she was remembering that on her sixteenth birthday David told her he was trying to enlist in the Canadian Corps. 'It seems terrible to be giving a party in the middle of a war,' Liz reiterated. Maureen knew that she harboured bad feelings for her mother for standing in the way of her marriage to David before he went away, that anything Caroline did would be wrong.

Maureen's face lighted at the sound of a faint, querulous cry from the nursery.

'Andy's awake from his nap. Let's go see him.' For an evanescent moment at Andy's christening she had considered writing Mama that she was married and had a son. But the old rage was not yet extinct. Sometimes, gazing down at Andy as he slept, she remembered the horror of her own childhood. As though it happened yesterday, she felt the pain and the hurt of being beaten by the mother she had tried to love because there was nobody else.

In the ensuing days, Maureen listened with avid interest to reports on the preparations for the party. Liz realized how she relished hearing every small detail. She took Liz with her to Chamberlin-Johnson-DuBose to help choose a dress for the occasion. Liz balked at trying on dresses herself. She would wear something from her closet. This was another reprimand for her mother.

Maureen had tried to coax Liz into agreeing to attend the graduation exercises, to be held the afternoon following Caroline's dinner. Liz went through the motions of rehearsing for graduation at school but vowed to her family that she would not show up on the occasion.

'I'm not going, Maureen.' Liz refused to relent. 'It's all so stupid. All that nonsense just because we finished high school.'

Caroline was hoping Eric would change Liz's mind. Maureen doubted it. Liz's rage extended to her father.

Two afternoons before the party, Liz arrived at the house in an aura of supreme happiness.

'I had a letter from David,' Liz effervesced, collapsing into a chair beside Maureen in the small sitting room, where a ceiling fan provided some relief from the heat of the day. 'I'd been frantic. It's been weeks since the last letter.'

'Mail moves slowly with a war going on,' Maureen commiserated.

'Oh, Maureen, David's wonderful.' Liz glowed. 'And he's the only person I know – except for you – who understands that I'm grown-up. Folks look at the calendar, and it says, "Liz is sixteen". They don't know I grew up ages ago.' Her eyes softened. 'Like Francis didn't grow up to his age for so long. I used to hate Mama for making such a fuss over him. I felt I didn't have a mother.'

'Liz, no.' Maureen was gently reproachful. 'Your mother has always loved you. Sometimes I envy that love. I wanted it so much when I was growing up, but my mother didn't have it to give. She was full of bitterness and anger. Andy will know I love him.' Her eyes glowed with this conviction.

'Oh, Victor told me yesterday that he's bringing his college roommate to the party. He asked Mama if he might,' Liz added. 'His roommate was partly responsible for his settling in Atlanta. That and Mrs Bolton. Victor

449

said his roommate never stopped talking for four years of college about how marvellous New Orleans was.'

Maureen tensed. She still seethed over the gossip that circulated around Atlanta about her. Now someone else from New Orleans was in town. 'What is Victor's college roommate doing in Atlanta?' Maureen tried to sound amused.

'He's on his way to New York. He's trying to get to France to join the French Army. He says there's going to be a draft, and he'll have to go anyway; but he'd rather fight with the French because they know what it's all about. They've been fighting for generations.' Liz shrugged. 'At least, that's the story he gave Victor.'

'Who else is coming?' Maureen probed. She wasn't going to worry about Victor's friend who was silly enough to rush into the French Army.

Maureen spent infinite care on her toilette this evening. Her first real party in Atlanta. The night was hot and muggy. She hoped there would be a breeze from the river to alleviate the heat. She felt recurrent guilt at going out tonight, because Andy was fretful. His first tooth was coming through.

'Andrew, do you think I should stay with the baby?' she consulted him.

'We're going to the party,' Andrew insisted. He knew how she had been looking forward to this. 'Carrie will be with him, and if he's crying, you can be sure Phoebe'll come in, too.'

'The doctor said there was nothing we could do except rub his gums with whiskey or paregoric,' Maureen worried. 'It's awful to see him in pain.'

'If he cries, Carrie will rock him to sleep,' Andrew consoled, his eyes moving over his wife with approval. 'Maureen, you look beautiful.'

'I want to be beautiful for you,' she said, and saw the arousal in his eyes. She exulted in his passion for her. Where once this gave her a sense of power, now she found pleasure in satisfying him. 'Andrew . . .' Maureen moved towards him, her eyes questioning.

'We can't be late for Caroline's dinner . . .' He wavered.

Maureen's fingers were already at the back of her frock.

'We won't be late, Andrew,' she promised. 'Lock the door.'

Maureen's exquisite pale green chiffon frock fell to the floor. She stepped from the green circlet and held out her arms to Andrew. She didn't care if they were late, she decided. It was the unexpected interlude of lovemaking that most pleased her.

'Maureen, how did I ever live without you?' he whispered while they moved together.

'Don't talk,' she urged. 'I just want to feel.'

Andrew helped Maureen into her dress again, managed the snaps at her back while she rearranged her hair. A quick look into the nursery and they hurried into the waiting car.

The lawn at Hampton House wore a fairyland atmosphere. Poles had been set into the lush green grass and adorned with colourful summer flowers. Japanese lanterns were strung from pole to pole, encircling the cluster of tables, each set up to accommodate six guests. A swift tally told Maureen that the guest list had been extended.

Already many guests had arrived and were being served a cooling wine punch from a pair of cut-glass punch bowls set on a table at one side of the lawn, presided over by Seth and Roland. Maureen fought against panic. These weren't the Red Cross ladies she knew casually, or the women she met at suffrage meetings. These were members of the old Atlanta families. How many of them had heard the stories about her parentage?

Liz and Janet spied Maureen and hurried to her side. Andrew moved away at a gesture from Eric, deep in conversation with Senator Bolton and a Georgia legislator.

'Your dress is so pretty,' Janet pronounced exuberantly.

'How's Andy?' Liz asked, as though she had not held him in her arms this morning.

'Still trying to cut that tooth,' Maureen told her. 'He *would* decide to cut his teeth with the weather getting so sticky.'

'It's nice out here by the river,' Janet said. 'Inside our house it was awful.'

The string quartet began to play a Strauss waltz. A couple whom Maureen knew only from photographs in the society pages of the Atlanta newspapers decided to dance, ignoring the lack of a proper dance floor. Why hadn't Caroline invited some boys Liz's age? Maureen asked herself, and immediately understood. Liz would have been upset.

'Maureen, you look beautiful.' Flanked by a smiling young couple, Caroline came towards them. Caroline was going to introduce her to the other guests. She mustn't let them know she was scared. 'That dress is perfect for you.'

'Thank you.' Maureen's smile was dazzling. Some of her tension was ebbing away. 'You're always lovely, Caroline.'

Though she enjoyed meeting so many people whom she knew only from the society pages, Maureen was relieved when the time arrived to sit down to dinner.

'Andrew and you are sitting with Janet and me,' Liz told her, drawing her to a table. 'Victor and his friend will be at our table, too.'

'We're the youngest, except for Josh and Francis, who're sitting with your parents,' Janet giggled.

'I haven't seen Victor,' Liz frowned. 'I hope some patient hasn't dragged him off to the hospital.'

'Here he comes.' Janet pointed to Victor's Ford.

Victor and his friend emerged from the car and hurried to Caroline to apologize for their lateness. Now the two young men were heading for their table. Maureen felt the colour drain from her face while her eyes focused on Victor's tall, dark-haired, dark-eyed companion. She had seen him no more than three times in her life, but the face was etched on her brain.

'Paul Beauchamp of New Orleans,' Victor introduced him in high spirits. 'Mr and Mrs Andrew Hampton, Miss Janet Porter; and my efficient assistant at the clinic, Miss Liz Hampton,' he finished with a flourish.

'How do you like Atlanta, Mr Beauchamp?' Liz asked politely.

'I like what I've seen of it. But please, call me Paul. My father was Mr Beauchamp,' he said engagingly.

He didn't know she existed, Maureen comforted herself. He knew only that his mother had killed his father in a family argument, and had retreated to a sanatorium. His grandmother – their grandmother – had reared the Beauchamp children.

Maureen contributed nothing to the table conversation. Her eyes were downcast. The others at the table seemed intrigued by Paul's Gallic charm. Liz was listening to everything Paul said with a look of agonized intensity. David was fighting in France, and Paul hoped to be there shortly. To Liz this was a bond between them.

All at once Liz lifted a hand to attract Seth's attention.

He came in answer to her summons, his face showing his pleasure in the festivities.

'Seth, would you please ask my father if we might have a bottle of champagne.' Liz managed a dazzling yet tremulous smile. 'We must drink to Paul's safe return from the war.'

'May it be soon,' Andrew said gravely.

Maureen watched while Seth leaned over to whisper in Eric's ear. She recalled that Janet said champagne had not been planned for the dinner out of deference to Liz's feelings about extravagance in time of war.

In a few minutes, as Maureen expected, Seth and Roland were distributing bottles of champagne among the various tables. Elvira and Patience were bringing Waterford champagne goblets.

Several toasts were offered, and then the three men became engrossed in war talk. Maureen wished she knew how to stop them. Liz looked distraught. Janet sat with mouth slightly parted, waiting for a moment when she might divert the conversation.

Paul's eyes lingered on her at errant moments, Maureen noticed. Her heart began to thump. He didn't know, did he? No, she sought to reassure herself. *How could he know?*

Mama would never believe that she was sitting here across the table from her brother. Fresh anger welled within her as she remembered the years of hating her father's other family, who had so much when she had so little. Paul said his grandmother *would have* loved the Metropolitan Opera. That meant she was dead. A nasty, bitter old woman who had denied her own grandchild.

While dessert was being cleared from the tables and coffee about to be served, raindrops began to fall. A clap of thunder warned of an imminent summer storm. Prepared for this, Caroline invited the guests into the house, where coffee would be served buffet style in the ballroom. A musical program had also been arranged.

Maureen sat at stiff attention, in one of the small gilt chairs set up in rows for the performance. She pretended to be absorbed in the music. Was Andy all right? Was he crying? When there was a brief pause in the music, Maureen whispered to Andrew that she was going into the library to phone the house. She wanted to check on the baby.

'No, stay here,' Maureen whispered when Andrew made a move to accompany her. 'I'll be right back.'

Phoebe answered the phone on the second ring. Andy was sleeping, she reassured Maureen. He had cried for a few minutes earlier in the evening, but Carrie but rocked him to sleep.

'You stop worryin' about him, you hear?' Phoebe clucked. 'You jes' enjoy yourself over there.'

'All right, Phoebe. We won't be much longer.'

'No rush, Miss Maureen. You have yourself a good time. It ain't gonna help them teeth none to have you frettin' here.'

Maureen put the phone down and turned around. She started at the sight of Paul Beauchamp. She had not heard him come into the library.

'Do you know that you have fascinated me all evening?' Paul moved towards her with an insouciant grin. 'I can't be rushing off to war without knowing you better.'

'You're drunk,' she said coldly.

'Why not? Soldier's entitled, isn't he?' He reached out for her hand and brought it up to his mouth. 'I sat there tortured because you're already married.'

'That was potent champagne.' She tried to be flippant.

'If you weren't married, I'd propose this minute,' Paul said hotly.

'I *am* married.'

His eyes rested on the rapid rise and fall of her breasts. Misinterpreting.

'Maureen . . .' He reached to pull her to him.

'Let me go!'

'I excite you,' he said in triumph.

'You frighten me,' she retaliated, and pulled herself away from him.

'I can't go off to war without holding you in my arms. Just for a few moments,' he coaxed amorously.

'Don't touch me!' Maureen recoiled from him. All the fury of her childhood, denied by her own blood, sought release. 'Do you know how your father died? Did no one ever tell you?'

Colour outlined his cheekbones.

'Are you from New Orleans?' Paul demanded. All evening she had prayed no one would remember and mention this.

'I'm from New Orleans,' Maureen confirmed.

'And you're too fine a lady for a man whose mother killed her husband?' His eyes smouldered.

'Do you know why she killed him?' Maureen's voice was unsteady.

'There were rumours,' Paul acknowledged, his face taut with shame. 'My father was not the first married man to dally with a woman.'

'He had a second family,' Maureen said passionately. 'My mother and me. I'm your half-sister.'

'I don't believe it!' He stared in shock.

'It's the truth,' Maureen told him. 'Your mother killed our father when she discovered his other family. Our grandmother knew. She turned my mother away when she came to your fine house for one final look at Papa. I'm your sister,' Maureen reiterated. 'My son Andy is your nephew.'

Paul staggered as though he had been struck a blow to the head.

'Excuse me,' he mumbled, and swung away from her. 'Excuse me . . .'

For several minutes Maureen stood alone in the library. She had met her brother. She could like him, she realized in amazement, though the champagne had made him momentarily obnoxious. He was Andy's uncle. Instinct told her she would see more of Paul when he recovered from the shock. She would come to know her family.

All at once she could think of her mother without hate. She'd write Mama and tell her about being married. She'd tell her about Andy. Let Mama know she had become a grandmother. Mama might still be consumed by hate. She was not.

37

Caroline attended Janet's graduation exercises the following morning with Ellen. In the way of the young, Janet accepted Liz's absence with an understanding Caroline could not share.

Caroline hoped that Liz would relent at the last moment and attend her own graduation in the afternoon. An hour before the exercises, with Liz refusing to emerge from her room and Eric swearing in exasperation, Caroline phoned the school to present the excuse of a sudden stomach upset.

To Caroline and Eric's astonishment Liz appeared at dinner, serene and friendly.

'I spent the afternoon typing a long letter to David,' she announced. 'That was much more productive than going to graduation.'

'I'm returning to Washington in the morning,' Eric reminded Liz, allowing his irritation at her behaviour to seep through. He had left Washington at a critical period, specifically to attend her graduation. 'Sit down with your mother and have a serious discussion about college.'

'I'm not going.' Liz lifted her head in defiance. 'I'll help Victor at the new children's clinic.'

'Papa, will you leave before the parade?' Josh asked while his father and sister engaged in a belligerent stare-down.

'I'll be leaving at just about the time it starts,' Eric guessed. 'I'd just as soon miss it.' His voice was ironic.

Caroline knew Eric was upset at Secretary of War Baker's announcement today that Major General John J.

Pershing would leave shortly for France with one division of soldiers. These would be the first soldiers ever to leave the United States to fight in Europe.

'Papa, I want to see the parade,' Francis said wistfully.

'I'll take Francis.' Liz astonished Caroline with the offer. 'So Mama and Josh can see you off.'

'Josh, would you like to see the parade?' Eric asked.

Josh wavered. 'No,' he decided, pleased with his decision. 'I'd rather go to Terminal Station with you.'

Caroline parked in front of the house with Josh, feeling the terrible loneliness she encountered each time Eric and she were parted. With the country at war, Congress would surely remain in session all summer.

'Mama, when will we go up to Hampton Court?' Josh asked as they walked up the steps to the veranda.

'Honey, I don't know that we will go up except for weekends this summer.' Caroline was apologetic. 'We'll be running the mill around the clock and – '

'I don't want to go to Hampton Court,' Josh interrupted, relieved at this disclosure. 'I want to stay in Atlanta and help Victor at the children's clinic.'

Caroline stared at him in amazement. 'Why, Josh?'

'Maybe someday I can be a doctor, too.' Josh was striving to conceal the intensity of his feelings, but his zeal shone from him. 'I'd like to know how to help people. Especially children. Remember how Francis used to be? Sometimes I hated him for being that way. But Victor helped him.'

Josh was not yet fourteen, but already he had a direction to his life. Eric would be disappointed for a while; he had expected Josh to go into law, join him in practice. But this was Josh's decision to make.

'Josh, have you talked to Victor?' Caroline felt a surge of pride.

All at once Josh was shy. 'I was hoping you'd ask him. Will you, Mama?'

'I'll ask him,' she agreed.

Josh's smile was brilliant.

Caroline sat in a rocker on the veranda. A poignant tenderness suffused her being. Josh would go to medical school.

Liz's refusal to attend college disturbed her. Or was she looking to see Liz acquire what had been denied her? A lack of a college degree had been no impediment to her running the mill, she acknowledged. Still, she doubted that Liz would follow in her footsteps.

Caroline abandoned introspection at the sight of Noah's car approaching the house. What was he doing away from the store on a Saturday afternoon? The busiest day on Decatur Street. Inchoate alarm brought her to her feet.

Noah's face was drained of colour. His eyes avoided hers until he stood beside her. 'Caroline, I couldn't tell you over the phone. It would be too terrible.' His voice was hoarse. 'We had a telegram from the Canadian War Department this afternoon. David was killed in action.'

A coldness crept over Caroline. *Not David. Dear God, not David.*

'Noah, they could be mistaken.' Her mind refused to accept what Noah had told her. 'Did they say "killed" or "missing" in action?'

'David's dead, Caroline. He died at Vimy Ridge.' Noah's loss was mirrored in his eyes. 'Will you tell Liz?'

'I'll tell her,' Caroline whispered. How would she tell Liz?

Noah leaned forward to kiss Caroline on one cheek, then turned and walked in silence to his car. Caroline stood on the veranda watching while he drove away. She was numb with shock. David and Noah had arrived in

460

Atlanta almost simultaneously with her. They were part of the tapestry of her life.

Caroline closed her eyes in anguish. How would she tell Liz? But it must come from her. *My poor baby. My poor, hurt baby.*

Caroline left the veranda and went into the library to wait for Liz to return with Francis. She sat in a haze of shock, struggling to accept the reality of David's death. So wrong, she railed inwardly. All his wonderful research left unfinished. *Why?*

Yesterday the President had signed the Selective Service Act, which required the registration of all young men between the ages of twenty-one and thirty. David had passed his thirtieth birthday. Even with a draft he would not have had to fight. How many more would die before this savagery was over?

Caroline tensed at the sound of the car stopping before the house. She heard the sounds of Francis' laughter. He had enjoyed the parade. She geared herself for the painful task ahead. Too numb to cry.

'Francis, you want to play catch?' Josh called from somewhere outdoors.

'Yeah,' Francis yelled back.

Caroline held herself back from going out to the veranda to exhort the boys to play in the shade on such a hot day. She paused at the library entrance, waiting for Liz to appear in the reception hall. *What could she say to Liz to make the truth less terrible?*

'Liz?' Her throat was constricted. 'Honey, come into the library, please.' She swerved and hurried into the room, seeking a few moments' respite before she must deliver the blow.

'Francis loved the parade,' Liz reported, walking into the library. 'But he was restless when General Wood began to speak, so I . . .' She paused, aware that Caroline was upset. 'Mama, has something happened?' Her eyes were suddenly fearful.

'Liz, I wish I knew a better way to tell you . . .' Caroline's voice was thick with emotion. 'Noah was here a little while ago. He . . .' She struggled to continue.

'What did he say?' Liz moved towards her mother. *'Mama, what did he say?'*

'He received a telegram from the Canadian War Department.'

'David's been hurt. Mama, is it bad? He'll be all right?' Liz's eyes searched Caroline's. 'Mama, tell me!'

'Darling, it's bad,' Caroline whispered. 'David was killed in action.'

'I don't believe it!' Liz's voice soared to the edge of hysteria. Her lips were bloodless. 'Not David.'

'Liz, Noah asked me to tell you. He couldn't bring himself to do it.' Now tears filled Caroline's eyes. 'David did what he felt he had to do. He gave his life for his country.'

'And you wouldn't let me marry him before he left!' Liz tried to rout out grief with rage. 'You denied us that! I might have had David's baby. I wouldn't be alone.'

'Liz, you're not alone,' Caroline protested gently. 'We all love you. We grieve with you.'

'You kept me from marrying David,' Liz lashed at her in fury. 'You wouldn't even let us have that. *You wouldn't let me have David's baby.'*

'Liz –'

'Don't talk to me about David,' Liz said with such contempt that Caroline flinched. 'You don't know what it means to love a man. You only love Hampton Mill!'

Caroline stood, white and shaken, while Liz fled from the library and upstairs to her room. The breach between Liz and her was impassable. She had lost Liz forever.

* * *

Day after day Liz hid in her room, refusing to see anyone except Patience, who brought up her meals. Both Janet and Maureen had come to the house, hoping to be admitted to Liz's room, only to be greeted by a muffled 'Please, go away.' Caroline sat down to dinner each night with Sophie and the boys, agonizingly aware of Liz's empty chair.

'Caroline, you'll have to let Liz work things out in her mind,' Sophie consoled. 'Stop torturing yourself.'

'I talked to Victor about having a psychologist come in to see her. He's sure Liz won't allow it,' Caroline said in despair.

'Wait,' Sophie insisted. 'Liz is too intense. It's going to take time.'

The country was busy promoting the first Liberty Loan of two billion dollars in 3½-per cent convertible gold bonds. A dinner was held at the Piedmont Hotel to make plans for Atlanta to become a ten-million-dollar stockholder.

On June 5 young men throughout the nation went to register under the country's first Selective Service Act. Atlantans poured out in a frenzy of patriotism. The *Journal* reported that more than 19,214 had registered from Atlanta. On Friday, July 20, the first drawing of draft numbers was scheduled to be held.

Eric wrote that on Registration Day, when ten million prospective soldiers signed up across the nation, the Confederate veterans held a reunion in Washington. For some it might be the last.

'It's hypocritical for us to say we're fighting to make the world safe for democracy,' Eric railed, 'when we're ruling in the Philippines, Haiti, and Santo Domingo.'

Eric wrote that Union Station was receiving thousands of new residents each week, most of them coming to fill war jobs. Government salaries of $1,100 or more a year were enticing young women from towns and cities where they had been happy to earn ten dollars a week, into War Department offices.

Brilliant college professors lent their services. Industrialists Charles Schwab of US Steel and Alexander Legge of International Harvester led a parade of 'dollar-a-year men' – though Eric suspected that some of these 'dollar-a-year men' took home more in expense accounts than they had earned in their big corporations.

The young women of Washington, Eric reported, were encouraged to entertain the homesick soldiers from nearby army bases. Formal introductions were hardly required in time of war. The young women were responding in vigorous delight.

About twelve miles out of Atlanta on Peachtree Road, Camp Gordon was under construction, with expectations of being prepared to receive soldiers by September 1. When the army insisted on a water supply of two million gallons a day, necessitating the building of thirteen miles of pipe – which the city could not afford – the Chamber of Commerce guaranteed to underwrite the cost. Mayor Chandler advanced funds to avoid any delay.

Atlantans, like people throughout the country, were learning to survive Food Administrator Herbert Hoover's 'meatless and wheatless days' each week. Sugar was becoming a precious commodity. Already Americans knew that the temperatures inside their homes and public buildings would be lower than normal when the cold weather arrived, because coal was required for the war effort. Public-spirited citizens hung an American shield in a wreath of wheat in their windows, to demonstrate their patriotism.

Caroline was distraught that Liz remained a recluse in her room. Patience reported that 'Miss Liz jes' picks at them good victuals Mattie sends up to her.' But for the past weeks Janet and Maureen were permitted inside at intervals. The summer was speeding past. Caroline knew she must soon return to Washington with Josh and Francis.

'Caroline, it won't help if you stay here in Atlanta. Liz has got to come out of this on her own,' Sophie insisted when Caroline stalled on making Pullman reservations for the trip to Washington.

'I'm her mother, and I feel so helpless,' Caroline mourned. Only with Maureen and Janet would Liz share her grief.

'Talk to Victor again,' Sophie urged.

'Liz won't see him. Victor's tried a dozen times. He told her he needs her in the clinic. We thought that would make her respond. Sophie, I'm scared to leave her.'

'You'll be back early in October for ten days,' Sophie consoled. 'It isn't as though you're going away for months. Liz won't even realize you're away,' Sophie pointed out, and Caroline flinched. She had abandoned going to the bedroom door each day to plead with Liz to talk to her.

'I'll speak to Victor again,' Caroline promised.

Victor sat behind his desk in the children's clinic office and listened in exasperation while his nurse explained why she was leaving. Like the previous nurse, she was running to Washington to become part of the war effort.

'These children are important, too,' Victor expostulated.

'They're so few of them.' The nurse dropped her eyes to the desk. 'And so many soldiers who'll be needing care.'

'I wish you luck.' Victor strained to be polite. His staff was reduced to a typist-receptionist. Last week Josh had

465

left for Washington with Caroline and Francis. All summer he had been a enormous help, dedicated to working with the children. Now, again, he was without a nurse.

When the nurse left, Victor sat in intense concentration. He would find a replacement, but how long would she remain? It was difficult to hold help in this critical period. Did he need a trained nurse? He turned this over in his mind. *No.* He needed someone with warmth and compassion and strength.

In sudden determination Victor left his office and drove to Hampton House.

'I'm going upstairs to talk to Miss Liz,' he said firmly to Roland.

'Yessuh.' Roland's eyes were troubled. He doubted that the doctor would be admitted.

Victor climbed the stairs and paused at Liz's door. He rapped. She didn't respond. He rapped again.

'Liz, I want to talk to you before I leave for the army.' He was deliberately sharp.

He waited, hope ebbing when she did not reply. How was he to get through to Liz? he asked himself in despair. All at once the door swung wide. Liz stood before him, pale and shaken, her dark-ringed eyes accusing. 'Why are you going into the army? What about the children you're working with?'

'The fourth nurse has quit on me to go into war work,' Victor fabricated. Two nurses had left him. 'I might as well enlist when I have to close the mill clinic and the children's clinic for want of help.'

'Victor, no!' Liz's voice was impassioned.

'I feel guilty at being out of uniform when so many Atlantans are joining up.' *Liz was talking with him. She wasn't running back into her room.*

'Have you enlisted yet?'

'No,' he conceded. 'My number hasn't been called.' As a physician, labelled essential to the city's welfare, he wasn't likely to be drafted. 'But why wait?' He had to involve Liz in the children's clinic. Bring her out of her grief. Out of that room where she had imprisoned herself.

'Victor, what's happening to you? What about your commitments here?'

'Liz, my staff consists of an office clerk. If, at least, I still had Josh . . .' He saw her eyes widen in amazement. She was becoming aware that life went on outside her bedroom.

'Josh?'

'All summer he came in to help with the children. The few patients I have,' Victor said ruefully. 'Five so far. The poor and desperate. I had hoped to bring in more.'

'Victor, you have a gift for working with these children. There'll *be* more. Look what you did for Francis.'

'I need someone who believes the way I do. Who isn't afraid of working twelve to fourteen hours a day. Josh was wonderful. Knowing Francis, he had a special compassion. But Josh had to go back to school.'

'If I come in to help, will you keep the clinic running?' Liz challenged. 'Will you swear you won't enlist?'

'If you come in to help – and work the hours Josh worked – I'll stay,' he accepted. 'It'll be an insane race,' he warned. 'I have to give some hours to my regular practice. I'll be out on house and hospital calls, but the rest of the time – when I'm not sleeping – I'll be with the children. And Wednesday afternoons and evenings at the mill clinic. I'll even expect you to learn to drive. That'll be helpful.'

Liz gazed intently at him. 'You buffaloed me into this,' she accused.

'Do you want to back out?'

'No,' Liz said. Her eyes desolate. 'Victor, I can't cry any more. Help me. Please, help me.'

Liz held out her arms. Victor brought her to him as though she were a tiny child to be comforted. Liz would find herself, he vowed, smoothing her silken hair while she clung to him. She would be whole again.

Liz flung herself into work with Victor, relieved to discover every waking moment occupied. Occasionally she saw Janet, engrossed in her studies at Agnes Scott, or visited with Maureen and Andy. Victor thrust increasing responsibility on her shoulders.

She talked with parents of children like Francis. They were eager for crumbs of hope, grateful that she talked without reserve about her family's experience. With brothers and sisters she shared her own rage at having to live with Francis in his difficult years. When parents admitted to doubts, her patience ebbed away, Liz became an avenging angel. How dare they abandon their child when there was hope. Not in six weeks or six months, but in time. *In their child's time.*

Liz dreaded her mother's return to Hampton House. The first night at dinner was agony. The presence of her mother brought back in painful sharpness their last encounter, when she learned about David's death. She was relieved when Victor appeared for dinner on her mother's third night at Hampton House. Mama had invited Victor because she, too, was uncomfortable, Liz theorized.

Much conversation in Atlanta these evenings revolved around the arrival in early November of Billy Sunday, the flamboyant evangelist who had chosen Atlanta as his first Southern destination in his fight against 'His Satanic Majesty'. A tabernacle was built to his own specifications at Jackson and Irwin streets.

468

Caroline was impatient at the city's fascination with Billy Sunday.

'The man plays on human emotions,' she dismissed him. *What does Mama know about human emotions?* 'It's fitting that the tabernacle is on the old circus grounds.'

'I hear the last time Sunday was in Atlanta was thirty years ago. He was playing in big-league baseball,' Victor contributed humorously.

'The whole city will turn out when he arrives,' Sophie grumbled. 'I never heard of such goings-on for one Presbyterian minister.'

'His advance man came into the city several weeks ago,' Victor recalled. 'He set up the whole operation. Three trained choruses, fifteen hundred ushers and doormen, a committee of one hundred laymen to help the ministerial committee. The advance man has even arranged for Bible classes at Camp Gordon.'

'Tell me about the clinic, Victor,' Caroline ordered. 'I want to hear every small detail.'

Liz listened in tight-lipped silence. She was glad when Janet phoned while they were sitting in the library over coffee. She could escape for a little while.

A week later Caroline returned to Washington. Liz grew less tense. She stayed away from the Kahn house. When Rae called to talk with her, she refused to go to the phone. She knew that Rae was hurt. After a few times Rae ceased to phone.

The Atlanta newspapers headlined Billy Sunday's arrival, fresh from evangelical triumphs across the nation, on Saturday evening, November 3. Despite her mother's contempt for him – perhaps because of it – Liz sat in the library on Sunday morning and read every word that was printed about him.

Sunday had hired an engine to catch the Dixie Flyer, en route from Chicago to Atlanta, when his train connection was two hours late. Newspapermen boarded the train and asked what message he was bringing to the South.

In his private drawing room, while Mrs Sunday did needlework across from him, the mercurial evangelist gave the reporters a statement for the Atlanta people.

'I expect Atlanta to come to the plate and line them out so fast that the devil will have his tongue hanging out, and when the game is called, the score will be one of which Atlanta will be proud. The time has come to clear the decks for action, to come out of the trenches and go over the top for God, home, and native land!'

Elvira came in with a fresh coffee for Liz and stared avidly at the photograph of Billy Sunday on the front page of the *Constitution*. Liz was astonished when Elvira admitted that she had been at the station the previous evening when Billy Sunday and his wife arrived on the Dixie Flyer.

'Oh, Miss Liz, you shoulda been there,' Elvira said fervently. 'The governor and Mayor Chandler and mobs of folks wuz there to welcome him. A brass band to play, and the biggest chorus. Musta been thousands of 'em singing.' Elvira's eyes grew misty. 'They sang "Sail On" and "Since Jesus Came into My Heart" – oh, some of the best songs.'

'Elvira, why did you go?' Liz asked.

'Miss Liz, when you got trouble, you go to God. And ever'body's got trouble sometimes.' Elvira's dark eyes were bright with sympathy.

'Should I go to hear Billy Sunday?'

'Wouldn't do no harm.' All at once Elvira was self-conscious. 'I better git back to the kitchen. I promised to help Mattie before I goes to church.' Elvira hesitated. 'Mr Sunday, he gonna have special meetin's for coloured folks. I plan on being there.'

Each day Liz read the newspaper accounts of Billy Sunday's activities in Atlanta. On Sunday he preached three sermons at the Jackson Street tabernacle, to thirty thousand people. He rested on Monday, which he called 'wash day', and on Tuesday preached in the afternoon and evening.

Everybody in Atlanta seemed to be attending. Atlanta society leaders, factory workers, politicians, churchmen, members of every profession. High-school classes, the middle-aged, the elderly, from every stratum of Georgia society hurried to hear the evangelist that seemed to offer so much to so many. Extra streetcars were scheduled to handle the crowds.

On Thursday Liz told Victor she was anxious to hear Billy Sunday. She was ashamed to ask Sophie to go with her. Janet was disrespectful in her assessment of the visiting evangelist.

'We'll go together,' Victor told her. 'Tomorrow evening.'

At Liz's invitation, Victor came to dinner. Aunt Sophie was pleased, Liz noticed, because she was going out in the evening for the first time in months. Sophie refrained from making any comments about Billy Sunday.

Victor talked to Liz about their work with the children while they drove to the tabernacle. He was making no conversational demands on her, content to ramble on about the subject closest to his heart. After some searching they found a place to park and walked to Jackson Street.

Thousands of young people were pouring into the tabernacle. This was high-school night, Victor explained. For a moment Liz was annoyed. *She* wasn't a high-school student. But she realized that Victor had spontaneously chosen tonight because last night he had been involved in a meeting with parents. Tonight was his first opportunity to come with her.

Liz and Victor were led to seats up front. A press box was set up on a site level with Billy Sunday's platform. Two grand pianos had been brought into the tabernacle. In moments the huge chorus, which had been rehearsing for weeks, began to sing. The tabernacle acquired the aura of an old-time revival meeting. Then the songs associated with Billy Sunday were sung. 'There's Sunshine in My Soul Today', 'Brighten the Corner', 'I'll Tell the Wondrous Story'.

Liz gazed about at the rapt faces, most of them young tonight. Why were they here? Because they were curious? Were they afraid of damnation? Or were they, like her, looking for salvation? *Would Billy Sunday bring it to them?*

Tonight's youthful audience was let into school songs, gave school yells. *When was Billy Sunday going to appear?* The question seemed to ricochet about the tabernacle. The suspense increasing by the moment.

All at once a hush fell over the tabernacle. Billy Sunday, in a dark grey suit and black four-in-hand tie under a hard white collar, had walked onto the platform. For a moment he paused under the harsh white electric lights. His eyes rested on the choir, moved on to survey the crowd in the tabernacle. He started to talk in soft, conversational tones. Talking to the Lord.

This his voice soared, his words rippling from his throat at breakneck speed. He leapt about the platform, pounded the pulpit, at one point mounted a chair. He lambasted the liquor trade, parents who drank at home before their children and gave them liquor.

At last Sunday stood before them, his eyes shut tight, his face contorted, his hand pounding the pulpit.

'Hurry up and don't wait any longer, Lord, before you

472

draw your sword and cut down those miserable cutthroats who have broken treaties, ravaged countries, and ruined women and girls. Oh, Jesus, if they haven't been stopped, they will be when they knock up against the Stars and Stripes.'

Afterwards multitudes from the audience pushed their way down the sawdust trail and waited their turns to shake hands with Billy Sunday when he came down from the platform. Liz was silent as Victor and she left the tabernacle and walked to the car. She was grateful that Victor made no effort to talk to her.

It became an obsession with Liz to hear Billy Sunday. Any night that Victor was free to take her, Liz went to the tabernacle. Nightly, except Mondays, hordes flocked to hear the evangelist, mesmerized as he leapt, perspiration-sodden, about the platform, declaimed, gesticulated, pounded the pulpit, or mounted a chair to emphasize a point.

More than three hundred neighbourhood prayer meetings were being held twice a week in private homes. Newspapers carried detailed accounts of Sunday's activities.

Victor strove to clear as many evenings as possible so that he could take Liz to the meetings. He concealed his own distaste for what had become a great emotional experience for Atlantans. But on the second Saturday evening when Liz and he took their seats in the tabernacle, Victor was grappling with a personal realization. *He was in love with Liz.* When had it happened?

Tonight more than a hundred soldiers from Camp Gordon were present and seated in a special section. At intervals Victor saw Liz's eyes leave the platform to rest on them. She was remembering David. Everywhere she looked in Atlanta these days, Liz saw men in uniform and remembered.

473

Victor struggled to conceal his restlessness, though tonight he felt this reflected in Liz. The Saturday-night crowd – though seven thousand strong – was smaller than usual. Billy Sunday had remarked earlier that 'most folks are out buying groceries on Saturday evening' and that it was 'tub night'.

Tonight the evangelist exhorted his listeners to 'stand up for Jesus'. He told them that 'Uncle Sam is fighting three things – Germans, booze, and prostitution.' Victor hoped he would avoid sermonizing on the war in Europe. He could sense Liz's torment each time this occurred.

At last, to Victor's relief, the meeting was coming to a conclusion. Sunday closed his eyes, gazed heavenward, one foot propped on his chair, perspiration running down his face in rivulets.

'Oh, God, help the man on the ship who aims the cannon to send to hell a submarine every time one sticks its dirty, stinking nose above the water. Oh, God, damn Germany and Turkey and all that gang of thieves and cutthroats. Oh, Lord, I don't want to bless them, and you can go ahead and damn them as soon as you get ready, as far as I am concerned; but, God, don't wait too long.'

Victor shuddered in revulsion as the audience applauded. He turned to Liz. Her hands were clasped in silence. She was frowning.

'Victor . . .' She turned to him, her eyes troubled. 'He's preaching hate. It took me two weeks to realize that. I'm a pacifist – I don't belong here.'

'I don't like what Sunday preaches,' Victor concurred, reaching to cover her hands with one of his own in reassurance. 'Liz, John McCormack will be singing at the auditorium-armoury on November 29. Why don't we go to hear him? I think you'll enjoy that.' Victor spoke on impulse.

'All right,' Liz accepted after a moment of hesitation. 'I love McCormack's records.'

Liz regarded him as a brother. He must never intrude beyond that point. He had no right. An afternoon at Hampton House two and a half years ago robbed him of that.

If Caro knew how he felt about Liz, she would be outraged. It was decadent, he berated himself, to stop loving Caro and fall in love with her daughter. *How had it happened?*

38

In the latter half of 1917 American young men, most of them churning with patriotic fervour, flooded the army camps. They discovered themselves faced with bad food, mind-numbing classes in French, four hours of drill each day, and demoralizing lectures on 'personal hygiene and the care of the feet'. The hero image fast evaporated.

The government enlisted the help of hundreds of celebrities in selling Liberty Bonds. Movie idol Douglas Fairbanks, opera star Ernestine Schumann-Heinck, even the President himself.

Women worked as mechanics, streetcar conductors, on factory assembly lines. They ploughed the fields, directed traffic, carried ice.

Liz awoke each day to the devastating realization that David was dead. She was grateful that Victor and the children's clinic consumed much of her time. Still, endless empty nights stretched ahead of her. After dinner each night she sat with Sophie or talked with Janet or Maureen on the phone. This was her social life.

The release of sleep was difficult to acquire. Often she lay until dawn, staring into the darkness. Why didn't women die when their men were killed in this senseless war? *Why must they make a pretence of living?*

Liz learned from Sophie that her parents and the boys would not come home for Thanksgiving.

'Your father's too busy with congressional committees. But they'll come home in time for your birthday.'

'No,' Liz said sharply. 'I don't want to hear one word about my birthday!' Her voice was jagged. On her last birthday David told her he was joining the Canadian Corps.

'All right, Liz.' Sophie understood. She'd relay the message to Mama. At irregular intervals Liz received brief letters from her mother. She never bothered to reply.

'Your mother suggests we invite some of the soldiers from Camp Gordon for Thanksgiving dinner,' Sophie told her. 'Everybody in Atlanta will be doing that.'

Liz tensed. How could Mama be so insensitive? She'd have to sit at a table where David had sat beside her and smile at other soldiers in uniform. Her instinct was to flee. She could go to Janet's house for Thanksgiving dinner. But Sophie would be upset. She would have to endure Thanksgiving dinner for Sophie's sake.

'May I invite Victor?' she asked.

'Liz, you know Victor is always welcome in this house,' Sophie clucked.

'This week after Thanksgiving Victor is taking me to hear John McCormack.' Liz frowned. Was she being disloyal to David's memory to go to the concert?

'If we weren't so rushed at the mill, I'd go.' Sophie sighed. 'We're breaking our necks to keep up with orders. What a blessing that your mother stockpiled all that cotton. The Cotton Advisory Board is urging the farmers not to sell a single bale until prices go up again.'

'The farmers say they're not making a profit,' Liz pointed out.

'At twenty-three to thirty cents a pound?' Sophie scoffed.

'They claim that's less than the cost of production.'

'The farmers all want to live like the rich,' Sophie snapped. 'Every farmer thinks he can't exist without a car. They buy all kinds of things they don't need at the exorbitant prices travelling salesmen charge them. When

477

the war's over,' Sophie predicted, 'they'll fall right down to earth again.'

Liz was grateful that Sophie invited Andrew and Maureen for Thanksgiving dinner. She contrived to sit between Andrew and Victor and talked with one or the other. She ignored the wistful efforts of their soldier guests to involve her in conversation. She looked at any man in khaki and remembered that David lay in a soldier's grave in France.

A week later Victor came to Hampton House again for dinner, scheduled early because of the McCormack concert. After dinner Victor and Liz left for the auditorium.

'I remember when McCormack sang here last year,' Victor reminisced while they drove from the house. 'It was almost down to zero. Not that the weather kept anybody away.'

'It's been cold even indoors these last weeks. Nobody has enough coal,' Liz fretted. 'Maureen says the only warm room in their house is the nursery. With us it's the dining room.'

'It's rough on the poor,' Victor commiserated. 'They're always the hardest hit.'

By the time Liz and Victor walked into the Auditorium, it was packed almost to capacity. As always these days, the presence of men in uniform was a poignant reminder that the nation was at war.

Liz felt a surge of guilt while she walked beside Victor to their seats. It was unfeeling of her to look forward to hearing McCormack with David dead only a few months. Liz's eyes moved compulsively to a box to their right where a party of French and English officers sat.

With an audience of five thousand waiting to hear him, the famous Irish tenor walked unheralded from behind the red curtain. His accompanist struck up 'The Star-Spangled Banner'. The entire audience rose to its feet while McCormack sang. The applause was thunderous when he sat.

To the audience's delight McCormack soon discarded the prepared programme to invite requests. They came with alacrity. 'Little Mother o' Mine', 'My Little Grey Home in the West', 'Mother Machree'. All the favourites. McCormack closed the programme with 'Keep the Home Fires Burning'. Tears blurred the vision of many of those in the auditorium.

Driving back to Hampton House, Victor told Liz he would go to Boston for Christmas. She listened in consternation.

'I'll be gone only until New Year's Day,' he reassured her. 'My family reminded me I haven't been home since I brought my grandmother out of Italy.'

'But the children,' Liz protested while her mind tried to cope with the prospect of all those days without Victor. Only now did she realize how much she clung to him. 'And the mill clinic,' she reminded.

'I've arranged for a doctor to cover for me. And the parents understand. I've told them that you'll work with the children while I'm away.'

'Victor, how can I?' Liz was appalled at this responsibility.

'You'll carry out my instructions as you always do.' Victor was unperturbed. 'If some serious problem arises, telephone me in Boston.'

The family arrived in Atlanta two days before Christmas. The same day Victor left for Boston. Liz contrived not to be at the station to meet her parents and the boys. At dinner that evening she spoke little. Her resentment towards her father for voting 'yes' on the country's entry into the war, her hostility towards her mother for refusing to allow her to marry David, rose to towering dimensions in their presence.

Over dinner Liz wrestled mentally with the prospect of leaving Hampton House. Leaving Atlanta. She could find a job in this year when so many women were needed to replace men who had gone off to war. She could manage without Hampton luxury. *She didn't want to be a Hampton any more.*

'Liz, is Victor making progress at the children's clinic?' her mother intruded. Reluctantly Liz allowed herself to be drawn into discussion about the clinic. Then she withdrew again behind her shield of silence.

The next morning a Christmas tree was set up in the parlour for the benefit of Francis and the cluster of servicemen from Camp Gordon and Fort McPherson who had been invited to share either Christmas Eve or Christmas Day with the Hamptons. At the clinic a tree was set up for the children.

At the appointed time on Christmas Eve a half-dozen self-conscious young soldiers – uniforms neatly pressed, shoes polished, hair brushed to a sheen – arrived from Camp Gordon for dinner and to spend the evening. They were impressed to be sitting down to a roast-duck dinner with a congressman and his family.

Mama knew how to make the soldiers relax, Liz admitted; yet this ability irritated her tonight. Papa talked to them about his experiences in the Spanish-American War. They listened with respect.

'That war was a play war compared to this,' Eric told them. 'Only the soldiers who were fighting in Cuba knew there was no glory in war. To most of the country it was a romantic adventure.'

'There's nothing romantic about dying,' a soldier in uniform less than a month blurted out, then flushed a violent red.

'No,' Eric agreed. To puncture the sombre mood that

480

laid a heavy hand over the assemblage, he ordered Roland to bring out two bottles of champagne.

Roland brought the bottles of Dom Perignon. Liz watched while her father popped the cork and poured. An infinite sadness shone from his eyes. Her mother's voice echoed in her mind: '*He's as devoted to pacifism as he ever was. But this is a time when it's important for him to be silent. You'll see, Liz. He'll fight when the time is right.*'

Suddenly she knew Papa hated this war as much as she. She could forgive Papa for voting for war. But she could never forgive Mama for refusing to allow her to marry David. She could no longer remain a member of this family. She would pack a bag and leave Atlanta. She would go far away and lose herself in some large city.

'Let's drink to a peaceful Christmas in 1918.' Her father lifted his glass. Everybody joined him. 'Let's drink to a world that will learn to live in brotherhood.'

'Amen,' a homesick Alabaman said, and the others echoed him.

'Amen.'

Atlanta had been experiencing one of its worst winters in history, with the coal shortage requiring furnaces and stoves to be utilized at a stringent minimum. Liz detested awaking to coldness each morning, when only a whisper of heat invaded her bedroom.

She awoke on Christmas morning to an awareness of unfamiliar comfort. Patience had slipped into the bedroom earlier and lighted the wood fire laid in the grate. Liz lay with the comforter drawn snugly to her throat and gazed at the splash of colour as birch logs crackled.

Last night's decision leapt into her mind. She would wait until Mama and Papa and the boys returned to Washington. Then she would put together what money she had – and what she could raise from her personal jewellery in a pawn shop on Decatur Street – and she would go as far away as her funds would take her.

Tears stung her eyes as she remembered the visit to Decatur Street with David. The tintype taken by a street photographer that day sat framed on her night table. Her only photograph of David. Why hadn't Mama let her marry him? She might have had David's baby.

A tentative knock startled her.

'Who is it?'

'Patience. I brang you some hot coffee, Miss Liz.' Patience's voice was cajoling.

'Come in, Patience,' Liz called.

Patience opened the door. She carried a full breakfast tray.

'Merry Christmas, Miss Liz.' Since her fourteenth birthday the servants had adopted the formal 'Miss Liz'.

'Merry Christmas, Patience.' Liz's face reflected her love. Patience had been a comforting presence in those months she had locked herself in this room. Patience's sympathy was special. Mama had told her about Zeke, whom Patience had loved. Zeke had saved Papa's life at the cost of his own on the battlefield in Cuba. Patience had mourned as she mourned.

'Ever'things smells so good downstairs,' Patience reported. 'Mattie an' Elvira been cookin' since five this mornin'. Francis already come downstairs and opened his presents. He so happy.' Patience radiated pleasure. 'Now, you eat up your breakfast. You don't want to hurt Mattie's feelin's.'

'I'll eat everything,' Liz promised. Patience would be unhappy when she went away.

When Liz arrived downstairs, shortly before two P.M., she found the family and five soldiers from Fort McPherson who would be their dinner guests in the library. A blazing fire had been nurtured in the grate; Roland was ushering the last of the guests into the library. The required smile of welcome on her face, Liz swung around to greet him. Mama was moving towards him with outstretched hand.

'I was hoping to find a bouquet of flowers,' the new arrival said, 'but I guess the cold froze everything.' He was handing Mama a five-pound box of Huyler's chocolates.

A coldness shrouded Liz as she gazed at the handsome newcomer. Dark hair, dark eyes, ascetic features. So like the face that haunted her dreams. *He might have been David's younger brother.*

She struggled to control her emotions while Mama introduced Cliff Fraser to them all. He was diffident and charming, and obviously drawn to her. Mama saw the resemblance to David, too. She looked nervous.

Roland brought in wine and glasses, and Papa poured for them. When they had drunk to peace in 1918, everyone went into the parlour to pick gifts from beneath the tree and to open them. Sophie had knitted scarves for each of their guests. Mama had chosen other small items. The atmosphere was convivial.

At a summons from Roland they went into the dining room. Mama had arranged no formal seating. Liz was disconcerted when Cliff Fraser pulled out a chair for her and promptly sat beside her.

'You don't know how wonderful it is to spend Christmas with a family,' he told her. A touch of David's shyness showed through. 'Christmas is a time when anybody away from home is homesick.' His dark eyes were sombre now. 'Especially when they don't know if you'll get home again before you're shipped out.'

'Where are you from?' Liz struggled to sound polite but impersonal.

'Miami,' he told her. 'Too far to go home for Christmas. It's mighty warm down there now,' he said wistfully. 'I've never been so cold in my life as up here.'

'It's the coldest winter I remember.' Liz was astonished that she was talking so easily with this soldier who resembled David. 'Folks were ice-skating out at Piedmont Park last week. That's rare in Atlanta.'

'Would you believe I'd never seen snow in my life until I came to Fort McPherson?' He was gazing at her in disconcerting intensity. 'I suppose you see a lot of snow up in Washington?'

'I don't live in Washington,' Liz explained. 'I stay here at Hampton House with my Aunt Sophie. I work with a children's clinic.'

'My father's a doctor down in Miami. A paediatrician.' He seemed delighted with this vague tie between them. For a moment there was an awkward pause. 'My mother told me to be sure to see the Cyclorama,' Cliff said. 'Her father fought at the Battle of Atlanta.'

'I saw it when I was a little girl,' Liz recalled. 'It's in an old circular wooden building near the Augusta Avenue entrance to Grant Park.'

'May I take you to see it tomorrow afternoon?' Cliff asked after a second's hesitancy. 'I have permission to be away from camp until midnight tomorrow.'

'I work at the clinic most of the day,' Liz stammered. 'And right now Dr Adams is in Boston. It's hard to get away . . .'

'You take time off for lunch,' Cliff pursued. 'Let me take you out to lunch. We'll be leaving for an embarkation point any day. I'd like to go to France remembering an hour with you.' For an instant Liz saw fear in his eyes. Cliff Fraser knew war was no glorious adventure.

Liz wavered, her heart pounding. Cliff was going to

France, where David died. Perhaps Cliff would die, too. How many would die before this war was over?

'I go to lunch at noon,' Liz capitulated, and gave him directions to the clinic. David was dead and Cliff Fraser was going off, perhaps to die. *This little she could do to make him happy*. 'But I have to be back at no later than one o'clock.'

'I'll have you back by one,' Cliff promised.

At twenty minutes to twelve the next day Cliff presented himself at the clinic. The reception room was deserted because Liz was working with a child in one of the treatment rooms, but she heard him arrive. At noon the little girl's mother arrived and rapped on the door. Liz was free to go out to lunch.

Over lunch Cliff talked with disarming candour about his dislike of the army. Yet a wheel had spun in Washington and his number had been drawn. He had no choice. He had been drafted.

'I'm lucky to have made officers' training,' he acknowledged. His eyes darkened. 'Maybe I'm lucky.'

It was almost like sitting with David. The resemblance was uncanny. Even Cliff's voice was like an echo of David's. Liz was sorry when her watch told her it was time to return to the clinic.

'Liz, I have to see you again.' Cliff's eyes pleaded with her. 'Dinner tonight?'

'All right.' She could tell Aunt Sophie she was staying downtown for a parents' conference. 'Will you be in the city?'

'I'm staying at the Georgian Terrace. We can have dinner there if you like.'

'I'll meet you just inside the entrance.' Sitting across a table from Cliff, she could pretend she was with David. 'At six.'

When the last child of the day was picked up at the

clinic, Liz phoned Hampton House to leave word for Sophie that she would not be home for dinner. She would be meeting with parents. Since Cliff walked into the library yesterday, she had been mesmerized.

Liz drove to the Georgian Terrace, parked, and hurried into the hotel lobby. Eager to see Cliff's face. *So like David's.*

Over a sumptuous dinner he confided in her, 'We're under orders to tell no one, but we're taking a troop train to New York at five A.M. tomorrow. We'll wait there for a ship to take us to France.'

'I wish the war would end tonight.' Liz's throat was tight. She was remembering those last minutes in Terminal Station when she told David good-bye.

'It won't,' Cliff said grimly. 'It won't end for months. Liz . . .' His hand reached across the table for hers. 'I wish we could go somewhere together so I could kiss you good-bye.'

David had not let her come to his apartment that last night in Atlanta. Why hadn't he let her come to him?

'We could go to your room,' Liz whispered. It would be like kissing David good-bye. 'Would anybody stop us?'

Cliff's hand tightened on hers. 'In wartime, Liz? Nobody'll stop us.'

Her hand in his, Liz walked with Cliff to the elevators. She tried not to look self-conscious. They pushed into a crowded elevator and went down a long, carpeted corridor to Cliff's room. In her mind it was David's room.

Cliff unlocked the door, reached inside for a wall switch, and pulled her into the room. With one hand he locked the door behind him and with the other drew Liz against him, too impatient to waste a moment.

'Oh, honey, you don't know how much I want to kiss

486

you.' Liz felt his heart thumping against hers. 'Since the moment you turned around in the library yesterday and looked at me.'

Cliff's mouth came down on hers. His hands moved about her back. While their mouths clung and bodies brushed, he sought for the buttons at the back of her chemise dress.

This was David holding her. David who was about to make love to her. She helped him pull the dress from her shoulders and thrust it to the floor. While his tongue taught her a new approach to passion, she reached behind to release the hooks of her brassiere. *Oh David, David!*

She closed her eyes and abandoned herself to emotion. *David*'s hands rippled about her body. *David*'s mouth burrowed at her breast. Then he was prodding her to the bed. A low sound of pleasure escaped her when she felt the weight of him above her. She whimpered in rising passion as he entered her.

'Liz, you're wonderful,' he told her, his voice husky, while they moved together. 'Oh, Liz, Liz!'

For as long as Liz dared remain, she lay in Cliff's arms and listened to him talk in candid trepidation about the long road ahead of him. In a few hours he would be aboard a troop train. Within days he would be sailing in a blackout across the Atlantic.

'I hope we'll meet again, Liz,' he said. 'Someday when this rotten war is over. If I come back . . .'

'Don't say that!' she ordered, and reached to kiss him again.

Cliff Fraser was going away to war – but for a precious little while she had given him happiness. All at once a kind of exultation seized her. She had discovered a purpose for living. Right here in Atlanta she would meet other soldiers she could make happy. And each time she lay in a soldier's arms, she would be making love to David.

39

Like many Atlanta girls, Liz spent New Year's Eve helping to entertain soldiers. In a spacious, festively decorated room provided in a Y building, she danced with a corporal from Camp Gordon.

'In three minutes and forty seconds it'll be 1918.' The tall handsome corporal drew her closer.

'We don't have to celebrate New Year's here,' Liz told him, all at once claustrophobic. A new year was coming in. A year that David could never know. 'Unless you want to.' Her smile was a blatant invitation.

She saw his eyes brighten for a moment, then cloud. The corporal had no hotel room, Liz interpreted. 'Where can we go?'

'My car,' Liz whispered while the music paused.

His hand pressed at her back in approval. 'Let's go.'

Liz and the corporal retrieved their coats and darted out into the cold winter night. He clutched at her in awkward haste outside the door and brought his mouth down to hers. Triumph welled in her. *David. David was with her again.*

'The car's right around the corner,' Liz told him. 'Let's hurry.'

While the church bells tolled in the new year, Liz and the corporal made love under a car robe on the rear seat of the Hupmobile. Afterwards Liz drove him to Camp Gordon.

Hampton House was in darkness except for the reception hall and the library. She walked into the library to exchange greetings with her parents. Sophie had gone to bed already. Tomorrow night Mama and Papa would be on the train with Josh and Francis; Sophie and she would be alone again.

'Was it a pleasant party?' her mother asked.

Liz shrugged. 'It was all right. The soldiers seemed to enjoy it.'

With the intensity that always coloured her activities, Liz plunged into a new way of life. She bobbed her hair. She learned new dances. She took up smoking. Her days were spent at the clinic. Every evening she was at one of the centres set up for the entertainment of servicemen.

Liz was ever conscious that the young soldiers with whom she socialized would leave at any moment for France. She gave them laughter and gaiety and passion. Each assumed David's face, David's arms, David's body.

Liz knew that Sophie was distressed that she was away from Hampton House every night in the week. She reproached Sophie for her lack of patriotism. Victor worried about the late hours she kept; he scolded her when she came into the clinic looking to coffee and cigarettes to wake her up.

She was struggling to block from her mind the realization that Victor was falling in love with her. Victor was her most cherished friend. Closer, in some ways, than either Janet or Maureen. That mustn't change.

The months sped past. At regular intervals her mother arrived at Hampton House for conferences at the mill. Her mother, too, protested her constant absences. Liz was cold to these reproaches. Let her, at least, help to brighten the evenings of the boys who would soon leave to fight for them. The Allied situation was critical.

In Washington Caroline was relieved that much of the insane socializing disappeared. It was now considered

490

unpatriotic to indulge in party-giving. The Washington tradition of calling was ignored. The Washington Chamber of Commerce introduced a 'Noonday Angelus', where at the stroke of twelve each day everyone stopped for two minutes to pray for victory. Posters reading 'Food Will Win the War' appeared everywhere.

Caroline and Eric prepared to return to Atlanta in early June. Caroline knew that Eric faced a battle to win the Democratic nomination for the Senate. He had voted for war, but it was well known that he had voted with reluctance. In the current aura of militarism, his pacifism was against him. Eric was going home to Georgia to fight for his political life.

Two days before they were scheduled to leave Washington, Caroline received a phone call from Victor.

'I'm worried about Liz,' he confided after perfunctory greetings. 'She's driving herself ragged. She works hard all day at the clinic, then goes partying every night. She thinks it's her obligation to entertain every serviceman in Atlanta.'

'Victor, she won't listen to me. Liz has put up a terrible wall between us. I've tried to talk to her, God knows.' She *should* be able to talk to her own child.

'Caro, somebody has to stop her.' Desperation coloured his voice. 'She's wearing herself thin.'

Caroline tensed. He's in love with Liz. With painful vividness the memory of the afternoon she lay in Victor's arms sprang into her mind. And now he was in love with Liz.

'We're leaving for home day after tomorrow.' Caroline fought to keep her voice natural. 'I'll try to talk to Liz.'

Once she would have welcomed the prospect of Victor as a son-in-law; now it was impossible. Surely Victor must know that. Even if Liz should decide to marry

491

Victor, *she* would block it. How could she accept the man who had been her lover as her daughter's husband?

Arriving in Atlanta, Caroline recoiled from the brevity of Liz's skirts, which reached only a few inches below her knees. She was upset by Liz's addiction to cigarettes and coffee. Yet at her first wary efforts to convey her anxiety, Liz cut her off.

Though distraught about the continuing barrier between Liz and herself, Caroline garnered comfort from the conviction that Liz was unaware of Victor's love for her and certainly didn't return it. She was still too entrenched in her grief for David.

Caroline concentrated on the demands of the mill. Eric commenced rigorous campaigning for the Senate. It was important that he win. Defeat could end his political career. Again Josh went to work at the clinic. Josh idolized Victor.

Like Eric, Caroline was pleased by President Wilson's Fourth of July pilgrimage to Mount Vernon in the company of representatives of every foreign-language group in the country. At a time when more than a million American men were overseas, the President spoke of a league of nations that could work to maintain world peace. Yet word drifted across the ocean that Lloyd George and Clemenceau ridiculed such a proposal.

After a mid-July dinner at Hampton House Caroline and Eric learned from Jim that the Communists, as the Bolsheviks now called themselves, had exterminated Czar Nicholas and the entire royal family. The world recoiled in horror before this news.

On the day of the late-summer primaries Caroline deserted the mill to be with Eric at his election headquarters. Even Jim, ever optimistic, was wary about predicting the outcome. But well into the evening it became clear that Eric had won the nomination. He would run for Harvey Bolton's seat in the Senate.

'It's not a heartwarming victory,' Eric admitted wryly while he sat over coffee with Caroline and Jim. 'I've never been elected by such a slim margin.'

'Except for Kitchen and Almon of Alabama, no candidate in the South who opposed the war resolution will be returned to Congress. Thank God, you voted as you did,' Jim said with satisfaction.

Caroline's pleasure at Eric's victory was overshadowed by her pain at Liz's alienation from Eric and herself. What was going to happen with the family? She would be relieved to return to Washington next week. She felt herself a stranger at Hampton House.

The parade of soldiers in Liz's evenings remained persistent. Even after the outbreak of a flu epidemic in mid-September, Liz went dancing nightly. She always found a soldier eager to take her to bed.

Though Liz gave no indication of being aware that Victor was in love with her, she derived guilty comfort from this knowledge. Then a fresh, unnerving awareness crept into her being. She found herself beginning to return his feelings. How could she love Victor when she loved David? She felt ashamed.

Endlessly Liz tormented herself. Sleeping with soldiers was not being unfaithful to David's memory. She didn't love those men. They helped her survive. But to love Victor was to be unfaithful.

Clinic hours with Victor became torture, yet perversely she longed to spend every moment of the day and night with him. In self-disgust she curtailed her social life. She left each evening's diversion alone or with Janet.

When Victor sprained his wrist, Liz undertook to be his chauffeur. She continued to drive Victor on weekend house calls even when his wrist healed. Both disregarded the lack of necessity. Liz was torn between fear and hope that Victor would say he loved her.

The flu epidemic was intensifying. Atlanta civilians and soldiers fell victim to the flu in terrifying numbers. At Camp Gordon deaths were a daily occurrence. Orders came through that soldiers were not allowed to visit Atlanta without special passes.

On October 7 the Board of Health ordered all schools, libraries, motion-picture houses, dance halls, churches, and every other place of public gathering to be closed. Streetcars were under orders to run with their windows open except in case of rain.

Liz awakened each morning to battle nausea. At first she suspected she was coming down with the flu. Then reality assaulted her. The calendar taunted her. As days passed, her suspicions could no longer be ignored. Locked in the bathroom with water pounding in the tub to mask the sounds of her morning sickness, Liz knew she was pregnant.

She remembered Maureen's pregnancy. She recalled all the early symptoms. Her symptoms. She moved about the house wrapped in alarm. A pale wraith. Each day that passed thrust her into deeper desperation.

The afternoon prior to the November elections, her parents, with Josh and Francis, returned from Washington. Her father's election was guaranteed, of course; the voting was a formality.

Sitting down to dinner that evening was agony for Liz. Nobody could know that she was pregnant, yet her mind conjured up sickening confrontations with her mother and father. She sat through dinner with her eyes fastened on her plate, conscious of her mother's worried stares.

At the earliest moment she escaped to the sanctuary of her room. She lay sleepless through the night, exhausted but too distraught to rest. She greeted another dawn with the nausea that had alerted her to her pregnancy. But in the course of the cold, dank night she had clutched at a possible solution. She would confide in Victor. *Victor must help her.*

Sick and frightened, she waited until the day's activities at the clinic were completed. When Victor and she were alone, she told him in one ragged, blunt sentence, 'Victor, I'm two months pregnant.'

He gaped at her in disbelief. Struggling to accept what she had told him.

'I don't want this baby. I don't even know who's the father.' Trembling, her mouth dry, she talked with compulsive speed. 'Nobody knows but you. Victor, you've got to help me. Take this baby from me!'

Victor's face was drained of colour. 'Liz, I'm trained to save life. Not to take it.'

'There's no life yet. Only a seed. Victor, remove the seed,' she pleaded. 'I can't have this baby!'

'Liz, I can't perform an abortion. It's dangerous,' he tried to dissuade her. 'We'll have to talk. We'll find some other way . . .' He stammered, searching his mind for a solution. 'Liz, we could – '

'Victor, answer me!' Her colour was high. 'Will you take away the baby?'

'I can't.' He shook his head. 'Liz, we – '

'I don't want to hear anything else!' She had counted on Victor's seeing her through this. 'I'll find somebody.' She reached for her coat and purse and ran from the room, ignoring Victor's exhortation to remain and talk.

She drove about Atlanta for almost an hour, unable to face going home. And then she parked the car and picked up a tall burly young soldier on Peachtree.

The soldier from rural north Georgia, slightly drunk and in Atlanta without a pass, had a seedy hotel room nearby. Liz accepted his crudely voiced invitation instantly.

'Sugar, it's awful out there at camp,' he complained, an arm about her waist as he piloted her into the small, bare hotel lobby, where a desk clerk did not bother even to look up. 'Everybody dyin' like flies from the flu. If they want to get me back to camp, they'll have to send a dozen MPs.' He grinned. 'It'll take that many to haul me in.'

'Can I stay with you tonight?' Liz asked. She was reeling yet from Victor's refusal to perform an abortion. *If Victor loved her, he would have done it.*

'You bet you can.' His eyes glittered in anticipation.

They walked up a narrow stairway with ragged carpeting. When Liz almost tripped, he laughed and scooped her up into his arms. Without putting her down, he found his key and opened the door. The room was small, with a faded blue chenille spread thrown across the bed, and matching curtains, in need of washing, at the one window.

'I'd like a cigarette,' Liz told him when he set her down on her feet.

'Sugar, you don't want to waste no time on a cigarette,' he objected, pushing aside her coat so he could fondle her breasts. 'I want a cigarette,' Liz insisted. Something about this soldier made her wary.

'Later.'

He was breathing heavily while he hurried to undress her. His hands were huge and rough. Liz shut her eyes, willing him to make her forget everything except her self-appointed task of giving another soldier pleasure. She winced at the stale wine scent on his breath when his mouth came down on hers.

His tongue thrust its way into her reluctant mouth while his hands cruised about her nakedness. It would be all right in a little while, she promised herself. She could stay here all night. She wouldn't have to go home. She wouldn't allow herself to think about tomorrow.

The soldier's mouth released hers.

'Lie down,' he ordered, and pushed her across the bed when she did not respond quickly enough to please him.

Liz lay immobile beneath his heaviness, steeling herself for invasion. He was wasting no time on foreplay, intent on burrowing within her. She cried out when he lowered his mouth to a nipple and bit.

'Don't do that,' Liz ordered. 'It hurts.'

'Come on, sugar. You like that,' he jeered, and bit the other nipple while he moved within her.

She shouldn't have come here, Liz thought in panic. This wasn't like the other times. He was pinching her all over – she'd be black and blue tomorrow. She didn't want him in her. Why didn't he finish!

But she didn't have to worry that he wasn't being careful, she told herself bitterly. She was pregnant. Where would she find a doctor who would take the baby from her?

At last the soldier lay limp. Heavy and sweaty. Why didn't he get off her? She hated this. She shouldn't have come here with him.

He lifted himself about her, pinning her prone on the bed between his hairy thighs. He brought himself between her breasts, crushing them together and groaning in passion at the impact. Liz shut her eyes in disgust. This soldier wasn't like the others. He was an animal.

'Kiss it,' he ordered, and her eyes opened wide in shock. 'Kiss it.' He thrust himself towards her.

497

'No!' All at once she was fighting to free herself while he swore in barracks language. 'No!'

He lost his balance and fell from the bed. Liz swung her legs to the floor, grabbed for her coat to cover her nakedness, and darted towards the door. He reached out for her as he stumbled to his feet.

'You ain't going no place.' He slapped her hard across her face.

'Let me out of here, or I'll yell my head off,' Liz warned. He was away from camp without a pass.

'You bitch!' His fist shot towards her, shutting an eye. The other fist drove into her stomach. She doubled over in pain. 'You goddamn, no-good whore. Get the hell out of here!' He moved to the door and pushed her from the room.

Liz fell to the floor. With painful slowness she rose to her feet and staggered down the dimly lit stairs and out of the sleazy hotel. Where had she parked? She struggled to button her coat while she prised from her memory the locale of the car.

She drove home. There was nowhere else to go. Her head pounded. Her eye was swelling. The pain in her stomach turned her sick. She left the car in front of the house and staggered up the steps and across the veranda.

'Liz?' She heard her mother's anxious voice when she dragged herself into the reception hall. 'Victor's been phoning every ten minutes. He . . . Oh, my God! Liz, what happened?'

Liz saw the foggy image of her mother's face as she collapsed. Mama was going to hate her for what she'd done. If Victor had helped her, nobody would have known. *Not Mama. Not Papa. Let me die. Please, God, let me die.*

Slowly Liz returned to consciousness. She knew she

498

was in her bed. She heard Victor's voice as he hovered above her.

'She's losing the baby, but she's going to be all right, Caro.'

Liz kept her eyes shut while mental anguish blended with physical pain. Mama knew she was pregnant. Papa would know. Nothing would ever be right for her again.

40

Caroline stood beside Liz's bed while Patience rolled up the soiled sheets and towels. Liz lay in a fresh nightgown, her face discoloured by bruises, eyes closed in slumber. A fire in the grate lent warmth to the room.

'Caro, don't look so distraught,' Victor chided in compassion. 'Liz is fine. All she needs is a good night's sleep.'

'That's all that matters.' Caroline was defensive. 'That Liz is all right.' Physically Liz was fine. But she had been pregnant by one of a procession of soldiers. In her anguish Liz had spilled forth the ugliness of the nights in which she sought for David in other men's arms.

When Patience left the room, Victor abandoned his professional role.

'I'd like to kill the man who beat her!'

'I could kill him, myself,' Caroline acknowledged. 'With no compunction.' She forced a wry smile. 'Despite my pacifist convictions.'

'If Liz wants to come into the clinic on Thursday or Friday, let her,' Victor said. 'It'll be good for her to be busy. If it seems too much for her, then I'll bring her home.' He hesitated. 'She's upset that you know she was pregnant.'

'Liz won't hear one word of reproach from us,' Caroline vowed. *She* could have been pregnant by Eric before they were married. She might have been pregnant by Victor after that stormy afternoon when they allowed themselves to be swept away. 'And no one else need ever know.'

'Nobody,' Victor agreed. He snapped his bag in preparation for departure. 'I imagine congratulations are in order. It's taken for granted that Eric's our new Senator.'

'He's staying at election headquarters till the bitter end. They must be celebrating about now.' Eric would wonder why she wasn't there. She had not called him about Liz. 'I'll go with you to the door.'

'You don't need to do that, Caro.' Victor leaned forward to kiss her on the cheek. 'I'll let myself out.'

Caroline pulled a chair to Liz's bedside and sat down. Sadness suffused her. How had she failed Liz? Was she wrong in not allowing her to marry David? But Liz had been so young. Was she responsible for tonight?

Caroline lay in restless wakefulness beside Eric, now asleep. He had been more shaken by learning of Liz's beating and miscarriage than she ever remembered. Only tonight did Eric comprehend that Liz was no longer his little girl.

Was Liz warm enough? She sought comfort in some small action that showed her love. Had the fire gone out in Liz's room?

Careful not to disturb Eric, Caroline left the bed. She slipped into her robe and went down the hall to Liz's room, cloaked now in shadows. The logs in the grate had been reduced to grey-edged charcoal, lending no illumination.

Caroline hesitated before the fireplace. If she tried to start a fresh blaze, she'd awaken Liz. She crossed to the bed and leaned forward to touch Liz's arm, flung across the comforter.

'Mama . . .' Liz's voice was low and tearful, her face hidden in the darkness. 'Mama, do you hate me?'

'Oh, darling, no.' Caroline reached for Liz's hand and

brought it to her mouth. 'Don't ever think such a thing. Papa and I love you. We all love you.'

'I've made such a mess of my life. I couldn't even be faithful to David's memory.' Her voice broke.

'Liz, you're not yet eighteen. Your whole life is before you.'

'It's over,' Liz insisted. 'First I loved David, and I lost him. Now I love Victor, and I've lost him, too.'

Liz was in love with Victor. A strange relief flooded Caro. But it was quickly replaced by misgivings. Was it too late for them? How could she have thought to stand in their way?

'I didn't mean to love him. It just happened. Mama, swear you won't ever tell Victor,' Liz ordered in sudden fear. 'Swear it.'

'I swear, Liz.' Caroline cradled Liz's head against her breast, as though Liz were a little girl again. 'But you should know that Victor's in love with you. I've seen it for weeks. Just by the way he looks at you.'

'He knows, Mama. He knows the way I've lived.' Liz shivered. 'All those soldiers. I don't even know how many. They'll always stand between Victor and me. It's too late for us, Mama.'

'Ssh,' Caroline murmured. 'Try to sleep, darling. I'll sit here with you.' *What could she say? Why could she do to make things right for Liz?*

Liz slept most of Wednesday. When she was not sleeping, she made a pretence of it. Patience moved in and out of the room, eager to bring her trays. To offer comfort. Mama came home from the mill at midday to look in on her. She heard Mama in whispered consultation with Patience. Papa was supposed to have left for Washington with the boys this afternoon. Instead he was waiting until Saturday. Because of her.

In the early hours of Thursday morning Liz lay wakeful, trying to fuse together the fragments of her life. She could not endure living at Hampton House any longer. Every time she looked at Mama and Papa – and Sophie – she would cringe in shame.

She could not return to the clinic. Loving Victor, whom she had no right to love. Knowing how she must disgust him. A convulsive shudder swept through her. How could she have talked to Victor the way she did? How could she ever face him after Tuesday night? Her life in Atlanta was over.

She should have left Hampton House all those months ago, when she first decided it. None of this ugliness would have happened.

She would wait to leave until Mama and Sophie went to the mill and Papa to his office, Liz plotted. On a special holiday from school, Josh and Francis would sleep late.

Too restless to remain in bed, she arose and dressed for the day, mindful that she would be travelling. Then she sat down at her desk to write a note to her parents: 'I'm sorry for all that's happened. I love you all, but I can't stay here any longer. Don't worry about me. I'll be all right. Please tell Victor I'm sorry to walk out on the children and him.'

Liz paused, then added another line: 'I'll leave the car at Terminal Station. *Please*, don't try to find me.'

She pulled a suitcase from her closet and packed necessities. For a poignant moment she held the framed tintype of David and herself between her hands. Loving David so desperately, how could she have turned to Victor?

She started at the tap on the door, bent to thrust her suitcase beneath her bed as Patience opened the door and walked into the door with a breakfast tray.

'I heard you movin' about, so I brang your breakfast,' Patience said, crossing to the table by the window to set down the tray. Patience had not seen the suitcase, Liz decided in relief; but her heart pounded from this unexpected encounter. 'You goin' in to the clinic this morning,' Patience decided, and smiled. 'Dr Victor, he be sure glad to see you.'

'He has two new little girls coming in,' Liz told her with a twinge of regret that she would not be there to greet them. 'People are beginning to hear about his work.' Victor would find somebody to replace her, Liz assuaged her guilt. But she would miss the clinic.

'You sit down and eat while your breakfast's hot,' Patience ordered. 'You eat up ever'thing.'

'I will,' Liz promised.

She would eat and wait until Patience came up to remove the tray. Then, with Patience down in the kitchen talking with Elvira and Mattie, she'd leave the house and drive to Terminal Station. She'd take the first train out. From some nearby town she would make a connection with the train to New York.

She hesitated for a moment over telephoning Janet and Maureen. She mustn't. They'd try to stop her. Tears stung her eyes. Would she ever see the family again? Would she ever see Hampton House? No. She had forfeited the privilege.

Caroline sat at her desk, talking with Victor on the phone. Searching for a way to ask him what she must ask without betraying Liz's confidence.

'Don't worry that Liz is sleeping so much,' Victor reassured her. 'It's good for her.'

'Victor, I have to ask you something.' Caroline forsook diplomacy in her anxiety. Her voice was tremulous. 'Are you in love with Liz?'

Momentarily Victor seemed speechless. Then he replied, 'Yes, Caro.' He was apologetic. 'I don't know when it happened. God knows, I didn't mean for it to happen. But I've been in love with her for months. I've said nothing to her . . .'

'Can you forget the mistakes Liz has made in her very young life?' Caroline pressed.

'That doesn't change my feelings,' he said immediately, but Caroline sensed a certain evasiveness in him.

'What bothers you, then?' she challenged.

'I've asked myself so many times if I dared to love Liz.' He paused. 'After what happened between us.'

'Victor, you mustn't let that stand between Liz and you. I told you then. That afternoon belonged to us. Nobody else will ever know. *That was ours.* If you love Liz –'

Over the phone she heard a commotion in Victor's office. 'Caro, there's someone banging at the door. Let me call you back,' Victor said.

Caroline put down the phone. She was trembling. Would Victor allow the one heated afternoon when they were lovers to stand forever between Liz and him?

She, too, had once felt this way, Caroline compelled herself to acknowledge. But if Victor loved Liz, then nothing should keep them apart.

Caroline started at the sound of the phone. She picked it up again.

'Hello.'

'Miss Caroline, I been tryin' to reach you.' Patience was talking loudly, excitedly. 'Your phone was busy.'

'Patience, is Francis all right?' Alarm surged in her.

'He fine,' Patience soothed. 'Miss Liz all right, too. But I think you best come home.' Her anxiety was obvious. 'Come home right away, Miss Caroline.'

'Patience – ' Caroline heard the phone click at the other end.

Caroline left the mill and drove the brief distance to the house. She hurried up the steps and across the veranda to the front door. Walking into the foyer, she could hear the lively voices of Francis and Josh at breakfast. Patience was coaxing them to drink their milk.

Caroline darted up the stairs. As she arrived at the landing, she saw Liz's door open. Liz emerged, carrying a suitcase. Caroline turned cold in comprehension. Oh, no. No!

'Liz, darling.' Fighting panic, Caroline moved towards her.

'Oh, Mama.' Liz's face betrayed her inner torment. 'Why did you come home?'

'Because I love you.' Caroline reached to take the suitcase from Liz's hand. 'Let's go back into your room and talk,' she coaxed.

'There's nothing to talk about,' Liz rejected, but she was following her mother into the bedroom. 'I know what I have to do.'

'Liz, you told me you love Victor. He loves you. Give him the chance to tell you.' *Would he?*

'Victor would like to sleep with me,' Liz said in brutal candour. 'I see that in his eyes. But that's not loving me.' Her voice dropped to a whisper as she lowered herself into a chair with an air of exhaustion. 'I lost David, and I can never have Victor. I've been so stupid.'

'Liz, your life has scarcely begun. Go to Victor.'

'He knows, Mama. He knows everything about me.'

'Give Victor a chance,' Caroline pleaded. Yet a part of her mind was fearful of Victor's reaction. 'Do you think you're the only girl in the world who's had an affair?'

'Dozens, Mama.' Liz closed her eyes in distaste.

Caroline took a deep breath, gearing herself for what must be said.

'Liz, you know that Papa was married when I came to Atlanta.' Her voice demanded Liz's attention. 'I think I was in love with him from the moment we met. I knew he had no real marriage. One afternoon at Hampton Court we allowed ourselves to forget he had a wife.' Liz was staring incredulously at her. 'Afterwards I swore it would never happen again. Not until we could be married. But I might have been pregnant, Liz. I might have been carrying his baby while he was still Tina's husband.'

'You, Mama?' Liz's eyes widened in amazement.

'He had been in Cuba. Wounded at San Juan Hill. He came home, and I was so grateful he was safe.' Caroline's eyes held Liz's. 'So you see, my darling, you're not alone. Let Victor know you love him. He loves you.'

'But it's wrong of me to love Victor. I loved David.' Her eyes shone with bewilderment.

'You were a little girl then. That was another kind of love. Precious, and to be treasured. But you're a woman now, Liz. You feel a woman's love for Victor.'

A rush of feet on the stairs jarred them. Then Victor's voice intruded. 'Liz?' He was knocking on the door. 'Liz?'

'Come in,' Caroline called, because Liz seemed incapable of speech.

'Have you heard the news?' Victor's face was joyous. 'A cease-fire order just went through. German officers are on their way to sign an armistice!'

'Oh, Victor!' Liz threw herself into his arms. Caroline breathed a prayer of thanksgiving. 'Victor, that's wonderful news!'

Caroline saw Victor's eyes settled on Liz's suitcase. Dear God, let him say something. Let him stop Liz from leaving.

His eyes rested uncertainly on Caroline, then moved to Liz. 'Liz, I love you,' Victor told her quietly.

'I love you,' Liz's face was luminous. 'Victor, could you ever bring yourself to marry me?'

'Anytime, anyplace you choose,' Victor declared.

Tears of happiness flooded Caroline's eyes. Her little girl was going to be all right.

In the midst of jubilant celebrations the nation was stunned to discover the report of an armistice was false. But on Monday, November 11, 1918, the news flashed around the world that the war was, indeed, over.

At dawn Atlanta newspapers filled the streets with 'extras'. At five A.M., in a drizzling rain, the Germans signed the armistice in Marshall Foch's railway carriage in the forest of Compiègne. Four hours later all firing ceased. The most terrible war the world had ever known was over.

Under a cloudless sky next day more than ten thousand troops and thousands of civilians marched in Atlanta to celebrate the return of peace. Caroline, Liz, Sophie, and Maureen – the Hampton women – stood with their men and watched the three hundred veterans of the Western Front in the post of honour at the head of the military division. These veterans drove in cars; their wounds did not permit them to march.

'Maureen, give Andy to Andrew so he can hold him high,' Liz ordered. 'Let Andy see the parade. Let him always remember.'

Like women throughout the nation, the Hampton women prayed that peace would be eternal.